The Dark Lady

Novels by Cothburn O'Neal

MASTER OF THE WORLD

THE DARK LADY

The Dark Lady

A NOVEL BY

Cothburn O'Neal

CROWN PUBLISHERS, INC. · NEW YORK

For nothing this wide universe I call,
Save thou my Rose, in it thou art my all.

SONNET 109

1

FORTUNATELY ROSALINE HAD THE TIRING ROOM ON THE SECOND FLOOR of the Rose all to herself. The other actors were on stage or in the large tiring room below. There was no one to complicate her already difficult task of changing clothes without revealing her sex. Her legs and hips were boyishly slender, but for two or three years now she had been forced to bind her breasts and pad her flat little belly to conceal the telltale signs of maturing womanhood.

The heavy court dress which she had worn while playing Lady Anne to Dick Burbage's Richard III was of course padded to make a buxom matron out of an ordinary boy actress; and the currently fashionable stiff doublet, once secured, defied detection of any human feature, male or female, in its wearer. It was such garments as the apprentice's tunic and the tight waistcoat worn under a doublet, neither of which was designed to minimize a high bosom, that forced her to exert extreme caution in choosing suitable times and places for her changes.

She was accustomed to wearing boy's clothes. She should have been, after five years of masquerading as a boy actor. So she felt easy and comfortable as she made the final adjustments to her hose and doublet and hung the discarded court dress in the wardrobe closet.

Through the thin plaster wall of the tiring house she could hear the piping treble of a twelve-year-old boy ranting through the dire prophecies of old Queen Margaret. She would have liked that part. It was better than hers. But she was afraid to risk playing prominent parts with a resident company. She was competent, too competent, so good that she would attract attention to herself. And personal attention was the last thing she wanted from London audiences. Exposure now would mean a term in St. Katherine's or Bridewell, or worse.

She could not help smiling at the boy actor's projection of the old hag's character. And her smile spread across her soft red mouth as she thought of the irony of her masquerading as a boy to play women's parts on a stage which forbade female actresses.

Act V was beginning. She wanted to see the fourth scene, to see how it sounded since she and her father had shaken it up. It had been her opinion that the scene was bob-tailed; and she had added two speeches, a total of six lines, which she thought would point up Richard's position—a king, on foot, defeated by Richmond, yet a king, arrogant even in despair.

She put on a cloak and a page's flatcap with a feather and climbed the back stairs to the lord's chamber on the third level. She found it vacant, Lord Strange, the company's patron, not being in attendance that day. She slipped into a seat at the railing and looked down at the stage. Directly beneath her was the musicians' chamber, sometimes used as a balcony or rampart on the stage itself. Underneath it, opening off the back of the apron stage, was the inner stage, a chamber of the same size as the musicians' loft and the lord's chamber but forming a part of the stage itself, a sort of alcove which was used variously as a boudoir or a study or a monk's cell or a tomb.

The house was full. She scanned the three balconies, one on top of the other, which ran around the circular walls of the tall building. The audience was leaning against the rails, intent on the play, forgetting to crack nuts or crunch apples or pop the corks out of fresh ale bottles. Many of the men neglected their pipes and let the tobacco smolder. Ladies had become careless of their vizards and fans, which dangled from their wrists or dropped into their laps and left their faces exposed to the stares of the stinkards in the pit, had the groundlings themselves not been too engrossed in Burbage's superb performance to notice the beauties above them.

Directly across the stage from Rosaline, in the third balcony along the back wall, she could see that the play was interrupting the usual employment in the "goose roost," that part of the house taken over by the Winchester Geese, or harlots who lived in the brothels of Bankside and paid rent to the Bishop of Winchester. The gallants had left off "heaving and shoving, itching and shouldering" to sit by the wenches; and for the moment there was little of the "tickling and toying, smiling and winking," which Stephen

Gosson had so roundly denounced in his *School of Abuse* a few years before.

On the big platform stage jutting far out into the pit, the battle of Bosworth Field was approaching. It was night in Richard's camp. An apparition representing the dead Lady Anne floated across the inner stage. Rosaline spoke her ghostly lines from where she sat in the lord's chamber:

> *"Richard, thy wife, that wretched Anne thy wife,*
> *That never slept a quiet hour with thee,*
> *Now fills thy sleep with perturbations.*
> *Tomorrow in the battle think on me*
> *And fall thy edgeless sword. Despair and die."*

The ghost of Buckingham followed, and then both apparitions vanished. Burbage played his recovery from the dream broadly and, as though in a daze, stared around the full circle of the balconies before he spoke. He winked solemnly at Rosaline as he cast his eyes up to the lord's chamber.

She followed the rest of Scene III from memory and waited for the added lines in Scene IV.

Burbage shouted:

> *"A horse! a horse! my kingdom for a horse!"*

Then Catesby:

> *"Withdraw, My Lord. I'll help you to a horse."*

> *"Slave,"*

Burbage said haughtily,

> *"I've set my life upon a cast*
> *And I will stand the hazards of the die.*
> *I think there be six Richmonds in the field;*
> *Five have I slain to-day instead of him.*
> *A horse! a horse! my kingdom for a horse!"*

As Burbage strode across the stage to signify a shift of scene to another part of the battlefield, the expressions on the faces of the entire audience assured Rosaline that she had been right. The

[3]

scene was perfect: Richard was the complete unregenerate villain. Burbage knew it. Even the stinkards knew it. If her father could only have seen it as it now stood, as she had written it!

She hurried downstairs to the tiring room while the short final scene was being played. If the audience demanded a post-performance jig or a tumbling routine, she would have to be ready. It was through her tumbling and dancing that Will Kempe had got her a place in the company.

But when she reached the lower tiring room she found that Kempe had failed the company. Nobody had seen him for the last hour. Since he had played no part in *Richard III*, he had simply left early and by that time was probably drunk or bedded down with some wench at the Blind Cupid just across Maiden Lane from the theater.

Upon learning that Will Kempe was not available, the audience cursed vehemently but good-naturedly and left without insisting on a jig. The theater emptied rapidly, the gentlemen leaving the balconies first, a few stinkards lingering in the pit or clambering up into the balconies to gather up any left-over nuts or oranges, to salvage any usable sea coals left unburned in the clay-lined fire pots over which the wealthier patrons had huddled during the cold hours of the performance.

Rosaline exchanged the light cloak and page's cap for a long heavy hooded cloak and fastened her costume trunk. Men were dressing all around her, but she paid no attention to their proud exposures and boasts of what they were going to do to the actor-smitten wenches waiting for them at the stage door. Rosaline was used to it all. Perhaps she even thought as a man, thought of herself as a boy, just as she was accepted by the company and had been accepted by a dozen other such troupes during her hazardous career as a boy actor.

"That would be young Ross Allen, the new boy," she heard the book-holder say; and at the calling of her name, the name she was currently known by, her heart sank.

Not another forward little wench who is afraid of grown men! she thought. That kind, who fell in love with her and could not understand why she had to refuse their favors, were hardest to get rid of. But it turned out to be a man who was asking for her this time.

[4]

"Ross, this gentleman wants to see you," the prompter said and indicated a tall fair-haired man in his middle twenties.

Rosaline looked around helplessly for Will Kempe. He was the only one who knew, who could make excuses for her; and he was gone. She looked back at her suitor; and when she saw his cool, friendly grey eyes, some of her courage returned.

"Ross Allen?" the man asked.

"Yes, sir," Rosaline answered.

"My name is William Strachey," he said. "I came to the theater with a party which includes the Earl of Essex, the young Earl of Southampton, Sir Fulke Greville, and Mr. William Harvey."

A procurer, Rosaline thought. Sir Fulke Greville's affair with the late Sir Philip Sidney was common knowledge, even among theater folk. So she judged the party by Greville's presence in it.

"Their lordships, all of the gentlemen in fact," Strachey was saying, "were much taken by the purity of your diction and the beautiful timbre of your voice."

Indeed? Rosaline thought. And what of my beautiful Italian face, my eyes black as night, and my silky raven hair? That was the usual approach. She looked around wildly. Will Shakespeare was the only man in sight whom she knew. He had sold her play for her.

"The party is repairing to the Pipe and Tabor for supper," Strachey continued. "Their lordships request that you come with me and read sonnets for the gentlemen after supper."

He smiled expectantly. His smile was as friendly as his eyes. It was hard to believe that he would pander for dissolute noblemen.

"There'll be a crown or two in it," he urged. She could use a crown or two.

"I'm only an apprentice," she hedged. "We must get my master's approval. Master Shakespeare."

Will Shakespeare, still fastening his doublet, stepped up beside William Strachey and faced Rosaline.

"Yes, lad?" He was as tall as Strachey, and much more handsome, his hazel eyes serious even when looking at a mere boy actor, and his auburn hair and youthful beard still groomed for the part of young King Edward V in the play just finished.

"Master," Rosaline began, feeding an impromptu line to Shakespeare, "this gentleman has asked me to read at a supper party. He

[5]

says there will be a few crowns in it for *us*. Shall *we* accept?" She hoped that her emphasis on *us* and *we* had been apparent to Shakespeare.

"So you want the lad to read for you?" he asked, turning to face Strachey and make a careful appraisal of the envoy.

"Yes, Master Shakespeare," Strachey said. Rosaline could have sworn that there was a twinkle in his eye. "Your apprentice referred me to you—on the matter of the few crowns."

He accented *apprentice* just perceptibly. He was as adept at catching cues as was Shakespeare the professional. And he was joining in the fiction.

"Will you bring the boy along, sir?" he asked and grinned full at Rosaline.

"And where is the supper?" Shakespeare asked.

"At the Pipe and Tabor, off Thames Street near Gracechurch."

"Aye," said Shakespeare. "I know the place, and the flavor of their beef. Yes, we'll go, won't we, lad?"

"If you say so, sir," Rosaline said obediently, and with considerable relief. From what she had learned of Will Shakespeare in the few days she had known him, she felt safe under his protection.

"What's this I hear about the Pipe and Tabor, and the flavor of their beef?" Richard Burbage asked. He was late dressing. Removal of the padding required for the character of the hunchbacked Richard III took a little time.

"The lad and I have been invited to supper," Shakespeare said loftily to the star.

"By the Earls of Essex and Southampton," Strachey added. "They want young Ross to read for them."

"I can understand that," Burbage said, taking a stand between the other two men and facing Rosaline squarely. He was somewhat shorter than either of the others, but within the last two hours he had proved how big he could be when he had heroic lines to read. "I am much impressed by the lad's reading myself. His Lady Anne this afternoon was one of the finest bit performances I've ever heard given by a boy."

"That it was," agreed Shakespeare.

"I too should like to hear young Ross give a private reading." Burbage's intense gaze, though quite friendly, made Rosaline uncomfortable. But she hoped Strachey would extend the invitation that Burbage was angling for. Burbage was almost a friend, as near as Shakespeare, as near as anyone since Will Kempe's defection.

"Then by all means join us," Strachey said. "After today's performance, I'm sure that Richard Burbage would be welcome at any supper table in London. In Ned Alleyn's chair, maybe?"

The three men laughed. Burbage had just begun to challenge Edward Alleyn, the pre-eminent tragic actor in England.

"Give me enough lines like those I had this afternoon, and I'll really make Neddie Boy look to his laurels." Burbage chuckled in satisfaction and added, "I accept your most gracious invitation, sir. Shall we join their lordships?"

"They have gone on ahead," Strachey said. "Let's take a boat from Winchester Stairs."

The three men and Rosaline left the relative warmth of the tiring room and went out a back door into the damp chill of the mid-January evening. A fog which had rolled in during the performance hung thick over the Thames. They drew their great cloaks tight around them and headed directly for Winchester Stairs. They passed the Bankside houses, each with its smock or little evergreen, just visible in the fog, to mark it as a brothel. Nearer the river the wharves were mere blurs in the mist, and the group had to feel their way to Winchester Stairs.

Most of the watermen were on the north bank of the river, where they had delivered their cargoes of theater patrons and waited for the evening brothel trade. After a time, however, Strachey found a five-passenger wherry and his party went aboard. With a cry of "Heave and ho! Rumblelow!" the oarsmen nosed the wherry out into the stream. Strachey and Burbage sat in the cloth-covered sternsheets and Rosaline and her Master Shakespeare sat amidships, facing aft. A small boy stood erect in the prow, holding a torch above his head and alternately blowing a blast on a conch shell and listening for the signals of other craft on the river.

Some of the boats marked their passage by bells, others by trumpet blasts, some by shouts. But whatever the signal, the traffic was orderly. The tide was full, not yet running out; so the wherry had little trouble holding to a course just west of London Bridge and parallel to it.

The passengers said little, considerately keeping silent so the watermen could navigate by ear in the thickening fog. Past midstream the boy began to toot his conch horn in short blasts, while his father listened to the echoes bouncing back from Fishmonger's Hall and the adjacent buildings. The oarsmen pulled slowly on their oars.

"Old Swan Stairs," the skipper called. "Old Swan, ahoy!"

"Old Swan, Old Swan," came back in a sort of singsong from about two points on the port bow.

The oarsmen swung the wherry to port and silently pulled toward the repeated chant of "Old Swan, Old Swan" until the flares on shore bit through the mist and the boat nuzzled against the pier, where the boy sprang ashore and pulled the wherry alongside with a sternline.

Strachey and Burbage stepped ashore. Burbage stopped to help Rosaline.

"Can I lend a hand, lad?" he asked. Rosaline, with an actor's ear for nuances, wondered at Burbage's inflection of *lad*.

"Thank you, sir," she said, accepting his assistance, though she was by far the most agile member of the party. If she had been of a mind to, she could have done a back somersault onto the pier.

The alley ahead was shrouded in fog. Lanterns hanging from brackets along the sheer grey walls cast balls of light no larger and but little brighter than oranges. Only the stench of the waterfront was as distinct in the fog as in bright daylight. The good smells of tar and rope and baled spices mingled with the foul breath of a fishmarket and then gave way to the odor of rotting garbage waiting in the gutters of Thames Street for a sluicing rain.

A block toward Gracechurch Street, the general conditions improved, and in the courtyard of the Pipe and Tabor, lighted by a score of flares, the members of the party were again able to see the others' faces.

A porter held a lantern up to the face of each one. The plague was bad that year—over six thousand deaths already—and the host had to make sure of his guests.

"Friends of his lordship, the Earl of Essex," Strachey said.

"Yes, sir," the porter said. "I recognize your face and your voice, Mr. Strachey."

He opened the heavy door and let the newcomers into the brightly lighted ordinary, where Lord Essex's party was already seated around the massive common table and a wood fire blazed in the huge fireplace. The room smelled of stout ale, mellow tobacco smoke, and the roasting flesh of a side of beef turning on a spit over the open fire.

"I brought the whole cast," Strachey announced as he handed his greatcoat to the porter.

"Ah, Burbage, glad you could come," Essex hailed from the table.

"And this is William Shakespeare, our little apprentice's master," Strachey continued with a hint of mischief in his voice.

"Welcome, Master Shakespeare," Essex said jovially. Pre-supper Spanish wine was already leveling the aristocracy.

"Our lad, Ross Allen," Strachey announced dramatically. And *Ross Allen,* as he pronounced it, sounded for the world like *Rosaline.* The similarity was, of course, no accident, but still Rosaline received a start when she heard her name spoken openly in London.

The commoners bowed low to the seated gentlemen, who nodded graciously. All of the men except the young Earl of Southampton wore their hats. Essex's blond curls shone brightly below the brim of his plumed blue velvet hat, blue like his eyes. William Harvey, the oldest man present, smiled cordially at Rosaline; and Sir Fulke Greville, older than the Earls but perfumed and powdered and painted like a young girl, outdid himself gushing over the beauty of Rosaline's speech during the afternoon's performance.

Though Rosaline thanked him perfunctorily, she did not hear a word that he was saying. Her entire attention was concentrated on Lord Henry Wriothesley, third Earl of Southampton. She did not wonder that he preferred to remove his hat: he had the most beautiful golden hair that she had ever seen on a man, or a woman, for that matter. And he obviously knew it, for he had let it grow long, much longer than Rosaline's own shoulder-length page-boy hair, and wore it brought around his neck in a loose tress and across his left shoulder, where it lay like a gilded epaulet.

His eyes too, blue like Essex's, but much clearer, as clear-blue as a bright winter sky, set off his other flawless features. Rosaline had heard that he was considered the handsomest young peer at court, even by the Queen herself, but she had expected no such beauty as she saw in his face. And withal a striking virility showed in his entire person, despite a complexion any woman would have envied and a sparkling diamond earring in the lobe of his right ear.

He wore a doublet of blue satin and, instead of a ruff, a broad lace collar which fell softly over a red leather gorget embroidered with gold thread. His broad trunks and upperhose, just visible under the edge of the table, were of red satin, matching the gorget, and they too were heavily brocaded with gold. And his silk stockings of a lighter shade of red were gartered about his long legs with cloth-of-gold bands. His soft leather boots, the short tops of which folded around his ankles, repeated the red in his gorget and upperhose. All in all, his elegant court clothes were in keeping with the perfection of his natural features.

Rosaline found herself confusing the young Earl with images of Adonis remembered from Ovid's *Metamorphoses*. He suddenly appeared nude before her, and she felt herself blushing, though she had spent most of her adolescent years in men's dressing rooms, among men in all stages of deshabille. This man was different, and the difference frightened her.

"Sit here, lad," Strachey said as he swung the end of a heavy bench closer to the table.

Rosaline stepped over the plank seat and sat down, almost directly opposite Southampton. The young Earl smiled at her, more graciously than she had any reason to expect. She was suddenly thankful that she was an entertainer; no other class of commoners could have mingled with the nobility on such easy terms; and at that moment the privilege of being near Southampton, of being favored by his smile, was the most important thing in the world. She had just learned the truth of Marlowe's couplet,

> *Where both deliberate, the love is light:*
> *Who ever loved, that loved not at first sight?*

"If old Fulke will give me a chance to get a word in," the young Earl was saying, "I too would like to commend you on your performance this afternoon."

"Thank you, your lordship," Rosaline said timidly, hoping Southampton would continue. His voice was pure music, or perhaps by then Rosaline was already too completely enamored ever to make another rational judgment about the young Earl.

"The illusion, too, was perfect," he went on. "I kept believing that Lady Anne was a real woman—a beautiful, charming woman. I think I might have fallen in love with her myself if she hadn't died in the fourth act. And to think it was you all the time, lad!" He chuckled delightedly, and again smiled warmly at Rosaline, his even white teeth catching the gleam from the candelabrum in the center of the table. His suggestion of falling in love with the Lady Anne set her heart to beating faster.

"Lucky for you it *was* a lad," Fulke Greville said. "Now we have the boy here with us to delight us and charm us. And there will be no messy entanglements for your lordship, as there undoubtedly would be if the lad were a lady."

"Speak for yourself, Fulke," William Strachey said. "Entanglements are only as messy as you make them."

"You should talk," Fulke said with a woman's inflection. "And you married, or practically so, to Frances Foster." He pronounced *married* petulantly, almost as though he resented the very idea of marriage. He carefully opened an ebony case and took out one of the new-fangled knife and fork sets just introduced from Italy. No one else at the table had a fork—or wanted one, in all probability.

"God's body, Fulke," Essex said in mock disgust at the sight of the fork. "First you won't touch a woman. Now you won't touch meat with your hands. What next?"

"No messy entanglements," Strachey repeated. "Not even with roast beef."

While the others laughed, Rosaline looked at the men in turn and wondered again why they were there together. William Strachey was soon to be married. Essex was already married to Frances Walsingham Sidney, Sir Philip's widow. Had he taken Sidney's place with Greville also? And what was the place of Southampton or William Harvey in this group?

All of the men had houses in the city, and families. Most of them were at court. Why then sup in a tavern and hire a boy to read love sonnets to them? Of course it was all to her advantage, Rosaline rationalized, in her present role. But was it normal? Was it natural? She so wanted Southampton to be normal, to smile at her again, really to fall in love with her, just as though she were Lady Anne. But he thought she was a boy, a twelve- or thirteen-year-old boy—not a woman almost eighteen, barely two years younger than the Earl himself.

[11]

The first luster of her infatuation was being dimmed already, dimmed by her own anomalous position as a boy actor, dimmed by the healthy skepticism she had learned during the years of her masquerade in the half-world of rogues and vagabonds, but dimmed most painfully by the air of complete adoration which the Earl of Southampton radiated whenever he spoke to the Earl of Essex. Rosaline felt a sharp surge of jealousy as a look of intimate understanding passed between the handsome young peers. They were ignoring her at the moment, unaware of all the rest of the world, it seemed. Then she was further enraged by the realization that there was not one single reason why either of them should pay any attention whatever to her—just a little boy, a hired reader to be brought on after the roast beef.

"Hold your bread over here, lad," Southampton said to her. The world brightened again. "Let me put a big piece of beef on it."

Mutely Rosaline picked up a heavy slice of bread from the wooden trencher which had been placed before her and held it across the table toward his lordship. He carefully laid a juicy slice of beef on the bread.

"Now your trencher for a hot Spanish yam." He slit open a roasted yam just dug out of the hot ashes and filled the steaming wound with fresh salted butter.

Rosaline capped her beef sandwich with a piece of rye bread and extended her trencher to receive the yam. Southampton placed the yam on the trencher and laid a pewter spoon beside it.

"Think that'll keep you busy for a while?" he asked.

"Yes, your lordship. Thank you."

It was annoying to be treated as a child, but it was wonderful to be served a savory supper by the beautiful Earl of Southampton. As Rosaline weighed the two emotions and munched on her sandwich, she was inclined to be more pleased than displeased. She took her spoon and stirred the melted butter into the yellow meat of the yam. The host passed behind her just then and leaned over her shoulder to pour a spoonful of Irish whiskey into the yam.

"Just a few drops, laddie," he said. "It makes a good Irishman of the yellow Spaniard."

Rosaline finished blending the butter and the whiskey into the yellow meat of the yam. She took a bite of the mixture. From that point on she was decidedly more pleased than displeased with the entire party. The host brought her a mug of cold milk, the ale being a little stout for so young a lad. And when rich Naples biscuits were brought on after the cheeses, Rosaline found that her wine was a very mild one, sweetened with honey and flavored with spices. She was being well taken care of by the host, though despite his efforts she was as fully stimulated as any of the men who had been swilling the heavy ale.

The host passed clay pipes to all the gentlemen and set a humidor of tobacco on the table. Then, as if by instinct, he brought Rosaline bound copies of Sidney's *Astrophel and Stella* and Spenser's *Shepherd's Calendar,* and a sheaf of manuscript containing unpublished poems by a score of literary noblemen. He placed them all on the table before her and hung a bright lantern to shine over her shoulder.

"Will that serve you right, laddie?" he asked.

"Yes, thank you, sir." She wondered if the host was being kind to her because of herself or because she was the guest of the Earls. She had never been quite so self-conscious before in all her life, life on the stage at that. She was just beginning to look on herself as a person in relation to other persons. And she was becoming increasingly conscious that she was a woman, and very happy about it. Or was she?

"What shall I read, my lord?" She spoke to Essex, who was the ranking peer present.

"Read from Sidney," he said. "We were all friends of his."

Rosaline opened the volume of *Astrophel and Stella.*

"Shall I read straight through, my lord," she asked, "or let the gentlemen suggest their favorites?"

"Begin at the first," Essex said. "Later you may skip if the gentlemen prefer."

"Thank you, my lord," she said and began:

"Loving in truth, and fain in verse my love to show—"

She was quite familiar with the collection of sonnets, having read them many times in just such groups as the one seated around the table in the Pipe and Tabor. Her voice, modulated for the intimacy of the small gathering, was even more appealing than it had been during the stage performance earlier in the afternoon. Before she finished the first sonnet, she had brought the gentlemen completely under her spell—hers and Sidney's. They relaxed contentedly, some lighting their pipes and settling comfortably against the cushioned backs of the benches, others leaning forward on their elbows and sipping after-supper wine.

Their eyes roved over her face, first its classic oval outline framed by loose black curls; then her alert black eyes set off by lustrous brows and lashes; her skin, paler in the glow of the lantern than in daylight; and her naturally red lips, deceptively soft in repose but fascinatingly flexible, even muscular, sometimes firm, as they shaped the words of Sidney's poetry. Her face appeared to be every bit as pleasing to her listeners as was her voice. By expert control of both she held the men in thrall.

She paused briefly after each sonnet and then continued easily when it was apparent that no one wanted to comment. She did glance around the circle to see what sort of impression she was making. The Earls were well pleased. Fulke Greville had drawn a lace handkerchief from his sleeve, and alternately dabbed daintily at his nose with it and passed a clove pomander under his nostrils. Whether his actions were prompted by affectation, grief at the memory of Sidney, or a mere indisposition brought on by the fog Rosaline could not tell; but his barely audible sniffs sounded the only discordant note in her reading.

William Harvey and William Strachey were the most relaxed, yet seemingly quite discriminating listeners. Strachey was inclined to nod agreement to lines which he especially liked, and Harvey wore a slight frown of concentration, as though he were trying to hold all the words of each sonnet in his mind for one total impression. Shakespeare smoked placidly and radiated a pride in the work of his apprentice.

It was Richard Burbage, however, who listened most intently. There was nothing passive in his entire appearance. His eyes were busiest, following every movement of Rosaline's facial muscles; and she sensed that his ears caught every inflection of her voice, reached perhaps for still other nuances which might have been there. He was the one who made her most actively conscious of her reading. But his listening served as a challenge rather than a hindrance. If anything, it improved her performance.

She read a half-dozen sonnets without interruption. After the seventh, the one beginning,

[14]

When nature made her chief work, Stella's eyes,
In color black why wrapped she beams so bright?

Rosaline allowed her usual pause for comment.

"That sonnet never sounded quite so well before," Harvey said softly, almost to himself, when Rosaline finished reading.

"It has been so much the fashion," Strachey said, "to write of fair ladies with blue eyes, that a sonnet to a dark lady, one with black eyes, has seemed a mere novelty, until this reading."

"Perhaps it's the lad himself," Harvey suggested. "His eyes may illustrate what Sidney meant by beauties flowing in blackness. If our lad were a lass, I warrant there would be more sonnets to a dark lady within a few years." He chuckled good-naturedly, to take away any embarrassment his remark might have caused a twelve-year-old boy.

"Indeed there would be," Strachey agreed. "Our lad has the eyes, the face, even the hair of a very lovely maid."

"A lad with a maidenhead," Burbage quipped.

It was a stock joke, but the men laughed politely. Rosaline looked quickly at Burbage, to try to read the enigmatic smile playing on his lips. It revealed nothing. She knew a moment of near panic. How much had Burbage guessed? How much would he reveal?

"Who was the black-eyed addressee, Fulke?" Harvey asked. "Was it Lady Penelope or the Countess?"

"I'm sure I don't know," Fulke Greville said with little grace. "Ask his lordship. Lady Penelope is his sister and Frances Sidney is now his countess."

Essex laughed under his breath. He seemed not to resent Greville's familiarity.

"I don't know either," he said. "Penelope has black eyes. Frances has blue eyes but black hair and brows. Each insists that the sonnets were addressed to her. The Queen hates both of them, and would probably behead the lucky lady if we ever found out which one it was. So, even if I knew, I'd hold a discreet silence."

"A wise man," Southampton said, pretending to a knowledge of women which Rosaline doubted in one so young. But she was glad to have the attention of the group diverted from her womanly beauty.

[15]

"He probably loved them both very dearly," Harvey said in a tone of complete seriousness.

"That may be," Fulke Greville said with a pronounced sniff at his pomander. "But I know one of his sonnets which is not in that book, one which casts some doubt on his love for either of them. I can assure you that he loved me more dearly than either of the ladies. Would you like to hear Sir Philip's—dear Philip's— view on lust for women?"

Though no one encouraged him, Greville began to recite in a strained falsetto:

> "*Thou blind man's mark, thou fool's self-chosen snare,*
> *Fond fancy's scum, and dregs of scattered thought;*
> *Band of all evils, cradle of causeless care;*
> *Thou web of will, whose end is never wrought;*
> *Desire, desire! I have too dearly bought,*
> *With price of mangled mind, thy worthless ware . . .*"

He ended on a note of defiance and looked around the circle as though he had just tossed a gauntlet on the table.

"Is that really Sidney's?" Strachey asked.

"Yes." It was Essex who answered. "I've heard Philip recite it. But I don't think he meant what Fulke reads into it."

"I should know," Greville insisted. "I was closer to him than Penelope or Frances."

His bravado had given way to a nervous grief. He was almost in tears, and his voice bordered on hysteria. Rosaline felt some embarrassment for him, and it was obvious that it would be unwise for her to read any more of Sidney's sonnets. She closed the book and laid it on the table, face down. William Harvey nodded approval as she caught his eye.

"Can you bear a part in pricksong, lad?" he asked.

"Yes, sir," she answered.

"Host," Harvey called. His age apparently allowed him to infringe on Essex's prerogatives as ranking peer present. "Bring us a book of madrigals and send us another treble voice from the scullery."

The other treble proved to be a pert little barmaid, who brought the songbooks to the table and who made Rosaline sing for all she was worth to hold her place as chief entertainer of the evening. The men all joined in on the madrigals, most of which were arranged for six voices, and the tensions created by Sidney's poetry were soon dissipated. When the men, the non-professionals, began to tire, Rosaline sang "Greensleeves" solo to her own lute accompaniment. Burbage was prevailed upon to read passages from *Richard III* and from some of the other tragic parts in which he was making a name for himself.

Then Rosaline read again, love sonnets, but none by Sidney. The party grew mellower with each sonnet and each fresh tankard of ale, and ultimately got around to the discussion of the relative merits of love between the sexes and friendship between men. Rosaline had listened to the arguments a hundred times, in a hundred taprooms, by a hundred different groups. But the thesis was the same: friendship is the nobler; true affection can exist only between men, woman being so much the weaker vessel, fickle as the moon. She knew all the arguments, all the allusions to the classical and medieval examples. She knew too the very sordid sequels to some of the sessions she had attended in the past, and she found herself listening in horror.

Perhaps it was the presence of Fulke Greville that colored the entire conversation. Whatever the cause, Rosaline followed the familiar clichés as though they were fresh pronouncements by the oracles of love. She imagined the young Earl of Southampton being stolen from all womankind before her very eyes. What had once been of academic interest, if of any interest at all, became a living threat charged with danger for the beautiful young Earl and for Rosaline herself.

Or so she thought, as she drank more deeply of the wine, the men's wine now. The wine might have been stronger than she supposed. She might have been tired. With her usual clarity of perception she would have been able to shrug off the feeling which settled over her, or to ignore the whole absurd colloquy, as she had in the past. But she found herself watching the fine features of the Earl assume wise and significant expressions as they softened and lost character in the fumes of wine and ale and tobacco. It was as though he belonged to her and were being seduced by a monster against whom she could bring no stronger weapon than the puny fists of a little boy. She felt a sudden urge to rip off her doublet and show him what a woman looked like, to destroy the friendship myth once and for all by giving the

[17]

golden boy one real taste of a woman's passion. She had never before thought of asserting rather than concealing her womanhood; but she became fascinated by the idea, even giggled slightly at the thought of the disturbance she might cause by shedding her masculine cocoon and bursting forth in all her female beauty.

"Will, don't you think we ought to put our apprentice to bed?" Richard Burbage said to Shakespeare. "It's late for a lad to be up."

Rosaline looked around at her Master Shakespeare. The quick jerk of her head made the tavern reel and spin. The wine—

"If the gentlemen have finished with our boy, yes," Shakespeare said.

William Harvey heard the conversation. He whispered to the Earl of Essex, who broke off the conversation long enough to dismiss the entertainers and to give them two crowns each. The gentlemen again complimented Rosaline on her reading, but seemed to be eager to get back to the profundities of their winey views on friendship.

William Harvey went with the three actors to the door of the tavern. He put a fatherly hand on Rosaline's shoulder.

"I don't think you understand your full charm, lad," he said. "Here in the stench and filth and vice and brutality—and right now the plague—of London, it is refreshing to hear a voice of such purity, to see a face of such beauty. You are like a flower growing out of a dunghill. You have delighted us all this evening.

"Their lordships, a little the worse for wine at this moment, were much impressed. I know—I know them both well. We enjoyed you too, Burbage. And Master Shakespeare, bring the lad again some time."

The porter let the actors out into the cold courtyard. The icy mist felt good to Rosaline's cheeks and brought some order to her errant mind. She felt in her codpiece for the two crowns. They were safe. And so was she, safe from some sort of nightmare hardly recognizable out of the overheated tavern.

"Where do you live, lad?" Shakespeare asked.

"On the bridge," Rosaline answered. "In a tenement near the Surrey end."

"Then we'd better walk," Burbage said.

"Yes, sir," she agreed.

The streets seemed to be completely deserted. The fog hid everything. Even the flares at street corners were visible for only

[18]

a few feet. But it was the quiet that told of deserted streets. The usual hum of the city was silent. There were no carts rattling on the cobblestones, no hawkers crying their wares. And the doors, barred against the plague, held domestic noises inside. Not even a baby's cry could be heard, only the clumping of the actors' own boots on the stones.

Shakespeare and Burbage each took Rosaline by an arm and the three walked down the middle of the street. It was the only way they could keep from losing one another in the foggy night.

"A fine night for a stroll," Burbage said. "No one abroad to force us to the wall."

"I rather prefer a bright spring day," Shakespeare said. "And a country lane." He wrapped his muffler about his throat with his free hand.

"And for a chat," Burbage continued, ignoring the interruption. "Suppose we talk about you, lad. Where did you learn to read lines as you do, as lightly as rippling water?"

"My father taught me," Rosaline answered. "He always said, 'Speak a speech trippingly on the tongue; mouth it not like a town-crier publishing his bulletin.' He coached me many hours."

"An excellent coach, I would say. Who was your father?"

"A schoolmaster, I think, with degrees from both universities. I am not sure, sir. He seldom talked of himself."

"And where were you reared, lad?"

"England." She was intentionally vague.

"England? What part? Your dialect eludes me."

"All over, sir. From York to Dorset, from Pembroke to Norfolk."

"Here's Gracechurch Street," Shakespeare said. He had taken the responsibility of piloting in the fog.

Gracechurch was as quiet as Thames Street had been. The trio of actors seemed to have all London to themselves as they turned down Gracechurch toward London Bridge.

"You mean traveling? With a company of players?" Burbage went on.

"Yes, sir. Ever since I can remember. First with a troupe of tumblers and jugglers and acrobats—Italians. Then with a number of companies of strolling players. Lord Pembroke's Men, and Sussex's Men, and Derby's, a dozen minor troupes maybe."

Rosaline sensed more than mere curiosity in Burbage's ques-

[19]

tions. She remembered how closely he had studied her performance at the Rose, and later at the Pipe and Tabor. In her attempt to make her apparent precocity seem plausible she talked a little more freely than was her custom.

"And your mother was Italian."

"An Italian tumbling woman," she said with some bitterness, remembering that horrible Sunday morning at Newington Butts.

"That accounts for your light *l's* and the trill in your *r's*," Burbage said. "They make fascinating little flourishes on our English speech." His voice held a note of envy, and at the same time a measure of satisfaction at placing Rosaline's dialect.

"Is your mother with you now?" he asked.

"No. She was stoned to death by a band of Puritans at Newington Butts five years ago, the summer of the battle with the Spanish Armada. We were playing in St. George's Fields during an archery meet and a patriotic rally."

Rosaline hesitated as the frightful images came crowding back into her mind. Then she continued slowly, deliberately, painfully.

"They sang hymns and called her and Aunt Olivia lewd Italian tumbling women—harlots—naked Jezebels—papists—all sorts of names—and then began throwing stones. They killed my mother and Aunt Olivia and Antonio, and Bassanio, the bear trainer. They even killed Ursa, his dancing bear.

"My father hurried me into the Newington Butts theater, which was nearby. He was hit by a stone and hurt badly just as we reached the front door of the theater. I dragged him across the pit and under the stage. He was unconscious. I sat holding his head in my lap, for hours it seemed, until some actors came into the theater.

"Will Kempe found us, he and Mr. Marlowe and Mr. Kyd, who were working on some plays for the Earl of Sussex's Men then playing at the Newington Butts theater. They took care of us. And when the Sussex troupe went on the road, Mr. Marlowe and Mr. Kyd stayed behind and my father went along as play dresser and scene shaker. We've played the provinces ever since."

Shakespeare put his arm around Rosaline's shoulders and hugged her sympathetically.

"That must be a painful memory, lad," he said. "I remember hearing of that incident at Newington Butts."

"I too," said Burbage. "Old Josiah Norton was leader of the Puritans. His cousin, Thomas Norton, was the first to point his finger at the 'unchaste, shameless and unnatural tumbling of Italian women.' In fact he tried to stop all kinds of entertainment, caused my father a lot of trouble at the Theater. He was imprisoned in the Tower about ten years ago for some of his fanaticism and died soon after, I believe. But old Josiah is still at large, still screaming at anything the people enjoy."

"The people enjoyed watching my mother," Rosaline said. "She was beautiful—and talented."

"I'm sure she was," Shakespeare said, "if you are anything like her."

"My father has always said that I am very much like her." Rosaline was not conscious of the circular compliment she paid herself.

London Bridge was covered over by tenement houses, many with shops on the first floor. Crossing the bridge was like going through a tunnel except for the two long spans which could be raised like drawbridges to let big ships pass through. The shops were all closed, but flares and lanterns still burned, warming the tunnel slightly and drying out some of the fog only to replace it with their own acrid smoke and fumes.

Rosaline's eyes smarted. The fog had been better.

"Your father," Burbage said. "You say he is a play dresser and a shake-scene? Did he dress *Richard III*? Will here has told me that you brought the play to him."

"Yes, sir. My father wrote most of it. I brought it to Will Kempe. He said that he owed so much money to Mr. Henslowe that he couldn't expect to get any cash for the play. So Mr. Shakespeare handled it for me."

"Why didn't you take it to Mr. Henslowe yourself?"

"He—he wouldn't buy a play from a boy," Rosaline answered. Something in Burbage's last question, a steeliness in his voice, made her suddenly wary.

"Even if Henslowe had bought it from the lad, he would have cheated him," Shakespeare said. "You know Phillip Henslowe, the old pawnbroker."

"Yes, I know him. Why didn't your father sell his own play?" Burbage asked.

"He—he was too ill to come to the theater."

[21]

"Does he have any more plays?"

"A few." Rosaline bit off her words.

"How many?"

"A dozen, maybe. I don't know." Actress though she was, Rosaline found herself doing a very poor job of evasion.

"A dozen. What kind?"

"We—he has eight or nine histories covering the wars from the time of King John to Richard III. The one I sold to Mr. Henslowe was the last in the series."

"Histories are good now," Burbage said professionally. "What else?"

"A play about twins, based on Plautus's *Menaechmi*. We call it *A Comedy of Errors*. And one about a shrew, and a husband who tames her."

"What else?" Burbage was almost demanding in his tone.

"A play about Titus Andronicus, which Derby's Men used at the Rose last year. Mr. Henslowe has a copy of it now. It's mostly by Thomas Kyd, but we—my father has worked it over, shaken up the big scenes."

"I'd like to talk to your father," Burbage said.

"He—he isn't well," Rosaline said.

"I won't disturb him. I just want to read some of his manuscripts. I liked *Richard III*."

"He—he isn't here," Rosaline said. They were approaching the south end of the bridge. Her room was only a few paces away. "He's at Brighton for his health," she lied. If only Will Kempe would be at home when they got there. Burbage was proving a little more than she could handle by herself. Shakespeare was a comfort. She was beginning to like him very much; but he, not being privy to her secret, could be of no help to her if Burbage insisted on prying into her affairs.

"Brighton? And he has the manuscripts with him, I suppose." Broad sarcasm in Burbage's voice startled Rosaline. Burbage had anticipated her answer to his next question. Furthermore he knew that she was lying. How much more he knew or had guessed she could only surmise.

"This is where I live," she said, stopping before a door opening off the bridge into the west side of a tenement house, the last one, next to the Surrey gate towers. "Good night, sirs. And thanks for bringing me home."

"Aren't you going to invite us in, lad?" Burbage asked as she placed her hand on the latch. "Or do you think it's proper?"

"Why do you ask that?" She froze at the implication of his question.

"Because you are a genius, a freak, or a woman!"

"May I have a choice?" Rosaline asked. Almost hysterically she took refuge in facetiousness as a new feeling of panic spread over her. Her action was practically a reflex, so frequently had she been forced to laugh her way out of troublesome situations or to distract a persistent admirer by a timely quip.

"I think you have been exercising a choice for quite some time," Burbage said soberly.

"Then I choose to be a genius. But what prompted you to make such a statement, Mr. Burbage?" She had to know how she was betraying herself.

"First, I sensed something more than met the eye in your reading of Lady Anne this afternoon. But that was brief and I was busy playing a part myself."

"Yes?" She would remember to be less womanly on the stage hereafter.

"Now I've had a chance to study you for several hours more. I've listened to your voice. I've watched your facial expressions. I've followed every move you made."

"So I noticed," she said.

"And quite aside from the fact that you have been lying like a jarkman for the last few minutes, you had already convinced me that you are not what you pretend to be."

"And why not, Mr. Burbage?" She was regaining her composure as it became apparent that she must fend for herself. Will Kempe was certainly not with her at the moment.

"The skill you show in reading and in singing, even in tuning and playing a lute, doesn't match your voice, lad."

"No?" She was calm now, deliberately so under pressure.

"No," said Burbage. "Bear in mind that my father built the Theater up in Shoreditch, the first playhouse in London. I grew up among actors. I've known scores of boys, some fully as accomplished as you are."

"Indeed?" She was normal enough to show some resentment at the slight to her competence.

"Yes. And invariably attainments comparable to yours go with

[23]

cambiata. There's not a trace of the cambiata in your voice. So you are a freak or a woman."

"Or a genius. Remember?"

"Or a genius. Now, won't you invite us in and let us discuss your genius in private, before it becomes a topic of conversation all over London?"

Rosaline was not sure that Burbage intended a threat. He could be warning her that others would be as observant as he; or he could be hinting at blackmail. She knew well the vanity of actors, the extremes to which they would go to discredit a rival. That Burbage should consider a mere boy—or a girl, as he now knew— as a rival was doubtful, though some boy actors had certainly been lionized by fashionable London. His interest seemed to be in the manuscripts; but that could well be a blind, a screen for his real motives. Burbage was a consummate actor, a better one than she was.

"Do come in," she said. The only way to find out what Burbage wanted was to have the talk he insisted upon. "I am ashamed of my quarters, just a storeroom on the first floor, but if you insist—"

She pushed open the door and led her guests down a long unlighted hallway to her room. First she knocked on Will Kempe's door across the hall. No one answered. Obviously Will had not come in, or he was too drunk to stir. She unlocked her own door and lit a candle.

The room, though fairly large, was cramped. Rosaline's cot and one stool were in the middle of the floor. The walls were lined to the casements of the windows with books, and boxes of manuscript littered the floor. A trunk and a three-legged deal table were crowded into what little floor space was not occupied by books and papers.

"Is this a bedroom or a library, lad?" Shakespeare asked in astonishment at the number of books in evidence.

"It's the only room I have, Master Shakespeare. The books are my father's. We sometime went hungry when he accepted a book instead of money for a performance, especially if he had to go into our purse to pay other members of the troupe. But we have a lot of books," she ended with a shrug.

"And you've read them all," Burbage said, more as a statement than a question. He lighted other candles and began scanning the titles of some of the books.

"Yes, sir," Rosaline admitted. "After my father was injured at Newington Butts, his eyes were never strong enough for him to read very long at a time. He loved his books so well that I read them all to him again. We had much free time together."

"Chaucer, Caxton, Gower, Halle, Holinshed," Burbage said aloud as he began to take stock of the room and all that was in it. "Ovid, Virgil, Plautus, Seneca, Mantuan. Here's old Lily's Latin Grammar." He chuckled as he remembered his own school days. "And Petrarch and Bandello, Cinthio, Ariosto, Boccaccio. You read Italian, of course."

"Yes, sir," Rosaline said. Burbage was beginning to nettle her. The least he could do would be to get to the point of his visit.

"Ronsard, Rabelais. Montemayor—and French and Spanish?"

"Yes." Rosaline was bordering on defiance. "I grew up among foreign entertainers—Italian, French, Spanish—all kinds of people joined our troupe. My father was their interpreter, a sort of manager, I suppose. He knew all their languages. And he was a schoolmaster without a school. He took it all out on me, his only pupil. He taught me the languages, among other things.

"Ever since I can remember, he has lavished on me all the care he would have given an entire form of boys in an academy. And I suppose you think I'm still lying like a jarkman."

"No," Burbage said, turning to focus his entire attention on Rosaline. "No, I think you've been goaded into telling the truth at last. But not all of it." He put down a copy of Halle's *Chronicles* which he had been examining.

"Is this your handwriting?" he asked suddenly, picking a sheaf of manuscript from the deal table.

"Yes," she said. "That's a translation of *Venus and Adonis* from Ovid's *Metamorphosis*. I'm putting it into verse. It's just an exercise that I was working on when my father—"

"Died!" Burbage supplied the word and stared into Rosaline's face, daring her to contradict him. "Your father has never been in this room. The manuscript of *Richard III* was in this same handwriting, not in the hand that scribbled the marginalia in these printed books. So are the copies of that other play over there. You copied them or you may have written them or dressed them or shaken up the scenes yourself. That's the genius I want to talk about! Now sit down and tell us about it. We won't hurt you."

He talked too fast for her to interrupt him; and at the end of his speech he grasped her by the shoulders and forced her to sit down on her cot. He pulled the stool away from the table and sat down directly in front of her.

"First of all," he began, still fixing his gaze steadily on her face, "you are no twelve-year-old boy. You are a woman nearing twenty."

"Eighteen," she corrected him. There was something hypnotic in his gaze. She realized that she could lie to him no more. "Eighteen next month."

"And your father *is* dead."

"Yes. Of the plague, two months ago. They wouldn't even let me bury him—just hauled him away in the death cart." She was dry-eyed, though both men probably expected her to break down. Shakespeare appeared to be on the verge of restraining Burbage in his almost brutal interrogation.

"And you have been dressing plays yourself. How long?"

"I don't know. Two years, three years. I had to read to my father after his eyes failed. I had to write for him at his dictation. Gradually I became more than his amanuensis. When we had plays to do and he wasn't able, I did them myself—just sort of carried on as I thought he would have dictated. Then I found myself doing it all. I had to, or we would have starved." She shook her head, as though trying to break the spell in which Burbage held her.

"You did *Richard III?*"

"Yes. Most of it—all of Richard's lines."

"Now, that's what I was trying to find out." Burbage relaxed visibly. "If you wrote that part and can write more like it, you are the genius I was talking about. Show me some more of your work."

Rosaline opened her father's trunk and handed the top manuscript to Burbage. He put more candles on a packing case and settled down on the stool to read. Shakespeare sat on a box and read from the exercise that Burbage had found on the table. Both men were quiet. Rosaline sat on her cot and stared mutely, first at one of them and then the other. They became completely absorbed in their reading. Still she felt trapped between them.

Occasionally Shakespeare would lower the manuscript and study Rosaline intently. Usually he found her watching Burbage just as intently. Once when Burbage stopped reading for a moment, Shakespeare said, "Listen to this, Dick. Venus is speaking:

> " 'Fondling,' she saith, 'since I have hemmed thee here
> Within the circuit of this ivory pale,
> I'll be a park, and thou shall be my deer;
> Feed where thou will, on mountain or in dale;
>   Graze on my lips; and if those hills be dry,
>   Stray lower, where the pleasant fountains lie.

> " 'Within this limit is relief enough,
> Sweet bottom-grass, and high delightful plain,
> Round rising hillocks, brakes obscure and rough,
> To shelter thee from tempest and from rain.
>   Then be my deer, since I am such a park,
>   No dog shall rouse thee, though a thousand bark.'

Does this mean what I think it does?"

"Yes," said Burbage with a chuckle and a speculative glance at Rosaline.

"I thought it did," Shakespeare said, well pleased.

Rosaline met neither man's gaze.

"It's from Ovid," she said self-consciously.

"But the imagery is yours," Burbage said. "I know Ovid in the original."

"And I thought she was just a little boy," Shakespeare said and went on reading. He whistled softly a few stanzas later, at the business of the stallion and jennet mare, and again appraised Rosaline carefully. Burbage was immersed in the history plays.

To cover her growing embarrassment at having her adolescent dreams read by a mature man in her presence, Rosaline began to rummage through her father's trunk, sorting manuscripts which she had not had time to arrange or catalogue. She hardly noticed the titles, however, busying herself primarily with evading the growing interest both men were showing in her.

When Burbage rested again, Shakespeare was ready with more choice stanzas.

"How's this?" he asked.

> " 'Good night,' quoth she; and ere he says 'Adieu,'
> The honey fee of parting tend'red is:

[27]

> *Her arms do lend his neck a sweet embrace;*
> *Incorporate then they seem; face grows to face;*

> *"Till breathless he disjoin'd, and backward drew*
> *The heavenly moisture, that sweet coral mouth,*
> *Whose precious taste her thirsty lips well knew,*
> *Whereon they surfeit, yet complain on drouth.*
> > *He with her plenty pressed, she faint with dearth,*
> > *Their lips together glued, fall to earth.*

"Or this?

> *"Hot, faint, weary with her hard embracing,*
> *Like a wild bird being tamed with too much handling,*
> *Or as the fleet-footed roe that's tired with chasing,*
> *Or like the froward infant stilled with dandling,*
> > *He now obeys and now no more resisteth*
> > *While she takes all she can, not all she listeth.*

This Venus woman grows on me. Adonis is a little stupid, though, don't you think?"

"Perhaps he values friendship between men more highly than love," Rosaline said angrily, lumping together her resentment at the foolish talk at the Pipe and Tabor, and her puzzling feeling for Southampton, and her displeasure at Burbage's high-handed manner with her, and Will Kempe's desertion of her just when she needed him, and Shakespeare's insistence on repeating the erotic passages from her poem—and all the cumulative frustration that had been building up inside her for two months or more.

"Your poem certainly casts new light on that problem," Shakespeare said. "The woman's point of view. It's the first time I've seen us men as a lady sees us, especially so passionate a pursuer as your Venus seems to be. You must—"

"All right, Master Shakespeare!" Rosaline blazed at both the men. She stood up and glared down on them angrily. "So I've lived an abnormal life, as a boy among men. I've grown into womanhood in the midst of the lechery and vanity of a man's world. Men forever bragging of their conquests and planning new ones. Men vile and cruel and lustful, forever seeking to despoil a virgin, always searching for an innocent.

"Can't I dream of a youth like Adonis? Pure and clean and shy? Can't I become the huntress in my own dreams? Remember I've had to live in these books and in my imagination. Must you leer at what I've written, Master Shakespeare? Men have composed a thousand poems a thousand times more erotic in their imagery than this one of mine."

"I'm sorry, lass," Shakespeare said gently. "I meant no harm. I like your poem very much. I think most men will like it, most women too. In fact I have a friend here in London who would like to publish it, I think. Richard Field, a former neighbor from Stratford, my home town. Would you let him print it?"

"And have every gallant in London seeking out the woman who wrote it, to see if she is as love-hungry as her Venus? No, I will not!"

"You don't have to sign it," Shakespeare urged. "Many gentlemen, some ladies perhaps, publish anonymously. Richard Field would pay two or three pounds for this, I'm sure."

"And a wealthy young patron might pay several times that if it were dedicated to him," Burbage said. "Say the young Earl of Southampton, for instance. His tastes lean that way, I hear."

Rosaline blushed scarlet. She was as surprised at her own reaction as she was at Burbage's unerring penetration into her thoughts. Ever since her first glimpse of the Earl of Southampton he had been the permanent image of Adonis in her mind. She felt that Burbage must have known that, though his face revealed nothing at the moment. What an actor! she thought as she stared at Burbage, trying to read just one of his thoughts. Just what did he mean?

"A patron would certainly want to know the real author," Rosaline objected, though she discovered that, quite irrationally, she really wanted to dedicate the poem to Southampton, to tell him how beautiful he was, to warn him of the wild boar—the image flashed through her mind:

> *'Tis true, 'tis true! thus was Adonis slain:*
> *He ran upon the boar with his sharp spear,*
> *Who did not whet his teeth at him again,*
> *But by a kiss thought to persuade him there;*
> * And nuzzling in his flank, the loving swine*
> * Sheathed unaware the tusk in his soft groin.*

[29]

The loving swine, Fulke Greville, or maybe Essex, *nuzzling in his flank!* Adonis talking of hunting and manly pursuits and friendship between men, rejecting Venus. Yes, the young Earl should be warned. Surely he would grasp the symbolism of her poem and be saved from such as Greville, *the loving swine,* saved for Venus. It was worth trying.

"Master Shakespeare," she said, shifting her attention from Burbage, "would you sign the dedication? You believe in the poem. Mr. Field is your friend. And I'll give you ten per cent of whatever we can get, just as I did on the play you sold to Mr. Henslowe."

"Why—I don't know." Shakespeare frowned.

"I can't possibly," Rosaline said. "I must keep my anonymity. I have to work in the theater, or—or work for the bishop," she said bitterly. She sat down again, most of the fire gone out of her. "The theater is my world, the only thing I know. My place is on the stage. And I'd like to keep it as long as I can—a place on the stage, not in the goose roost. It is true, I need two or three pounds, and whatever else a patron would give. But I can't risk exposure."

It was difficult to tell whether or not she was acting. Perhaps she herself did not know. But she was giving a touching performance.

"Do it for her, Will," Burbage said. "It may be the wisest move you'll ever make in your life."

Both of the others, struck by some earnest quality in Burbage's voice, looked at the actor quizzically and waited for him to continue.

"I know the theater, as much about the theater as any man in England." He spoke with deliberate authority.

Shakespeare nodded, as most actors in London would have nodded agreement to Burbage's statement.

"And unless I'm mistaken," Burbage went on, "I have found right here the beginning of a great dramatic career." He held up a fistful of manuscript.

"Some of it is rough; I'll grant it is spotty; but already I can pick out those passages which show your mark, young lady, the mark of your genius, as I recognized it in *Richard III.*"

It was Rosaline's turn to doubt Burbage's sincerity. He was being impressive, quite convincing. It was hard not to forget that the man was an accomplished actor.

[30]

"I find Marlowe and Kyd and Greene all here, and, I believe Lodge in this play about King John. I've played parts by all those men and I've seen Ned Alleyn in plays by all of them. I know their work."

"My father and I have worked with each of them at one time or another," Rosaline said in defense of her plays. "Some of those manuscripts are dressings of plays by the men you mention. In *Titus Andronicus,* we've merely shaken up the scenes written by Thomas Kyd."

"So I guessed," Burbage said. "And the things you've done are improvements. Do you grasp the full significance of that, Will? This child has *improved* upon the work of the foremost dramatists of our time."

"Unbelievable!" Shakespeare said.

"Is it?" Burbage asked. "Perhaps she is uniquely fitted to do just that—having grown up in the theater, lived as a boy among men, and yet every bit a woman, as the poem you just read proves. Coached by a devoted scholar, who could be better prepared to present both men and women understandably on the stage?"

If the excitement in Burbage's eyes was feigned, he was a better actor than Rosaline accounted him; and she had utmost respect for his ability. His enthusiasm was infectious. He stood up and began to pace the little free floor space in the cramped room. And he seemed big again, perhaps because of the space restrictions, perhaps because of the size of his idea. Suddenly he stopped and faced Rosaline.

"Do these men know about you?" he asked.

"Not Marlowe or Kyd. We haven't seen them in two or three years. They never did know I was a girl. I was dressed as a page boy, for our tumbling act, when they found us. And after what happened to my mother, I never dressed as a girl again."

"What about Greene?"

"He's dead. He died three or four months ago."

"Yes, I know. Did he know that you were a woman?"

"No. But he did know that I was dressing plays and shaking scenes after my father could no longer work. In fact, he resented it. He called me an upstart crow, my being so dark and so young."

"I remember," Burbage said and quoted verbatim from Greene's *Groats-worth of Wit:* " '. . . there is an upstart crow, beautified

[31]

with our feathers, that with his tiger's heart wrapt in a player's hide, supposes he is as well able to bombast out a blank verse as the best of you; and being an absolute *Johannes fac totum,* is in his own conceit the only Shake-scene in a country.' So you are the upstart crow?"

Burbage laughed in sheer delight.

"Yes," Rosaline said.

"I don't wonder that he resented your youth," Burbage said. "But that's our gain. Greene is dead. Marlowe and Kyd are getting in so deep with the authorities that they're likely to be arrested any time. Lyly and Peele are finished, now that the children's companies are dissolved. And you're only eighteen, and already privileged to pick the best brains in the business and to 'bombast out a blank verse with the best of them.' Yes, young lady, you have a place in the theater, and we'll do all we can to preserve it for a long, long time."

Burbage pushed the deal table over in front of Rosaline's couch and motioned for Shakespeare to draw his packing case up closer.

"By the way, what's your name?" he asked suddenly.

"Rosaline, Rosaline Lee." Her mother had named her Rosa Lena.

"Very well, Rosaline. Your work is not perfect, but it shows the most promise I've ever seen. Now, would you consider joining a syndicate to realize the most out of your talent?"

"Yes."

"Then listen to this. You write for me, and we'll organize a company that will make Ned Alleyn a faded memory, even though he has married old Henslowe's stepdaughter and insured himself a job for life. His writers are already through or dead. You are just beginning."

"But if people find out I am a woman—well—aside from the law forbidding women to work in the theater—"

"The Queen herself would resent you. I know." Burbage waved the objection aside impatiently. "That's one of our problems. We can't let it be known that there is such a thing as a woman playwright. I can't pretend to write your plays. I'm too well known, and there are my father and Cuthbert, my brother. But William Shakespeare—"

He turned to face his brother actor.

"Will, you have a family. You live to yourself, keep pretty much to yourself. You have a house. You are practically unknown, and frankly your future in the theater doesn't look so bright—"

"Now, Dick—" Shakespeare remonstrated.

"Face it," Burbage went on. "You are adequate in bit parts, and you make a handsome king, but you're no Edward Alleyn."

"Or Richard Burbage," Shakespeare said with a broad show of sarcasm.

"Well—no, now that you mention it, you're not. But you are a shrewd business man, the only actor I know who doesn't owe his next year's earnings to Phillip Henslowe. Now, why don't you take Rosaline in, sort of look after her, you and Anne? You represent her, handle her plays for her, let her use your name in business.

"We can keep her secret for her. We can all make money out of the partnership. And I firmly believe we can bring the London stage to heights never before reached. That's what I think of the girl's talent, and of my own!"

"You realize the risk she is taking, don't you, Dick?" Shakespeare asked calmly.

"Yes. I certainly do."

"And the risk Anne and I would be taking? You know the law. If we took her into our home we would be liable for everything she did."

"Yes."

"And what are you risking?" The question was quite pointed.

"I'll stake my professional career," Burbage said. "And I'll pledge my interest in my father's theater to show my good faith."

"What do you think about it, Rosaline?" Shakespeare asked. His matter-of-fact approach was a comfort to Rosaline in the face of Burbage's militant enthusiasm.

"I don't know. It does offer me the chance I want more than anything else in the world. I shall have to trust someone. I think I trust you, Master Shakespeare. What would Mistress Shakespeare say?"

Shakespeare rose and walked over to the window. The three had read and talked all night. The sun had risen and was bringing a light grey into the fog outside.

"We have three children already," Shakespeare said. "Our house is crowded. And Anne is none too friendly toward theater people.

[33]

She would rather I returned to Stratford and went into the glover's business with my father."

Rosaline and Burbage joined him at the window. They sensed that the decision was his, he being the oldest and by far the most stable member in the proposed partnership.

"I'll talk it over with Anne," he said at length. "Find us a piece of parchment, Rosaline, and I'll draw up an agreement binding Dick to his bargain."

Rosaline returned to her father's trunk and opened the portfolio in which he had kept his writing materials. It was the first time she had opened it since his death. She found a sheet of heavy paper easily enough, and a fat bundle of notes addressed: *To Rosaline.*

She gave the blank paper to Shakespeare; and as soon as the two men started phrasing their agreement she opened the bundle and began to read. Her hands trembled and she caught her breath unconsciously at the first shock from the message her father had left. As she read on she became oblivious of Shakespeare and Burbage, of all her surroundings. She did not hear Will Kempe come blustering down the hall after his night of carousing, not even when he burst into the room and greeted his fellow actors with a bluff, guilty heartiness.

Only when Shakespeare spoke directly to her and read the agreement to her did she bring her mind back to the present. Then she listened dully until Shakespeare asked her if she and Will Kempe would sign as witnesses to the agreement.

She nodded.

Shakespeare had written the compact three times on the same piece of paper, with three places for signatures. He and Burbage signed as principals. Then Will Kempe signed as witness.

Rosaline took the quill from Kempe and wrote *Rosaline* in the first space. She hesitated and turned to Will Kempe.

"Do you know about this?" she asked, handing him the letter from her father.

"Yes," he said.

"Is it true?"

"Yes."

Her name then was Rosaline de Vere; but instead she wrote *Rosaline Lee* in the spaces left for her signature. Shakespeare tore the paper into three pieces. He gave Rosaline the center piece and he and Burbage took the end pieces. Thus she held the key, the piece to be matched by both of the others to make the agreement legal.

"Now you have a hold on both of us," Shakespeare said, preparing to leave. "The business arrangements are binding. I'll let you know how I come out with Anne; that is, if she'll talk to me after my staying out all night." He grinned wearily. "Finish up that poem about Venus and Adonis. I'll sign the dedication and make arrangements with Richard Field."

Burbage and Shakespeare left, but Rosaline insisted that Will Kempe stay behind.

"I'm sorry, Rosaline—" he began, a look of complete misery spreading over his disheveled red hair and beard and clouding his pale blue eyes. "About last night."

"That's all right. Will, am I really Rosaline de Vere, the bastard daughter of the Earl of Oxford?"

"Yes. Didn't your father—I mean Allen—ever tell you?"

"No. Until I found this letter just now, I thought Allen Lee was my father. I haven't read all of it, just his note. There are pages and pages of old manuscript with it."

"His reports. Reports he never sent," Will Kempe said and sat down wearily on Rosaline's cot. "I knew your mother, and your grandfather Monarcho, the clown, many years ago. We trouped together.

"The young Earl of Oxford, who was active in the theater then, fell in love with your mother; but old William Cecil, now Lord Burleigh, who was his guardian, had practically forced him to marry Anne Cecil. Nevertheless, his lordship left England with your mother's troupe in 1574 and got as far as the Low Countries, where Cecil's spies caught up with him and brought him back.

"The next year, with the Countess Anne pregnant and a Cecil heir to the Oxford name fairly well assured, Cecil let the Earl travel abroad—under proper surveillance of course.

"Naturally his lordship searched Europe for your mother. He found her in Venice in October, 1575, I believe. And he found you, of course, a daughter some four or five months older than Lady Elizabeth de Vere, the legitimate Oxford heiress.

"That complicated matters for the Earl, for Viola, your mother,

[35]

and for you. Fortunately Cecil's spy, one of the Earl's old tutors—and the man you knew as Allen Lee—also fell in love with Viola and sent in false reports to the Cecils.

"You have the true reports there in your hand, a sort of insurance your father left you to do with what you will. They could prove embarrassing to the Earl, or to the Cecils, though Countess Anne has been dead five or six years now and the Earl has married again, one Elizabeth Trentham.

"Anyway Allen brought you and Viola back to England. I don't know whether the Earl ever knew about it or not. I am reasonably sure that the Cecils didn't, or they would have caused trouble long ago. That's about all I know."

"That's enough," Rosaline said. She was numb. Neither the discovery of her true parentage nor the wonderful prospect that Richard Burbage had opened up for her could prevail against the buffeting that her emotions had taken during the long night.

When Will Kempe left her room, she lay back on her cot in utter exhaustion and fell asleep before he had closed the door behind him.

2

RICHARD BURBAGE WAS NEVER A MAN TO LET HIS PARTNERS IDLE away their time. As soon as Rosaline finished *Venus and Adonis* and turned the manuscript over to William Shakespeare to deliver to Richard Field, Burbage started her to work revising an old play based on Montemayor's *Diana Enamorado*.

It was the story of two young gentlemen of Verona—one a faithful friend, the other faithless. In the light of the current popularity of the friendship theme, Burbage thought the play had possibilities. And even though Rosaline considered the whole plot rather silly and the bandying of Silvia between the two friends positively absurd, she did agree to dress the play for revival.

She worked with Burbage practically looking over her shoulder, too; whether because he had some tardy doubts about her having dressed the other plays or because he merely wanted to see that things were done properly, she could not tell. Naturally their collaboration was not always smooth. First he objected to her inclusion of Will Kempe's already famous skit with his dog.

"It has no place in the plot," he argued. "It simply doesn't fit— a typical English clown going through a quibbling routine with a mongrel on the streets of Verona. Don't you consider that just a trifle absurd, my child?"

"I consider the entire play just a trifle absurd, Mr. Burbage," Rosaline said, looking up from the table at which she was writing. She ignored his referring to her as a child. "Indeed, the absurdity of Launce's speeches to Crab may lend reality to the rest of the dialogue."

"But Will Kempe has given that skit in every tavern and stew in Bankside."

"And in most of the villages and towns in the provinces," Rosaline agreed, with an indulgent chuckle, "and the people love it. I have seen this very skit save many a dull performance.

"I remember one afternoon in Bristol. We were playing in an innyard. The play was *The Widow's Apron Strings,* as I recall, and it was all but stalled—dull, uninspired. The audience, mostly sailors, had already begun throwing things, mushy, rotten things, at us."

Rosaline shrugged and laughed again, comfortably, reminiscently.

"Then Will Kempe borrowed a dog from a little boy in the audience and slipped in between scenes and began this nonsensical patter. He drew chuckles, then guffaws, and then raucous, good-humored cheers.

"He kept coming back between scenes, in a sort of running skit quite independent of the plot, but he saved all our skins. From then on Crab was a regular member of the troupe, and it became standard practice for Will to bring him on whenever and wherever a play started dragging."

"And you think this play will drag?" Burbage was slightly miffed at the suggestion that a play with him in the cast could drag, but it was evident that he had been listening.

"I think it might," Rosaline said, facing him. "But not if Will and his dog play Launce and Crab; that I promise you."

"Very well," Burbage said. "I'll trade out with you. What I

really came to see you about was a song for Tom Downton. He will be cast as Proteus, and he has a beautiful tenor voice. Let's use it."

"Where?" Rosaline asked.

"Oh, where he helps Thurio woo Silvia. You could include his song as a serenade. Here, I have it with me."

He unfolded a single sheet of paper and laid it on the desk before Rosaline.

"Sing it," she urged as he took his place behind her, where he could read over her shoulder. "Can you?"

"I can try," Burbage said agreeably.

He cleared his throat and began to sing in his rich but not very tuneful baritone:

> *"How I love thee, how indeed?*
> *With all my heart I love thee.*
> *Thou art mine only passion's need;*
> *That is how I love thee.*
> *My heart for thee doth ever bleed."*

When he had finished the first stanza, he paused, but Rosaline made no comment. She just sat, quiet, frowning and rereading the lyric before her. Burbage walked around the table so he could see her face by candlelight.

"No?" he said quizzically, when she looked up at him.

"No," she said.

"Remember our bargain," he said, "a trade-out, Will Kempe's silly low-comedy skit for a really fine tenor solo."

"No, Mr. Burbage," Rosaline insisted. "Not a really fine solo. Will Kempe's 'silly low-comedy skit,' as you call it, is a classic in its field. It is sheer clowning, but it is superb clowning, time-tested, comparable in quality to your Richard III.

"But this poem, which purports to be a love lyric, is really silly. It's trite and insincere and—and, well, it just isn't good poetry. Will Kempe's nonsense *is* good fun. Do you see what I mean, Mr. Burbage?"

"Perhaps," Burbage said reluctantly, "but a bargain's a bargain. Let's include Tom's song, even if it is inferior. His voice will carry it."

"Mr. Burbage," Rosaline said, "before we write that lyric into the play, let me see what I can do with the tune, maybe fit some

[38]

pertinent words to it. Hum it again, will you?"

Burbage was hesitant, if not skeptical, but he began to hum the tune, uncertainly and slightly off key. Rosaline tapped out the meter with her left hand as she wrote a few tentative lines.

"Who is Silvia? What is she, that all the men pursue her?" she said aloud after a time.

"Not 'all the men' and not 'pursue,' " Burbage countered. *"Pursue is not the word for a serenade."*

"Not all the men?" Rosaline said. "It seems that most of the *young* men in the play are enamored of the fair Silvia. 'That all young men pursue—do court—her." She looked inquiringly at Burbage.

"No," he said, shaking his head.

"That all our swains commend her," Rosaline suggested; and while Burbage was nodding, she started over and added still another line: "Who is Silvia? What is she, That all our swains commend her? Holy—fair—and wise is she— I think I've got it. May I work on it another day before we decide which to use?"

"I consider that a fair compromise," Burbage agreed, smiling broadly at Rosaline's earnest countenance. "Leave Kempe's lines in. And I think I already know whose lyric Tom will sing."

"Thank you, Mr. Burbage, for me and for Will. He needs a part in every play—and he does draw people to the Rose, the same as you and Mr. Alleyn. He knows instinctively how to please an audience."

"So do you," Burbage said, as he drew on his greatcoat. "If a thorough understanding of the theater and a willingness to work are the stuff playwrights are made of, you should go far."

Rosaline rose to show him to the door.

"And I think you will, you little upstart crow," he added with a chuckle, as he stepped out into the long hall.

The Two Gentlemen of Verona ran for one performance; and although the play as a whole was not enthusiastically received, Will Kempe and Crab were called back four times, and Tom Downton got three encores when he sang "Who Is Silvia?" But Rosaline had little chance to polish up the rough passages. The Rose was closed before the first of February by a new edict of the Privy Council.

Indeed the theaters had been closed since September except for the single month-long season at the Rose which had offered a few days' work to the Admiral's Men and Lord Strange's Men and some stray actors like Rosaline.

The prospect of another year of closed theaters and other plague restrictions was a dismal one; and Rosaline found herself staring at a blank wall. Since her mother had never mentioned the Earl of Oxford, she decided against taking any immediate notice of her true paternity. And she rejected further dramatic composition as being rather futile for the time being. She could, of course, live by reading in taverns, but that would become increasingly hazardous. It would be practically impossible to conceal her sex in such intimate surroundings, especially if she read for the same groups for any length of time.

Nor did she expect anything from her bargain with Shakespeare and Burbage. But that alliance proved to be her one hope. Shakespeare knocked on her door two days after the Rose closed.

When she opened the door, he merely jingled three bright gold sovereigns and dropped them into her hand.

"We struck a good bargain with Richard Field," he said. "He liked your poem—or rather my poem." He laughed self-consciously.

"Three pounds!" Rosaline exclaimed. "He must have liked it, to pay in advance."

"I told you he was an old friend. Now he wants a dedication, and he too favors the young Earl of Southampton. If you'll write it, we'll drop it off at Paul's on our way."

"On our way?" Rosaline was puzzled.

"I think it's time you saw Anne. I've mentioned you, but something has always come up. Now that the theater is closed and Will Kempe is likely to be moving on, you can't stay here by yourself, not on this end of the bridge."

Winchester Row was little more than a stone's throw from her window. Shakespeare's implications were all too clear.

"No," she said. "I must go somewhere."

"And I think your selling a book of poetry may impress Anne more favorably than your talent as a playwright or an actress."

"She knows, and she doesn't approve," Rosaline said uncertainly.

"She may approve. Anyway, write that dedication and we'll be on our way. We live all the way across the city—in St. Helen's Parish, Bishopsgate."

"Very well, come in," Rosaline said and sat down at the table to compose her dedicatory preface to *Venus and Adonis*. She began with a Latin quotation from Ovid's *Amores:*

Vilia miretur vulgus: mihi flavus Apollo
Pocula Castalice plena ministret aqua.

Then she wrote:

To the Right Honorable
HENRY WRIOTHESLEY,
Earl of Southampton and Baron of Titchfield

Right Honorable,
I know not how I shall offend in dedicating my unpolished lines to your lordship, nor how the world will censure me for choosing so strong a prop to support so weak a burden. Only, if your honor seem but pleased, I account myself highly praised, and vow to take advantage of all idle hours, till I have honored you with some graver labor. But if the first heir of my invention prove deformed, I shall be sorry it had so noble a god-father, and never after seed so barren a land, for fear it yield me still so bad a harvest. I leave it to your honorable survey, and your honor to your heart's content; which I wish may always answer your own wish, and the world's hopeful expectation.
                                        Your honor's in all duty,

She left the space blank for Shakespeare's signature, though she wished with all her heart that she might have signed her own name to it. If she were only a legitimate daughter, the Lady Rosaline de Vere, how simple it all would be!

She put on a heavy cloak and a page boy's cap while Shakespeare read the dedication.

"I'm ready," she said, without much enthusiasm, when Shakespeare had signed the paper.

"It's a pretty morning," Shakespeare said, trying to cheer her up. She smiled wanly as she opened her door.

Little of the beauty of the morning was immediately apparent, however. The two actors had first to go through the long tunnel of London Bridge to the Middlesex end. The passage was two carts wide, and almost free of traffic, since the plague had grown worse. Some of the shops facing onto the bridge were open, and others left little windows ajar through which ginger cakes or glasses of wine or handfuls of hot roasted nuts might be passed to customers on the bridge.

Most of the people walked, keeping well to the wall and holding powerfully scented pomanders to their noses whenever they met pedestrians going in the opposite direction. They nodded greetings cautiously, but no one spoke; all seemed loath to open their mouths in public. Rosaline gave a sigh of relief when she and Shakespeare came out into the open on the south drawbridge over the current.

"It *is* a pretty day," she said, and lingered long enough to take several deep breaths before she went into the second section of the tenements built over the bridge. She welcomed the sunlight in the next open span even more eagerly and was in much higher spirits when she passed through the third tunnel and came out into Gracechurch Street, inside the City.

Rosaline had seen little of London. Her father had always shunned the city—for fear of discovery by the Cecils, she guessed. Since his death she had seldom ventured out except in the company of Will Kempe, who went abroad mostly at night and then only to nearby taprooms. But the place stimulated her. Every street, every bend in every street, had its odor—usually foul and pungent, but nevertheless exciting—and its own little view, sometimes a sordid reminder of misery and vice, but just as frequently a breathtaking vignette of stone and timber and living humanity blending harmoniously into a single mood of the city itself. She loved it, as indeed she had loved the smaller towns and the familiar fields of the provinces.

West on Eastcheap, past butcher shops and bakeries to Watling Street, to St. Paul's Churchyard, she strode beside Shakespeare, savoring the thousand and one sensations that came out of the city to greet her.

Paul's Churchyard was busier than London Bridge or Gracechurch Street had been. In spite of the plague, the place was crawling with hawkers of popular pamphlets and ballads and sensational broadsides; and the walls were lined with stalls kept by the more reputable booksellers. Few people bought anything, but nondescript scholars and students rubbed elbows with foppishly dressed gallants as they all browsed through the bookstalls and openly read the broadsides without paying the hawkers a farthing.

Shakespeare stopped at the sign of the White Greyhound, where he left the dedication with an apprentice who was keeping the shop for Richard Field.

"Just tell him Will Shakespeare left it," he said.

Rosaline could hardly keep her hands off the books displayed. She had never seen so many books before in her life. She wanted them all. She understood why her father had collected so many, finally so loading down the wagon in which they had traveled that they themselves had been forced to walk during their last few months on the road. She laughed softly to herself as she thought what would have happened if she and her father had ever come to Paul's together: they would have had to get two wagons and another horse to help old Caesar haul them around.

"Come along, lad," Shakespeare said. "We still have over a mile to go."

He led the way through the cathedral itself, down the center aisle, known then as Duke Humphrey's Walk. The old church was noisier than the yard had been. Out-of-date playbills, hand-scrawled rental notices, and signs advertising services of all kinds hung on the pillars and hid the elaborate carvings of the railings before the altar. Money lenders and brokers crouched in the shadows waiting for surreptitious borrowers and clutching their purses in their hands, away from pickpockets and cutpurses who lurked in still darker shadows.

Instinctively Rosaline placed her hand over her codpiece, a tasseled purse hanging from the swordbelt of her page's costume. She had never been in St. Paul's Cathedral before, but such a crowd was no novelty to her, and her eye for rogues was probably much keener than the eyes of the two stupid-looking catchpoles assigned to police the churchyard.

Cheapside, a wide thoroughfare lined with well-kept shops, fairly glistened in the winter sun, which was by that time almost directly overhead. The buildings in Goldsmith's Row, the pride of London, shone like open jewel boxes. Rosaline found herself lagging behind to look at wares intended strictly for ladies. Recently she had been becoming more and more keenly aware that she was a woman, in spite of the masculine appearance she was forced to assume. She was discovering feminine yearnings quite aside from those expressed in *Venus and Adonis*.

Shakespeare indulgently loitered with her until they reached

Threadneedle Street, which he took as a short cut to Bishopsgate Street. Between Bull Inn and the gate, they came upon a crowd of jeering citizens.

"What is it?" Rosaline asked.

"A carting, I think," Shakespeare said and opened a passage through the crowd. The parting citizens revealed a two-wheeled cart drawn by a broken-down Barbary roan. Two offenders against the citizenry were tied to the rear of the cart by a few feet of cord.

One was an arrogant young apprentice stripped to the waist, presenting a bare back already striped by the whip of the beadle who followed along behind, lashing the culprits and proclaiming their crime in a monotonous singsong.

The crime was harlotry, and the other culprit was a young country wench with the face of a child but the ripening body of a woman. She too was stripped to the waist and her hands were tied behind her, the more to accent the fullness of her high young bosom, which was the feature attracting most of the crowd and drawing the most vociferous comment from the old lechers who leered at the girl from upstairs windows. Her upper arms were marked by the beadle's whip as were her out-pointing breasts, purple-tipped in the cold air and only partially hidden by the luxuriant blonde hair which hung loose around her shoulders. Her dejection presented a perfect contrast to the apprentice's bravado in the face of their humiliation.

"Which house will you be in tonight, Doxie?" a bold gallant called above the beadle's droning recital of the culprits' sins. The crowd laughed and suggested the names of a half-dozen brothels farther out in Bishopsgate, beyond the city walls.

Shakespeare hurried Rosaline on past the scene and through Bishopsgate. About halfway to Artillery Garden, he turned into a sidestreet and stopped at the second house, one of a row of two-storied tenements built to house the influx of foreign artisans whom the guilds would not allow to live inside the City.

"This is where we live," he said. "Wait here on the stoop. I'll fetch Anne."

He went inside. The front room of the lower floor was given over to a glover's shop run by a Fleming, whose name was inscribed across the body of a wooden calf hanging from a bracket by the door. Rosaline heard Shakespeare climbing the stairs to the second floor. She wondered why he had left her standing outside. Perhaps

Anne was even more hostile than Rosaline had expected her to be.

Presently Shakespeare clumped down the stairs again and ushered his wife out onto the stoop. Anne was a tall gaunt woman, wearing a clean linen apron and cap. Her mouse-colored hair was drawn back severely into a bun on the back of her neck, and her thin face looked harsh in the clear sunlight. She appeared to be eight or ten years older than her husband.

"This is Rosaline," Shakespeare said, "the girl I told you about."

"In boy's clothes." Anne was shocked; deliberately so, Rosaline guessed.

"I've explained all that," he said.

"Yes, I remember. How do you do."

"How do you do," Rosaline said as primly as Anne had spoken the words.

"So you want to live with us?" Anne asked, disapproval patent in every word and expression.

"I should like to rent a room. I can pay."

"Richard Field bought her poem for three pounds—in advance," Shakespeare said.

"It's unnatural for a woman to read and write—especially for money," Anne said. "And to dress in men's clothing. That's sinful; it says so in the Bible."

Rosaline's eyes widened. Was it possible that Anne Shakespeare was a Puritan? And she the wife of an actor?

"I have three children, young lady," Anne went on. "Two little girls and a little boy. This neighborhood is a disgrace as it is, nothing like Stratford, where we came from." She scowled at her husband.

"And to take in a girl—a girl who wears boy's clothes and acts in the theater. It's against the law—"

There was a steadily growing clamor in Bishopsgate Street, just one house away. It finally drowned out Anne's speech.

"What's that noise?" she shouted above the din.

"Oh, just a carting," Shakespeare said. "We passed it on the way. Some little country wench, with no place to live probably, got into trouble and got caught. Nothing serious." His voice was elaborately casual, too casual to be cruel.

The cart stopped at the corner, in full view of the party on the Shakespeare stoop, while the beadle mumbled his charges and gave each of the culprits five lashes with his whip. Welts on the young offenders' backs glowed red, and the girl especially winced under the blows as though she could not stand another beating.

Rosaline watched indignation spread over Anne Shakespeare's face, and her heart sank. She was inclined to blame William Shakespeare. He could not have chosen a more inopportune time to ask his wife to take in a stray girl—an actress at that. He knew of the carting, and yet he had deliberately allowed their meeting to take place on the stoop about the time the cart could have been expected.

When Anne spoke, her voice carried the same measure of indignation apparent in her face.

"She's—they're mere children," she said. "Being whipped in public like that. The poor girl will never have a chance, after the humiliation of being carted. It's an outrage!"

She slowly shifted her gaze to Rosaline and speculated for a moment. Her face lost its harshness, her grey eyes their habit of stern appraisal. And her voice had a new warmth in it when she spoke again.

"We do have a room," she said softly, her speech barely audible above the hubbub moving on out Bishopsgate Street. "It's small, but it's warm. When can you move in, child?"

It was several years until Rosaline learned that Susanna Shakespeare had been conceived three or four months before Anne and William were married. So, at the moment, she could not account for Anne's sudden change of heart. Her puzzled glance at Shakespeare was met by a broad grin and a sly wink. Obviously he understood his womenfolk, as well as the timing which made for effective drama.

3

THE SHAKESPEARE CHILDREN TOOK TO ROSALINE AT ONCE. HAMNET and Judith, both perfect images of their handsome father, were eight years old when Rosaline moved in, and as lovable a pair of twins as could have been found in all England; or so they appeared to Rosaline, who was tasting real family life for the first time. Susanna, lacking a few months of being ten, was more like her mother; and her insistence on sharing Rosaline's room somehow made Rosaline feel that Anne herself approved of "Our Sister Rose," though Anne's reserve seldom cracked as it had that once under the impact of the carting.

Rosaline got off to a bad start with Anne, when the older woman insisted that she immediately quit wearing the shameless hose and doublet and get herself some decent dresses. Rosaline complied willingly enough, even to allowing Anne to supervise the buying and sewing of her wardrobe. And she let Anne dress her for the first time as a simple, normal girl, not as a great lady on the stage in heavy court dresses hastily thrown on over hose and waistcoat. Naturally the new clothes seemed strange.

"So this is how it feels to be a woman," Rosaline said as Anne backed away to survey her handiwork.

"How do you mean, my dear?" Anne was pleased with what she saw. Any dress would have been an improvement on those disgraceful boy's outfits.

"I don't know exactly what I mean," Rosaline said upon being pinned down to a literal explanation. "Maybe it's—I mean, don't women wear *anything* under their petticoats?" Her mother and Olivia, "the shameless Italian tumbling women," had worn tight knit drawers under their circular skirts, but of course in the tumbling business—

"Something under our petticoats?" Anne frowned in mild puzzlement as she adjusted a pleat.

"I mean—well, I've worn hose and breeches so long, it feels strange not to have anything between my legs—so naked."

"Something between your legs, indeed!" Anne said, suddenly shocked into attention.

Rosaline felt herself blushing at the construction Anne placed on her words.

"Naked!" Anne continued archly. "Well, I never! No, to feel naked certainly is not to feel like a woman!"

Anne knelt to pin up a hem and to hide her own embarrassment at the turn the conversation had taken. The bite she took on a mouthful of her precious pins further accentuated the set of her jaw. Obviously she did not equate nakedness with femininity.

But now the matter had presented itself, Rosaline wondered. Her acquaintance with women, for the last five years at least, had been through literature. The poets had little to say about nakedness in men. But of women—the recurring image in Ovid was that of a naked girl at the poet's bedside, and there were countless others. Her own image of Southampton as a golden-haired Adonis was but a turnabout. She wriggled slightly inside her voluminous petticoat. Yes, the freedom of her thighs, her own flesh on flesh, did make her feel more like a woman—irrationally perhaps, but there it was. And she rather liked it. She wriggled again, comfortably, sensually.

"Hold still!" Anne snapped. "How do you expect me to measure a hem with you squirming like an eel?"

"I'm sorry," Rosaline said. She stood perfectly still and looked down at the top of Anne's neat linen cap. She *was* sorry. She had not meant to shock her benefactress. But after having lived among men for so long, having become accustomed to their frankness, even their vulgarity and jocular obscenity, she wondered that she did not scandalize Anne every time she opened her mouth. She was finding out how it felt to be a woman; she had to learn how to talk to a woman, to live as one. She resolved to study Anne, to study every woman she met, until she understood them as well as she had grown to know men.

She began teaching Susanna to read and to make her letters. And upon the insistence of Richard Burbage she spent some time reading a number of old plays from his father's library.

Then the bound copy of *Venus and Adonis* came from Richard Field, and a few days later a letter forwarded by the printer from the Earl of Southampton.

"Want to read my mail?" Shakespeare asked, handing her the note.

She glanced hastily at the signature and then read eagerly:

Master William Shakespeare,
Only today has my copy of your most excellent *Venus and Adonis* caught up with me. First it went to my lodgings in the Strand, thence to my mother at Southampton House in Holborn. Her ladyship brought it to me here at Titchfield, where I was called on business a few days ago. I am delighted to be named god-father to "the first heir of your invention," and the prop to support the

burden which you so modestly term "weak," but which needs no support at all. Indeed it can stand alone in any company.

So pleasing a literary gem deserves a more elaborate setting than the mere printed page. Therefore I request, indeed I command, that you be at the Mermaid Tavern, a fortnight hence (May 9) for the debut of my god-child. Bring your talented young apprentice, if you will, since the same group who heard him read at the Pipe and Tabor some time ago will be present, as will others of similar tastes. I look forward to hearing him read your graceful lines to the noble company. Richard Burbage too will be welcome and perhaps interested in a proposal I shall make at that time.

From Titchfield this 25th of April, 1593.

Your assured friend,
H. Southampton

"May I keep it?" she asked, hugging the letter to her bosom.

"I see no reason why not." Shakespeare chuckled. "It's yours, you know. I only hope our mixed identity doesn't complicate matters too seriously." He sounded a little disturbed.

"And we do accept the invitation?" The vision of the young Earl filled her mind, even to the exclusion of her pride in her own published poem.

"It's a command," Shakespeare reminded her. "It is the privilege of a patron to command."

"Yes," she said, and she wondered how much it was his privilege to command; no more than she was willing to grant at that moment, she was sure. She looked away from Shakespeare, lest he read her thoughts.

"You of course will resume the role of my boy apprentice." He *had* read her thoughts. He was smiling knowingly, if indulgently, when she glanced his way again.

"Yes," she said again. She could not keep a hint of dismay out of her voice, or out of her face. She had to remind herself that the Earl had written a polite letter from a patron to a poet whom he knew as a thirty-year-old man, not a silly, moonstruck eighteen-year-old girl.

But her spirits were not damped. Her imagination ranged from the careful planning of how she would act at the Mermaid Tavern to fantastic dreams of how the golden-haired Adonis would see through her disguise, discover the true love in her heart, and, flouting all conventions, carry her away on his snow-white charger.

Then she would practically writhe in embarrassment at the absurdity of her own childish thoughts, and start giving reasons why it was impossible for the Earl to think of her as a girl, much less as one worthy of his personal attention.

First, she would have to play the boy so well that not even another Burbage could penetrate her disguise. Second, the Earl could have any woman at court if he wanted her. And that brought back the disturbing memory of his infatuation with Essex, and the presence of Sir Fulke Greville in his circle and the stories she had heard of Sir Francis Bacon and Lord Henry Howard. She remembered "others of similar tastes" from Southampton's letter, and of course placed the worst possible construction on the words. Then she began to brood over that possibility.

Her *Venus and Adonis* was supposed to arouse normal passion in the Earl, or in any man, for that matter; so to fill the days until she would actually see his lordship she began a series of sonnets, a sort of sequel in the same vein, or in a slightly more serious vein. Following the conventional pattern of urging a young man to marry and produce a son in whom to perpetuate his beauty and his virtues, she started out rather impersonally:

From fairest creatures we desire increase,
That thereby beauty's rose might never die,
But as the riper should by time decrease,
His tender heir might bear his memory:
But thou, contracted to thine own bright eyes,
Feed'st thy light's flame with self-substantial fuel,
Making a famine where abundance lies,
Thyself thy foe, to thy sweet self too cruel.
Thou that art now the world's fresh ornament,
And only herald to the gaudy spring,
Within thine own bud buriest thy content,
And, tender churl, mak'st waste in niggarding
  Pity the world, or else this glutton be,
  To eat the world's due, by the grave and thee. (1) *

*The numbers of the sonnets quoted follow the order established in the 1609 edition published by Thomas Thorpe, who however paid little or no attention to the sequence in which the poems were originally composed.

But in her own enthusiasm she quickly became urgent. And quite in the mood of her poetry, she actually began to feel that if the Earl did not have a son almost momentarily, the world might well lose its brightest ornament before a copy could be made. With the terrible prescience of the young she visualized the horror of Southampton's reaching lonely middle age, faded and childless. The thought was more than she could bear. The young man had to be warned that long years were ahead; a second sonnet spoke of forty winters.

> When forty winters shall besiege thy brow,
> And dig deep trenches in thy beauty's field,
> Thy youth's proud livery, so gaz'd on now,
> Will be a tatter'd weed, of small worth held:
> Then, being ask'd where all thy beauty lies,
> Where all the treasure of thy lusty days,
> To say, within thine own deep-sunken eyes,
> Were an all-eating shame, and thriftless praise.
> How much more praise deserv'd thy beauty's use,
> If thou couldst answer—"This fair child of mine,
> Shall sum my count, and make my old excuse—"
> Proving his beauty by succession thine.
>   This were to be new made, when thou art old,
>   And see thy blood warm, when thou feel'st it cold.   (2)

And by the time she started the third sonnet, she had placed herself right in the middle of the problem. Already she had gone beyond the mere feeling that the Earl should leave a son: a woman would of necessity be involved, and Rosaline could not imagine a woman anywhere who would be unwilling to oblige. Perhaps the idea came to her quite unconsciously, or perhaps her realization that the young Earl had hardly known his father, who had been dead for many years, gave her poem its added emphasis on motherhood.

> Thou art thy mother's glass, and she in thee
> Calls back the lovely April of her prime:
> So thou through windows of thine age shalt see,
> Despite of wrinkles, this thy golden time.

[51]

> *But if thou live, remember'd not to be,*
> *Die single, and thine image dies with thee.* (3)

After a half dozen more sonnets, and over a week spent in their composition, she found herself ending one,

> *Make thee another self for love of me,*
> *That beauty still may live in thine or thee—* (10)

and addressing her patron as "Dear my love" in still another (13). But by that time she was so completely at home in a world of her own creation that she could see nothing exceptionable in the familiarity of her language.

She told no one what she was writing; but when she put on her page's costume and joined William Shakespeare and Richard Burbage for the long walk to the Mermaid Tavern, she had seventeen sonnets hidden in the copy of *Venus and Adonis* from which she was to read. And she carried with her still other poetry, poetry which was never written but which sang in her ears as she started to see the Earl of Southampton for the second time in her life. Had she not been a poet, she might not have been capable of building up the one-sided romance which had taken possession of her during her short experience as a woman.

Shakespeare and Burbage were full of news which they considered more important than her reading before a company of noblemen. Three days before, the Privy Council had issued a license to the Lord Admiral's Men and Lord Strange's Men to travel and present plays in any towns free of the plague and not within seven miles of London. Since Edward Alleyn was to lead the combined troupe, and had indeed arranged for the license, Burbage was none too happy, though he seemed willing to travel under almost any conditions so long as he had an opportunity to appear in those roles which he considered his. Shakespeare was not at all eager to leave London unless he could send his family to Stratford-on-Avon. He could make more money helping the Flemish glover than he could on tour with a company of players. Of that he was sure.

Rosaline had no particular interest in the matter. It would be practically impossible for her to go on the road again, even though Will Kempe was named in the license and Shakespeare and

Burbage might go along. Without her own gypsy-like caravan, which she had lived in and used as a dressing room even when it was loaded with books, she could hardly make her changes and conceal her sex from a company made up of strangers, especially when there were so few jobs and a plethora of unscrupulous actors in the most vicious competition for those jobs.

So her feeling was principally one of relief that the two men had something to keep their minds off her while they walked through the streets of London. It gave her leisure to collect her wits—and her dreams—and to plan how to make the most of those precious hours she would be privileged to spend in the presence of his lordship. In her musing she never once considered the possibility that the young Earl she was building her fantasy around might be a figure of her own creation, the Adonis of her poetic improvisations, quite unlike the real nobleman who had reserved the Mermaid Tavern for the evening.

Nor did Southampton do anything to dispel the picture that was growing in her mind, not that evening anyway. Even though the three actors arrived early, the Earl was already preparing to receive guests, and a consort of eight viols was playing softly behind a painted arras. The entire ordinary of the Tavern was decorated for the occasion. Much of the plate and all of the fine damasked napkins displayed the Southampton crest. Other noble guests had lent their flags to the occasion, which began to take on the air of an affair of state. The Mermaid looked like a room at Whitehall.

"Your lordship shows a remarkable flair for the dramatic," Burbage said as he surveyed the room from the Friday Street entrance. "This setting would do justice to any professional in London."

Rosaline, shocked by Burbage's audacity, was in turn surprised to see the Earl flush with pleasure at the compliment. Burbage knew his audience, baseborn or noble.

"I have always been interested in the theater," the Earl said modestly. "What little I know of dramatic values I picked up in your father's Theater, Mr. Burbage."

"No, your lordship," Burbage insisted. "Such gifts are instinctive, inborn."

A less partisan observer than Rosaline might have accused Southampton of being coy in response. But for her his smile was the rising sun, especially when he turned it full upon her to give point to his next suggestion.

"I was especially eager to have you professionals arrive early," he said. "I want to know what you think of this idea. Master Shakespeare, your poem is so passionate—yes, I've read every word of it—and the images so erotic, I wonder how it would be if the boy"—he warmed Rosaline with the full radiance of his smile— "were to dress as a Grecian maiden and read from here." He moved a panel of the arras and revealed a set of marble steps leading up to a classic façade painted on a screen.

"The host was so good as to have these properties prepared in advance," Southampton explained.

The properties were obviously rented from Phillip Henslowe, the three actors thought at once. Host William Williamson was a sly one. He had probably charged his lordship for having the entire scene specially built.

"I have also arranged for the costume," the Earl went on.

Rosaline felt the amused stares of her partners concentrating on her.

"Why yes, I think that would be most effective, my lord," Burbage said, almost gleefully.

"Yes, indeed," Shakespeare agreed.

After Rosaline had resolved to play the boy apprentice with such skill that no one could guess her sex! It was a conspiracy. Shakespeare and Burbage were struggling to restrain their mirth. Fortunately all eyes, even those of William Johnson, the host's apprentice, were on her instead of her companions, or someone would surely have suspected that very strange things were in the offing.

"The guests are arriving at the Bread Street entrance, your lordship," the apprentice announced.

"What do you think of the plan, lad?" Southampton asked Rosaline. He was impatient to greet his guests.

"Why—yes, your lordship, whatever you wish." She spoke meekly, suggesting strictest obedience. It was the privilege of a patron to command. And with her erstwhile protectors abetting him, she could not hope to have her objections sustained. Nevertheless she was seething inside. And yet she had wanted the young Earl to see her as a woman. Very well, she would play Venus for all she was worth. She met the eyes of Burbage and

[54]

Shakespeare as Southampton turned to leave. She withered both men with a single glance and then tossed her head arrogantly. If she must stand alone—

"Where shall I find the costume?" she asked, addressing no one, but aiming her question at his lordship, who was just leaving the room.

Something in her voice made him stop and turn around before he answered.

"The host will have it," he said.

Rosaline still faced the other two men. Southampton studied the back of her head for a moment before proceeding toward the Bread Street door to meet his guests.

"I have the costume," William Johnson said. "Come with me."

He was about Rosaline's age, an alert grave-eyed youngster who seemed eager to set everything in order for the party. Already he was showing signs of becoming a host in his own right.

"His lordship has been spending money like a sailor on leave," he said professionally to Rosaline as he led her to a dressing room off the scullery. "If you give a good performance, lad, he'll pay you a bagful."

"I'll do my best," Rosaline said, assuming her little-boy modesty again.

"That's what he wants. He's been ordering the best all day. Here's the dress."

He opened a cupboard and showed her a Grecian maiden's costume hanging on the wall. It was a simple white gown with a gold cord for a sash. A pair of gold sandals hung from a peg nearby. Rosaline held the dress up before her. The length was right.

"You'll make a pretty girl," William said admiringly.

"I play women's parts on the stage."

"I thought so. Well, do your best, as I said."

"I will. May I dress here, after dinner?"

"Sure. You know how to find the place?"

"Yes. I can find it."

"Then I'd better get back to work."

Rosaline followed the apprentice back to the ordinary. She was glad to see William Harvey and William Strachey among the guests. They spoke to her, as did the Earl of Essex. Sir Fulke Greville was a less pleasant sight to her.

[55]

"I've been looking forward to hearing you read Master Shakespeare's divine poem," he said. He took her hand and held onto it, stroking her palm annoyingly. "I've never seen a lovelier boy, nor read a more fascinating poem. Ah, those images of Adonis! You should make them live."

Rosaline retrieved her hand and said something unintelligible. She would certainly spoil his evening when she appeared in woman's clothes, as Venus rather than Adonis. The thought gave her some malicious satisfaction, as she took a seat in an obscure corner of the room and studied her audience. Sir Walter Raleigh was there, as well as several other members of the Friday Street Club who were attending Southampton's party in lieu of their regular May meeting. And Rosaline was immediately attracted to the Danvers brothers, Sir Henry, about the same age as Southampton, and Sir Charles, some two years older. They were obviously the Earl's best friends, except for Essex, and they seemed to be just the sort of men she would choose as companions for his lordship. There was certainly nothing effeminate about either of them.

She knew Giovanni Florio and several others by sight, or by reputation when their names were mentioned. But she spoke to no one, not even to Shakespeare and Burbage. In fact she deliberately avoided the two actors, who joined various conversational groups before the supper was served, but who always managed to pass her way and remind her, by the amusement lurking in their eyes, that they looked forward to her performance more eagerly even than did the Earl of Southampton himself. Very well, she repeated to herself, let them have their little joke.

As the meal progressed, Rosaline managed to stay in the background. She drew no attention to herself, not even the attention of the young Earl, who was palpably impatient to have the supper over and to get on with the treat he had arranged. His eagerness was for the poetry dedicated to him and for the setting he had devised, however; he was not yet conscious of Rosaline as more than a talented boy who might read the poem to best advantage. So she was free to study his handsome young face, animated as it was by the compliment of the dedication and the almost unanimous approval of the poem by all who had read it. And she found him more beautiful than she had remembered him. Like a servant-girl she stored up images of each of his expressions; she listened for his voice that she might memorize its timbre, that she might recreate him at will in the privacy of her own night thoughts.

She ate sparingly, hardly tasting what little she did eat; and when the dessert course was served, she stole out and made her way to the dressing room. Hastily she threw the Grecian robe over her page's costume, just as she had always dressed for her parts in the theater. She reconsidered, however, and took off her round-hose, or breeches, and her stockings. Then, after a thoughtful moment, she removed her doublet and waistcoat and wore the dress exactly as the Greek maidens had worn similar gowns thousands of years before. She felt like a woman again, finding sensuous, almost sensual delight in the texture of the soft cloth as the toga clung to her bare body, and in the smoothness of her own flesh when her thighs were freed from the separate restrictions of round-hose.

She carefully combed her hair and bit her naturally red lips until they were a shade or two darker. Then she drew on the sandals, gathered her book and manuscripts together, and sought her place on the marble steps. She sat down casually, as she thought a Greek goddess might sit during her more relaxed moments. She looked down at the sandals, kicked one off, and studied her foot. Then she kicked the other one off and hid both of them in a potted palm. She was proud of her feet; they were beautiful, as were her legs, which had been widely exhibited in page boy's stockings, though never fully appreciated for the shapely feminine features that they really were.

Looking around to see that everything was in order, she recognized the musicians as men who had played at the Rose. She spoke to the leader and suggested the music she would like played as her introduction. She too knew a thing or two about dramatic effect, and she was prepared to present the illusion of an illusion which would impress everyone in the house. If his lordship wanted to present a Greek maiden, she would show him a Greek maiden whom the Greeks themselves would have accepted as one of their own. Her coloring was right; and her figure, draped in the authentic Grecian gown, was all any sculptor could have wished for. She wondered if the audience would think that the garment was padded like the court dresses standard in the theater. For once she was willing to take the risk. Within moments the career of a boy actor playing women's parts would reach its peak, or a sensational ending.

Burbage and Shakespeare came behind the arras to assist in the performance. Both stopped in amazement and started to speak at once, but seeing the musicians seated in sight of Rosaline they merely stared in mute surprise. She smiled at each of them, condescendingly, as Venus, or even Minerva, might have smiled on a pair of bewildered mortals.

Burbage recovered first. He shook his head slowly in admiring disbelief.

"Are you ready, Venus?" he asked, a broad grin breaking over his countenance.

Rosaline nodded. She did not deign to speak. Already she was tasting her triumph over the two traitors who had let her in for this. Shakespeare regained his wits in time to help Burbage move panels of the arras to one side when Rosaline signaled the musicians to begin their overture.

The effect on the audience was instantaneous. A gasp of surprise was followed by an awesome silence. Rosaline's memory of her mother's grace in tableaux brought simple beauty to all she had learned in her portrayals of great ladies on the stage. She presented exactly the picture she intended. The music stopped and she began:

> "Even as the sun with purple-colored face
> Had ta'en his last leave of the weeping morn,
> Rose-cheeked Adonis hied him to the chase.
> Hunting he loved, but love he laughed to scorn.
>   Sick-thoughted Venus makes amain unto him
>   And like a bold-faced suitor 'gins to woo him."

As she continued she found the images which had first inspired her lines recurring to give color to her reading. She read more from memory than from the printed page and soon she let her eyes go roving over the faces of the men seated about the room. It was almost as though she could see the same images forming in the men's eyes, which followed every movement of her lips. How much she herself formed a part of those images, how she became Venus to every man before her, she could not have known. But she did feel that the audience was a lute in her hands, strings at

[58]

her finger tips, sensitive to her slightest pressure, a rich sounding board to amplify the softest whisper of music in her poetry.

For an hour she read, remembering every nuance she had written into the poetry and responding to every outgoing impulse from her entranced audience. At the end,

"Thus weary of the world, away she hies,"

Rosaline let her voice fade to little more than a whisper, as though Venus were truly disappearing from the world. No one seemed to know exactly when she quit speaking. There was a pause, a moment of dead silence. Men rubbed their eyes as though they distrusted their vision—or perhaps it was their hearing. Then to a man they broke into unrestrained applause which threatened to shatter the sturdy oak beams of the Mermaid Tavern.

Rosaline rose and bowed, shyly as she had been taught by Viola and Olivia, but effectively, as she had learned in a hundred provincial inn yards when her next meal depended on the number of bows she could take, each drawing a shower of pennies. There were no pennies thrown in the Mermaid, but the confident smile on Will Johnson's face assured Rosaline that the guests were going to pay: they had been treated to the best.

When the applause had changed into a clamor for an encore, Rosaline raised her hand for silence. She still had her audience under control. The noise stopped at once.

"I do have an encore, gentlemen," she said. "A sequence—the beginning of a sonnet sequence which Master Shakespeare has addressed to his lordship, the Earl of Southampton."

She could not resist a glance at Shakespeare to see how he was going to react to his latest poetic offerings.

"These sonnets, like most sonnets, are of course quite personal—but with his lordship's permission?"

She waited for Southampton to grant her request.

He stood up at his table near the marble stairs. He more than any other man present seemed to be dazed by what he had just witnessed. He looked at Rosaline in bewilderment, in disbelief, almost in awe, as though he had seen a miracle. She smiled at him expectantly, and felt a surge of pleasure course through her body, a half-erotic, half-malicious satisfaction in the power that she knew she was exerting over the handsome young peer.

[59]

"Yes—yes—lad, by all means read Master Shakespeare's sonnets," he mumbled at last.

"Thank you, my lord," she said.

She re-opened her book; and facing her audience again, she read the sonnets from manuscript. In them what had been impersonal and abstract in *Venus and Adonis* became an intimate appeal to one man. And what might have been an anticlimax to the featured piece of the evening actually gave particularity to the longer poem, because every man present believed that the sonnets were addressed to him alone and that Rosaline was his own beloved, actually composing her sentiments before his eyes.

Without waiting for the second round of applause Rosaline bowed briefly and ducked behind the arras and hurried to make her change back into the page boy's costume with its stiff-fronted doublet. If she knew men, and she thought she did, there would be some pawing when she returned to the ordinary, pawing which would surely discover her secret in the soft folds of a Grecian maiden's dress. She drew on her stockings and round hose before she took off the gown. Then she got into her tight-fitting satin waistcoat and buttoned its twenty small buttons down the front.

Will Johnson suddenly opened the door and stared at the shape of her waistcoat. He showed no surprise, however, in his grave eyes. Rosaline's reaction was one of panic; here was the discovery she had feared, and by a common tavern apprentice.

"Do your friends know you are a woman?" he asked calmly.

"Yes." There was no need to lie.

"His lordship?"

"No."

"The gentlemen are asking for you," he said, his curiosity seemingly satisfied. "They are complimenting Master Shakespeare and his lordship, but they are asking for you. They'll pay a bagful."

And I shall have to split with you! Rosaline said to herself. Just when her chance came, she had laid herself open to blackmail—after all these years.

She encased herself in the stiff doublet and adjusted her ruff. William Johnson hung up her discarded dress carefully and untied the knots in the golden cord.

"The sandals are in the potted palm," Rosaline told him.

"I know. I was watching."

So were the barmaids, Rosaline discovered as she passed through the kitchen on her way back to the ordinary. They stared at her in wonderment at her performance and giggled when she smiled at them. The boldest openly winked at her. What a situation! she thought: caught between admiring young wenches whom she could not accommodate and lecherous old men who thought her portrayal of a woman was but a clever illusion.

And his lordship—she hoped his lordship had been impressed, one way or another; but that line of thought led to an equally anomalous situation. By that time she was back in the noise of the crowded ordinary. The tables had been cleared of everything except ale tankards and wine glasses. The men had relighted their pipes, but most of them stood and talked in little clusters, or in three large groups, of which Shakespeare and Southampton and Burbage were the respective centers. With her return, however, all eyes again sought her face, and she was greeted with still a third round of applause.

Back among men, she felt more comfortable in her boy's clothes and moved freely about the room, accepting the compliments tended her and evading exploratory contacts with men who wanted to assure themselves that their eyes had really deceived them or with a few, like Fulke Greville, who accepted her as a most desirable boy to be courted and fondled.

She welcomed the friendly greeting of William Harvey.

"Master Shakespeare will never know how much he is indebted to you, lad," he said, "for the way you introduced his fine poem."

"Thank you, sir," she said modestly. She smiled and looked around for Shakespeare. He was frowning and mopping his brow as he tried to hold his own in the conversation.

"Let's have another round of ale at our tables," Southampton called out. "I want to talk to Master Shakespeare myself for a few minutes."

"The illusion was complete," Harvey went on. "I was thoroughly convinced that you were the maiden you pretended to be. And I must read the poems carefully. As you read them they sounded as though only a woman could have written them. I must find out for myself how much of the feminine quality was due to your interpretation and how much Master Shakespeare actually put into them."

Rosaline found a new source of uneasiness in Harvey's words.

Suppose discriminating readers did sense that a woman had written the poems. Or—she suddenly understood Shakespeare's frown and obvious discomfort. The tone of the poems, especially the sonnets, which she had introduced without his knowledge, could very well put him in a highly questionable light, if they were as patently feminine as Harvey considered them. She hoped Shakespeare would not give her away to protect his own virility.

"His lordship is beckoning for us to sit at his table," Harvey reminded her.

She smiled her thanks and made her way across the crowded room to a table already occupied by the Earl, the Danvers brothers, Giovanni Florio, and the two actors.

"You wanted me, your lordship?" she asked.

"Indeed I do, lad," he said. Though there was a trace of his earlier bewilderment still in his face, he seemed relieved to see Rosaline dressed as a boy again. Obviously she had been entirely too disturbing in her Grecian gown. "We have big plans in the making, and we want you to be a part of them," he went on.

Rosaline sat down at the table and looked quizzically at both Shakespeare and Burbage for clues to the big plans. Shakespeare continued to frown miserably, and he returned her gaze with an accusing look, as though she were a criminal. Burbage, however, exuded charm and confidence.

"I have asked Master Shakespeare to write a play especially for me, a sort of masque to be given at my country seat at Titchfield," Southampton explained. "Mr. Burbage assures me that your master is an accomplished play dresser and dramatist, fully competent to execute my commission."

"We have confidence in Master Shakespeare, haven't we, Ross?" Burbage said. He leveled his steady hypnotic eyes on Rosaline. "He could write a masque to please his lordship if anyone could, couldn't he?"

"Yes—yes, Mr. Burbage," Rosaline said hesitantly. "But with the license issued for the company to travel—" She left Shakespeare an opening to refuse; she certainly owed him that much. It was obvious that he was beginning to wonder where the deception might ultimately lead.

"We have discussed that, Mr. Burbage and Master Shakespeare and I," Southampton countered. "Mr. Burbage says that these

[62]

provincial tours barely pay expenses at best, just enough to keep the troupes together."

Trust Mr. Burbage to refute any objections to his plans, Rosaline thought. If Mr. Burbage approved, they were all practically at Titchfield already.

"The masque will be worth far more to me," Southampton continued, "than Master Shakespeare's services will be to Lord Strange's Men on tour. Besides it will be a chance for him to take his family away from London during the bad plague months. Titchfield is delightful in the spring and summer, an ideal place to write poetry. I—I even try a few lines myself now and then." He laughed self-consciously.

His laugh was poetry, at least to Rosaline. She wondered if he would stay at Titchfield.

"I will see that you are all well paid," Southampton went on. "Fifty pounds for Master Shakespeare. Comparable remuneration for you, Ross, as a performer in the play, and for Mr. Burbage when he comes down to help us amateurs produce it."

Rosaline looked at Burbage again. He nodded very slightly. Obviously he had anticipated or, more likely, directed Southampton's thinking.

"I told his lordship that you had a lot of influence on your master, since you lived as a member of his family and were completely in his confidence," Burbage said.

"So we are enlisting your aid," Southampton said. "Master Shakespeare seems somewhat hesitant or unduly modest, especially in the light of his very fine poems which you have read for us this evening."

At the memory of her performance, Southampton narrowed his eyes and studied Rosaline intently. Some of the look of disbelief returned to his eyes, and a sort of wistfulness came over his countenance. Despite his eagerness in planning the masque, he was still disturbed, haunted, if Rosaline could judge him as she had come to judge most men.

"I'm sure Master Shakespeare could write your play, my lord." She looked straight at Shakespeare. "And I'm sure that he will do what he thinks best for his family. It would be good for them to get away from London for the summer. When will you want the play finished, my lord?"

"By autumn. For Michaelmas, let us say. We—I mean Sir Henry

[63]

and Sir Charles Danvers, and my Italian tutor Florio, perhaps Messrs. Harvey and Strachey—will be at Titchfield for the harvest." The men seated around the table nodded. "We should like to present the play during the fall festival. Will that give you enough time, Master Shakespeare?"

"Yes—I suppose so, my lord." Shakespeare sounded resigned. "My apprentice is my amanuensis. I dictate to him. How fast can you write, lad?" At last there were friendly crinkles at the corners of Shakespeare's eyes.

"Fast enough," Rosaline said.

"Then it's settled," the Earl said eagerly. "I'll send word to Thomas Dymock to get Whitley Lodge ready for your family, Master Shakespeare. You may go down within the week. You'll be quite comfortable I'm sure."

The decision made, the party entered into a session of more detailed planning. The play should be designed for a large cast, perhaps contain a lot of topical allusion, and by all means have a few songs to give the amateur singers a chance to make up in song what they lacked as actors. It would be presented out of doors, in the garden.

Since most of the conversation was addressed to Shakespeare and subtly directed by Burbage, Rosaline had a good opportunity to study her cast, that she might subtly slant her characters to fit the performers and thereby make casting much simpler when the time came. Southampton and the young Danvers brothers were perfect courtier types, merry madcap lords; Florio, when he spoke, cried out to be cast as a pedant; William Harvey would probably enjoy doing a burlesque on the braggart soldier. The conversation made reference to a Miss Cordelia Annesley, a witty young woman, and one or two other ladies who would like to take part in amateur theatricals, since the professional stage was of course closed to women. And of course Shakespeare could always be cast as a king, and Burbage could do anything assigned him.

The present conversation was sprightly, spiced by the affected witticisms currently fashionable at court, and nostalgically perfumed by Florio's dated euphuisms. Actually it seemed to Rosaline that the men were already rehearsing their parts. Certainly she had begun composition by the time the guests came by the table to compliment her and Master Shakespeare and to take leave of their host.

After the others had gone, the Earl gave Shakespeare twenty pounds in appreciation of the poem dedicated to him. Then he gave Rosaline a handful of gold half-angels.

"These are symbols, lad," he said to her. "I've never seen a creature look more like an angel than you did this evening—a dark angel, perhaps, but a lovely one. I may mean a pagan goddess —or maybe I don't know what I mean," he ended in confusion.

He smiled, but his eyes were troubled. No, he did not know what he meant. Rosaline hoped she did know. If she could only tell him that she was a woman—and end up a cheap punk kept in Bankside, she thought realistically.

"Anyway, I say angelets to an angel, even if I can't reconcile the symbolism." He laughed more uneasily than was his custom and looked away in embarrassment.

"Thank you, my lord," Rosaline said softly. "I'm no angel, but I do appreciate the angelets." Her voice was without conviction. Actually she felt a sense of shame at accepting his money. It was as though she had sold him something which she wanted desperately to give to him.

The Earl walked away with Shakespeare and Burbage. Rosaline opened her codpiece and dropped the angelets into it without counting them.

"I told you he would pay a bagful," Will Johnson whispered at her elbow.

She looked around in rising fear to find him grinning triumphantly. She had forgotten all about him.

"Very well," she said in resignation. "How much do you want? All of it?"

"How much do I want?" he asked in surprise. "None of it. Why?"

"You mean you aren't going to tell that I am a girl? Or threaten to?"

"Certainly not. Why should I?" He was beginning to redden in anger.

"I don't know. I thought— Well, exposure would mean Bridewell or worse. You—you are the only one who knows."

"God's blood!" Will Johnson exploded, "I don't care how you dig your gold out of the lords of London. What you're doing is better than working for the bishop. And you're good—good for

[65]

business, good for the tavern trade. The host made plenty off you tonight. Keep it up."

"Oh, thank you, Will," she said with a deep sigh of relief. She wanted to hug him.

"Keep it up," he repeated. He looked cautiously over his shoulder. "I'll own this place one of these days. I hope you're still around."

He gathered up an armload of tankards and bounded away toward the bar. Rosaline closed her purse and joined her companions at the Friday Street door. His lordship appraised her again, his expression still puzzled, or wistful, as the three actors took their leave.

4

TITCHFIELD FULFILLED ALL SOUTHAMPTON'S PROMISES. FROM THE start, the undertaking assumed a holiday air. The leisurely journey by carrier—two longwagons, each drawn by three horses harnessed in tandem and decorated with gay tassels and tinkling bells—was more of an informal tour of the byroads than a purposeful business trip along the Queen's highway. The drivers followed trails through bright burgeoning reaches of the downs and wound in and out of the fresh May green of New Forest to deliver freight and re-load with fleeces and bales of fluffy combed wool.

For Rosaline it was a return to trails familiar since her earliest childhood. It seemed strange not to bound off the wagon and do cartwheels down the village streets, as she had done with her mother's troupe to advertise the big performances to follow. She missed Bassanio and Ursa, his dancing bear. And she missed Antonio's lute, and the jigging music of Will Kempe's pipe and tabor, both of which used to precede the troupe's entry into a town. But she felt a sense of security, a feeling of safety, at being a part of Anne Shakespeare's family, which she had never known before. Anne was nothing like her mother, and yet despite her sternness she was more motherly than Viola had ever been. Perhaps if Viola had lived, had been allowed to grow old—but she would never have been old, never as old as Anne Shakespeare.

Anne seemed to grow younger though, and less stern, the farther away she got from London. The downs were not her native Warwickshire fields, nor New Forest the Arden she had known, but her smile flashed from gay to sad and her grey eyes brightened and grew wistful more frequently than they were wont to do in London. Her whole face seemed more alive. Rosaline could sense Anne's alternate joy in this country and her yearning for her own midlands; and the very knowledge that Anne was so readily sensitive under her prim exterior drew Rosaline closer to the older woman.

The children, of course, were on an extended picnic made still more exciting by the necessity of pretending that Rosaline was a boy. They now had a new big brother before the novelty of a big sister had worn off, and they took to the fiction with an avidity which promptly dispelled any fears Rosaline might have had of their accidentally revealing her sex. She had forgotten a child's capacity for make-believe, she who had lived by make-believe all her life.

Hamnet profited most from Rosaline's masquerade, since he most wanted a brother to even up the two-to-one advantage which the Shakespeare daughters had always held before. Frail, but agile and quick to learn, he was readily impressed by Rosaline's acrobatics, and teased his new "brother" into performing at every out-of-the-way stop. He was in fact doing simple tumbling feats with her by the time the wagons reached the village of Fareham, where Thomas Dymock was waiting to take his lordship's guests to Whitley Lodge, since the carriers were going around the harbor to Portsmouth rather than up the estuary to Southampton.

Thomas Dymock, Southampton's bailiff, greeted the guests as though they were nobility.

"His lordship instructed me to take you to the lodge," he explained, somewhat apologetically. "I am sure he would have put you up at the Place, had he been in residence. But his mother, the Countess Mary, is now mistress of the household, and his lordship is loath to impose upon her."

"The lodge will be quite satisfactory, I'm sure," Anne answered; with some relief, it seemed to Rosaline. Perhaps the move from a

London tenement to one of the finest manor houses on the south shore would have presented too great a contrast. But the lodge—

"The lady and the children will ride in the caroche," Dymock continued, indicating a small ornate carriage, with a liveried driver standing by. "I have brought horses for the gentlemen."

Rosaline was reminded that she qualified as one of the gentlemen by a groom who held a stirrup for her. She liked the looks of the small Barbary roan which Dymock had provided. He was much like Caesar, the horse she had first learned to ride in the academy run by Pignatelli brothers, friends of her mother—indeed the Italian riding masters had given Caesar to Viola when he was retired from the academy, and the old horse had drawn Rosaline's wagon along this very road many times in the past.

Whitley Lodge, overlooking the Place and a wide stretch of Southampton Water, required no apology. Though nothing like the magnificent Titchfield Place, with its acres of formal garden, the lodge was by far the finest house that Rosaline had ever entered as a guest. Arriving as she had, on an Earl's horse, beside a crested caroche, she was inclined to forget that she was included in "the statute" along with "rogues, vagabonds, and sturdy beggars." She was learning what it meant merely to be the guest of an earl. To be the daughter of an earl, Lady Rosaline de Vere; or the wife of an earl, the Countess—

Anne sought Rosaline soon after the guests had been assigned to their rooms. She knocked softly, almost timidly, on Rosaline's door.

"Come in," Rosaline said. She was still wandering about the room fingering the texture of the bed linen and testing the softness of the feather mattress.

Anne entered and came to her, humbly it seemed.

"I don't know whether this is wrong or not," Anne said. She stood beside Rosaline, and they both stared out of a window overlooking the water. "I mean this deception, and your dressing like a boy and writing plays. I just don't know. But it did get my children out of plague-infested London."

She was silent for a moment. Rosaline could think of no comment.

"We all will have a chance to live in this lovely house for the summer," Anne went on. "It will be something for my daughters to remember forever. There's nothing in Stratford as fine as this, except perhaps New Place. Oh, it isn't new; it's a hundred years old, but it's like this—substantial—comfortable—nice.

"I wish our Stratford friends could see us now." An unexpected note of gloating satisfaction in Anne's voice caused Rosaline to look at the older woman. Anne's eyes were steely, fixed on some point across Southampton Water. "In Stratford they look on Will as a ne'er-do-well. They laugh at us—at his being an actor—and expect us to come home poor and hungry and penitent. If they could only see us now!"

At last she faced Rosaline.

"I love Will," she said. "I had to come with him, even if I didn't want him to be an actor. I couldn't stand the humiliation of staying behind in Stratford or in Shottery and living with our people. I was miserable in London, too. But this—a decent place for my girls to live, even for a little while—this is wonderful.

"And I'm not forgetting that it's not really Will," she continued, smiling wanly, "but you, Rosaline, who are responsible. I know what we owe you."

"Nothing," Rosaline said. "Nothing by comparison to what I owe you. A home, the only one I've ever known. I might be working for the bishop, or walking around London behind a cart, or rotting in Bridewell if you hadn't taken me in."

"Not you, Rosaline!" Anne said in horror. "You're too good, too fine." She blushed at the compliments she was paying this girl in a man's hose and doublet.

Suddenly she threw her arms about Rosaline and drew the girl to her.

"I do thank you, Rosaline," she said. "Even if this doesn't last, you're giving us a few months of happiness."

"It'll last," Rosaline said, resolving to make it last. "Dick Burbage says this is only the beginning of our partnership. If we make good here—and we will—all of us will live in luxury."

"I hope so," Anne said, backing toward the door and trying to cover her embarrassment with an unnaturally bright smile, "I know so, Rosaline—I mean Ross. I must get used to calling you Ross—used to another son in the house."

She turned and hurried out but closed the door gently behind her without a sound.

Rosaline stared thoughtfully at the closed door for a full minute after Anne had left. Then with a resolute expression set on her features, she began to unpack—first her notes and writing materials, then her clothes.

And she kept her writing materials foremost throughout the summer. She took time to give lessons in reading and writing to Susanna, who would spend hours writing her own cramped exercises while Rosaline, seated nearby, worked on her play. There were trips with the other children, tours of the gardens of the Place, trips in the dog-cart drawn by an old mare so gentle that Hamnet could do most of the driving, trips down the three-mile lane to Fareham and on to the ruins of Porchester Castle with its old Norman keep and Roman walls. Rosaline explained the sights to the children, as her father had explained hundreds of such places to her during their wandering about England. Then there was boating on Southampton Water, with William Shakespeare and various members of his lordship's staff pulling on the oars.

But always the play took precedence. When the traveling troupe played in Southampton and moved on toward Bath and Bristol, Richard Burbage slipped away from the other actors and spent a day at Titchfield. He read what Rosaline had written and offered a few suggestions, though he approved of most of her work. He congratulated her and Shakespeare on the easy life they were living. He was full of bad news. Traveling was terrible; road companies were things of the past; London had become intolerable for actors. Both Marlowe and Kyd had been arrested and brought before the Privy Council within a week after the Shakespeares had left the city. Both had been released; but Marlowe had been murdered by the end of May, and Kyd was a dying man.

There was a bright side, however, as Burbage's almost gleeful accounts of the playwrights' misfortunes clearly indicated. The theaters would re-open sometime, and when they did, most of the writers and all of the actors would be starved to death, or so nearly starved that Burbage could recruit a company of the best talent in England to produce Rosaline's plays. Yes, they were all very fortunate to have the present commission from the Earl of Southampton. Burbage urged Rosaline to do her best on the comedy and start thinking about tragedy, which was his forte. With that he left, after promising to return when the road company headed north to Shrewsbury, or when his lordship needed him to produce the play, whichever was earlier.

So Rosaline worked for some four months under almost ideal

conditions. She sometimes allowed herself brief periods of keen disappointment because his lordship had not come to Titchfield; but her better judgment told her that his presence might have occasioned the distraction which would have marred her best work, or perhaps kept her from producing anything at all. His image was with her constantly, however; and fully aware of her rashness she built the most attractive role, that of Biron, around him and wrote herself a part, "a wightly wanton, with a velvet brow, with two pitch-balls stuck in her face for eyes . . . a beauty dark" called Rosaline, to play opposite him.

When his lordship did come, he came alone; and after paying his briefest respects to his mother, he hurried to Whitley Lodge for a report on Master Shakespeare's progress. He wore a dusty shoulder cloak over a green doublet. His leather riding boots came up to his roundhose, and all his clothes carried the exciting smell of a hard-ridden horse when he burst into the main hall and rapped on the center table with his riding crop.

"Anybody home?" he called.

Everybody was home, and expecting him, though Thomas Dymock had warned the Shakespeares and the staff to let his lordship spring his surprise. The room filled quickly. Rosaline noticed happily that the young Earl sought her first with his eyes and smiled at her, though he spoke first to William Shakespeare after he had dismissed the staff and the women.

"How is the play coming along?" he asked.

"It's finished, your lordship," Shakespeare said. "That is, it's ready for your reading and suggestions, my lord."

"Excellent! Let's see it at once. Bring some ale, Tom."

"Ross, will you fetch the manuscript?" Shakespeare requested.

Rosaline went into the study and picked up her copy of the play, which was ready to hand; but she waited long enough to make it look as though she had had to search for it. She tried to return slowly, but she found herself hurrying to place the manuscript in Southampton's hands. Her own trembled as she let go of her offering and basked in his smile of acceptance.

"Tell me a little about it," the Earl said, reading over the *Dramatis Personae*.

Rosaline held her hands behind her and crossed her fingers. She and Shakespeare had read the play several times together, and

[71]

she had coached him on what to say in just such circumstances. She hoped he would carry through. This was the first test.

"I have laid the scene in Navarre, your lordship," Shakespeare began, "in the King's park. I remembered that you wanted the play presented outdoors, and so I have adapted all of the scenes to fit the gardens of Titchfield Place."

"Excellent!" the Earl said.

"I have taken a very slight plot, based in some measure on the visit of Queen Catherine of France and Marguerite de Valois to the court of Navarre some years ago.

"The entire treatment is quite whimsical, I believe, a little bit of everything. Some sonnets, some lyrics, some rhymed verse, some blank verse, some prose, a few songs, something for everybody."

"Sounds good," his lordship commented. He was reading while he listened, and Rosaline was pleased to note that he was quite alert enough to grasp both what he read and what he heard.

"There are a king and princess, and three pairs of young lords and ladies, as well as the usual cast of stereotypes: a pedant—your Italian tutor Florio, if you have no objections, my lord—a rustic, a parasite, a bragging soldier and his *zanni*. The braggart soldier owes something to Sir Walter Raleigh, my lord, again if you raise no objections."

"Objections? Indeed not. Raleigh is no great friend of mine or of Robin's—the Earl of Essex, I mean. So poking a little fun at him will please us well." The Earl laughed.

Rosaline smiled at his lordship's reaction. She was proud of her grasp of affairs at court. Obviously her satire was accurate enough to be pleasing.

Thomas Dymock arrived with tankards of ale. He served his master and Shakespeare and took a tankard for himself. The three men sat down together. The Earl motioned for Rosaline to join them, though no ale had been provided her. She sat down facing his lordship, her eyes constantly roving over his handsome face and shoulders.

He laid the manuscript aside as he drank.

"I like what I've read so far," he said. "I'll take it with me and read it as soon as I have had a bath and got into some comfortable clothes. I'm delighted that the play is finished.

"I've sent word to Burbage to come here," he continued. "I'll begin assembling our cast at once."

[72]

After that speech the Earl seemed suddenly self-conscious, as though he had something more to say but felt at a loss for words to say it. There was no opening for anyone else to speak; so the pause grew awkward. The other two men busied themselves with their tankards. Rosaline forced herself to glance toward the door.

"I too have—have been composing," Southampton began finally. "Master Shakespeare, I could not bring myself to address my work to an acknowledged poet of your stature, but I would like you to hear what I have written."

"By all means, my lord," Shakespeare said in some surprise. "But certainly you overrate me as a poet."

Southampton opened the leather purse which he wore as a codpiece and drew forth a piece of paper folded several times.

Rosaline's heart sank into a well of jealousy. She expected a sickening amateurish sonnet to the Earl of Essex, or worse still, to that nauseating Sir Fulke Greville.

"As you chose to address your sonnets to one several years your junior, so have I written my lines to a younger man—a very talented boy."

He smiled at Rosaline as he unfolded the manuscript.

"To you, Ross," he said suddenly, almost blurted, and began to read a poem that began:

> "O thou, my lovely boy!" (126)

"Of course it really isn't much of a sonnet," his lordship said apologetically. "It's only twelve lines, in fact, but that was all I could think of at the time."

"Very good," Shakespeare said, the forced quality of his voice fortunately lost on the flustered young Earl. "The thought is most provoking."

"I have another—one I wrote with an image in my mind of Ross, as the Grecian maiden, reading *Venus and Adonis*." Southampton paused for a moment and then read with considerably more confidence:

> *"A woman's face with Nature's own hand painted*
> *Hast thou, the master-mistress of my passion;*
> *A woman's gentle heart, but not acquainted*
> *With shifting change, as is false women's fashion;*
> *An eye more bright than theirs, less false in rolling,*

[73]

Gilding the object whereupon it gazeth;
A man in hue, all 'hues' in his controlling,
Which steals men's eyes and women's souls amazeth.
And for a woman wert thou first created:
Till Nature, as she wrought thee, fell a-doting,
And by addition me of thee defeated,
By adding one thing to my purpose nothing.
    But since she prick'd thee out for women's pleasure,
    Mine be thy love and thy love's use their treasure."   (20)

The expressions of amazement on the faces of his audience at the end of the sonnet were far more flattering than any words of praise would have been. His lordship was quick to recognize the effect of his poem; and before anyone could speak, he rose and gathered up the manuscript of the play.

"Well, I must return to the Place. I'll read the play tonight and we'll discuss it in the morning."

The others rose and bade him goodbye. He left in a hurry, obviously both embarrassed and pleased by the reception his poetry had met.

Dymock shrugged off the sonnets and gathered up the empty ale tankards. He left Rosaline and Shakespeare alone in the great hall. She slowly turned and faced Shakespeare, her countenance a playground of mixed emotions. Shakespeare was fittingly sympathetic.

"You are haunting his lordship, Rosaline," he said.

"Yes, I know." Her voice was low.

"Did you intend to?"

"Yes—I think so. I didn't ask to appear as a Greek maiden. But I tried to make the most of it. And I did write the sonnets to him."

"Before you appeared as a Greek girl," Shakespeare reminded her.

"Yes," she agreed again.

"Do you know what all this may lead to?"

Rosaline made no answer. She looked away.

"Shall I tell his lordship that there are some faulty lines in his sonnet?"

"What do you mean?" she asked, looking back into Shakespeare's eyes, searching for his implications.

"Till Nature, as she wrought thee, fell a-doting,
And by addition me of thee defeated,
By adding one thing to my purpose nothing—"

Shakespeare quoted accurately; his quick memory was his strongest asset in the theater. "Shall I tell him that Nature really did not add that 'one thing' to you, Rosaline, that you really are not 'pricked out' for women's pleasure?" He had missed none of the Earl's suggestive play on words.

"No," Rosaline said quickly, "that would spoil everything, right now."

"But later?" Shakespeare sounded like Burbage in his insistence. Perhaps he was deliberately doing what he thought Burbage would do to preserve their partnership in a similar situation. He must have guessed that she intended to play opposite the Earl in the play: Rosaline to his Biron.

"I don't know, Will," she said in dejection. "Honestly, I don't know. Don't tell him anything. I'll—he'll—"

"He'll find out for himself, I suppose." Shakespeare supplied the end of her thought. "If he's interested enough."

He threw an arm affectionately around her shoulders and walked with her toward the study.

"It's your life, Rosaline," he said. "Do with it what you will. You are talented; you are beautiful. I can't tell you where your talents and your beauty will serve you best. His lordship would certainly be infatuated with you if he knew that you were a woman. How long it would last—" He no longer sounded like Burbage.

"Aye, there's the rub." She unconsciously quoted a favorite expression of her foster father, Allen Lee. Perhaps she half realized that she needed him more at that moment than ever before in her life. When she looked up at Shakespeare, there were tears, unaccustomed tears, in her eyes. She leaned her head against his shoulder, the nearest thing to a fatherly shoulder that she had. If she could talk to Anne, but Anne—

Anne Shakespeare came around a bend in the stairs and surveyed the great hall.

"Has his lordship gone already?" she asked and then stared at her husband and Rosaline. Her face clouded over at what she saw. There was about the same difference in age between her and Will that there was between Will and Rosaline—all in Rosaline's favor.

"Are you crying, Rosaline?" she asked sharply.

"Yes, Anne," Rosaline said. She blinked her eyes and turned away from Shakespeare, completely unaware of Anne's little flare-up of jealousy. "I'm all right now."

"Something his lordship said," Shakespeare explained. He caught the inflection of his wife's speech, but did not bother to take note of it.

Rosaline went into the study and sat down at her desk. She repeated such lines as she could remember from his lordship's sonnet. She conjured up carefully stored images, each heightened by the recent appearance of the Earl at Whitley Lodge. She remembered the cultivated modulations of his voice, the warmth of his smile when it favored her, the entirely gratuitous consideration which he had shown Ross Allen—his gentleness toward her own boyish self. And she was engulfed by her feeling for him and an irrational fear that he might change, or grow old, or even die. She moistened a pen and began to write.

> *Shall I compare thee to a summer's day?*
> *Thou art more lovely and more temperate....* (18)

5

MICHAELMAS WAS THE GAYEST TIME OF THE YEAR AT TITCHFIELD, A season of all-day feasting and all-night dancing, the house full of noble guests and the spacious gardens given over to his lordship's sturdy yeomen. And that Michaelmas day on which *Love's Labor's Lost* was presented was long remembered as the peak of all festive occasions in Hampshire. The young Earl combined the holiday with the celebration of his twentieth birthday, which came a week later, on the sixth day of October.

The September rains that year had been light, too light for the end of a drought year; but the month had been ideal for the rehearsal of an outdoor masque.

His lordship had assembled a cast of note, if not of recognized histrionic ability. He and the Danvers brothers were cast as Biron, Longaville, and Dumain. Sir Charles and Sir Henry Danvers provided Maria and Katherine, respectively, from among the girls of the local gentry. Rosaline was successful in her plan to be cast as Rosaline opposite Southampton. Miss Annesley played a charming Princess of France to Shakespeare's King of Navarre. Florio played himself, called Holofernes, and Sir William Harvey openly burlesqued Sir Walter Raleigh in the part of Don Adriano de Armado.

William Strachey played Costard, and Sir Fulke Greville took great delight in being cast as Jaquenetta, a country wench but at least a woman. Rosaline had coached little Hamnet, over Anne's objections, until he made an extravagantly precocious Moth. Burbage, besides directing the play, took the role of Boyet, which he of course built into a part intended to dominate the entire production. He was too good a director, however, to feed his personal vanity, and the finished play was a well-balanced piece of fluff which danced and sang and sparkled with sophisticated witticisms and good-humored satire.

Coming, as it did, after an elaborate mid-day feast served outdoors to the tenants and laborers and in the great hall of Titchfield Place to some three hundred house guests from London and Southampton and all the south shore, *Love's Labor's Lost* played before two thousand people assembled in the garden. And not one of the two thousand failed to find something for himself in the play, whether it was a sly reference to an intrigue at court, the sheer joy in language for its own sake, or poignant nostalgia in such homely lines as Winter's song:

> *When icicles hang by the wall,*
> *And Dick the shepherd blows his nail,*
> *And Tom bears logs into the hall,*
> *And milk comes frozen home in pail,*
> *When blood is nipp'd, and ways be foul,*
> *Then nightly sings the staring owl,*
> *To-who,*
> *Tu-whit, to-who, a merry note,*
> *While greasy Joan doth keel the pot.*

[77]

But it was the players themselves who got the most pleasure out of the performance. During the month of rehearsal together, with caste lines suspended and class barriers ignored, they had learned to respect one another, sometimes to love one another, and to work together in the creation of an artistic masterpiece. So the final performance had a bittersweet quality about it, a last delicious taste of easy comradeship before a permanent farewell to the make-believe court of Navarre.

No one felt the full poignancy of that last performance more keenly than Rosaline, unless it was the Earl himself. The two played the most intelligent parts in the masque with a conviction and a convincingness which lent whatever reality there was to the plot. They could be lovers without reserve—it was all make-believe. They could trade quips with delightful sauciness; they could flirt outrageously with each other.

He could say:

> *"Vouchsafe to show the sunshine of your face*
> *That we (like savages) may worship it."*

And she could urge:

> *"O vain petitioner, beg a greater matter!"*

And they both could mean it. For two hours Rosaline could be a dark beauty dressed in gowns, costumes provided by his lordship, which were the equals of any worn by the fine ladies in the audience. For two hours his lordship could pretend that she was the true flesh of the dark mistress he had dreamed of for almost half a year.

Towards the end of the last scene, played by torches in the early autumn twilight, Rosaline found herself dreading the closing song, hating to pair off in the finale, really the finale, the end of a glorious summer, of a painfully ecstatic month of lighthearted banter, repeated again and again in her half-dreams during the nights in Whitley Lodge—the end of everything.

Southampton, too, was loath to let go of the illusion. He held her hand in a tight insistent grip while they sang the Spring song with half the cast on the *Ver* side, and throughout the Winter song, sung by the rest of the cast from the *Heims* side of the stage

[78]

area. He tightened his fingers even more, until they hurt her hand, when the entire cast formed a single rank behind Sir William Harvey while he read Don Armado's last line, addressed to the audience:

> *"The words of Mercury are harsh after the songs of*
> *Apollo. You that way, we this way."*

The musicians struck up a jig and the cast divided and danced away down two narrow avenues of sculptured box and yew leading off in opposite directions from the playing area. A short distance outside the torchlit circle the young Earl suddenly darted through a gap in the shrubbery, drawing Rosaline with him into a secluded arbor.

Savagely he swung her around in front of him and hugged her to him with all the strength he could muster. When his lips found hers, she responded, open-mouthed, with all the pent-up passion that had been rising in her awakening body for nine long months, ever since that first night at the Pipe and Tabor when she had read from Sidney's love sonnets. They clung to each other hungrily until it seemed that his lordship had drawn all the strength out of her body.

Then he released her as suddenly as he had drawn her to him. Limp, she would have dropped to the ground but for the support of a convenient trellis. Southampton took one step backward and stared at her in the dim flickers of light which penetrated the arbor.

Suddenly he slapped her across her mouth with one open hand and wiped his own lips on the back of the other.

"You stinking little catamite!" he said in a vicious, rasping half-whisper. "I might have known!"

Rosaline was too shocked by both the blow and his verbal abuse to realize that his brutality was but an explosion of rage at himself growing out of his own shame at having been the aggressor in so loathsome a business. She had forgotten till that moment that he still thought she was a boy, that he had succumbed to an uncontrollable impulse generated, so far as he knew, by an illusion—and he was ashamed, once the impulse had passed.

"No! No, your lordship," she said in rising panic, as the truth came home to her. "It's not what you think!"

[79]

But there was no time to explain. In a moment he would be gone, and he would shun her forever—if he did not kill her on the spot to erase his disgusting behavior. What could she do in that one remaining second? She was never sure, thereafter, whether she was thinking of herself or of him in that moment of decision.

Acting as precipitately as he had moved in the height of his desire, she flung herself against his chest and turned in his arms so that her back was toward him. Catching him by surprise, she had no difficulty in drawing his right arm over her shoulder and guiding his hand down inside her bodice and cupping it around her firm bare breast.

"There!" she said triumphantly. "I'm no catamite—no stinking little boy. I'm a woman, fully as mature as you are, my lord."

Then she broke away and faced him again. Her words stung him, placed the entire responsibility for his unnatural behavior right back on him, where it belonged, though her intention had been to reassure him. For a moment he bristled, then relented, softening visibly in the flickering light.

"Thank God," he said simply, humbly. "Thank God for you, my darling. Thank God that you *are* a woman."

He drew her to him again, gently this time, as though he had found something precious, to be cherished not ravished. Rosaline buried her face in his jasmine-scented doublet.

"You had to be a woman," he went on, quickening in his speech. "I think I knew that you were. I *must* have known. I couldn't have fallen in love with you otherwise."

"No," Rosaline mumbled through his ruff. "I'm sure you couldn't."

"Did I hurt you? I'll cut my hand off if I did."

"No, my lord. You couldn't hurt me, not physically; I love you too dearly."

"By the way, what's your name?" he asked after a pause.

"Rosaline."

"No, I don't mean in the play. I mean really."

"Rosaline," she repeated. "That's my real name, Rosaline—Lee."

"Then Master Shakespeare deliberately wrote your part in the play to—"

"Don't you know now, my lord? I wrote the play—and the

sonnets—and *Venus and Adonis*. I told you that I was no child—no stinking little boy. Master Shakespeare represents me, as my business agent. A girl wouldn't have a chance as a poet in her own right."

"I see it now," his lordship said, "or I begin to—"

He held her away from him just far enough to try to see her eyes in the dark.

"There's the ball," he said rapidly. "I'll have to put in an appearance, but since it's a masked affair I can slip away. And you—do you still have the mask you wore in the last scene of the play?"

"Yes. Here." She dangled the jeweled vizard in front of him.

"Then wear it, and the dress you have on—you are beautiful in it. And here, take this." He hastily removed his own ring and put it on her thumb.

"Wear this," he continued rapidly, "so I can find you if someone else should have a dress like yours."

"You mean come to the ball—as a woman?"

"Certainly. You've just convinced me that you *are* a woman." He laughed softly. "I'll find you and dance with you—in the gallery. Then we'll find a place where we can talk—all night—forever."

"Yes, my lord," she said demurely.

"Yes, my lord," he mimicked. "You'll be calling me Hal before daybreak, beloved."

With that he kissed her soundly again and ushered her back into the crowded garden, where she soon lost herself among the dancing commoners and made her way to the gallery on the second floor of Titchfield Place. People were dancing there, as well as in the great hall below and both the parlor and winter parlor.

Rosaline had hardly entered the long narrow room before she was drawn into the pattern of a stately galliard. She danced with three masked partners before she was given a chance to get her bearings. When she finally did manage to free herself, she sidled along the wall, ducking under the massively framed portraits of his lordship's ancestors and side-stepping the cushioned chest-settles along the way, until she found a fairly inconspicuous spot which commanded a view of the dance floor and the head of the front stairs.

She sat on a farthingale chair, smoothed out her hooped petticoats, readjusted her mask, and prepared to wait quietly for his lordship. She had reckoned without considering the demand for her as a dancing partner, however. One minute after she considered herself settled for her vigil, she was back on the floor dancing a coranto.

But her second partner whispered "Guess who" just as she caught the jasmine scent on his doublet; and at the end of the set he whisked her down the back stairs, out through the garden, past several teams of Morris dancers, to a rowboat tied up in a creek which ran through the kitchen garden. Without ceremony he lifted her into the boat and cast off. The tide was running out; so his lordship made good time toward Southampton Water.

"We have two tides here," he said, irrelevantly it seemed to Rosaline. "One through the Solent and another by way of Spithead about two hours later."

"Indeed?" she said. "And where are we going? To the Solent or Spithead?" She felt sufficiently at ease to be a little tart in her speech.

"Oh, I forgot to tell you. My pinnace is anchored out in the Water a little way. It's called the *Ictis*, the old Greek name for the Isle of Wight."

"Yes, I know," Rosaline said, somewhat piqued either because he was treating her like a child or because he seemed willing to do such commonplace things as row a boat and discuss tides on so important a night. He had not even kissed her when he lifted her into the skiff.

"The pinnace goes with the Island. It's all part of Hampshire. I'll assume governership some day. I'm already responsible for the maintenance of the *Ictis*."

He rowed in silence for a few minutes, his breathing becoming labored after a time.

"Here it is," he said as the hulk of the sixty-ton pinnace loomed in the moonlight. "*Ictis,* ahoy!"

"Ahoy," the sleepy watch replied. "Who is hailing?"

"Southampton."

"Aye, aye, your lordship." The watch was suddenly wide awake. He threw a line and drew the skiff alongside a ladder suspended from the quarterdeck.

His lordship boosted Rosaline up the ladder ahead of him and followed her on board.

"How would you like to join the dancers up at the Place, lad?" he asked the watch.

"Very much, sir."

"Then begone and don't come back before sunrise."

"And if I see Mr. Strachey, sir?"

"Tell him I relieved you."

"Aye, aye, my lord." The sailor slid down a rope to a ship's boat and cast off. He began to row rhythmically against the tide.

"At last!" the Earl said. "We have the world to ourselves." He already had a firm grasp on Rosaline.

For several minutes there was no talk of tides or pinnaces or islands or governorships. No talk at all. His lordship made up for his earlier negligence, and Rosaline had completely forgotten her pique by the time he led her into the luxurious master's cabin and lighted the lantern above the chart table.

"I want to look at you," he said, blinking at the yellow light. "I have to make up for so much time—all the time I've seen you as a boy."

Rosaline, accustomed to being looked at, pirouetted, flaring out her voluminous petticoats.

"All right, look," she said, completely unabashed, and faced him, returning his bold appraisal in kind. "I like to look at you, too. Of course, I'm way ahead of you. I've known all along that you were a man."

"You little witch," he said. "Looking is not enough. Come here."

It never entered Rosaline's mind to play coy or tease by restraining her own desire, which was certainly equal to his. By acknowledging authorship of the sonnets and of *Venus and Adonis* she had tacitly recognized all the promises made or implied by the poems. Already he was familiar with her innermost feelings, the love yearnings expressed in her erotic poetry addressed to him.

Now she was consciously grateful, for a moment, for the ease with which a woman's dress could be put off. By that time she and his lordship were discovering what millions of lovers before them had known, the one perfectly blissful union that is fresh and new to all the world. Two eager, beautiful young bodies found their meaning in the romantic old cabin of the *Ictis*, which had

[83]

been fitted out many years before to accommodate the Earls of Southampton on honeymoon cruises.

Later there was time for conversation, though at first they clung desperately to each other as they talked, fearing it seemed that their new-found ecstasy literally must be held in their arms or else be lost forever. Whatever self-consciousness they might have felt was soon dissipated by their joint conviction that their meeting had been a miracle.

"Wouldn't it have been terrible if I had been a boy?" Rosaline said in the awed voice of one whom death has just missed by inches. She clutched Southampton's hand convulsively. "What if we had missed each other?"

The thought was more than either could bear. His lordship held her tight against him.

"Don't think about it. Here we are together. That's all that matters."

"But how did it all happen?" she asked, still fearsome.

"I was searching for you," he said. "I would have found you."

To answer his questions Rosaline hastily ran through her life, selecting details here, omitting a few there, exercising her privilege as a playwright and perhaps unconsciously dramatizing those incidents which seemed inevitably to have been drawing them together.

Southampton had traveled most of her routes. They both loved the canals in Salisbury—like Venice, they thought—and the broad streets of Gloucester and Newcastle; and they had been cramped in the narrow lanes of Bristol and waterbound in Oxford after a heavy rain. They found that they had much in common, despite their difference in station. Soon they were very much in love again, and silent for a time while more urgent diversions replaced conversation.

Then it was his turn to tell her about himself, about his life at Cecil House and Theobalds, as a royal ward under the guardianship of Lord Burleigh, with Lord Essex, also a royal ward, as a sort of older brother and certainly an idol.

Rosaline had a vaguely disturbing memory that her own father, Lord Oxford, had been a royal ward of an earlier generation. He too had been reared by William Cecil, Lord Burleigh. Her acute ears told her that Southampton bore no love for the Cecils. That

[84]

was one more thing that she and his lordship had in common—but the last one she would ever reveal to him.

"I was nominated for the Garter last May," he was saying, "but I was not approved."

"Why?" Rosaline asked. His rejection was unthinkable.

"Too young, maybe. Then there was the matter of the prize ship pending at the time."

"The prize ship?" Rosaline asked. He had spoken the words as if they were vastly important.

"A little venture of mine into privateering," he explained. "Ralph Bowes and Carew Raleigh and I financed a ship for Sir Martin Frobisher, who subsequently captured a vessel off St. Malo in Brittany with a load of sugar from Brazil. Her Majesty contested our claims when the ship was brought into Portsmouth last September. The affair was finally settled to our advantage early in the spring, but I am not yet a Knight of the Garter."

"But you will be."

"I hope so. Robin, Lord Essex, is certain of Her Majesty's favor sometime; and his fortune is my fortune at court."

That was but one of his many references to the Earl of Essex, who had not been able to come to Titchfield for Michaelmas because his active sponsorship of Francis Bacon for the office of Attorney-General had kept him at court throughout August and September. Rosaline could detect jealousy in her reaction to the mention of his name. Yet Southampton's progress at court was obviously dependent upon Essex's preferment. She had to wish Essex well.

"Raleigh was Her Majesty's favorite," Southampton continued. "But after his affair with Elizabeth Throckmorton last year, her Majesty sent him to the Tower, and his influence has declined steadily ever since. Soon Robin will be the favorite. Then he'll make things right for us."

His optimism expressed itself in a resurgence of his affection for Rosaline, after which he slept awhile from sheer physical exhaustion.

Rosaline was too excited to sleep, too deeply disturbed, too jealous of her few hours with his lordship to close her eyes. She sat up on the bed beside him and brushed his golden hair out of his face. She compared his fair skin to her own tawny flesh. Lying nude on the silken sheet he fulfilled completely every image of

Adonis which she had ever cherished in her night thoughts. Nothing she had written, she felt, had said enough.

She got out of bed and, throwing a blanket around her bare shoulders, sat down at the chart table and dipped a pen into the inkhorn. The sonnet she wrote began with an actor's apology for imperfect expression, and ended with the true lovers' plea,

> *O, learn to read what silent love hath writ:*
> *To hear with eyes belongs to love's fine wit.* (23)

But sitting alone before the chart table in the chill of the September night, Rosaline began to see difficulties which had not presented themselves in their early fervor. Looming largest of all was the Queen. Her Majesty did not take her courtiers' love affairs lightly. Raleigh was not the only favorite she had punished for marrying her own maids-in-waiting without her permission. She had indeed refused to let Frances Walsingham Sidney live in Essex House after her marriage to Lord Essex. For one of her gentlemen to marry out of court was to commit political suicide.

And then there was Lord Burleigh, who had control over the Earl of Southampton for another full year, until the Earl reached his majority. He probably had some marriage plans of his own for young Southampton. And further, his lordship had made no mention of marriage—simply of a powerful undying love, which she did not doubt, but which he might not associate in any way with matrimony.

She grew afraid of the night. She wanted his lordship to awaken and reassure her. She rose and stood by his bed. He was breathing easily, but his body was cold to her touch. She took the soft blanket from around her shoulders and spread it over him. Then she slipped into bed beside him to warm him with the heat of her own body.

In warming him, she woke him.

"Have I been asleep?" he asked in dismay.

"Yes."

"How long?"

"I don't know. Hours, maybe. It seemed like hours to me."

"How could I?" he asked guiltily, drawing her into the crescent formed by his relaxed body. "When time is so short and we've missed so much of it already."

"You were tired, my lord. Michaelmas was a busy day."

"Yes, and a busier night. A deliciously busy night." He fondled her breasts and inhaled the perfume of her hair.

"It will be morning soon," she said. "I shall hate it."

"Why?" He nuzzled the back of her neck and breathed against her ear.

"Because it will end this night. Always I have loved the sun. Long nights and dark days depress me. I've welcomed the sun every morning of my life. But now I hate it—I dread to see it rise. I wish morning would never come."

"Why?" he repeated.

"Oh, you know why, my lord. This night is all we have. It can't last." A note of hopelessness crept into her voice.

"Face me when you say that," he said and forcibly turned her body so that her lips met his.

She responded to his caress in feverish desperation, as though she were trying to wring every drop of distilled ecstasy from her last hour on earth, or to give her lover all that he could normally have hoped for in a lifetime. When she did relax, her emotions fell apart completely and she spilled out all her fears in a rushing torrent of words generously salted by an equally heavy flood of tears.

His lordship let her continue uninterrupted. He petted her and soothed her, wiping her eyes for her and absorbing the sobbing rigors which racked her body from time to time. When she finally grew quiet, he began to answer her fears one by one, even the Queen's objections.

"It's just a matter of time until Robin will be back in Her Majesty's favor. Then she will grant him anything. I'll get him to present you at court and everything will be all right."

"You mean we can be married?" She ventured her question timorously and held her breath while she waited for his answer.

"Be married?" he said, rising on one elbow and searching her eyes. "We're married already, aren't we? I mean I consider us married, don't you?"

"Yes—yes, my darling, I do. I do. But I wasn't sure about you." She drew his face down to hers, wet again with sudden tears.

"Then let's complete the ceremony," he said a moment later. "I've heard somewhere of a custom on some island or other. The bride and groom take locks of their hair and tie them in a love

[87]

knot and cast them into the sea. That's all there is to it, but it's as binding as a chapel ceremony."

He got out of bed and found a pair of shears in the chart cupboard. With them he snipped a strand of his blond hair and then cut a similar lock from her black curls. Together they tied the love knot and then stood side by side while he opened the stern port and threw their marriage token into Southampton Water.

"With this symbol I thee wed," he said solemnly. Then just as solemnly he took her in his arms and kissed her exactly as he would have done before the altar in Titchfield Church.

"If you mean it, my lord, I shall honor this pledge all my life," Rosaline said softly. "And I'll not reveal myself or do anything to embarrass you or prejudice you with Her Majesty until you are ready to acknowledge me openly as your wife."

"I mean it," he assured her. "My pledge given here is as good as the honor of Southampton. And you needn't call me 'my lord.' Call me 'husband' or Hal."

"Very well, Hal. I believe you. I know that betrothal is as binding as marriage among the simple folk. I am not so familiar with court practices."

"Betrothal?" he repeated. "This is not betrothal. This is marriage. I've been betrothed since I was seventeen." He laughed lightheartedly, but his remark fell heavily on Rosaline's ears.

"Betrothed?" she said in a tight voice. "To whom?"

"To Lady Elizabeth de Vere."

Rosaline stiffened in his arms.

"Daughter of the Earl of Oxford?" she asked fearfully. First, the Lady Elizabeth had stolen Rosaline's birthright, and now she held prior claim to her lover.

"Yes, and granddaughter of Lord Burleigh. The Earl and my mother and Lord Burleigh arranged it," his lordship explained. "I never intended to marry her." He laughed again, as though the whole thing were a joke.

"But you're expected to."

"How can I? I'm already married."

"How will you get out of the betrothal?"

"I'll manage it," he said with complete confidence.

Just then the first rays of the sun glistened on the still water outside the stern port. But they carried no warmth. Rosaline shivered as an icy rigor ran outward from her heart.

"You're cold," his lordship said, suddenly solicitous of his bride. "Let me find you some clothes. You can't wear that gown back to the Place, not at this time of the morning."

He let go of her and hastily wrapped her in a blanket. Then he put on his own clothes and went forward to the crew's quarters in search of something for her to wear. She sat in shivering misery, staring at the bed which had held her brief moment of paradise. She had been cast out by Southampton's light-hearted admission of his betrothal. Not that she doubted the honor of Southampton, but she well knew the power of Oxford and Burleigh, the Queen's own Lord Treasurer. The Cecil curse which had plagued her mother had lived on to blight her life as well.

His lordship returned with a pair of canvas slops and a seaman's sweater. She greeted him with all the gayety she could muster, dropped the blanket, and stepped into the wide-legged slops. After tying the rope belt she drew the tight-fitting sweater on over her head and tucked it in at the waist.

"Hey, that's no disguise," his lordship said in admiration, his eyes on the pointed bulges made by her proud young breasts so recently initiated into full womanhood. "I must try again."

He disappeared and returned a minute later with a loose seaman's jerkin and a Monmouth cap. He held the jerkin while she put it on. It was completely shapeless, hiding all her features, including her hands. He turned up her sleeves for her and surveyed her again.

"There, that's better," he said, "or worse, depending how you look at it. Now your hair. Turn around and hold still."

She already felt like a little boy again.

His lordship plaited her hair into a single queue, sailor fashion, and tied it with a piece of tarred line. Then he set the Monmouth cap on her head and, grasping her shoulders, turned her around again. He eyed her critically.

"Now, you'd pass anywhere as an able-bodied seaman," he said, nodding his head in approval. "Or a cabin boy, anyway."

Together they folded her woman's clothing and packed it in a duffle bag. Then, with a long last look at the master's cabin, they went out on deck and Southampton pulled his skiff up to the foot of the ladder. He went down first, caught the bag, which she tossed to him, and held the boat steady while she backed down the ladder into it. He seated her on the thwart beside him.

"Man the starboard oar, sailor," he commanded gaily.

"Aye, aye, sir," she said and began to pull, matching his strokes as she had learned to do when she and her foster father had rowed together on Derwentwater.

Halfway to the shore, they met William Strachey and the seaman returning to the *Ictis*. The seaman looked half asleep.

Strachey hailed them.

"Is there anyone aboard, my lord?" he asked.

"No," his lordship replied shortly. "I pass the command to you, Mr. Strachey," he added as an afterthought.

"I take command, sir," Strachey said and managed a token salute, certainly no more perfunctory than his lordship's transfer of command had been.

Rosaline tried not to face Strachey; but when the boats passed she found herself staring directly into his cool grey eyes. They seemed to hold disappointment or perhaps reproach, though Strachey said nothing; and she felt herself blush in shame, not for herself but for his lordship, who had spent the night aboard the *Ictis* with a pretty boy.

She dug the blade of her oar deep into the water and hauled back hard against the creaking thole.

She was tired, and her shoulders were aching by the time the boat rubbed against the kitchen garden pier, but she doubted that it was the rowing which caused her pain.

She took leave of his lordship without ceremony. The Place was quiet. A few late revelers still sang drunkenly on the lawn and occasionally one of the less hardy souls could be seen lying exhausted under a shrub. Whitley Lodge, too, was quiet, so Rosaline made her way to her room without being observed. She exchanged her sailor suit for a smock, but she did not lie down immediately. She sat on the edge of her bed and relived the last twenty-four hours, taking stock of what she had, what she had lost, and what she was likely yet to lose. Despite the brightening sunshine outside, she felt that dark clouds were closing in around her, threatening to shut all light out of her life. Happily his lordship could be in no way responsible for the evil things in store for the two of them. A line came to mind:

Yet him for this my love no whit disdaineth ...

She crossed over to a table by the window, drew a fresh sheet of paper from a portfolio there. She might be able to catch that last moment before it too was gone. Slowly she wrote and used the line in a sonnet which began with her image of the sun, rising in splendor on happiness too short.

> *Full many a glorious morning have I seen*
> *Flatter the mountain-tops with sovereign eye,*
> *Kissing with golden face the meadows green,*
> *Gilding pale streams with heavenly alchemy;*
> *Anon permit the basest clouds to ride*
> *With ugly rack on his celestial face,*
> *And from the forlorn world his visage hide,*
> *Stealing unseen to west with this disgrace:*
> *Even so my sun one early morn did shine*
> *With all-triumphant splendor on my brow;*
> *But out, alack! he was but one hour mine;*
> *The region cloud hath mask'd him from me now.*
>   *Yet him for this my love no whit disdaineth;*
>   *Suns of the world may stain when heaven's sun staineth.* (33)

She read the sonnet over and placed it loose in the covers of her commonplace book. Then she slipped off the smock and slid between soft linen sheets on her featherbed. She sank into a sleep of sheer exhaustion. She had to be strong enough the next day to prepare for the journey back to the dismal tenement off Bishopsgate.

6

BACK IN LONDON, SETTLED AGAIN IN THE SHAKESPEARE HOUSEHOLD, Rosaline sank deeper into the fears which she had brought with her from Titchfield. Without his lordship by her side to reassure her, the absurdity of their wedding ceremony became clearer with every sunrise. At night, though beset by doubts during long hours of fretful tossing, she invariably returned to the *Ictis* in her dreams; and half waking she would believe in all her early hopes, until judgment rather than yearning returned to discipline her thoughts. Then in daylight everything that had happened at Titchfield would recede and become unreal, everything except the image of Southampton himself. She hardly knew whether the vision was a blessing or a curse; but it haunted her, coloring every commonplace sight in the city, every rustic scene in the fields outside the wall. As she wrote of the lover's mind,

> *The most sweet favor or deformed'st creature,*
> *The mountain or the sea, the day or night,*
> *The crow or dove, it shapes them to your feature.*   (113)

This sonnet was one she would send to her lover if their affair proved not to be at an end. For his part, his lordship had promised to send a letter to her at Richard Field's shop in St. Paul's Churchyard. She invented excuses to slip into boy's clothes and visit Paul's every day. She pretended to be looking for books that she needed in her writing; and even Anne Shakespeare, happy in the unaccustomed affluence resulting from Southampton's excessive generosity to all who took part in *Love's Labor's Lost,* looked on Rosaline in a more favorable light and was agreeable to almost anything that would further so profitable a business. So Rosaline spent hours hovering near the sign of the White Greyhound, jostling and being jostled by the mob as she browsed through the bookstalls. But after a week of disappointment she was ready to class the promised letter with all the other promises made at Titchfield.

Then it came, a fold of heavy paper sealed with the Arms of Southampton and addressed to Ross Allen. Rosaline rushed back into the sunlight, where she broke the seal with trembling fingers and read:

> My Darling:
> My poetry is improving, thanks to you. How is this?

There were two sonnets, one beginning,

> *Is it thy will thy image should keep open*
> *My heavy eyelids to the weary night?*

> *Dost thou desire my slumbers should be broken*
> *While shadows like to thee do mock my sight?*   (61)

and the other,

> *When most I wink, then do mine eyes best see,*
> *For all the day they view things unrespected;*
> *But when I sleep, in dreams they look on thee,*
> *And darkly bright are bright in dark directed.*   (43)

She laughed at his precious play on words, reminiscent of some of her lines in *Love's Labor's Lost*. But the sonnets expressed feelings in such perfect consonance with her own that all of her assurance in Southampton's love returned in one welcome rush. Of course his lordship meant every word that he had ever spoken, just as she had pledged her very soul to him. They were in complete rapport. They were one: one body, one flesh, one love. How could she ever have doubted him? She read the short note attached to the sonnets.

> I have been in correspondence with the Earl of Oxford. His lordship has agreed to see me at his house in Hackney next Wednesday morning at nine, at which time I shall inform him that my betrothal to his fair daughter has been terminated. Wish me luck.
>
> Your impatient lover,
> H.
>
> From Titchfield the 10th of October, 1593.
> P.S. My business finished here, I shall be at my lodgings in the Strand after Tuesday.

Hal would be in London Tuesday! It was Tuesday already, Rosaline remembered. And the very next day— Dear, silly, impetuous Hal. He was going to "inform" the Earl of Oxford that the betrothal was at an end. Rosaline, feeling far wiser than the young Earl, was suddenly horrified by his rash intentions. He would brave a peer of England and tell him that he was spurning the granddaughter of the Lord Treasurer of England—blithely, with not a single argument that he could bring to justify his rejection of Lady Elizabeth de Vere. He had no chance at all. He would be fortunate if the Queen did not send him to the Tower.

And then he would have to give reasons. And that would involve Rosaline and bring disgrace. And if an Earl had to be disgraced—

Her nimble wit, intoxicated by the words of her lover, produced an alternate plan at once, a brilliant plan. It was she, Rosaline de Vere, not his lordship, who had the means by which Lord Oxford could be brought to terms. It was almost noon. Time was so short that she must think through her plan on her way to Hackney. And it was three miles to Hackney. She would have to hire a horse, and someone to go with her. Not Burbage or Shakespeare; there was not time, and besides she was not ready to tell them about Southampton, not until she was sure.

Already she was rushing through the churchyard, nimbly dodging around the slow-moving scholars and rogues and hucksters who cluttered up the place. By the time she realized that she was heading for the Mermaid Tavern she knew who it was that she was seeking: Will Johnson, the host's apprentice.

She found him cleaning pewter mugs in the scullery.

"Remember me, Will?" she asked.

"Sure," he said, looking cautiously over his shoulder. "You're the girl."

"Yes. Can you take the afternoon off?"

"I don't know."

"I'll pay you half a crown."

"What do you want me to do?" He was becoming interested.

"To ride with me out to Hackney, to see the Earl of Oxford."

"Oh, about reading for a party?"

"Something like that. Can you come with me?"

"Sure, sure. I don't have to clean this pewter. I'm just doing it. The host's not here, anyway."

"Hurry then. We'll have to hire horses."

"We have horses right here in the stable," Will Johnson said, taking off his apron and reaching for his blue apprentice cloak and white flatcap. "They'll cost you another shilling for the two of them."

"Very well. I'll pay in advance."

"You needn't to. I trust you. Be at the Friday Street door in ten minutes."

Will Johnson disappeared through a door opening toward the stables. He led the horses out into Friday Street a few minutes later. He boosted Rosaline into the saddle and mounted his own horse. Then he respectfully reined his horse in behind hers, since she was dressed as a smart young squire and he perhaps thought it fitting to ride as her groom.

They threaded their way slowly through the city traffic, but once outside Bishopsgate they urged their horses into a lively gallop out Shoreditch as far as St. Leonard's Church, where they turned right on a country lane which Will said was a short cut to Hackney. He proved to be a dependable guide, right up to the front gate of Lord Oxford's estate. There being no guard on duty, Rosaline boldly led the way up to the hitching post before the broad house front.

Still in a state of high exhilaration, sparked by Southampton's letter and fanned by her feverish planning for the encounter with her father, she had not considered the recklessness of her actions. Had she slept on her plans, or even considered them calmly for one hour, she probably would have abandoned the whole idea and let the Earl of Southampton break his own engagement.

As it was, she tossed the reins over her horse's head to Will Johnson, dropped lightly to the ground, and asked her groom to wait. Without hesitation she knocked on the front door and told the answering servant that although his lordship was not expecting her he would be glad to see her. Her clothes, the finest young gentleman's costume in her theatrical wardrobe, evidently impressed the lackey, for he led her down a long hallway directly into the library, where her father was seated behind a rich mahogany desk.

The Earl of Oxford was a slightly built man of finely chiseled facial features framed by reddish-brown hair and beard. When he raised his hazel eyes to appraise his guest, Rosaline was startled by his resemblance to William Shakespeare. Perhaps for that reason she was involuntarily attracted to him, though she was determined to hate him.

"You wish to see me, young man?" he asked without rising from his chair.

"Yes, your lordship. Alone."

"Very well, lad." The Earl changed his form of address when he heard her treble voice. He nodded dismissal to the servant, who left and closed the door behind him.

Rosaline advanced into the center of the room and removed her plumed hat. Her black curls hung full around her shoulders.

"Do you know who I am, my lord?" she asked boldly.

He rose slowly and stared at her with rising incredulity.

"You look like a woman that I was very much in love with once, a long time ago," he said, obviously startled by her appearance.

Feeling perhaps that her performance lacked dramatic appeal, Rosaline took two running steps and went into the tumbling routine which Viola Nigrone had made famous from one end of England to the other. Finished with her acrobatics, Rosaline faced his lordship again and curtsied in perfect impersonation of her mother.

"No! It can't be," Oxford said in astonishment. He passed his hand across his eyes and forehead, as though brushing aside a vision. "You're no ghost."

"I am Rosaline de Vere," she said in loud firm tones, "daughter of Viola Nigrone and Edward de Vere, Viscount Bolebec, Lord of Escales, Sandford, and Badlemere, Earl of Oxford, Lord Great Chamberlain of England." She glibly repeated the titles listed by Lyly in his dedication of *Euphues and his England* to his lordship. The Earl regained his aplomb during her recital.

"I must say that you are well informed on your pedigree," his lordship said, and coughed discreetly behind his hand.

"I, sir, am a disgrace to my family."

"Indeed? That sounds ominous."

"First of all, my lord, I am a bastard, as you very well know. I have toured all England, not only as a lewd, unchaste tumbling woman but also as a boy actor. I have written plays for the common public theater." She paused for breath.

"I can believe that," the Earl said solemnly. "You show great promise as a dramatist of bizarre imagination."

"These things, if known, would bring shame upon the house of Oxford," Rosaline went on gravely.

"My, my. So they would." His lordship indicated a chair for Rosaline and sat down again behind his desk. "Surely you have your reasons for revealing these terrible truths. Suppose you tell me what they are."

"In addition to all these things, my lord, I am the mistress of the Earl of Southampton, who loves me very dearly and wants to marry me. If you will release him from his betrothal to the Lady Elizabeth, I give you my solemn promise that I shall never reveal my true identity as long as I live. If not, I shall rock England with my story."

The Earl studied her face intently. A faint smile which played about his lips enraged Rosaline. That he would laugh at her was the one reaction which she had not anticipated. Her hopes began to fall, draining away her confidence and leaving her with a strong suspicion that she had just given an absurdly childish performance.

"I think the Lady Elizabeth should be consulted on this matter, don't you?" her father asked. "After all she's the one concerned." He pulled a bell cord hanging beside a tapestry on the wall behind his desk.

"Yes, my lord," Rosaline answered meekly.

When a servant answered the bell, he sent for Lady Elizabeth. "You are very much like your mother," he said during the wait. "Every bit as proud and independent, too, I'm afraid."

Rosaline made no answer. His speech sounded like a friendly overture, which of course would necessarily be false. She would not be trapped. She might have made a fool of herself, but all that she had said was true. Lady Elizabeth, whom she knew to be five months younger than she, might be easier to influence after all.

His lordship rose when the door opened again. Rosaline stood with him and faced Lady Elizabeth as she entered.

Rosaline's heart sank at the picture her sister made in the doorway. Elizabeth de Vere was perhaps half an inch shorter than Rosaline, and as fair as the older girl was dark. Her hair was very blonde with the slightest tint of red in it, and her eyes blue and clear. Though small of bone, her figure was just a little fuller— "riper" perhaps was the word—than Rosaline's in every curve. In a blue satin gown, she appeared to be an exquisitely wrought doll grown to woman's size. Surely Southampton had no intention of deserting this beauty for a tawny acrobat!

"Betty, this young gentleman is no gentleman at all," the Earl said as a preface to his introduction. "This is your sister, Rosaline. I believe your uncle Robert Cecil has hinted that you might have such a sister somewhere."

"Yes," Lady Elizabeth said. "How do you do, Rosaline." She maintained perfect composure.

"Your ladyship." Rosaline curtsied instinctively.

"Rosaline has made some startling revelations," the Earl continued. "She is a disgrace to the family, an ex-tumbler, a shameless boy actor, a common playwright, and the mistress of your fiancé."

Lady Elizabeth gasped.

"Furthermore," his lordship continued, "she threatens to tell her story to all the world and scandalize the House of Oxford if you don't renounce your claim on the young man. Imagine what your grandfather would think."

Her ladyship either sobbed or giggled into a scented lace handkerchief.

"I feel that the decision is yours, Betty," her father continued, "since it's your betrothal. Shall we risk everlasting disgrace or are you willing to free the Earl of Southampton from his vow?"

Rosaline began to seethe inside at the cruel banter. They could just throw her out; they had no call to humiliate her. Or perhaps they had. All she wanted at the moment was to be dismissed. She was in far beyond her depth. If she had only waited to consider! Just one hour! Haste, haste, haste. Haste always led to disaster, to humiliation, to tragedy.

"I have no wish to shame you, Father," Lady Elizabeth said obediently. "You were a party to the betrothal. In fact, I believe you arranged it, you and Grandfather. If you think I should relinquish my hold on Hal, I certainly will."

"There, Rosaline," his lordship said, with that same irritating smile. "Is that what you wanted to hear? Is that what you want me to tell his lordship in the morning?"

"Yes, yes, my lord," Rosaline said wearily, hopelessly. Both of them were tormenting her, having their little joke at her expense. "Now, may I be excused, your lordship?"

"Certainly." He reached for the bell cord.

"No, Father," Lady Elizabeth said. "I'll show Rosaline out."

Lady Elizabeth hurried her sister out into the hall and closed the massive library door. Then she impulsively flung her arms about Rosaline's neck and exclaimed, "You dear, you darling! How I've longed for someone to do what you've just done!"

Rosaline disentangled herself in sudden fear that her ladyship intended to strangle her but there was no stopping the flow of gratitude. Her sister kept pace with her down the hallway toward the front door.

"I've been trying to wish Hal off on Bridget Manners," Lady Elizabeth ran on, "but she considers him too young and fantastical and volatile; as, indeed, do I. I couldn't break the engagement myself. Grandfather would have had a fit. But you, marvelous, beautiful you, beloved sister, are making him ask for his release himself. I love you, I love you, I love you. Wait till I tell William."

She paused for breath, but only momentarily.

"William Stanley, you know—of Derby. But his brother Ferdinando has just succeeded to the title, and of course Grandfather wants me to be a countess. But what do I care about titles? William and I are so much in love. He'll love you, too, and be oh, so very, very grateful to you."

Her ladyship broke into a trot to keep up with her sister.

"Can't you stay and visit awhile?" she urged. "And meet Elizabeth? Elizabeth Trentham, my father's new countess. She's called Elizabeth—that's why I'm Betty. You must call me Betty. And see our new baby brother, little Henry. He's just nine months old, and such a little dear. And Bridget—she's nine. And Susan— she's six. They're sweet little girls, my full sisters, but I've so wanted a sister my own age. I don't know why my mother waited so long to have a sister for me. Oh, I'm glad you've come home."

They had reached the front door. Rosaline stopped on the porch and faced her sister.

"I haven't come home," she said distinctly, slowly, as she would have spoken to a very young, very excitable child. "I have just broken all ties with the House of Oxford. I promised his lordship. I shall never enter that door again."

"Then I must visit you. Where do you live?"

Rosaline gave her address without thinking. Certainly her sister was not serious.

"Then I shall visit you tomorrow."

"No. You can't. I live in a dismal tenement. You wouldn't like it. And you're not to visit me or tell anyone that I am your sister— not ever. I've promised his lordship. I keep my promises. I hope he keeps his, if he means them."

"Oh, fie," Betty said, blithely dismissing all objections. "I'm going into the City tomorrow afternoon. If I can't visit you in your house, I'll pick you up in my coach—Elizabeth's coach, I mean. Be ready at three o'clock."

Rosaline eyed her sister speculatively. The girl was half Cecil, and all Cecils were dangerous. Perhaps a long sensible conversation, if such a thing were possible, might calm her ladyship down and prevent her broadcasting the family secret and spoiling everything. Rosaline was afraid of this fantastical young lady, afraid, at least, of what she might do.

"Very well," she said, resignedly. "You may pick me up tomorrow at three, if you still want to." Lord Oxford might have no intention of releasing Southampton from the betrothal. Betty might be pretending, deliberately trying to hurt her bastard sister. Or if she were serious she might be of an entirely different mind after the Oxford-Southampton conference. The whole affair was insane, as crazy as her coming to see his lordship in the first place.

Betty again hugged Rosaline and kissed her on the cheek. "Until three o'clock tomorrow, then."

Rosaline stumbled down the steps and made her way to the hitching post. Will Johnson helped her into the saddle.

"Does she think you are a boy?" asked Will. He had been too far away to catch her ladyship's words.

"Obviously," Rosaline answered. That was the easiest explanation.

"Jesus!" Will exclaimed. "I wish I was in your shoes. You can't do anything for her."

"Not a thing," Rosaline agreed. She was in no mood for further conversation. Things—strange, unbelievable things—had been happening entirely too fast.

7

LADY ELIZABETH DE VERE CALLED FOR ROSALINE IN HER STEP-mother's coach, an elaborate new vehicle bearing the Oxford coat of arms. Drawn by four matched Irish hobbies and manned by liveried coachmen and footmen, it created a sensation in the narrow sidestreet, which barely afforded it turning room. The neighbors turned out to see Rosaline carried away by the great lady with whom Anne Shakespeare had assured them Rosaline had business.

[100]

As the coach pulled out into Bishopsgate Street her ladyship waxed voluble in her account of Hal's interview with her father on which she had shamelessly eavesdropped.

"You should have heard Father," she said. "Stern, firm, incensed by Hal's rejection of the flower of the House of Oxford."

"Did either of them mention me?" Rosaline asked. It was not vanity that prompted her question.

"No, not by name. Father said, 'Surely, young man, you have found another woman or you wouldn't be so precipitate in this matter.' Hal said, 'That, my lord, might be a valid conjecture, but its truth or falsity would be entirely irrelevant to the matter at hand.' Doesn't that sound terribly important? Oh, they were both on their most pompous behavior.

"When Father demanded five thousand pounds he said, 'You may break my daughter's heart, and that sum is poor recompense indeed for a maiden's broken heart!' Imagine breaking my heart! Oh, Father was wonderful." Betty giggled.

"Five thousand pounds?" Rosaline repeated indignantly. "That's outrageous! That's a fortune, a king's ransom."*

"Oh, fie, Rosaline. Hal owns half of the south of England. He can afford it. Anyway, Father probably had to demand enough to make things look good to Grandfather."

"But do you want the money?" Rosaline was still angry.

"Certainly not. And I'm sure Father has no intention of giving it to me. In fact, he didn't even mention it, when he told me about his talk with Hal. He didn't know I was listening all the time." She giggled again. The coach jolted over a stretch of unusually rough cobbles.

"Where are we going?" Rosaline asked, when she realized that the coach was well inside the City.

"To meet William."

* The amount (£5000), which would probably be equivalent to a quarter of a million dollars today, does seem fantastic, but the sum is established by Henry Garnet (an alias of George Fenner, agent of Father Parsons). About a year later in a letter concerning Lady Elizabeth's marriage to Stanley, Garnet wrote, "The young Earl of Southampton, refusing Lady Vere, payeth £5000 of present payment." His letter is found in Foley's *English Jesuits*, IV, 49. The estimated value (£1 = $50) conforms to the reckoning of Sir Sidney Lee, G. B. Harrison, and other eminent Elizabethan scholars.

"Oh, no!" Rosaline exclaimed. William was the brother of Ferdinando Stanley, recently Lord Strange, until his succession as Earl of Derby. Ferdinando was the patron of the troupe with which William Kempe and Richard Burbage had been touring the provinces. William might even recognize her, if he had attended the Rose while his brother's troupe was playing there. "We can't meet him together," Rosaline said.

"Indeed we can," Lady Elizabeth insisted. "I was going to meet him anyway, secretly. Now that I am no longer betrothed I can see him openly. He'll want to meet you, to thank you."

"But you aren't going to tell him that I'm your sister—your bastard sister."

"Certainly. He won't mind. Do you know, Rosaline, I was supposed to be a bastard myself, if I can believe my Uncle Robert. He said that Father once ran away to the continent—with your mother, I suppose—and when Grandfather's spies brought him back he wouldn't have anything to do with my mother. Uncle Robert said that they tricked Father into sleeping with my mother, thinking she was someone else, and I was conceived."

"Your Uncle Robert must hate you to tell you things like that," Rosaline said.

"Oh, no. Uncle Robert likes me. But he hates Father, and Hal, and Robin Essex—all of the royal wards whom Grandfather reared. I suppose it's because they were of the real nobility and handsome and rich, and he's so ugly and hunchbacked, and Grandfather was only created Lord Burleigh to make my mother eligible to marry my father. I'm glad he told me. I mean I don't mind your being a bastard, and my being an intended bastard. It makes us sort of equal, gives us something in common, don't you think?"

Rosaline found it as hard to restrain her laughter as it was to follow her sister's reasoning.

"I don't wonder that Father preferred your mother to my mother," her ladyship went on. "Or that Hal prefers you to me. You're so beautiful, so dark and Italian-looking. You'd cause a sensation at court. You know Italians are all the fashion now. Everyone has an Italian tutor, like Hal's Giovanni Florio. Do you speak Italian, Rosaline?"

"Yes, your ladyship."

"No, no—Betty, if you please."

"Yes, Betty. I read, write, and speak Italian."

"Then couldn't you be my tutor? I don't mean really, but pretend to be. Then you could live with me and go places with me, even if you don't want to admit to being my sister."

"Don't be absurd, Betty." But in spite of herself Rosaline was being charmed by her noble-born sister.

"I'm not being absurd. Anyway here we are."

The coach pulled up before the Blackfriars Gatehouse, which had been converted into a four-family dwelling. Betty sent her coach on into the courtyard and rang for the porter.

"I have my own key," she explained, "but I brought Henry's quarterly wages. Henry Walker, I mean. He's Elizabeth's dumb man. Elizabeth owns this building and keeps him on as caretaker. He really is deaf and dumb, and oh so discreet."

Countess Oxford's "dumb man" appeared presently and let the two young women into an apartment on the second floor. He made elaborate, if mute, signs of thanks for the money Betty had brought him and then disappeared.

"We reserve these rooms to use whenever we want to stay overnight in the City," Betty said.

"It's lovely here," Rosaline said, surprised by the exquisitely appointed interior, in striking contrast to the austere façade of the centuries-old gatehouse.

"Elizabeth lived here before she married Father. She seldom comes here any more. In fact, I think she keeps the building just to give poor Henry a job. I've been meeting William here but— oh, Rosaline, why don't you move in here?" She fairly sparkled in her sudden inspiration. "I won't be needing the place any more. You could live here until you and Hal are married, get out of that dismal tenement, have a nice place for Hal to visit you—or do you—" For once Betty was at a loss for words.

"Yes, we do," Rosaline said, divining her sister's meaning. "Oh, Betty, we are already married, though of course we must keep it a secret."

Rosaline became as talkative as Betty had been and rapidly ran through her whole affair with Southampton, including the pagan wedding ceremony. Her sister seemed the immediate answer to her urgent need for a confidante, a woman of her own age. Somehow she felt that Betty would understand and keep her secret.

"I guess you really couldn't say that we're married," Rosaline ended lamely.

"Oh, but you are," Betty insisted. "I just know you are—and so romantically, so much nicer than a stuffy old church wedding."

Rosaline hugged Betty impulsively. They were sisters after all, similar in many ways, or quick to pick up each other's mannerisms. Although Rosaline had intended to slip away before Betty's suitor arrived, William Stanley found the two contrasting beauties deep in conversation when he entered unannounced.

Rosaline was surprised to learn that he was in his early thirties, though she felt that Betty probably needed a husband several years her senior. Stanley, in turn, showed no surprise at anything Betty said or did, not even her frank introduction of her favorite, though bastard, sister. He accepted Rosaline quite graciously and admitted his indebtedness to her for breaking Betty's engagement to the Earl of Southampton. He even listened to Betty's account of Rosaline's wedding; and although he did not commit himself as to the validity of the ceremony, he did think it would be a good idea for Rosaline to live in the Gatehouse.

So it came about that Rosaline was persuaded to take up residence in Blackfriars. She explained to Anne Shakespeare that the young Lady de Vere had employed her as a tutor in Italian. Of course she made no mention of the relationship. And she assured Anne that she would live up to her compact with Shakespeare and Burbage, the arrangement which was already proving so profitable to all concerned. As earnest, she immediately began a new poem about the rape of Lucrece, an adaptation of a story from Ovid's *Fasti,* to satisfy Richard Field's demand for another "Shakespearean" poem like *Venus and Adonis,* which was proving to be a most gratifying commercial success.

To Shakespeare and Burbage, who helped move her things into the Gatehouse, she told a slightly different story. They were her kind of people, not to be shocked by her becoming Southampton's mistress, though she told them of the love-knot wedding ceremony for whatever it was worth. Shakespeare already had his suspicions, based on what he had observed at Titchfield.

Richard Burbage volunteered the cogent remark that *"phallus erectus* knows no caste lines or class distinctions," but he urged Rosaline to develop her literary talents to "fall back on when his lordship no longer wants to push you back on a featherbed." He sounded like Tom Pope playing a low comedy part in a Bankside brothel.

Rosaline replied heatedly that she fully intended to continue writing, to pay her own way by prostituting her dramatic art so she could *give* her favors freely to her beloved husband until such time as he could openly establish her in a household of her own, as the Countess of Southampton. Hers was an extravagantly ambitious speech, but Burbage had the power always to draw out the worst or the best in her. At any rate by the time he left the Gatehouse he had so aroused her ire that she was resolved to supply him with the best plays ever heard in London, if and when the theaters ever opened again.

Southampton, when he finally learned of her new address from a note left for him at the sign of the White Greyhound, required still another set of explanations. Not at first, of course. They spent the first night reassuring themselves that the delights they had discovered aboard the *Ictis* were indeed capable of being recaptured. It was morning, well along in the morning, before his lordship thought to wonder at the sumptuous surroundings in which he had been reunited with his bride. Perhaps he thought that she had wasted all her slender resources to provide this setting for their reunion.

"Could we—could we keep this place?" he asked, still lying in bed, looking up at the gilded cornice molding and giving her the benefit of the doubt, if any.

"I have already arranged for it permanently," she said. "It belongs to a friend of mine."

"A friend?" There was a doubt.

"Now, Hal," she said, snuggling closer in his arms, "you just listen to me quietly for a few minutes. This friend is a lady, a real lady." Of nimbler wit, she had been anticipating his question and was ready with her answer.

"Who is this friend?"

"Now, Hal, don't get upset. It is the Lady Elizabeth de Vere."

His lordship did get upset. He released his grasp on his bride and sat bolt upright in bed beside her, his fair-fleshed body and golden curls glistening in the morning sun to rival the angry fire that flashed from his erstwhile adoring eyes.

"You—you went to Elizabeth de Vere?"

"No—no, of course not. I never in my life ever intended to set eyes on her." That was technically true. "She came to me."

"But how, how did she know about you, about us?" The anger in his eyes was now becoming mixed with a growing fear, as well as a look of bewilderment. The play of emotions across his face was an exciting thing to see.

"Intuition, perhaps. We women have it, you know. Now, don't get excited. If someone were stealing you from me I'd know it, and I think I would find her to see what she was like."

"But how?" That was his immediate worry. What had betrayed his secret? If the Queen should learn as much—

"I don't know," Rosaline lied. "She's a Cecil, you know. And the Cecils have spies everywhere. They can find out anything." She suddenly wondered how much they had actually found out about her and her mother. She could understand his fears, though it was her job to allay them.

"Does anyone else know? I didn't even tell Lord Oxford about you," he said.

"No, I'm sure no one else knows." She felt that it would be unwise to mention William Stanley. Anyway Betty's affair with him had been kept secret so far. "And I'm positive that Betty will tell no one."

"So it's Betty, is it? How close are you two? And just why did her ladyship do all this for you?" Southampton got out of bed and slipped into a dressing gown. It looked for a moment as though his married life was rapidly coming to an end.

Rosaline also got out of bed and followed him.

"Had it ever occurred to you, my lord, that she might have done it for you, that she might have loved you very much, so much that she wanted you to be happy—even with me?" She was a little surprised at the sound of her own voice reciting the carefully composed explanation.

But it gave his lordship pause while she put on a robe and combed the worst tangles out of her hair. It *was* a flattering thought, and one quite in keeping with some of the sentiments expressed by noble gentlemen who thought only of their beloved ladies' happiness, even in rejection. At least such things happened frequently in the literature of court romances, usually a man giving up his mistress to a dear, dear friend. Perhaps women could feel as deeply, be as chivalrous. At least he deigned to face his wife and allow her to proceed, and she did with careful timing.

"Perhaps in seeking out your mistress, she wanted to be sure that yours would be no tawdry, clandestine affair carried on in inns and taverns."

"But I could have provided as fine a place," he said petulantly.

"Could you, my lord? Could you so conceal your accounts and properties that no one would have discovered our hideway before we were ready to publish our love openly?"

His lordship pondered that question.

"Men don't always understand how we women feel, or how we love and plan." She hated to resort to the sophistry of which "we women" was the core, but it *was* a line of argument which no man had yet satisfactorily refuted. "I think it was sweet and unselfish and thoughtful of Betty. And I know that she will keep our secret. We women understand one another."

"Have you got to know her very well?" he asked cautiously.

"Yes, my lord. I love her."

"And how does she feel about you?"

"The same, I think."

"She loves you? How could she, after—"

"Perhaps she loves me, my lord, because she knows that you love me. Can you understand her loving you so much that she would love whatever and whomever you loved?" If Rosaline had known the precedent she was setting in that speech, she would probably have bitten off the tip of her too-glib tongue.

"Yes," Southampton said, flattered by the speech and dazzled by the picture his wife made during her earnest appeal, like a lawyer pleading the case of her beloved before a wavering judge. "I think I might understand such a love. At this moment, I might feel just that way about you. I might even like Betty more, for your loving her."

The thought disturbed Rosaline, gave her a moment of panic. Just whose case was she presenting? Her knowledge that Betty was infatuated with Stanley, and that her own argument was pure fabrication came quickly to her rescue. Still she felt herself forced to resort to coquetry, which she had intended never to employ on his lordship.

"Well, now, don't go falling in love with Betty all over again," she said with the show of a pout, "just because I'm fond of her."

[107]

"Again?" his lordship repeated. "I never was in love with her. I hardly knew her."

"I could understand if you did," Rosaline continued, gambling as she well knew. "She's so beautiful, so fair and blonde and lovely, all pink and white. Just the sort of woman men love. Why you ever rejected her for a black-eyed crow like me, brown as a Tartar—"

She won. His lordship gathered her into his arms and whispered through her hair.

"I have the answer to that," he said. "I worked all night on it, one night. My sonnet to a dark lady. Listen:

> *"In the old age black was not counted fair,*
> *Or if it were, it bore not beauty's name;*
> *But now is black beauty's successive heir,*
> *And beauty slander'd with a bastard shame;*
> *For since each hand hath put on nature's power,*
> *Fairing the foul with art's false borrow'd face,*
> *Sweet beauty hath no name, no holy bower,*
> *But is profan'd, if not lives in disgrace.*
> *Therefore, my mistress' eyes are raven black,*
> *Her eyes so suited; and they mourners seem*
> *At such, who not born fair, no beauty lack,*
> *Slandering creation with a false esteem:*
> *Yet so they mourn, becoming of their woe,*
> *That every tongue says, beauty should look so.*   (127)

Does that explain my feelings to your satisfaction, beloved?"

"Oh yes, Hal. Yes. It's beautiful."

"Then let's forget all about fair ladies and devote all our attentions to a dark one."

"I shan't forget Betty, my lord. I'm too fond of her. But you may. Indeed I shall insist that you forget her."

"And she'll forget me, though Lord Oxford insisted that I might break his daughter's heart."

For the first time Rosaline noted the ambiguity of her father's statement. Which daughter had Lord Oxford had in mind when he said those words? She wondered. She wondered too that Southampton said not one word about the £5000.

But not for long. Their first crisis past, the two lovers plunged into their first full day together, learning to live waking hours of daylight in other occupations than heated embrace. They took time to savor their passion, rather than rush greedily to each feast as if it were the last. And there was a sweetness in their slower-paced love making which they both learned to cherish, a new kind of accommodation which neither of them had ever had to make before. So their hectic first love ripened by the hour into a more stable affection which promised everlasting satisfaction.

"I never guessed that love could be like this," Rosaline said, lying relaxed late at night, tired but too happy, too grateful, to go to sleep without thanking someone or at least making acknowledgment of the bliss which was hers. "I mean such complete beauty in everything, and confidence that it can last."

His lordship said nothing but gave her shoulders a little squeeze to assure her that he was listening.

"Still Titchfield was wonderful," she continued. "Despite our impatience, our desperate clinging to what was too good to last, that night aboard the *Ictis* held something that I never want to lose, something that I wouldn't trade this for, but still—a painfully sweet—a bittersweet—Hal, do you know what I'm trying to say?"

"Possibly," he mumbled. "You usually say what you have to say very well."

"And then that terrible week before I heard from you—and all the rash things I thought of, and your impulsiveness. Impatience, haste, unwillingness to wait even for one moment. It's all there, Hal. It's all part of young love. But it's tragic, tragically sweet—not like this, but wonderful, gloriously poignant, positively lyrical in its very desperation."

"It is all that," his lordship said with a yawn.

"But I can't say it, not in a word. It would take pages—a whole play. And I shall do it, Hal! I know a story of a pair of star-crossed lovers. Bandello has told it; and Arthur Brooke used it in his *Romeus and Juliet*. Hal, I shall tell it again, for I know now the exquisite pain of Juliet's first love. Our love shall live after us, dearest, in the greatest lyrical tragedy the world shall ever know. I can do it. I know I can, all because of you."

"Sure, sure you can, darling. You'll tie our love up in a neat little bundle and sell it to Richard Burbage. But wait until to-morrow. This is not a play; let's go to sleep. To listen to you, one would think the whole world was a stage and men and women merely players."

"Yes, Hal. That's it. You're wonderful. All the world's a stage and all the men and women merely players. Why it even scans. I'll use it sometime. Thank you, you dear, wonderful inspiration."

"Tomorrow," he said, half asleep.

"Tomorrow," she repeated.

8

ROSALINE SAT AT A SMALL TABLE ON A LOW PROTECTED BALCONY overlooking the bar and ordinary of the Dolphin, the least rowdy inn that she had been able to find in Plymouth. The first ships to return from the Cadiz expedition were riding gently at anchor in the harbor while the victorious crews squandered their spoils in the waterfront taverns and brothels. With few exceptions only officers and gentlemen came into the Dolphin. Rosaline had spoken to none of them so far but she listened to their casual talk. Sooner or later one of them would bring news of the *Due Repulse,* Essex's ship with the Earl of Southampton aboard.

She had sat at the table for three days now with only her commonplace book for company. She opened the book to a clean page and wrote of his lordship's three months' absence from London, a lonely quarter that seemed a full year to her, the first three months that they had been apart in her three years' residence at Blackfriars Gatehouse.

> *How like a winter hath my absence been*
> *From thee, the pleasure of the fleeting year!*
> *What freezings have I felt, what dark days seen!* (97)

Finished with her poem, she turned to the one Southampton had sent her when he had first ridden to Plymouth, back in April, after that call to arms on Easter morning, 1596. How like him were his words! Though she knew that he was eager to join his beloved Essex in the Cadiz venture, he had written to her as though he were being torn away from all that was dear to him, and already impatient of return:

Then can no horse with my desire keep pace . . . (51)

But next to it was the one he had written in the last letter she had received from him, now a month old, in which he vowed that nimble thought could jump both sea and land.

As she read, she became aware of the presence of someone near her, a presence first announced by a heavy perfume which had insinuated itself into her consciousness during the last few lines of the sonnet. The scent was hauntingly familiar, though unpleasant in its memory. When she looked up, she was startled to see Sir Fulke Greville standing at her elbow.

"Have no fear," he said softly. "I won't reveal your secret."

She had no idea that he knew of her relationship with Southampton. She had not seen him since the performance of *Love's Labor's Lost* at Titchfield three years before.

"Do sit down, Sir Fulke," she said. Fulke Greville was in Raleigh's camp; and although Essex and Raleigh were now working in harmony, Rosaline felt that she must find out whether or not Sir Fulke knew enough to do any damage at court.

"Then I was right," he said, obviously pleased that he had been recognized. "You are Ross Allen, aren't you?"

"I was," Rosaline said with a smile. Sir Fulke had a sense of humor.

"You've hardly changed at all," he said, and studied her face and eyes while he drew a scented handkerchief from his sleeve, sniffed daintily and passed his clove pomander twice under his thin nose. "No trace of a beard yet."

"Not a whisker." Rosaline laughed softly. She was beginning to like Sir Fulke. He could be a tease when he wanted to be.

"Oh, how I envy you, lad. Dressed up so prettily, like a lady, and waiting for his lordship."

Rosaline stifled a little gasp as it dawned on her that Fulke Greville still thought that she was a boy.

"Yes, you *are* fortunate," he continued. "Dear Philip and I had one delicious month in Paris together. Sir Philip Sidney, you know."

"Yes," Rosaline said mechanically.

"While we were in the Low Countries fighting the Spaniard, he took leave and spent it in Paris. I joined him there. But within a year dear Philip was dead. You know how nobly he died, his poor bleeding side, and his last thoughts for that thirsty wounded soldier to whom he gave his last swallow of water."

"Yes, I've heard the story," Rosaline said, recovering her voice. There were tears in Sir Fulke's eyes, and he suddenly looked old and wrinkled and tired under the rouge and powder on his face. He was a sight to be pitied rather than loathed.

"But you," he said with an attempt at brightness, "you are young and his lordship is young, and you have a lifetime before you. Yes, how I envy you. If only dear Philip—"

It was more than Rosaline could bear. She interrupted him.

"No, no, Sir Fulke. You don't understand," she said rapidly. "I am not a boy masquerading as a woman. I have always been a girl—the boy's costume was the disguise."

"Oh," Sir Fulke said. Disappointment spread over his face. "I thought—I thought—"

"Yes, Sir Fulke, I know what you thought." On sudden impulse she clasped one of her hands over his and squeezed gently. "Anyone might have thought the same. I'm sorry, Sir Fulke."

"I always knew that young Southampton was attracted to you, especially that autumn at Titchfield, but I thought—" He looked dazed, still unwilling to accept the fact that Rosaline was a woman. "And I envied you—I so envied you."

He turned to leave, but stopped for one last word.

"Forgive me, my dear, for my mistake," he said. "For a moment— I hardly know what to do sometimes. I think I may return to the wars myself. Perhaps I can die, as dear Philip died, and join him in valor. I should welcome that. Perhaps my recklessness would pass for courage. I might even be considered a great soldier, like Philip."

He was moving away, down the three steps from Rosaline's balcony, when his last words, or the last words Rosaline heard, died on his lips.

Rosaline thumbed through the pages of her commonplace book. They contained the record of the three years she and the Earl of

Southampton had lived together as lovers. She read his lordship's answer to her worry, upon reaching the age of twenty-one, that she was getting old:

> *To me, fair friend, you never can be old ...*   (104)

To think that he could have taken her remark so seriously and answered it as gravely as if he had thought she really feared the loss of her youth! A warmth of feeling engulfed her and she started reading near the beginning of the book, with the first notes written in the Blackfriars Gatehouse. Odds and ends in the scrapbook recalled everything that had happened during those three eventful years.

She turned to the dedication of *The Rape of Lucrece,* published over Shakespeare's signature of course:

To the Right Honorable

HENRY WRIOTHESLY,

Earl of Southampton and Baron of Titchfield

————

The love I dedicate to your lordship is without end; Whereof this pamphlet, without beginning, is but a superfluous moiety. The warrant I have of your honorable disposition, not the worth of my untutored lines, makes it assured of acceptance. What I have done is yours; what I have to do is yours; being part in all I have, devoted yours. Were my worth greater, my duty would show greater; mean time, as it is, it is bound to your lordship, to whom I wish long life, still lengthened with all happiness.

Your lordship's in all duty,

In his lordship's copy of the book she had written a sonnet beginning "Lord of my love," with the double meanings both enjoyed. Now reading the messages brought back the whole year to her mind. After finishing *The Rape of Lucrece* for Richard Field, she had begun work on *Romeo and Juliet* immediately, while the glow of young love was still on her world. And at Betty's insistence, she had written a masque for the Stanley–de Vere wedding. She had called it *A Midsummer Night's Dream* and in it she had parodied *Romeo and Juliet.*

[113]

Rosaline remembered Betty's disappointment at the delay in her wedding, occasioned by the death of Ferdinando Stanley within six months after his becoming Earl of Derby. Since he had left the Countess Alice pregnant, William and Betty had had to postpone their marriage until the baby was born to determine succession to the Earlship. A stillborn boy had left William's title clear; so Betty had become a countess after all. But her wedding coming as it had, on January 26, 1595, had made the midsummer masque appear just a little absurd. Still Betty had insisted that the play be given in conjunction with her big court wedding at Greenwich Palace. And since Rosaline had considered the play absurd to begin with, she had dressed the play for the occasion and even dared to resume her disguise as a boy actor and play Hermia in the production.

Rosaline sighed. Now her little sister was Countess of Derby— and a mother. She envied Betty the daughter, born earlier in the summer, which Rosaline had not yet seen.

A collection of playbills reminded Rosaline of the other plays she had written to please Burbage. After the reopening of the theaters in June following her removal to Blackfriars, Burbage had recruited most of the players from the company of the late Earl of Derby and had organized a troupe of his own under the aegis of Sir Henry Carey, Lord Hunsdon, Lord Chamberlain of England. And since the Lord Chamberlain's Men had been strong rivals with the Lord Admiral's Men from the very first, Richard Burbage had driven Rosaline hard to keep him supplied with plays equal to Edward Alleyn's repertoire.

For him she had written, in addition to the lyrical love dramas, two histories: *Richard II,* which Burbage had made a success although he contended that Richard was more of a poet than a king; and *King John,* in which Rosaline seemed to have worked all the youthful self-conscious poetry out of her system. To compete with Alleyn's *Jew of Malta,* by the late Christopher Marlowe, she had written *The Merchant of Venice;* but still very much in love and bitter at no one, she had been kind even to her Jew, and Burbage had pleased all London with his sympathetic portrayal of Shylock.

But the plays had not been the only outlet for the lyric impulse engendered by her first blissful months with the handsome young Earl. From the very first both she and Southampton had kept on adding to what was becoming one of the best-known sonnet sequences of their day. Under the tutelage of Rosaline—or Rose, as he chose to call her—his lordship was soon writing in true iambs and creating acceptable imagery, especially in tribute to Rosaline's black eyes, his favorite theme even when they looked askance at some of his meters.

Certainly Rosaline could not question the playful sincerity of such a poem as the one that ended,

> *Then will I swear beauty herself is black*
> *And all they foul that thy complexion lack.*   (132)

Though some of his broader sentiments sounded a bit extravagant, as when he wrote,

> *So are you to my thoughts as food to life,*
> *Or as sweet-season'd showers to the ground,*   (75)

he had been quick to quote a dozen sonnets, from greater pens than his, which tended to cloy in their clichés. He even cited a recent contribution of hers which he playfully called the greediest proposal ever made by a virtuous woman:

> *Sweet love, renew thy force; be it not said*
> *Thy edge should blunter be than appetite,*
> *Which but to-day by feeding is allay'd,*
> *To-morrow sharpen'd . . .*   (56)

Then he had delighted her with a teasing parody of all the far-fetched metaphors poets might employ:

> *My mistress' eyes are nothing like the sun;*
> *Coral is far more red than her lips' red . . .*   (130)

"Now you're learning," she had said in open admiration. " 'My mistress, when she walks, treads on the ground'—I like that. I don't think I ever read a sonnet just like this, but then I never met a man just like you."

"And I know that no man ever had quite so dear a subject," he had countered. "I suppose that's the secret. Most poets write of

[115]

ladies 'painted red and white,' artificial ladies to begin with—
and so, artificial sonnets."

"Would you like me painted red and white?"

"Indeed not. And I'm not satisfied with a whimsical parody. Let
me try again."

He did try again, with carefully faint praise for his dark lady,

> *O, let me, true in love, but truly write,*
> *And then believe me, my love is as fair*
> *As any mother's child,*

but ending with the line,

> *I will not praise that purpose not to sell.* (21)

There had come a time, however, when Southampton was forced
to put in an appearance at court. Although the plague was bad
that first winter and the Christmas festivities were radically cur-
tailed, his lordship of necessity had to be away from the Blackfriars Gatehouse occasionally, first for a few hours, or half a day,
and then overnight, and ultimately for days at a time. The competition for preferment required constant attendance upon Her
Majesty, an hour's absence sometimes requiring three hours of
flattery in recompense. So either Southampton or Essex had to be
present to protect their joint interests.

But it could hardly be said that his lordship's mind was always
in the court chamber. Foreseeing the bleak months ahead when
he might have to spend whole weeks at Whitehall or Greenwich
or Hampton, he could only justify his absence from Rosaline as a
sort of self-denial to be rewarded somehow by the pleasure in
anticipation of his return to her. He spent many hours at court
not flattering the Queen, but composing still more sonnets to his
Rose. One spoke of "feasts so solemn and so rare, since seldom
coming."

And on his return he had been so conscious of Rosaline's hours
spent in lonely solitude that he sometimes spent half the night
explaining the necessity of his absences and the nature of all his
business, lest she suspect him of mere dalliance in the court chamber. Rosaline, still as much in the throes of lyric ecstasy as her
lover, responded with a closing couplet to reassure him:

So true a fool is love that in your will,
Though you do any thing, he thinks no ill.   (57)

But before the mood had begun to cloy, the lovers were forced to think of other things than themselves. The Earl of Essex, though unsuccessful in his attempt to have Francis Bacon appointed Attorney-General, was nevertheless rising in the Queen's favor and confidence. Essex House became the center of a buzzing foreign intelligence service. Through his organization Essex uncovered, among other things, a plot to poison the Queen. And since the poisoner was the Queen's own Portuguese physician, Roderigo Lopez, whom the Cecils defended at first accusation, the final trial and conviction of the culprit represented quite a victory for Lord Essex, and of course for Southampton, who had spent the winter months helping on the case.

In May of that first year the Countess Mary Southampton, the Earl's mother, married Sir Thomas Heneage, the Queen's Vice-Chamberlain. So his lordship's fortunes seemed to be on the upturn, as he enthusiastically maintained on his less and less frequent visits to the Gatehouse. It was in this mood of gay confidence that he and Rosaline had planned to observe their first anniversary aboard the *Ictis* during the celebration of Michaelmas and his lordship's twenty-first birthday. With his engagement to Betty broken, his preferment at court assured, he felt that he would be able to present Rosaline at court soon after he had reached his majority and become free of Lord Burleigh's guardianship.

Rosaline closed the commonplace book, with her handkerchief inside for a marker, and leaned against the balcony railing as she remembered her second visit to Titchfield. She sipped at her glass of wine and closed her eyes for a moment. A vision of Whitley Lodge replaced the busy ordinary of the Dolphin, a vision almost as clear as the lodge itself had been that morning—it was Saturday, October 5, two years before, she remembered, his birthday coming on Sunday that year.

The main Michaelmas celebration was already over and she and Southampton had stolen aboard for their second night in the master's cabin of the *Ictis,* but the Place was still full of gayety in anticipation of his lordship's birthday. She was posing then as a maidservant to Thomas Dymock, to account for her presence at Titchfield. The regular guests that year were many, including the

Countess and her new husband, Sir Thomas and Lady Mary Arundel (his lordship's sister), Lord and Lady Essex, and, most disturbing of all, Essex's beautiful cousin, Elizabeth Vernon. That name jerked Rosaline back into the present. Southampton had considered it necessary to be attentive to Essex's cousin, and though the affair was supposed to have been sheer rumor, she wondered if Mistress Vernon were also waiting his lordship's return with some degree of eagerness in her heart.

Rosaline had been almost glad that the fatal quarrel involving the Danvers brothers had spoiled his lordship's birthday celebration. She remembered how she herself had dressed Sir Henry's wound and heard Sir Charles take all the blame for the death of Henry Long. She remembered too the dangerous exciting days during which his lordship had interfered with the Queen's justice, hidden Sir Charles and Sir Henry from Sir Walter Long, who insisted that murder had been done. Yes, she had been pleased that her lover's attentions had been shifted, temporarily at least, from Elizabeth Vernon, even though his aiding the fugitives to escape to France had earned him the appellation of "outlaw," which had plagued him at court for nearly a year and effectively blocked whatever chances he may have had for immediate advancement. He was bitter, very bitter at those who censured him and exaggerated his crime, for he had always felt that he had been in the right and that his detractors were slandering him. There had been times when he threatened to do something really vile, for as he wrote:

> *'Tis better to be vile, than vile esteemed...* (121)

In his dejection he had even accused her of siding against him, had written to her of his self-pity:

> *Then hate me when thou wilt; if ever, now;*
> *Now, while the world is bent my deeds to cross,*
> *Join with the spite of fortune, make me bow...* (90)

And she had answered to comfort him:

> *That thou art blam'd shall not be thy defect,*
> *For slander's mark was ever yet the fair...* (70)

[118]

But that was all over. Rosaline hugged the commonplace book to her bosom, mutely thankful that her lover was back in the good graces of Her Majesty. Despite the near disastrous effect of Father Parson's seditious *Conference About the Next Succession to the Crown of England* which the Jesuit had dedicated to Essex, much to the Earl's embarrassment, the Queen had favored Essex of late and had indeed commissioned him Lieutenant-General in charge of the Cadiz expeditions. By all reports the campaign had been eminently successful and Essex, with Southampton in tow, should be the Queen's favorite at last.

Rosaline feared to hope, but did hope, that Southampton might now acknowledge her as his wife and present her at court. She honestly felt that she wished it more for his sake than for her own. She knew the strain under which the deception kept him. For herself, she would have been happy to remain in the background, though Betty was unfailingly optimistic, enthusiastic in fact, over Rosaline's prospects at a court which was becoming increasingly Italianate in tastes and manners.

She worried for a moment about Betty, and her baby, which was sickly. Then she wondered about little Hamnet Shakespeare, who had been very ill when she left London. But the longing to see her husband drove such thoughts out of her mind, and she hugged her book to her and waited for his lordship.

"Madame, Madame Rose," she heard from a door opening off the balcony behind her.

"Yes?" She turned and met the calm grey eyes of William Strachey.

"Oh, Mr. Strachey, is he here?" she asked, rising eagerly.

"No, Madame. The *Due Repulse* put into Portsmouth. Lord Essex changed his course at the last minute."

"Then Hal—his lordship—will not be coming to Plymouth?"

William Strachey's eyes clouded at her show of disappointment. He seemed always sensitive to her feelings.

"No, Madame. He and Lord Essex will post to London immediately. Perhaps they are already on their way. It—it was urgent that they do so," he added, to soften the blow, it seemed, by showing that the delay was not of his lordship's wish or making.

"Then—then, I suppose I should return to London."

"Yes, Madame. There is a pinnace sailing for London tonight. I can arrange passage for you if you wish."

[119]

She smiled her gratitude to him, though her eyes were brimming with tears. Good, capable William Strachey. He seemed always to be standing by when his lordship disappointed her. It had been he who had got her out of the Danvers affair and spirited her away and back to London before the conspirators had become embroiled with the Queen's officers.

"But do you think—his lordship—" she stammered.

"You'll be safe, Madame," William Strachey assured her with whimsical wrinkles forming at the corners of his eyes. "You'll not be left to the mercy of sea-weary sailors. My wife, Frances, and our son will be aboard. They'll protect you."

"Indeed, they will." She laughed easily. "When do we sail?"

"With the tide, Madame Rose."

9

At the Gatehouse Rosaline found a note pinned to her pillow:

Beloved Rose:
It was the great disappointment of my life to find you gone from this bed. Henry Walker finally explained to me that you had journeyed to Plymouth to meet me. I might have known—so characteristic of your sweet self! I'll see you, darling, at the earliest possible moment. I am due at court now. We expect great things. I haven't even time to pen a sonnet, though my heart is full of poetry.
Your devoted lover,
H.

It was dated two days before. She kissed the note a dozen times and then prepared to refresh herself from her voyage so she would be ready when her husband returned "at the earliest possible moment." She bathed and perfumed her body and tied her hair back the way he liked it—like the groomed tail of an Irish hobby, he always said teasingly. Then she put fresh silk sheets on the bed and waited.

But his lordship did not return that night, and her vigil extended into the next day. Her eagerness did not abate one whit. First she rushed to her door at the sound of boots, tired boots, on the stairway—but it was only the lazy clumping of Henry Walker, the porter, coming to spread a fresh carpet of dried rushes in the hallway. About midmorning, she heard other footsteps, rapid, businesslike footsteps on the stairs. Instead of rushing to the door she sat tensely on a farthingale chair in the drawing room—he needed to be disciplined for his tardiness—and waited for his key to turn in the lock.

There was a knock instead. He was being very formal. Perhaps, after time for consideration, he had begun to doubt Henry's dumb explanation that she had gone to Plymouth. He was in a jealous pique! Very well, she could cure that.

She sprang lightly from the chair and raced to the door. She turned the lock and flung the door open wide enough to admit her lover in all his demonstrative exuberances. The door fanned her sheer silk gown against her, revealing her body in fascinating contour.

And Richard Burbage stared at her in open-mouthed admiration.

As her face fell, he said, "I gather that I wasn't expected. Or was I?" He leered at her with mock lasciviousness.

"No," she answered shortly. "But come in. I'll be right back."

She fled to her bedroom for a robe. Burbage unloaded an armful of manuscript on the center table and sat down in a window seat.

"How is little Hamnet?" she asked, as she re-entered the room, still tying the sash around her dark red robe. "I suppose you came by the Shakespeares'."

"Hamnet is dead," he said, all the facetiousness gone from his voice.

"No!"

"He died a few days ago. Will and Anne have taken him to Stratford for burial."

"Poor little Hamnet," she said. "And Judith. She'll be lost without him. Twins are so close."

"And Anne," Richard Burbage said. "She blames it all on London. I doubt that she ever comes back."

"How did Will take it?"

"Hurt, of course, but calm."

"Will he be back? To London I mean."

"He has to come back. There's nothing in Stratford for him. And that share in the Lord Hunsdon's Company which you and he hold jointly in his name is a valuable property. Someone has to be on hand to count the profits." At last the true Burbage was speaking.

"You mean, of course, that I'm neglecting our interests," she said.

"Well, yes. A troupe has to have plays."

"I've been away from London less than two weeks and you accuse me of neglecting your precious Theater!"

"Have you written anything while his lordship was away?"

"Well, no," she admitted. She sat down on a carved stool at the center table. "No plays. A few sonnets."

"Sonnets!" Burbage exclaimed. "A farthing a bundle. Plays, we need plays. That's what people pay for. You should be writing plays while his lordship is away, so when the time comes—"

"Richard Burbage, stop your intolerable insinuations." She stood up beside the table and glared at him angrily. "I don't have to write another play as long as I live. His lordship—"

"Where is he?"

"At court."

"Fine. Now, while he's at court, let's talk about that manuscript there." He rose and pointed dramatically at the paper on the table. "Your Earl and the Earl of Essex and Sir Walter Raleigh and the other brave gentlemen who fight our wars are playing right into our hands. Their glorious victory at Cadiz has whetted everybody's patriotism. There will be a new increased demand for historical plays."

"They are brave men!" Rosaline said, with weakening defiance in the face of Burbage's frontal attack. "To cheapen their victories by calling them theater advertisements is to—"

"I did nothing of the kind," Burbage remonstrated. "I have utmost reverence for their lordships. But their stories, as they spread, will recall older stories. The audience will clamor for them. We don't create the public taste; we cater to it. Or we can let Ned Alleyn and Phillip Henslowe take all the business across the river. They are acquiring a stable of young writers who are eager to please."

"What's this play about?" Rosaline asked, idly fingering the manuscript pages on the table beside her.

"It's called *The Famous Victories of Henry the Fifth*. Henry V was the famous rakehell Prince Hal, you remember. I thought you might start with his youth, back in the reign of Henry IV, and come on down through his victories at Harfleur and Agincourt. Maybe write a series of two or three plays, to keep the people coming back to the theater. You could fill in the gaps in history from Holinshed's *Chronicles*. Can you do it?"

"Certainly I can do it!" She was still on her mettle.

"Your own Hal might provide a sort of pattern for the reckless Prince Hal."

"His lordship is not reckless!" she said.

"Have you forgotten the Danvers affair? Anyway it was just a thought. Prince Hal turned out well, made an excellent king."

Mollified somewhat, Rosaline sat down again and began to read the old play.

"And see what you can do for Will Kempe," Burbage continued when he sensed that her interest was rising. "He does have quite a following and he's always complaining that there's nothing for a comedian to do in history plays. The character of the fat old knight offers possibilities; but if you keep him, change his name from Sir John Oldcastle. Lord Cobham, the present Lord Chamberlain, objects—it seems that the old boy was a relative of his, way back yonder. See what you can do; a good comic part in a history play might give it a double appeal."

"Might," Rosaline said abstractedly, her mind on the worn pages in her hands.

Sensing her preoccupation with the play, Burbage stole out quietly, easing the door shut behind him so as not to disturb Rosaline. But she heard him go; and realizing that he had practically tricked her into reading the manuscript and promising to dress it for revival, she flung the bundle of paper against the door and stamped her sandaled foot on the Turkish rug. Then she gathered up the manuscript and stowed it in a cupboard. She had no time for such things, when his lordship might come home at any minute.

She went back into her bedroom to restore her appearance. She exchanged her robe, and the gown it had wrinkled, for a fresh smock. Then after careful attention to her lips and eyebrows and lashes, she combed her hair and retied it into a fresh pony tail. She resumed her seat at the center table, but she read from her commonplace book, rather than from *The Famous Victories of Henry the Fifth.* The sonnets recreated her vision of Hal and sharpened her eagerness to greet him.

She sat for another hour before she heard the key turning in the lock. She was startled by the sound. There had been no footsteps audible on the stairs. She stood where she was and faced the door expectantly.

It was Betty who entered unannounced.

"Betty!" Rosaline exclaimed, disappointed but pleased.

"Rosaline, you darling."

The two women rushed into an embrace.

"I'm so glad you're here," Betty said. "I came by last week, as soon as we returned from the north. But you were gone. I missed you."

"I went to Plymouth."

"So Henry explained," Betty said. She threw off a light cloak which she had worn over her court dress. Obviously she had just come from court, for she was dressed in elaborate fashion—the fashion of unwed maids-in-waiting or newly married women. Her full breasts were high embusked and bare, to their rouged tips.

Rosaline appraised her sister. Hers was not the usual attire of a young mother with a nursing child.

"How is the baby?" Rosaline asked, shifting her attention to Betty's face.

"She's tiny. She's ill. She's been sickly for months now."

"What seems to be the matter? What does the doctor say?"

"Doctors lie," Betty said positively. "The baby doesn't like me, Rosaline."

"Nonsense," Rosaline said. She shook her sister playfully. "Of course she likes you."

"No, Rosaline. No. she doesn't. She won't nurse." Betty turned to face her sister, with an expression of such complete, miserable despair that Rosaline feared for her sanity.

"It felt so good—when she did try at first," Betty went on. "You've no idea what it's like to have a dear little baby tugging at your breast! Then she stopped. She doesn't love me. And she's breaking my heart." Betty began to weep soundlessly, but tears soaked into the shoulder of Rosaline's smock where Betty had nestled to have her cry.

"The baby doesn't know," Rosaline soothed her. "She can't

[124]

know. It's just that there's something wrong with your milk. It should clear up. Do you have a wet nurse?"

"We've tried several," Betty sobbed. "She doesn't like any of them—because she hates me, I know. We have to give her goat's milk sopped up in a sugar teat."

"Then it isn't you, Betty. See? It's something in the baby's constitution." She pushed Betty away from her and looked steadily into her eyes. "The baby couldn't hate you. She couldn't even know how to hate. She has no control over her appetite. Don't you understand that, honey?"

"I don't know," Betty said. Her eyes were as disturbing as her voice. "William doesn't love me any more either. He doesn't like my breasts either. He wants me to cover them, like old married women who are ashamed of their limp, sagging dugs. But Robin and Walt appreciate me, even if my husband and daughter don't."

Rosaline could understand William's position, what with Raleigh and Essex turning their attention to his young wife. Besides, something in Betty's eyes, a sort of glazed wildness, disturbed Rosaline.

"Are Lord Essex and Raleigh at court now?" Rosaline asked.

"Yes, for three days," Betty said. "They are all the rage. Heroes of Cadiz. They're so popular—and they both sought me out to compliment me, said my breasts were the loveliest at court."

"Hal. Have you seen Hal, Betty?"

"Yes, I've seen Hal, but not to talk to him. With that Elizabeth Vernon hanging on his arm all the time, no one can talk to him. I declare, Rosaline, I don't see why you don't tell her— But you can't, can you, Rosaline?"

"No, Betty. I'm in no position to tell anybody anything."

"Then I'll tell her—" Betty's eyes were almost normal again, full of their adoration for Rosaline, and indignation for her cause.

"No, you don't! Don't you say a word about me at court!" Rosaline warned her.

"But someone ought to. That Elizabeth Vernon is none too virtuous. I can tell you that. Like her uncle. Do you know that Robin has been carrying on with Elizabeth Southwell, and Elizabeth Bridges, and Elizabeth Russell?" Betty was counting the Elizabeths off on her fingers. "Not to mention Lady Mary Howard. And then there's his wife, Frances Walsingham Sidney Devereux, of course. And he finds me quite attractive. But my baby and William don't love me."

Rosaline drew Betty to her again, but it was she who wept at her little sister's crooked reasoning. There had been times when it had amused her to follow the erratic course of Betty's thinking. Now it was heartbreaking to listen to her.

Gradually she got Betty to talk of the spring and summer spent at Knowsley and Castletown on the Isle of Man, of which the Earl of Derby was governor. Still, when Betty finally drove away in her coach, Rosaline was deeply disturbed about her sister's obsession. Her report on Elizabeth Vernon's attachment to the Earl of Southampton was, in its way, somewhat disturbing as well. Rosaline, though perfectly sure of his lordship's constancy, nevertheless allowed herself some moments of jealousy and downright resentment at his continued absence. Then in contrition she began to write on a fresh sheet of paper:

> *That god forbid that made me first your slave,*
> *I should in thought control your times of pleasure,*

and, after some thought, ended:

> *I am to wait, though waiting so be hell;*
> *Not blame your pleasure, be it ill or well.* (58)

As she mulled over the words of Betty, Rosaline became more and more firmly convinced that Elizabeth Vernon was at fault. Obviously she was the huntress in the affair. And she was a formidable huntress, both in her own right and in her relation and resemblance to the Earl of Essex, whom young Southampton adored. Poor Hal, even if he did allow himself to be seduced, he was not to be blamed. How could he resist? Almost fondly she composed lines just to prove how noble she could be if such were really the case:

> *Gentle thou art, and therefore to be won,*
> *Beauteous thou art, therefore to be assailed . . .* (41)

That was early in the afternoon. By nightfall, she had shed all her pretenses at nobility, and was pacing the floor in rising anger.

[126]

The very least his lordship could do was send her a message. "The earliest possible moment," indeed! A whole night and day, now— three days since he had pinned that note on her pillow. She was ready to raise her voice at him. But his ears were not in hearing distance. Very well, she would write him a warning. Savagely she added still a third sonnet to her day's output of poetry; this one ended with a warning:

> *That I may not be so, nor thou belied,*
> *Bear thine eyes straight, though thy proud*
> *heart go wide.* (140)

Then she pulled on a light wool street dress, stepped into a pair of sandals, and went out for some food. She had not eaten for twenty-four hours. But she could wait just so long for food— or for his lordship. She went into a fashionable little inn farther inside Blackfriars and spent an hour on a hearty helping of roast beef, with cheese and sweet wine for dessert.

She felt better on the way back to the gatehouse; and when she saw candles burning in her upstairs window, she fairly ran the rest of the way and up the steps into Southampton's arms.

It was Hal! Hal at last, smelling of tobacco and musk, and feeling bristly in a kiss. She stood back and looked at him when he finally released her. A beard, he had grown a beard, a full square brush of golden whiskers, carefully trimmed and groomed; that is, until she had disturbed their symmetry.

"A beard!" she exclaimed.

"The Cadiz Cut, it's called. All of us heroes grew them during the voyage. You should see Robin's."

"Robin's indeed! Yours is enough. But I might get used to it. Let's see if I can."

They saw. The beard interfered with nothing they did. In fact Rosaline grew to like what the beard represented, a new manliness which his lordship felt called upon to justify in every manner he could devise. Yes, the Cadiz beard should enliven court life no end.

Late in the night, after his lordship had worn himself out and talked himself out in his enthusiasm for his new stature at court, Rosaline stole out of bed to destroy the premature sonnets she had written. She gathered up the sheets of paper and took them into the kitchen. When she lit a candle to decide which to burn, she recognized his lordship's handwriting on the last sheet. Below her bitterest poem he had written:

> *O, never say that I was false of heart,*
> *Though absence seem'd my flame to qualify.*
> *As easy might I from myself depart*
> *As from my soul, which in thy breast does lie . . .*   (109)

She felt warm all over. How could she help loving a man like that? She returned to bed without burning any of the precious poetry.

10

ROSALINE LAY QUIET IN THE TOMB, DRUGGED, PRESUMABLY DEAD. Soon it would end, this rashest of all the mad things she had done in the past four or five months. Hal, intoxicated by the favor of the Queen, had shared most of the risks with her. In the gayest season at court in many years, gay because of the success against the Spaniard at Cadiz, his lordship had brought her to Whitehall several times. There had been masquerade balls, to which she had come disguised each time as a different character. Once before they had attended a big, crowded function at the Banqueting House, where she had remained a mysterious anonymous beauty still privileged to mask her face at will, while admirers complimented her bare bosom with flattering comparisons to the lovely breasts of the Little Countess of Derby.

Now this, on Twelfth Night, during the festival of Epiphany, this risk which she had had to take alone. Beside the tomb Richard Burbage spoke his lament:

> *"—Ah! dear Juliet,*
> *Why art thou yet so fair? I will believe*
> *That unsubstantial Death is amorous;*
> *And that the lean abhorred monster keeps*
> *Thee here in dark to be his paramour. . . ."*

[128]

After drinking the lethal toast to his love he leaned over her for a moment, as though kissing her, and then slid to the floor beside her bier. She lay still through the short scene between Friar Laurence and Balthasar, waiting for her cue: *The lady stirs.* Then she sat up, asked about her Romeo, dismissed the others, and stabbed herself with Burbage's dagger. As soon as the small curtain was drawn across the makeshift inner stage which had represented her tomb, Rosaline and her fellow corpses, Romeo and Paris, arose and adjusted their costumes for the final bow.

William Shakespeare as Escalus, Prince of Verona, at last reached the closing couplet:

> *"For never was a story of more woe*
> *Than this of Juliet and her Romeo."*

The audience stood and applauded vigorously as Burbage and Rosaline joined the rest of the cast on the apron of the platform stage erected in the huge old Banqueting House at Whitehall. Rosaline bowed and swept the hall full circle with her eyes as she smiled at the cheering courtiers. There must have been two thousand in attendance, filling all ten of the elevated tiers of stools and benches on the main floor and crowding the galleries so full that many, no doubt, had been unable to see the stage at all. But they had enjoyed what they heard, and the painted canvas roof of the pavilion billowed upward with their shouts of "Bravo," a fashionable new Italian expression of approval.

It was over. Rosaline had made good her resolve to play Juliet before the Queen and her court, mostly the court, though no one outside her circle of intimates would ever share in her satisfaction at being acclaimed by the most fastidious theater audience in the world. Even her intimates had tried to discourage her from running the risk involved in impersonating a boy actor in a performance before Her Majesty; all except Richard Burbage, who welcomed her as a Juliet to challenge and stimulate his Romeo. And that she had done. So happy had she been with her husband these last few months that she had known again that ecstasy which she had first captured as she wrote the lines of the play; and she had brought those lines to life in the Banqueting House within the last two hours.

Before the cast could clear the stage, a messenger came from the Queen.

"Her Majesty requests Master Shakespeare, Mister Burbage, and the lad who played Juliet to wait upon her in the presence chamber," he announced pompously.

So it was not all over, Rosaline realized with a skip in her heartbeat. She might still be discovered. She took some little confidence in the mask provided by her make-up. The thick coats of "red and white" which the audience demanded of their heroines had exaggerated her features to the almost grotesque proportions required for projection in so large a hall. She would not be recognized as a person anyone had ever seen, unless some enemy had already discovered her secrets and tattled.

But there was no refusing the Queen's command. Rosaline followed Shakespeare and Burbage and the page single file through the milling crowd backstage to a small private room reserved for Her Majesty in the Banqueting House. The room was empty, except for a carved oak throne-chair cushioned with ermine robes.

"Wait here," the page said and went out through another door.

"What do you make of it, Dick?" Shakespeare whispered.

"Her Majesty was impressed by our performance," Burbage answered with complete confidence.

"But why me? The Prince's part is nothing to attract notice."

"You wrote the play. Remember?" Burbage grinned at his two companions. "As well as half a dozen others which have been given here at court this Christmas season. Her Majesty no doubt knows which plays are by Shakespeare. Maybe she likes them."

"Do you suppose she knows about the deposition scene which we had to cut out of *Richard II?*" Rosaline asked. If the playwright were accused of sedition, she would have to admit authorship; she could not let Shakespeare go to jail for her. Partially allayed fears began to rise again.

"We'll soon know," Burbage said.

Preceded by nobles bearing the Scepter, the Sword of State, and the Great Seal Purse, the Queen entered the room after the formal procession from her box near the stage. The three actors knelt and kept their heads bowed until the Queen made herself comfortable among the ermine robes and dismissed her staff. Only one lady, a stout greying countess, remained after Her Majesty had cleared the room. It was the countess who signaled that the actors might look on Her Majesty, though all three continued to kneel throughout the interview.

Upon raising her eyes, Rosaline thought her own make-up less bizarre. The Queen had fully as much white lead smeared on her face and neck and bosom as Rosaline had used to make her features visible to the farthest gallery of the Banqueting House. Yet Her Majesty's wrinkles still showed; and her lips, painted vermilion and parted to reveal decaying teeth, presented a travesty of a human mouth. The white silk dress trimmed in bean-sized pearls and the black mantle embroidered in gold thread did nothing to ameliorate the Queen's ugliness. Neither did the crooked auburn wig and the collar of gold and jewels which framed Her Majesty's face. Only her sharp little old eyes seemed alive in a hideous painted cadaver. The lying words of the court poets! Rosaline thought. The Queen was an old hag.

Her Majesty scratched indelicately under one of her breasts, which she still wore exposed, since she claimed the privileges of unmarried women long after her aging bosom had made the practice repulsive. When she spoke, however, Rosaline forgot some of the unpleasantness associated with her person. Her voice was clear and strong.

"Mr. Burbage, I enjoyed your play very much this evening," she began.

"Thank you, Your Majesty."

"God's death, don't thank me, man. I had nothing to do with it. Thank your two companions, the lad for playing a perfectly charming Juliet, and Master Shakespeare for composing so touching a poem."

Burbage bowed, the best court bow he could manage from a kneeling position.

"You, lad. I don't think you knew what you were doing, but you did it beautifully. When I was about your Juliet's age, I was very much in love with Tom Howard. You wouldn't believe that I was ever a young girl, lad, but I was. I know exactly what Juliet felt. You were a charming Juliet, though. From where I sat, you appeared to be a lovely one. Upon closer inspection, the illusion vanishes."

Rosaline could have returned the compliment. She was thankful, however, that she was wearing her horrid false face.

"But you read the lines convincingly. At times I—I thought I was back at Hatfield, dreaming of Tom Howard—

"That brings me to you, Master Shakespeare. You have no

right to know so much about the heart of a lovesick maiden. If I didn't know—if I weren't familiar with your work by now, I would swear that a woman wrote *Romeo and Juliet*. Some of your sonnets to that flighty young Southampton—yes, I've seen them circulating around the court—sound like the work of a woman too.

"But of course there is not so talented a woman in all England. If there were, I—I would destroy her." The Queen clenched her long slender fingers into vicious fists and pounded the arms of the throne-chair. Her small eyes flashed. Rosaline believed her.

"I would not tolerate a woman with your creative talent, Master Shakespeare. I fear that you are building a world in your plays which may one day seem more real than the England I have created by the sheer force of my will." Her hands were still clenched. She seemed to be addressing Shakespeare almost rhetorically. Her words were for herself, or for all the world.

"It is possible that your world and mine will always be linked together, perhaps even confused in the minds of posterity. I shall be forced to share my fame with a dozen men—you, perhaps among them—but no woman shares in the glory of Elizabeth Rex. Be thankful that you are a man, William Shakespeare."

She managed a smile at last.

"Were you a woman, I would have you beheaded. As it is, I resent very much your skill in laying bare a virgin's soul, but I shall reward you for a beautiful play. Countess, my purse!

"Give Burbage and the lad a sovereign—the old heavy ones, the twenty-three carats," Her Majesty instructed. "Give Master Shakespeare two. Playwrights are not properly valued, I fear, either by the audience or by skillful actors like Mr. Burbage. Your Queen appreciates you. You are part of the glory of England —at least two sovereigns' worth—in coins, of course." Her Majesty chuckled at her own pun and dismissed the actors, who backed out of the presence chamber.

"Well, that settles your status, Madame Playwright," Burbage said as they made their way to the tiring rooms. "Elizabeth *Rex* brooks no *regina*—politic or dramatic."

"She meant it, Dick," Rosaline said. "She would kill me if she knew. I'm sure she would." She shuddered at the memory of Her Majesty's threats.

"She probably wouldn't believe it, if it came to a test," Burbage said casually. "She wouldn't believe that any other woman could do a man's work, none but Her Majesty."

"I don't think I'd risk another performance at court, if I were you," Shakespeare said. He had been skeptical at first, uneasy all along.

"I won't, though I don't see that my appearance at Whitehall has anything to do with my writing plays."

Rosaline entered a little cupboard of a room which she had managed to reserve for herself. The share-holding members of the Lord Chamberlain's Men (or Lord Hunsdon's Men, as they were called for a few months in 1596) knew, of course, that Rosaline was a woman; they knew also that it was her plays that gave them the advantage over the Lord Admiral's Men, and consequently they took all possible measures to protect her anonymity. So she had privacy where formerly it had been impossible.

Instead of changing into her boy's clothes she cleaned her face down to her naturally dark complexion and put on a court dress similar to the ones the ladies in the audience were wearing. Then putting on a mask, which was entirely in order on such huge occasions when half the women present were court mistresses, she went to meet Southampton at a side door.

"Let's go home," he said. "I have exciting news."

"How was my Juliet?" she asked, a little disappointed that he had not complimented her.

"Wonderful. I still don't approve, but you were wonderful— what I saw."

"Hal! You mean you didn't see the performance?" She was trotting along beside him, hurrying toward a wherry at the foot of Whitehall Stairs.

"I'm sorry, Rose," he said. "You know I love your performances, especially your private ones, which I know best. But we just received intelligence from some Portuguese seamen, and Robin called a special conference at the cockpit in St. James Park." He laughed a little apologetically at the choice of a conference place.

"And what was this important bit of intelligence? Am I privileged to know?" It would have to be something indeed to be important enough in her eyes to tear her husband away from the greatest portrayal of Juliet yet seen in England.

"A storm. We knew that King Philip was sending the Adelantado with twenty fighting ships and seventy troopships to avenge

Cadiz." Southampton guided her carefully down Whitehall Stairs. "We were prepared for attacks on the Isle of Wight, Portsmouth, Southampton, or London—if the Spaniard were so daring. Now we've received word that the Spanish fleet was caught in a storm, with a loss of forty ships and hundreds, maybe thousands, of men."

That hardly seemed important enough to justify his absence from the play; but she allowed him to continue, in whispers, after they were seated in the sternsheets of the wherry and snugly wrapped in blankets to protect them from the January air. The sky was clear, with a bright moon glistening on the water. The conversation could have been more romantic; but, tired as she was, she listened half-heartedly.

"Robin thinks this is the time to prepare for a campaign on Ferrol and then to the Azores to intercept the Indian Fleet with its cargo of gold and silver and jewels and spices. We could harry the Spaniard and fill Her Majesty's coffers at the same time."

The Indian Fleet, tall treasure galleons, spice-laden carracks. The moon shone on York House and the Savoy Palace as the rowers pulled the wherry around the bend in the river. Flares were burning in the gardens of Arundel House and Essex House. Torches, marking their respective stairs, lighted rippling avenues on the surface of the Thames.

"That's the secret of preferment with Her Majesty: military success and rich spoils of war." His voice was eager, young.

Her Majesty would behead a talented woman, would she? She would not share her glory with any woman. What would Her Majesty give to be snuggled up in a blanket with "that flighty young Southampton," held tightly in his arms, tickled by his Cadiz cut beard? Rosaline no longer feared the Queen's envy. She could have gone to sleep without a qualm.

"The Earl of Cumberland would merely attack the Spanish reserves at Ferrol, a purely preventive measure, no spoils, no real battle. Robin's plan is much the bolder, the more spectacular, the more likely to please Her Majesty."

Bridewell Palace always gave Rosaline the shivers. Only the Fleet Ditch separated it from Blackfriars. How close she lived to it! How near she sometimes came to being liable to a term in Bridewell Prison for Women. But not with his lordship's arms around her. She cuddled deliciously.

[134]

"Blackfriars Stairs," the waterman called, and eased the boat alongside the wharf.

Southampton lifted Rosaline bodily and deposited her on the pier, high and dry, without getting so much as a drop of water on her red velvet shoes.

"Now, you mustn't tell a soul of Robin's plans," he cautioned on the walk to the Gatehouse. "Even when we start provisioning we shall keep our ultimate destination a secret."

"Oh, I shan't tell a soul," Rosaline said in awed tones. "Dark mysterious woman of intrigue that I am, I shan't breathe a word to my countless foreign lovers. When does all this begin?" Walking in the sharp air awakened her.

"Now. I mean we're in the planning stages already. We'll begin provisioning and levying men in April or May, then be ready to sail by the middle of June at the outside." They had reached the outer door of the Gatehouse. Rosaline was beginning to tire.

"And how long will the campaign last?" Rosaline asked. She was becoming aware that he was actually thinking of leaving her again.

"Six months or more. We'll intercept all the shipping from the Indies during the summer and fall."

"Six months," she repeated on the way up the stairs. "Twice as long as the last time."

"And twice the progress. Look how much favor we won with the Queen by the Cadiz expedition. Twice as much glory, twice the spoils—ten times the spoils—and Robin will be the biggest man in England."

His lordship unlocked the door and struck lights in the drawing room. Henry Walker had kept a fire of sea-coals going. The apartment was warm.

"The biggest man in England," Rosaline said. "With the young courtiers and the people in the streets, you mean. Will the Queen like that?"

His lordship turned toward her. He studied her face as he took off his heavy cloak.

"It's strange that you should ask that, Rose," he said. "Francis Bacon posed exactly the same question. Oh, he knows nothing of Robin's plans; but he's been lecturing Robin on his popularity. He says that the Queen wants her people's love for herself alone and prefers her favorites to be hated—and Robin is the best-loved man in England right now."

"Mr. Bacon has Her Majesty's ear, if reports are true." Rosaline began to take off her elaborate court dress. She spoke wearily.

"Granted. But who is he to lecture the Earl of Essex on his behavior? He said Robin was too independent, not easily ruled; that his estate was not equal to his greatness; that he was entirely too popular; and that he was a soldier. Can you imagine? Those are the very things which will lead to Robin's advancement. Nothing can stop him. Certainly no upstart lawyer like Francis Bacon." His lordship laughed.

"Her Majesty doesn't welcome competition of any kind. Did you know that I had an audience with the Queen tonight, my lord?"

"No." His word was more than a simple negative. It was an expression of disbelief.

"Well, I did. She gave me that." She tossed her gold sovereign on the table.

"An old twenty-three carat," he said, weighing the gold piece in his hand and then dropping it noisily on the table again.

"By Her Majesty's express command. She gave me one and Richard Burbage one and Will Shakespeare two."

"Shakespeare two?"

"Shakespeare, the playwright, you know. Double pay for genius." Rosaline put on her most superior air. "She thinks that Shakespeare's make-believe world may one day rival her own in the memory of man."

"Her Majesty is a shrewd judge of literary and dramatic merit. And she's honest in such matters. Did she really say that?" Perhaps his lordship glimpsed another avenue through which Rosaline might arrive at court.

"She said that," Rosaline stated. "And she said further that Shakespeare's understanding of women was incredible. It was almost as though a woman had written *Romeo and Juliet,* as well as some of his love sonnets which are floating around the court in manuscript."

"She likes them? That's wonderful. Perhaps—" His voice was eager.

"But she declared that there was not so talented a woman in all England, and if there were she would have the female genius beheaded. She would brook no woman rival to share in the glory of the Age of Elizabeth."

She faced Southampton and stared steadily into his eyes.

"I believed her, Hal," she said. "I believed every word she said. And if I were the Earl of Essex I would study Sir Francis Bacon's advice very carefully before I rejected it."

"Rose, darling, do you know what you're saying?" He laughed a little uneasily. "You, a mere slip of a girl, if I may be trite, are presuming to advise a peer of the realm. You and young Mr. Bacon!"

"Perhaps."

"Has the Queen's commendation of your plays gone to your head? Do you honestly believe that these characters you have created in your history plays, these—these figments of your imagination are real kings and lords? Do you think the success of *Richard III* and *Henry VI* qualify you as an authority on contemporary court policy?" His pride, both for himself and for his beloved Robin, was even more sensitive than Rosaline had guessed.

"These 'figments of my imagination,' my lord, are well grounded in history." There was pride in authorship too. "I am not entirely ignorant of the nature of monarchs. Otherwise my kings would sound hollow; and they don't! I know of none who preferred to risk sharing his authority with the people's choice."

"Indeed? Her Majesty—"

"Her Majesty favors Lord Burleigh and his two sons, as she formerly favored Walsingham—four of the most widely hated men in England. And she has consistently passed over Lord Essex's candidates for high offices, including Francis Bacon for Attorney-General. It is possible that Mr. Bacon now considers Lord Essex's sponsorship the worst possible recommendation for office."

"How do you know all this, Rose?" Now he was calm, in marked contrast to his animated eagerness upon their arrival at the Gatehouse.

"How do I know? It's common knowledge. I have to know. It's part of my business as a playwright. I have to keep my work topical or the crowds will cross the Thames for their entertainment."

"Oh, yes, about your business as a playwright."

"What about my business as a playwright?"

Rosaline recognized a danger signal in the rising pitch of her voice. Until that moment she had not realized how much her portrayal of Juliet had taken out of her. Added to it was the hurt of learning that her husband had walked out on her performance to meet with Essex.

"I think you ought to give it up. You don't have to write another line. You know that." It was not the first time he had raised objections.

"As I've given up everything else," she said bitterly, but against her will. She simply could not stop. "My very identity. To live like a ghost, nameless, faceless, friendless—well, almost. My writing is all that I can claim—and I can't even put my name on that."

"Not unless you want your lovely head cut off," Southampton said gently.

Thank God, he knew her limits as well as she did. She fell into his arms and clung to him desperately, fearfully. Some day she would say too much, or he would.

"Oh, Hal, I'm so tired. Forgive me. You undress me. Put me to bed. I try to play grown up with you, to talk big, to be old and wise. But I'm not. I'm little and I'm tired." She *was* tired, but she knew perfectly well that she was acting, retreating from the position she had almost established by her analysis of Her Majesty's attitude toward favorites.

"It's just that the thought of your being away for six months upset me." She had to act. She had to withdraw. She could not stand against Essex, not yet. "But if you must go, you must. Let's make the most of the four or five months we have before you leave."

"I'm willing, darling."

"Then let's begin now."

"Let's."

11

THE INTERVENING MONTHS WERE BUSY ONES, AND EVENTFUL ONES. On February 2, James Burbage died, leaving his theater holdings to Richard and Cuthbert. In March, Lord Cobham died and Lord

Hunsdon succeeded him as Lord Chamberlain, restoring the name of Lord Chamberlain's Men to Burbage's company of players. Betty's baby died about the same time. All of these events posed new interlocking problems to Rosaline and her associates both in the theater and at court.

Essex was interested in placing Robert Sidney in the late Lord Cobham's position as Warden of the Cinque Ports; Burbage was jealous of the prestige given his company by the patronage of the Lord Chamberlain; Southampton was indirectly involved with both besides his own affairs, one of which was a duel with the Earl of Northumberland, canceled just in the nick of time by order of the Queen; and the Little Countess of Derby, after the loss of her child, began to cast her shadow over all concerned.

And, though Rosaline and the Earl of Southampton might not have made the most of their months together, they certainly made more of them than they had intended: neither had intended that Rosaline should become pregnant. But despite the precautions she had taken—tricks learned from certain disreputable hangers-on at the theaters—or perhaps because of untimely laxity in those precautions, she did conceive, sometime in February as best she could judge. She had her suspicions in March, and in April she was sure.

Her first reaction was one of dismay. Then, remembering her earliest sonnets, how insistently she had urged his lordship to engender a replica of himself, she wondered who better than she could nurture that replica. Who had the greater right? In fact, should he fail to return from the island voyage, he might, but for her, leave behind a world bereft of its finest ornament. Thinking thus, she was able to recreate all the feeling she had put into those first sonnets, written before she had acknowledged, perhaps before she had even realized, the true nature of her love for Hal, her yearning to bear his child. Now she wrote:

> *Mine eye hath play'd the painter and hath stell'd*
> *Thy beauty's form in table of my heart;*
> *My body is the frame wherein 'tis held.*

But how would his lordship receive the news? How well did she know his heart? Would he rejoice over the prospect of a son? Or would he reject her as just another mistress who had borne him a bastard? Had he loved her only for her companionable wit, her lithe young body?

She rose and hurried into her bedroom. There, before a large mirror, she dropped the smock from her shoulders and studied her nude image critically and fearfully. So far her figure did not show any change; but her imagination supplied visions of a misshapen body, distended, clumsy, awkward, lame. Lame, that was it. She who had prided herself on her perfect control over her body—a tumbler, an acrobat, as light and graceful as any nymph—would be lame by comparison.

She saw herself as she would be in a few months, and her fears mounted still higher. Her hold on his lordship was so tenuous—a mere lovers' knot of gold and black hair—so completely subject to whim that one sight of her in a condition of less than perfect physical grace might make her ugly forever in his eyes. If only she were established as his wife, recognized by the Queen, acknowledged by the Church, her condition might bind her lover to her. Her son would be the Southampton heir, the Fourth Earl. If—but her hold on him was her beauty, her wit, her accommodating body; and that body would soon be deformed out of all semblance of the Greek maiden who read verses about Venus and Adonis.

She resolved not to let him see her until she was slim and lovely again. But how? Where could she go?

Her uneasy musings were interrupted by the sound of a key in the outer door. Hastily she drew her smock on again. As she knotted her sash she unconsciously measured to see if her waist was perceptibly larger.

"Rosaline?" It was Betty's voice.

"Yes. Coming." Rosaline felt unaccountably relieved that it was Betty. Of course she had to see Hal; she wanted to see him, but not just yet, not until she had made some plans for the next few months. She went back into the drawing room.

"I wasn't sure I would find you here," Betty said. She was struggling with a mite-sized lap dog as she tried to get out of an ermine wrap and muff and hood to match.

Rosaline helped her. Betty wore a sheer woolen dress which, although not cut low enough to expose her now famous bosom, was fitted to reveal the voluptuous contours of her maturing figure.

"You'll find me here most of the time," Rosaline said. "I'm so glad you did drop by. I have something to tell you."

[140]

"It's dull at court," Betty said, showing no curiosity concerning Rosaline's news. "All that the men think about is some old campaign against the Spaniard. There's no gaiety."

"Is my Lord of Derby planning to go on the voyage?"

"William? No, of course not. He doesn't plan to do anything but scold me." Betty crossed the room and backed up to the fire of sea-coals burning in the grate. She never did look directly at her sister.

"Scold you, honey?" Rosaline said. "Surely not. William wouldn't scold you. He's entirely too gentle."

"You just don't know. He thinks I'm no good as a wife. My baby didn't like me. I didn't have a healthy baby. She was always sickly. She died." Betty clutched the little dog to her bosom. The dog let out a high-pitched yelp.

"Did William say that?" Rosaline asked.

"No, but I can tell. I can tell that he thinks I'm not a complete woman, not a satisfactory wife. But he doesn't know." Betty looked very wise, with an air of extreme secrecy.

"Doesn't know what, Betty?" Rosaline asked, disturbed.

"He doesn't know what kind of a woman I really am, does he, Jolie?" The little dog squirmed excitedly at the mention of her name and licked at Betty's chin. "Jolie is a Meletei, direct from Malta. Isn't she a dear? Robin gave her to me."

"Robin?"

"Lord Essex, you know."

"Does Robin know what kind of woman you really are, Betty?" Rosaline asked. If Betty were in her right mind she would resent such a question. Rosaline risked it as a test.

"What kind of woman I really am?" Betty appeared to be puzzled for a moment, as though she had forgotten her own recent words. "Oh, yes. He knows all about women."

"So I've heard. Does he know all about you?"

"I know what you're thinking, Rosaline." Betty was looking wise again.

"Have you been carrying on with Raleigh and Essex?" Rosaline allowed her question to sound severe.

"Walt is at Sherborne," Betty answered evasively. She showed a measure of cunning if not of rationality.

"What about Robin?"

"He has a lot of girls worried. The Queen banished Elizabeth

[141]

Bridges and Elizabeth Russell from court for three days for taking physic without leave." Betty giggled and squeezed Jolie. "And for going through her Majesty's galleries to watch Robin at tennis. He strained himself showing off—now he's home in bed."

Obviously Betty was not going to answer a direct question. Indeed Rosaline had no right to ask such a question. But she was convinced that Betty was not morally responsible, and she hated Raleigh and Essex for taking advantage of Betty's condition, if they had. Whatever Betty did in her right mind was her own business. But if she were temporarily deranged, then her behavior became Rosaline's business—and Lord Derby's.

Rosaline had almost forgotten her own problem. She remembered that she had intended to share her secret with Betty; now she was afraid to tell Betty anything. So she held her silence or filled in gaps in Betty's chatter with meaningless platitudes. She took a growing dislike for Jolie, and for the Earl of Essex as it became increasingly apparent that he was intent on taking Betty to bed, if he had not already done so.

"Could I stay here with you, if William drives me out?" Betty asked while she was preparing to leave.

"Certainly. Your room is always ready—I never use it. But I—I may be leaving." Rosaline made a sudden decision or voiced a decision which she had made earlier. "I may be gone for—oh, for a year. Why don't you just go back to Hackney, to your father? You'd be lonesome here, without me."

"Yes. I'd be lonesome here," Betty said, fastening the ermine coat around her neck. "I'm lonesome anywhere."

After Betty had gone Rosaline became more and more worried about Betty's condition. She wondered what she could do. Certainly Lord Derby knew that his wife was not normal. So, probably, did Lord Oxford. Or did they? Did they ever talk to her or listen to her? Were they aware of all the dangers confronting her?

Rosaline dressed carefully, conscious of her waistline, and arranged her hair. She studied her features as she powdered and rouged. Some women grew more beautiful during pregnancy, but only in the face. They were wives, secure in their places, loved by husbands who wanted sons, and who probably consorted with mistresses while their wives were most grossly misshapen. She smiled a wry bitter smile at her reflection in the mirror. The bonds of a mistress held more firmly—when they held at all. There had been times when she took pride in her ability to hold his lordship by the sheer force of her person. Now she began to long for something more tangible, something legally binding. Or did she? She squared her shoulders and tossed her head arrogantly.

Southampton arrived early.

"I hear that court is dull these days," Rosaline teased after he had kissed her, "with Raleigh gone to Sherborne and Lord Essex at home in bed."

"You hear correctly," his lordship said, removing his heavy cloak. It was an exceptionally cold day for April. "By the way, where did you hear all this?"

"Betty. She stopped in for a minute."

"Oh. Betty."

"Hal, does Essex know about me?" It was strange that she had never thought to ask that question before.

"Does he know what about you?" Southampton sounded evasive. He faced the fire and opened his hands to the flames.

"Anything—everything—who I am."

"He knows that you exist."

"That you have a mistress, in other words." But she was not bitter.

"No—I don't know what he thinks our relations are."

"But you haven't told him that we consider ourselves married?"

"No. Not in so many words," he answered guiltily. "I thought when the time was right, when Robin and I were both in Her Majesty's good graces—favorites."

"Oh, don't apologize, don't explain, Hal. I'm not censuring you. Would his lordship know me if he saw me?"

"No. He's never seen you without a mask, at least not in several years."

"Good. Then I want you to take me to see him."

"What?" His lordship spun around to face her, his surprise apparent in every feature.

"You don't have to acknowledge me or even introduce me. Just take me to him."

"Why?"

"To discuss a mutual friend. Not you," she said with a reassuring smile. "And I'd rather not tell you who it is. Can't you trust me with your Robin? I trust you with him—and with his cousin Elizabeth."

[143]

He had to smile. To mention Elizabeth Vernon was to tread on thin ice. There were a number of sonnets dealing with that lady, sonnets by both of them. The issue was closed, but it was a lever Rosaline could still use when she chose to move his lordship without too much argument.

"Very well," he said, somewhat reluctantly. "I'll take you to him."

"Just tell him that you know me, that you are doing a favor for a friend. I'll name the friend."

"Yes, I'm sure you'll work out a convincing story. You're the playwright in the family." His good humor sounded just a little forced, but he put back on his heavy cloak and helped Rosaline into her topclothes. She covered her face with a black domino which she usually wore when she went abroad with him.

Since it was only half a mile from Blackfriars to Essex House, they walked, stopping for a moment to warm their feet at the Bel Savage Inn. At Essex House his lordship gained immediate entrance and arranged for Rosaline to be shown into Essex's presence. As she followed a liveried servant up the stairs to Essex's bedroom, she felt like a punk brought in off the streets by a procurer. Her mask only aggravated the feeling. And Southampton waited downstairs, just as a pander might have been expected to do. She wondered what the servant would report to the household staff or to the Countess, or to Elizabeth Vernon, since it was Southampton who had brought her. She felt dirty, but she hoped to prevent some business still dirtier.

Even with the curtains of the great chamber drawn against the afternoon sun, Rosaline could still make out the elaborate carving on the walnut bedstead and tester, from which heavy brocaded tester valances hung above parted base valances of figured satin. Two featherbeds forced pillows high against the paneled headboard, but she could not distinguish his lordship's features. On closer inspection she could not even detect the bulge of his body under the embroidered quilts.

After the servant closed the door behind her, she approached the bed cautiously.

"You are a forward wench, aren't you? You don't even wait to be invited to bed." His lordship spoke, not from the depths of the featherbed but from a high-backed chair facing the fireplace.

"Oh. Your lordship." Rosaline curtsied. "I didn't know where you were."

"Well, I'm not in bed." Essex rose and came out from behind his chair for a look at Rosaline after she had removed her mask. "Of course, we could remedy that," he added when the firelight fell full on her face.

"I came to talk, my lord."

"Indeed? About what?" He was tall, tending to lean forward or to thrust his head forward as he talked.

"About the Countess of Derby."

"Which one? There are three at the moment, I believe. No, two—Countess Margaret died in November." His voice was testy, his mood vile, if Rosaline was competent to judge.

"The Lady Elizabeth, my lord, wife of the present Earl—neither of the dowagers."

"The Little Countess."

"Yes. I believe she's called the Little Countess."

"Come closer. It must be cold over there by the bed."

"Yes, my lord." Rosaline joined him before the fire.

It was the first time she had seen him that close since the night in the Pipe and Tabor, several years before. His blond hair had grown darker, or so it seemed; and his blue eyes had lost some of their luster. He looked ill.

"And just what is your connection with her ladyship, may I ask?" He studied Rosaline, feature by feature.

"I am her Italian tutor, my lord. And—and I love her very much."

"And is that what we're to talk about? Her Italian lessons?"

"No, my lord. Her ladyship is ill. I fear for her."

"So am I. Why doesn't she see a doctor? Are you privy to her secrets?"

"Yes, my lord. I think so." Rosaline wondered how accurate her guesses had been.

"Then you mean that her ladyship is too ill to see me, and perhaps has sent her tutor as a substitute. Not a bad idea." He leered cynically at Rosaline.

"No, my lord." Rosaline was beginning to loathe the man. What Southampton saw in him— "Her ladyship is sick in her mind, not responsible for what she does. Do you understand me, my lord?"

[145]

"Possibly. I am considered reasonably intelligent."

"And by all reports, your lordship is a man of honor, of true chivalry, one who would not duel a crippled adversary."

"No."

"Then, my lord, surely you would not seek or value the conquest of a woman who was not aware of what she was doing."

"There's a difference."

"Is there, my lord? Surely you know the state of her ladyship's health. Surely you know that her seeming attraction to you is but an obsession, that you as a man can mean nothing to her but a sort of test for her to pass—a substitute for something she missed in her unhappy experience with her baby."

"Aren't you somewhat presumptuous, Mistress Meddlesome, to counsel your mistress or me on our behavior?" His lordship was in his very worst mood, if reports of him were at all accurate.

"I've said nothing to her ladyship," Rosaline said softly. She did not trust her full voice; it would have rung with anger.

"And it would have been wiser of you to have said nothing to me. The very idea! A woman is a woman. Her body is as sweet with or without a healthy mind in it. No woman ever thought clearly for five consecutive minutes anyway. So your argument falls of its own weight."

"Her Majesty is a woman. Perhaps she sometimes thinks for several minutes at a time." Rosaline was not sure that she intended her words as a threat.

"Her Majesty," Essex started to shout, then caught himself and watched Rosaline's face warily.

"Just who are you?" he asked again. "I've seen your face somewhere before. Are you one of Her Majesty's spi—servants, here at her behest?"

"No, your lordship. I am exactly as I represented myself, a friend of Lady Derby. I am very fond of her. I pity her in her present state. I should hate very much to see anyone take advantage of her and perhaps do her permanent injury, possibly break up her marriage. I considered your lordship a man of highest integrity; I thought that I might be able to appeal to your honor. You are rational. She is not."

"Did the Earl of Derby send you?" Essex asked, taking no notice of her plea.

"No. I am sure that he knows or suspects nothing. I doubt that

[146]

he would send anyone. I think perhaps he would come himself."

Essex laughed. He might be sick too. Rosaline considered that possibility for the first time. Lord Essex deranged? Or maybe Rosaline herself was crazy. She saw the hopelessness of her visit. What had she expected? Would she grow worse as her pregnancy progressed? The sooner she got out of Essex House—out of London, in fact—the better off she would be.

"I see that I was mistaken," she said.

"You have, indeed, made a mistake," Essex said. "Are you sure that you won't reconsider the bed?" His tone was insulting.

"Positive, my lord. Now may I be excused?"

"By all means." He rang, and the door was opened by his lackey.

Rosaline curtsied and followed the servant out the door of the great chamber and down the stairs to where Southampton was waiting. He rose from a bench near the door. Presumably he had spent the time alone. The entire house seemed deserted, with the Countess living in Walsingham House and Elizabeth Vernon at court.

"How was the interview?" he asked, but his manner sought for more than his words.

"Disappointing," she said through clenched teeth. What her husband saw in his precious Robin!

"Disappointing?" he asked after the lackey had let them out the front door of Essex House. "You must have asked a lot of Robin. He's the most generous man I know."

"I asked very little."

"And he refused?"

"Yes, he refused. Then he asked me to bed." She could not resist telling that much. "I refused, too."

"Asked you to bed," he repeated, with a weak little laugh. "That's Robin for you. 'Give every woman her opportunity,' he says."

"I've had mine. I declined it. Now, let's forget all about it." Rosaline was anxious lest she be prodded into a full explanation.

"Robin didn't find out who you were?" Southampton asked. She wished that he had not asked. "I mean about us."

"No. Let's not talk about it any more."

Traffic was getting heavier in Fleet Street, forcing pedestrians to take the wall. Southampton pressed to the north side of the street at Temple Bar; and throwing his left arm protectively around Rosaline's shoulders, he drew his rapier and warded off titled horsemen and swaggering ruffians alike. The lightening of the plague had made people less fearful of physical contacts, so that the crowd streaming under Ludgate practically forced the young couple to take refuge in the Bel Savage until the laborers and artisans were all safely home for the night.

Rosaline remembered the innyard vaguely, from the time she had played there as a child with her mother—a very young child, not more than five, for Monarcho, her grandfather, had been alive then. He had carried her on his shoulders. She had worn a little bear suit and had danced with Ursa, the real bear in the troupe. She even remembered how Monarcho had taken her down to the Thames afterwards and claimed all the ships on it for her and told wonderful stories of the far-off lands from which they came. She had been a precocious child, she decided as they entered the ordinary.

Southampton chose a corner table set off to itself by half-walls and curtains. He seated Rosaline and sat down facing her.

"One would think we were lovers," Rosaline said, "holding a forbidden tryst."

"Aren't we? Lovers, I mean."

"Oh yes, my lord. And more, much more." She thought that she might make an opening to reveal her secret. But a waiter came to take their order. Southampton ordered with great care and then seemed hesitant to begin the conversation.

"What is it, Hal?" Rosaline asked, sensing his reluctance to introduce something unpleasant.

"It's—well, Rose, I promised you that the campaign would not begin before June or July. But it looks as though I must leave now, for the south coast, I mean."

Rosaline was silent. His plans just might coincide with her own.

"Much of our work has to be done in secret—the court is full of spies—but we must begin at once. It falls my lot to attend to the recruiting of men and provisioning of ships in the south ports. I can go to Southampton without arousing any suspicion. I'd like to take you with me but—"

"Oh, that's all right," Rosaline cut in, sincerely. Perhaps the relief in her voice startled him, for he looked up in surprise. "I can't go—I understand that," she said agreeably. They were both silent while their dinner was served to them. Then he continued.

"I'll be back in London occasionally; frequently, I hope. It isn't as though I were leaving England. I'll see you from time to time."

"No," Rosaline objected. "No, you mustn't see me until after you return from the voyage." By that time everything would be over.

"Indeed, I shall. It isn't that secret. Nothing has changed except that I shall be at Titchfield instead of Whitehall or Greenwich or Richmond or Windsor. You'll hardly know the difference."

"Something has changed, Hal. I—I've changed."

"You? You've changed?"

"Yes, Hal. I'm going to have a baby."

"A baby?" His immediate reaction amounted to no reaction at all. He just stared.

"Yes, a baby. And I don't want you to see me while I'm fat and clumsy and lame. When you get back from the Azores, you'll have a healthy little boy and I'll be as slim and pretty as ever. But until then you mustn't try to see me. I'm going away too."

"Going away, where?"

"I don't know yet, but I'll find a place. I won't be seen in London, nor the baby, not until you are ready to claim us."

"I'll see that you are taken care of," Southampton said. Rosaline wasn't entirely pleased with his choice of words. "Well taken care of. I'll make arrangements the first thing in the morning."

"Don't, Hal. You make me sound like a high-priced harlot. I'll make my own arrangements and I'll pay my own way and I'll have my own baby." She was on the verge of tears.

"It's a little late for you to take all the credit, isn't it?" There was a twinkle in his eyes. "I trust that I was in at the beginning of this. I insist on seeing it through. I claim my share."

"You needn't be so businesslike about it. It isn't a commercial venture."

"Very well, I'll have my business dealings with Will Shakespeare as usual. Good old Will. I'll make a nice settlement on him, just in case I decide to stay in the Azores."

"Oh, Hal, I hadn't thought of that; I mean your not coming back." She *had* thought of it, and she felt guilty as she denied it; but the idea of a financial settlement had never entered her mind.

"Well, think of it now, and forget that nonsense about going away where I can't see you again before I leave. I can't imagine

[149]

your being awkward under any conditions. And as for your getting fat—the more there is of you, the more I'll love you."

"No." Rosaline would not be swayed. She had taken risks all her life, but the risk of suddenly becoming ugly and gauche in his eyes was one that she would not take. "No. You shall not see me after tonight."

The argument continued in a lower key during the meal and gradually played out after they returned to Rosaline's apartment. Their last night together held some of the poignancy and insistency of their first night aboard the *Ictis*; and when Southampton left the next morning, without waking Rosaline, he probably felt that he had won his point. He fully expected to see Rosaline every week or two, but he was careful to make the arrangements he had mentioned. He drew a thousand* pounds and dispatched it to William Shakespeare before he left London.

So it was that Will Shakespeare came to Blackfriars Gatehouse before noon on the very day of his lordship's departure. Rosaline was up and dressed and worried about what she should do next. She *knew* that she had won the argument. She was going away. But where?

She let Shakespeare in and took his wet cloak. The weather had turned warmer, but it was raining outside.

"What have we written this time?" Shakespeare asked, as he took a seat before the fire and propped his feet up on the grate to dry out the soles of his boots.

"Nothing except those two plays about Henry IV. You know, the ones now in rehearsal."

"No, I mean for our patron. His lordship is most generous this time—a thousand pounds." Shakespeare read his line for maximum effect.

"A thousand pounds?"

*There is no record of this transaction in the Southampton accounts, but the amount is verified by Sir William D'Avenant, Shakespeare's godson, whom Nicholas Rowe quotes as saying "my Lord Southampton gave him [Shakespeare] a thousand pounds to enable him to go through with a purchase which he had a mind to. A bounty very great and very rare at any time." A sum equivalent to $50,000 today is indeed such a bounty, and the fact that there is no record of Shakespeare's ever having made a purchase of such proportions points to Rosaline as the recipient.

"Yes. Is that enough? What have we done? I was told merely that it was the usual arrangement."

"I'm not sure, Will," Rosaline said seriously. "It may be far too much and it may be far too little. I'm going to have a baby."

"Oh, I see." Will was not shocked.

"So, if his lordship is merely sending expense money, it's far too much. If he is paying for his pleasure—if this is the end—"

"It's far too little," Shakespeare said, to finish her speech. "I can't believe the latter, Rosaline. I might have doubted his intentions in the beginning, but not after three—no, it's four years now, isn't it? I would trust him, Rosaline. He is merely being generous. And it's not too much."

"Thank you, Will. I needed reassurance." It was good to confide in him again, and in Anne. She had an idea. "Will, do you think Anne would take me in again as she did before?"

"What do you mean?"

"I mean I want to go to her to have my baby. I don't want his lordship to see me pregnant. I want to leave London."

"I don't know, Rosaline." Shakespeare spoke without any confidence. "She's living with my people at Stratford or with hers at Shottery. She has no home right now. I—well, you know how things have been in the theater. We are just now making up the time lost during the plague."

"Oh, Will, what was that New Place Anne used to talk about? Could you buy it for her?" Rosaline eagerly knelt on the floor beside Shakespeare and clutched at his arm.

"I buy New Place?" He chuckled at the absurdity.

"I mean with my money—our money—the thousand pounds that Hal gave us." Her whole body was alive.

"Not ours. I won't take a commission on this deal. Not a penny. I'm no—"

"Stop, William Shakespeare!" Rosaline shouted and stood up rigid beside him. "Don't you say this money makes you a bawd and me an expensive harlot! I won't hear it. Do you understand?"

"Yes, Rosaline, I understand. I won't say it. I don't even think it." He rose and Rosaline fell against his chest, sobbing in near hysteria. He soothed her and held his silence. She spoke first after her storm had passed.

"Really, Will, can't I give New Place to Anne? I love her. I want her to have it, if it can be bought." Rosaline shook with one final sob. "I could never repay her in full for taking me in when I had nowhere to go. I'd like her to have a respectable place to rear her daughters. I'd like my baby to be born in such a place. Now, can we talk about it?"

"Yes, we can talk about it." William Shakespeare deposited Rosaline on a sewing stool by the fireplace and resumed his seat.

"Can you buy New Place?" she asked.

"Perhaps. It is run-down—not so fine as Anne remembered it, but it can be repaired."

"How much?"

"Oh, fifty or sixty pounds; and a like amount to make it like new again."

"So little?" She sounded somewhat disappointed that it would not take more, all her money perhaps.

"So little?" Shakespeare repeated. "That's enough, more than I've made in the last five years. You aren't losing your money sense in your new-found wealth, are you, Rosaline?"

"Oh, no, Will. No. But then I never did have any money sense. You just go ahead and buy New Place for Anne, whatever it costs, and look after the rest of my money for me. Will you do that for me, Will?"

"Yes."

Rosaline could not tell whether he was doing it for her or for Anne, but it did not matter. The result would be the same.

"When?" she asked.

"As soon as I can get away for a few days."

"Now," she insisted. "Tomorrow. I want to be in Stratford when Hal comes back to London. He mustn't see me again."

"I'll see about it," Shakespeare agreed, rising.

"And, Will, I'm his wife. You know that, don't you?"

"Yes, Rosaline. You're his wife."

"And we must explain that to Anne."

"We'll try," Shakespeare said as he drew his cloak around his shoulders.

12

ROSALINE PUNCTUATED HER JOURNEY WITH SONNETS. IT WAS A HABIT that both she and Southampton had grown into, a way of preserving solitary thoughts for conversation, of keeping emotions fresh until they could be shared. Her commonplace book bulged with such sonnets already, a hundred perhaps, some passionate, some censorious: lyrics of devotion, lyrics of suspicion and reconciliation—her life with his lordship.

In the company of a carrier and a half-dozen other riders, she had begun her journey to Stratford on a joyous note, for Southampton had returned unexpectedly near the end of April and they had had one more precious night together—positively the last that she dared risk, for her belly was beginning to show signs of plumpness. Hal still insisted that he would come again before she left London, since William Shakespeare had not been able to consummate the deal for New Place at once and consequently she could not tell exactly when she would leave London. But Shakespeare had made the purchase on May 4; and within three days, as soon as his note got to London, she was on her way to Stratford-on-Avon.

With the memory of his visit still fresh in her mind she could write joyously of her condition:

> *Then happy I, that love and am beloved*
> *Where I may not remove nor be removed.* (25)

At High Wycombe, the first overnight stop on the way to Stratford, a tiring day's journey from London; in a dismal rented room in contrast to the rich appointments of her apartment in the Gatehouse; among simple country folk who noted her occasional nausea, guessed her condition, and smiled benignly at her or leered suspiciously, since she was traveling alone, Rosaline found her mood changing. She began to see the difference between her position, her responsibilities in the matter, and those of her husband. Without him to reassure her, she told her commonplace book of the beginning of her resentment toward the pregnancy which had robbed her of the remaining months with her lover, and she recorded the incipient fear that he might suffer shame because of her:

> *I may not evermore acknowledge thee,*
> *Lest my bewailed guilt should do thee shame;*
> *Nor thou with public kindness honor me,*
> *Unless thou take that honor from thy name:*
> *But do not so; I love thee in such sort,*
> *As, thou being mine, mine is thy good report.* (36)

As she composed the sonnet, she began to feel guilty for the first time, perhaps because of the prospect of having to explain her plight to Anne Shakespeare who might be less receptive than the pages of the commonplace book.

Her second day in the saddle tired her still more and plunged her deeper into despondency. At Oxford, where she stopped to spend the night, she laughed bitterly at the thought that she was the daughter of the Seventeenth Earl of Oxford, entitled to honor by the mayor himself. And yet she sat alone in another loveless room in an inn full of strangers. To the rhythm of plodding hoofbeats still pounding in her ears, every thud of which raised fears for the living burden in her womb, she wrote a dirge that began,

> *How heavy do I journey on the way,*

and ended,

> *My grief lies onward and my joy behind.* (50)

Normally Rosaline would have enjoyed the trip, for there was no part of England that she loved better than Oxon or Warwickshire in May. The meadows flaunted their wild patchwork of short-stemmed flowers as a challenge to the neat fields of fresh young oats and barley, or the hardier blades of winter wheat and rye. She had traveled the road many times in former springs—as a child, as a little girl, as a boy actor—and loved every view it presented. Always it had been a joy. But the charm of the country-side went by this time unnoticed. Rosaline's vision turned inward, or backward, or forward toward Anne, never to the sunlit banks of May flowers on either hand.

Though she had always enjoyed the peace of Stratford at sunset, she found herself relieved that it was after dark when the carrier with whom she was traveling crossed Clopton Bridge and pulled up into an innyard in Back Bridge Street at the corner of Warwick Road. She was relieved because she did not want to face Anne Shakespeare that night. She wanted to lie down, to have a night to herself. She went directly to her room and undressed. Then, sitting up in bed with her commonplace book on her knees, she wrote:

> *Weary with toil I haste me to my bed,*
> *The dear repose for limbs with travel tired;*
> *But then begins a journey in my head,*
> *To work my mind, when body's work's expired ...* (27)

and stared into blackness for half the night.

The next morning, after the usual applications of wet towels to her throat to allay the nausea which had been plaguing her every morning for the past two months, she brushed a light touch of rouge on her pale cheeks and lips, dressed in a plain street dress, and set out to find New Place. Since it was the second largest house in Stratford, the first person she met at the Market Cross in High Street pointed it out to her, only two blocks down at the corner of Chapel Street and Chapel Lane.

Even by comparison to the Gild Chapel on the next corner, New Place was an imposing structure of brick and timber. Sixty feet wide, its façade rose three stories, with three ornamented gables fronting on Chapel Street. It boasted four chimneys and numerous glazed windows, some with tinted panes leaded into geometric patterns. Already stonemasons were making repairs on the walls, and a pile of stones cluttered up the otherwise neat plot of grass between the gate and the heavy oak front door. Rosaline could visualize its former splendor, and her spirits rose at the picture of what it would be like when Will and Anne completed its restoration.

She crossed the front garden and lifted the heavy knocker. Before she could let it drop again, the door swung inward, and Susanna rushed out eagerly and threw her arms about Rosaline.

"Rosaline!" she cried. She was within two weeks of being fourteen years old and already as tall as Rosaline.

"My, how you've grown!" Rosaline said, almost painfully pleased by her first cordial reception into New Place. Judith, a gangling twelve-year-old, rushed out next with equal effusiveness, and Rosaline found herself fighting back tears at the memory of Hamnet, Judith's twin.

"Mother and Father are getting your room ready," Judith said. "I'll show you upstairs. Susanna has to wash the dishes." She smiled triumphantly at her sister and pointed the way.

They climbed the stone stairs to the second floor, and Susanna led the way to a corner room with large bay windows on the south and west. Will and Anne Shakespeare were arranging the pleats in the tester valances atop a huge poster bed.

"Mother, she's here!" Judith exclaimed, leading Rosaline by the hand. "Isn't she beautiful?"

Anne stepped down off a stool and faced Rosaline, who approached to embrace her. Her mouth full of pins, her precious pins again, Anne turned a cheek for Rosaline to kiss. She held on to a bed post with one hand and gave Rosaline a token hug with her free arm.

"Go help Susanna with the dishes," Will said softly to Judith, and Rosaline tensed herself for unpleasantness.

Obediently but reluctantly, the girl went back downstairs.

"You are looking well," Anne said impersonally. "A bit pale, but you aren't showing much yet."

"Then you know," Rosaline said.

"Yes. Will told me about it."

"Everything?" Rosaline asked, looking toward Will.

"I tried to explain it all," he said. "I thought it would be easier for me. I've been explaining things to Anne for a long time." His voice gave evidence of the sort of conversation they had had.

"He shouldn't have taken advantage of you," Anne said, but there was little sympathy behind her words, either for Rosaline or his lordship.

"It's as much my fault as it was his," Rosaline said, quick in

[156]

his defense. "I am as much to blame as he is. If you don't want me here, I'll—"

"Oh, no, I don't intend to drive you out. But you should have waited." There was a lot of bitterness in Anne's voice.

"But I can't stay, knowing how you feel." She turned to leave at once.

"Yes, you must. We'll have to—"

"What Anne means is that she knows exactly how you feel," Shakespeare said. He had been standing by as though deliberately studying Anne's performance or waiting for his cue. "You see Susanna was—"

"I'll tell her!" Anne said sharply. "Will is saying that I was over three months' pregnant with Susanna when he married me. He won't let me forget it."

"Not now, not when Rosaline needs a home. I've never mentioned it before." Will was calm, coldly deliberate in his statement. Anne flamed red at his words.

"I realize that. But he married me," she said, speaking to Rosaline. "Will married me before the baby was born. I don't know whether he wanted to or not, but he did. You should have made your man marry you—if he were free to do so."

"But we are married." Rosaline spoke defiantly. She was always defiant on that point. Either the love knot cast into Southampton Water was binding or she was a common punk. "In our own minds and in the sight of God we are married."

"Maybe," Anne said skeptically. "But before a child is born there should be a license, a ceremony, everything in perfect order in the sight of God, and of the community." She too was defiant.

"Now, Anne," Shakespeare said gently. "Our license is entered in the bishop's register as follows, '*eodem die similis emanavit licencia inter Wm. Shaxpere et Annam Whateley de Temple Grafton.*' You are Anne Hathaway of Shottery, I believe, not Anne Whately of Temple Grafton."

"Very well, shame me," Anne said, on the verge of tears. "It's just a mistake. Everybody knows that. We were married right and properly before Susanna was born. The entry is a mistake."

"Sure, it's a mistake," Shakespeare agreed. "Perhaps Rosaline and his lordship have made a mistake. Who is to judge? Not we, surely."

Anne's tears began to flow at last. Shakespeare put his arms around her, somewhat clumsily it seemed. His face was sad. Obviously he had found no pleasure in what he had been forced to say.

"What shall I do?" Rosaline asked.

"Just make yourself at home," Shakespeare said. "Anne will get over this. She's just in one of her spells." He spoke as though his wife were not even present. "We'll just tell people that your husband is at sea."

"And if I never see him again, we'll just say he was lost at sea," Rosaline said wearily. To be so tired so early in the morning. "I'll have to stay. I have nowhere else to go. I shan't like it any better than Anne will. But I have no choice."

"I had a choice," Anne said, her tears dry, her features set in a stoic mold. "I chose New Place. I accept what goes with it. This is the best room and the best bed in the house. It's yours. I trust you will be comfortable. While you are with us I will be content with the second best room and the second best bed." She allowed her jealousy to show.

"It's Rosaline's room, bought with her own money," Shakespeare said. "And so was the best bed."

"That I know," Anne said. "So is all of New Place. I should be grateful. At least, I shall say no more. Will and Edmund will fetch your things. Where are they?"

"At the inn," Rosaline said.

That first day set the pattern for Rosaline's life at New Place. Shakespeare returned to London the next day. The girls were quite companionable, but Anne held firmly aloof and made her disapproval perfectly clear though she never said another word about her feelings. Rosaline, perhaps misunderstanding the natural curiosity of village folk, took all of their inquisitive stares and whispered comments as pointed condemnation of her. She wrote of herself:

> *When in disgrace with fortune and men's eyes,*
> *I all alone beweep my outcast state,*
> *And trouble deaf heaven with my bootless cries,*
> *And look upon myself, and curse my fate ...* (29)

Her nausea, instead of lessening at the end of three months, seemed rather to get worse and in general she felt wretched. For a time she was sure that she was going to die. She had moments when she wanted to die, in fact moments of deep self-pity, and maudlin, almost morbid, pity for her dear beloved Hal because of the mess she had got him into by her love. She imagined herself dying and wrote:

> *No longer mourn for me when I am dead . . .*
> *Lest the wise world should look into your moan,*
> *And mock you with me after I am gone.* (71)

All she wanted was complete oblivion for herself, for her child, for her name. She had always been nameless, a peer's bastard, a peer's mistress, a boy who never lived, hiding a girl who was nobody. Yet Hal loved her, and she him. How could he love her? Better that he forget her than be shamed by her. Better deny her. Indeed how could he acknowledge or explain his love for her? He should be warned.

> *After my death, dear love, forget me quite . . .* (72)

But she did not die. And as the people of Stratford saw more of her, they began to smile at her and speak to her. Her attacks of nausea grew lighter and less frequent. She found herself eating hearty meals and gaining weight. As the summer wore on, she even saw some humor in her awkward stance and ungainly gait, and was able to compose some lighthearted as well as some serious sonnets about her "lameness." She was actually in quite good spirits, when the news reached Stratford that the fleet had sailed from Plymouth on the tenth of July. She had had no word from Southampton. Indeed she had not told him how to communicate with her except through William Shakespeare in London. And since the company was having a busy season—and a profitable one primarily because of the success of Rosaline's two plays on Henry IV with Will Kempe portraying Sir John Falstaff, as she had rechristened Sir John Oldcastle—Will had written only the briefest of notes to his family.

Rosaline could not resist the fine summer weather, and she was happy in spite of herself and of Anne. She worked on the last play of her series, the one in which Prince Hal, whom she had patterned on her Hal after all, proved himself a good and just king. She looked forward to composing it, as a sort of vindication of her husband, whose escapades were frequent subjects of court and tavern gossip. It was her opportunity to bring out all the fine, noble qualities which she knew lay dormant in his lordship's character.

She sat on the ground in a grassy plot near the kitchen garden and leaned back against the trunk of a shade tree. A breadboard, held upright on her knee, served as her writing desk. She had written nothing so far, preferring rather to sit in a semi-reverie and steep herself in memories of his lordship until the character of Prince Hal came alive in her mind. It was still early in the morning, the sun just getting warm enough to make her light jacket unnecessary.

Judith, having finished washing the breakfast dishes, came running out the back door and then slowed down to a hesitant walk and approached Rosaline shyly. She brought writing materials with her.

"Could I write, too, Rosaline?" she asked.

"Certainly," Rosaline said. "Sit right here beside me. What shall we write?"

"Anything," Judith said, spreading her full skirt and sitting down crosslegged in front of Rosaline. "I won't bother you."

"Of course, you won't," Rosaline said and scribbled a few tentative lines. When looking over her board she saw Judith watching her expectantly, she asked, "Now, what have you written?"

"Nothing." Judith sounded a little surprised. "I—I can't write, Rosaline. It was Susanna you taught to write."

"And now you want me to teach you," Rosaline said, grasping what Judith meant.

"Yes—I hoped you would. Susanna is about the only girl in Stratford who can write. She brags and shows off and—"

"We'll change that," Rosaline said gaily. "Hand me your board and I'll write a pattern for you to follow. Before you know it you'll be writing better than Susanna."

Judith scrambled eagerly across the grass and laid her board on top of Rosaline's. She watched every movement of Rosaline's hand as it formed the capital letters of the alphabet in precise Italian script.

"Now," Rosaline said at last. "Start with 'A' and make ten copies of each letter on this page. This is the way to begin."

Rosaline clasped her hand over Judith's and guided it through the formation of the first letter.

"There!" Rosaline said, and Judith sighed happily.

Neither of them had seen Anne approach and take a firm stand beside the tree where she could watch over their shoulders.

"Just what do you think you're doing?" Anne asked ominously.

"Writing," Rosaline said, looking up at Anne. "I'm teaching Judith her letters, as I taught Susanna in London."

"Give me that paper, Judith," Anne commanded.

The girl rose and handed her writing board to her mother, who snatched the paper off and wadded it up into a tight little ball.

"I don't want you teaching my daughters to write," she said angrily.

"But why? Why, Anne?"

"It's unnatural for a woman to read and write. Look at you! You wouldn't be in this mess if you had never learned to read and write." Anne drew Judith away from Rosaline and stood between them.

"I was merely helping them improve themselves, or so I thought," Rosaline said, rising awkwardly to her feet.

"Do you think you've improved yourself?" Anne asked accusingly. "Writing makes a woman think she's a fine lady and she begins making eyes at fine gentlemen, and what does it get her? What did it get you, Rosaline?"

"Mother!" Judith cried. "I asked her to. I asked Rosaline to teach me."

"You be quiet, Judith. You don't know what's good for you. I say it's sinful for a woman to read and write and I forbid you to learn." Anne faced Rosaline. "My girls love you, Rosaline. I guess we all do. But I don't want my girls to be like you. I don't want them to read and write. Do you understand?"

"Yes," Rosaline said.

"You may have ruined Susanna already; I don't know. But I am not going to let Judith learn to read and write—not even how to write her name."

Anne turned and hurried Judith into the kitchen before her. Rosaline stared after them for a time and wrinkled her forehead into a thoughtful frown. Then she sank back down against the trunk of the tree and gathered her writing materials into her lap.

Perhaps I learned just in time, she said to herself. Never again, as long as I live, will I ever try to teach anything to anybody.

Now she wrote rapidly from sheer self-discipline, and three hours later she was surprised at the volume and the quality of the poetry that she had produced. The dull plodding lines of the old play which she used as her source and the factual incidents drawn from Holinshed's *Chronicles* had come brilliantly alive under her hard-driven hand. She found a new pride in her work, a confidence in her ability to write without a thought of his lordship as her inspiration.

She was still producing, precisely and competently, when William Shakespeare returned unexpectedly a week later with bad news from London. In fact, he found her in the same spot under her favorite tree.

"My, but you look busy," he said as he came upon her without her seeing him.

"Will!" She scrambled to her feet. "What are you doing home? We weren't expecting you."

"Be careful," he cautioned. "Remember you're not a tumbler at the moment." He kissed her on the cheek and led her to a bench near the kitchen porch.

"The theaters are closed," he explained in answer to her question.

"But I thought the plague was no longer a threat."

"It isn't the plague. It's a play by Thomas Nashe, *The Isle of Dogs,* which the Earl of Pembroke's Men performed at the Swan last week. The Privy Council declared that it contained seditious and scandalous matter. So the Council closed all the theaters and put the offenders in Marshalsea prison."

"Nashe?" Rosaline asked. Imprisoning playwrights always gave her a start.

"No, he ran away. But they imprisoned Robert Shaw and Gabriel Spencer. You know them."

"Yes, I've seen them perform."

"And a minor actor, Ben Jonson, who Nashe said wrote most of the play—all of the offensive passages."

"Did you see the play? I mean a copy of it?"

"No, the Privy Council ferreted out and burned every known copy."

"And closed all the theaters?" Rosaline was not surprised. Such was the usual reaction to theatrical improprieties.

"They even issued a public order that all playhouses in the vicinity of London be plucked down." Shakespeare chuckled. "But I understand that the sheriffs got secret instructions not to carry it out. The Lord Chamberlain and Lord Admiral interceded for their players, I presume."

"You don't seem worried."

"No. We're going on tour—to Bath and Rye and Bristol and Dover. By fall we'll be allowed to play in London again."

"I hope so. By fall—what do you know about the fleet?" She hesitated to ask about his lordship directly.

"They ran into a storm and put back into Portsmouth. The Earl of Essex was back in London when I left, but the word was that he would sail again at once. No direct word from the Earl of Southampton. I came by the Gatehouse and picked up these." Shakespeare drew some papers out of his doublet and handed them to Rosaline. "As best I could understand Henry Walker, these were pinned on your pillow."

"Yes." How like Hal. He always pinned notes on her pillow when he came to the Gatehouse and found her gone. The first one said, "To Rose," and the little pat of wax bore the imprint of Southampton's signet ring. She broke the seal and read a sonnet that began:

My love is as a fever,

and ended,

For I have sworn thee fair and thought thee bright,
Who art as black as hell, as dark as night.   (147)

Suddenly numb in every tissue, Rosaline read the closing couplet again. It was unbelievable. She skipped to the next sonnet. It too oddly condemned:

For thou art covetous, and he is kind . . .   (134)

"More bad news?" Shakespeare asked.

She paid no attention to his question, but stared dully at the poems she had just read. Surely there was some mistake. It was all a joke. She broke the seal on the second letter. It would clear the misunderstanding, explain everything. It had to.

> Two loves I have of comfort and despair,
> Which like two spirits do suggest me still:
> The better angel is a man, right fair,
> The worser spirit a woman, color'd ill.   (144)

More confused than ever, Rosaline turned the paper over to see the address, which in her haste she had neglected to read. In his lordship's hand, exactly like the address on her first letter, she saw "To Robin." With a sigh which seemed to breathe the life out of her body, she slowly turned the page back over and read the second sonnet addressed to Essex:

> That thou hast her, it is not all my grief,
> And yet it may be said I loved her dearly;
> That she hath thee, is of my wailing chief,
> A loss in love that touches me more nearly.   (42)

There were other sonnets, in the same vein, addressed to each of them; but Rosaline had read enough to grasp the false suspicions which had prompted her husband to write them. In addition to the shock, the injustice of the implications of the sonnets, she felt a surge of resentment at the readiness with which Southampton seemed to relinquish all claim on her, to blame her entirely, and to forgive Essex. Since the grounds for suspicion were not only false, but patently absurd, her feeling was one of anger rather than dismay. After all the poems she had written, all the arguments she had advanced, all the proof she had given, it seemed that her lover still held to the silly belief that friendship between men was nobler than love between the sexes.

If he had believed his suspicions he should have challenged Essex and run him through with a rapier. He who had challenged Northumberland over a trifle! And he should have hauled her out of bed and beaten her half to death—if he really loved her.

"That's better," Shakespeare said as the color rose in her cheeks. "You had me worried there for a moment. I thought it might be really bad."

[164]

"It is," Rosaline said. She handed him the papers. "Read those and see what you make of them."

Her anger cooled somewhat while Shakespeare read; and she found herself trying to solve the puzzle. Why had his lordship thought that she had been having an affair with Essex? True, she had asked him to take her to Essex and she had never explained why. But surely he had trusted her. Or had he? The sonnets certainly sounded otherwise.

And she had told him that Essex had invited her to bed. Did he think no woman could resist his precious Robin? Had Essex himself boasted of a conquest which he had never made? Had Essex guessed who she was and deliberately lied to free Southampton from what he might have considered undesirable ties? She was getting angry, angry at Essex again.

"You haven't been unfaithful to his lordship, have you?" Shakespeare asked.

"No, of course not."

"Who is this Robin?" he asked.

"The Earl of Essex."

"Whew! That does pose an interesting problem, doesn't it? What basis does your husband have for his suspicions?"

"None. Absolutely none that I know of."

"Then I wouldn't worry, if I were you. When they get back to London, all this will be cleared up and everybody will be happy again."

"If Essex has done this deliberately, it won't be cleared up easily," Rosaline said.

"He's not like that," Shakespeare said. "At least the people seem to love him, to think that he is fine and noble."

"I hope the people are right. I'm not so sure. And I don't know how happy I'm going to be if it is cleared up. I don't like his lordship's willingness to give me to his friend."

"A woman's pique," Shakespeare said. "You're speaking in the heat of a woman scorned. Remember his lordship wrote these in a fit of jealousy. Jealousy does strange things to a man, drives him crazy sometimes. You'll both see things differently when you cool off."

"Thanks, Will," Rosaline said with an attempt at a smile. "I know you mean well. Excuse me, will you?"

"Certainly."

She went upstairs to her room and sat staring out her west window at the setting sun. She still loved sunsets in Stratford. She remembered other evenings when she and her foster father had crossed the Avon just to look back across as the sun went down. It was hard to be angry or bitter as she remembered him. It was hard to be angry when she remembered Hal, not his poetry, which was typical of his impetuosity, but Hal himself. Her love was surely strong enough to survive her fit of pique.

It was her love that counted, too. Her fidelity was what made her good, what gave legitimacy and honor to her unborn child. He must learn the truth, must forget his jealous suspicions. But if he did not, then still her love was her integrity. Almost unconsciously she phrased her thoughts in the meter of a sonnet:

> *Let me not to the marriage of true minds*
> *Admit impediments: love is not love,*
> *Which alters when it alteration finds . . .* (116)

Then she slept for half an hour and rose and bathed her face in cool water. She had regained her composure and some of her confidence by the time she joined the Shakespeares downstairs. Will and the two girls welcomed her into their circle of stools in the back yard, but Anne remained aloof.

"Feel better?" Shakespeare asked.

"Yes, much better."

"Hungry?" Susanna asked. "We've had supper, but I could get you some berries and cream. We'd like some more."

"No. A glass of milk, maybe."

Susanna went into the buttery and began rattling a dipper against the sides of a crock of milk.

"Would you care to hear a sonnet to cheer you up?" Will asked.

"Yes. By whom?"

"By me, Will. Just listen:

> *"Whoever hath her wish, thou hast thy Will,*
> *And Will to boot, and Will in over-plus;*
> *More than enough am I, that vex thee still,*
> *To thy sweet will making addition thus.*
> *Wilt thou, whose will is large and spacious,*
> *Not once vouchsafe to hide my will in thine?*

[166]

Shall will in others seem right gracious,
And in my will no fair acceptance shine?
The sea, all water, yet receives rain still,
And in abundance addeth to his store;
So thou, being rich in Will, add to thy Will
One will of mine, to make thy large Will more.
*   Let no unkind, no fair beseechers kill;*
*   Think all but one, and me in that one Will."*   (135)

Rosaline studied Anne's stern features lighted by a pale beam from the lantern which Susanna had carried into the buttery. She feared what Anne might think of Will's sonnet; so she listened intently to his play on words, the half-dozen broad puns that he made on his name. At the end she laughed at the absurdity of his poem. She did not even try to keep the note of raillery out of her compliment.

"Wonderful, Will. I don't believe I ever heard anything just like it."

"Or, like this one," Shakespeare said, untouched by Rosaline's gentle derision. He rattled off twelve more lines of puns, and ended with the couplet:

"Make but my name thy love, and love that still,
And then thou lov'st me—for my name is Will."   (136)

Rosaline's laugh escaped spontaneously.

"That's precious. One couldn't say that you were ashamed of your name. But I didn't know you loved me."

Anne suddenly burst into tears.

"Judith, go help Susanna," she said.

Judith rose uncertainly and looked at her mother.

"Run along," Shakespeare said. "You heard your mother."

Judith scampered across the porch to the buttery.

Rosaline crossed over to Anne and put her arms around the older woman, who was almost convulsed by that time. To her surprise Anne clung to her and wept into the folds of her skirt.

"I didn't mean it, Anne," Rosaline said. "I was joking. And I meant no slight to Will when I laughed at his sonnets. They are terrible and he knows it."

[167]

"I'm glad you laughed," Anne said between sobs. "It was your laugh that did it. For all these months I've thought—I don't know what I've thought. With you and Will in London, and you so pretty and young, and me eight years older than he is, I thought—I guess I thought it was his baby and you two had made up the story about his lordship. But your laugh. No mistress ever laughed at her lover like that. Then I knew that I was mistaken."

Anne hugged Rosaline tightly around her waist, and for the first time Rosaline felt completely welcome at New Place.

"Just when I was about to suggest a little friendly fornication," Will said, to keep the affair from getting maudlin.

"Will!" Anne said in rebuke. "The girls. They'll hear you."

"Well, would you like to hear another sonnet? I still have one more."

"No," Rosaline said. "I've heard quite enough. Write them out and I'll put them in my book as horrible examples."

"Glad to. I've always wanted to be a horrible example."

"I've been one," Anne said in contrition. "I'll make it up to you, Rosaline. You don't know how wretched I've felt. But I'll make it up to you."

Susanna and Judith returned bearing berries and cream and cheese and rye bread. Rosaline gave Anne another quick hug, and started in on the food with a ravenous appetite. She forgot for the moment that his lordship had cast her out.

13

THE BIGGEST DAY IN ANNE SHAKESPEARE'S LIFE WAS THE DAY THAT brought the Countess of Derby to New Place. The arrival of the caroche, embossed with the Derby coat of arms and drawn by six white horses, was enough in itself to impress the neighbors; but the Countess's entourage—consisting of three baggage wagons, two longwagons full of women servants, and three dozen liveried men on horseback—formed a procession which clogged High Street and Chapel Street from Market Cross to Gild Chapel and taxed not only New Place but also Stratford's limited hostel facilities to the limit during the Countess's overnight stop.

The Little Countess herself won the hearts of all Stratford by her graciousness to the townspeople. Most endearing of all was the picture she made upon her departure when she insisted on acting as Rosaline's nursemaid and personally carried the infant Miranda out to the caroche. As the procession pulled out of Stratford she was still holding the baby in her arms, lifting it up to the windows of the caroche for the townspeople to admire and acknowledging their adoring smiles as though the child were her own.

Rosaline's triumphal departure was full vindication of all Anne's modest accounts of the Shakespeare's fine London friends. Betty's relation to Rosaline was never quite clear to Anne, but that merely added to the fascinating mystery of the beautiful dark lady who had come to Stratford to have her baby while her husband was away at sea. Whatever had been the town's first reactions, influenced perhaps by Anne's coolness toward Rosaline at the beginning, the Countess's visit, coming after Anne's almost slavish devotion to Rosaline during the last few months of her pregnancy, established the dark lady as a woman of mystery. And as a woman of virtue, for even if a nobleman had called for her there might have been a few raised eyebrows; but when the Countess of Derby, daughter of the Earl of Oxford, came for her and greeted her practically as a sister, who could hold on to a single doubt?

Rosaline was aware of all this, and she loved Betty for what she had done. She lay back against the luxurious cushions of the caroche and closed her eyes. She was happy for Anne, for her new status in Stratford now that New Place had been restored to its former elegance and already visited by a countess traveling in state. She was happy for Betty, who seemed to be improving in spirits with every hour she spent tending the baby. She even felt happy for little two-months-old Miranda, who from the very first glimpse of Betty seemed to prefer her to all other people in the world. Rosaline was not the least bit jealous. The affection growing between her two companions in the coach was perhaps the best thing that could happen to either of them. It might restore Betty's mental balance and it certainly insured Miranda's future.

"How did you find out where I was, Betty?" Rosaline asked without opening her eyes. She had not tried to carry on a coherent conversation with Betty at Stratford. She had no wish to reveal anything to the many straining ears, and Betty had been so completely taken by the baby that she had talked of nothing else.

"Henry Walker," Betty said. "I mean I learned from him that Master Shakespeare had picked up your mail. Then I found Master Shakespeare and he told me. Do you think the baby is warm enough?"

Rosaline felt Miranda's arm.

"I think so," she said. The baby was as warm as an ermine robe could keep her.

"That was just last week," Betty said. "That I went to the Gatehouse, I mean, to take Henry's wages—Elizabeth sends the first quarter payment about the end of January. I've been at Hackney since William left me."

"Since William left you?" Rosaline sat up with a start.

"Or I left him. I'm not sure. Anyway William was jealous of me because I was so popular at court, and he took me north last July, to Warrington and Knowsley and Lathom. He wasn't at all like himself. We had a terrible row at Knowsley. Rosaline, sometimes I think William is losing his mind."

"Surely not. Jealousy does strange but temporary things to a man." She modified Shakespeare's words which were supposed to have comforted her; but she felt that they did not apply here. Obviously the aberration was Betty's, not the Earl's.

"I don't know, Rosaline. He got some letters that made him furious. He locked me in a tower. I don't know what he would have done if Tom Ireland and Dr. Dee hadn't quieted him down. Do you think the baby is too warm, Rosaline?"

"No, I think she's just right."

Betty rearranged the robes and shifted the sleeping Miranda so the sun would not shine in her eyes.

"Then the most amazing thing happened. Countess Alice—you know, Ferdinando Stanley's widow—got hold of a letter that Thomas Audeley wrote to Edward Smythe in Paris telling stories about me and Robin.* Then she wrote to William. Can you imagine such a roundabout way to spread scandal?"

* Audeley's letter, written on Sept. 20, 1597, is still preserved in the Hatfield Manuscripts. It says: "My Lord of Essex is in no great grace, neither with Queen or Commons: with Queen for that he lay with my lady of Darbe before he went."

[170]

"No." Rosaline was afraid to ask whether or not the stories were true.

"Of course Alice would do anything to break us up. And I suppose she succeeded. William flew into another tantrum and I came to Hackney. I don't really know whether he drove me out or not."

"I'm sure he didn't," Rosaline said. "He's too gentle. He loves you too much."

"No he doesn't—he didn't. You talk like Uncle Robert. He said that Tom Ireland wrote him that William was most lovingly kind and that he was grieving over my absence. But I don't believe it. He was cruel to me. Rosaline, the baby's wet."

Rosaline offered to take Miranda.

"No, let me," Betty objected. "Just hand me a dry diaper."

Rosaline could not restrain her amusement at the sight of the Countess of Derby performing all the duties of a common nursemaid.

"Father was wonderful to me while I was at Hackney. He didn't blame me a bit. And then when I went to the Gatehouse and asked about you and learned from Master Shakespeare that you had a baby— Rosaline, why didn't you tell me sooner?"

"I tried to," Rosaline said. "The last time I saw you at the Gatehouse."

"You did?" Betty was intent on straightening the baby's long dress over the fresh diaper. She really expected no answer. "Well, I just had to see the baby. Isn't she a darling? Like my Elizabeth except for her eyes—I believe they're going to be black like yours, Rosaline. And she loves me. You can see the way she reaches for me and holds on to me and smiles at me."

"Yes. She loves you," Rosaline agreed.

"So, I just got my things together and moved into Stanley Palace in Westminster to provide a home for you and the baby. I'm still the Countess of Derby; I have a right to the Palace. And while I had the wagons and things I just drove up to Stratford to get you."

"Did you have to bring so many people?" Rosaline asked. "Your entire staff?"

"So many people?" Betty asked blankly. "When we went north in July, Sir Edward Fitton went with us and brought five hundred people on horseback, not counting the coaches and wagons. I didn't bring a hundred to Stratford. I just wanted to be comfortable."

"I'm glad you did," Rosaline said with a laugh. "Anne will remember your visit for the rest of her life."

Rosaline took full advantage of the comforts afforded by Betty's affluence. At Oxford she reveled in the homage paid Betty by the mayor and the college dons. She wondered if they would have been twice as obsequious if they had known that they were entertaining *two* daughters of the Earl of Oxford. And at High Wycombe she was struck by the contrast her second visit made with the first miserable night she had spent on her way to Stratford nine months before.

But there apprehension set in. She had tried to forget the vituperative sonnets Southampton had written, to assure herself that there was only a slight misunderstanding which could be cleared up when they saw each other. Yet Southampton had been in London since the end of October, three months now, and he had made no effort to find her.

She had not told Betty that there was anything wrong. She still was not sure just how clearly Betty was thinking, or how much credence to put into her casual gossip. All was not well with Essex; Rosaline had gathered that much. Her Majesty blamed him for failure to burn the Spanish fleet at Ferrol, for failure to capture the treasure fleet from the Indies, for making too many knights, for discriminating against Raleigh and Monson, and for continuing in his affairs with half a dozen women at court on his return. Rosaline decided that Betty herself was free of Essex, if she had ever really been entangled with him. Betty's information was all secondhand, however, since estranged countesses were not welcome at court and Lord Oxford seldom went near the Queen.

So Rosaline was established in Stanley Palace, as Betty's Italian tutor, when Southampton was finally mentioned. Betty brought up his name so matter-of-factly that Rosaline was stunned.

"Now, we'll just send word to Hal that you are here," Betty said, as though they had been talking about him all the way from Stratford. "He can call on you here, or you can meet him at the Gatehouse. But there's one thing I want understood: you're not to give him the baby. He can see Miranda whenever he wants to, but he's not to take her away from here."

"I'm not sure he wants her," Rosaline said, looking down at

[172]

her daughter lying in the fussy, satin-lined cradle which Betty had provided for her. "Or me either."

"Well, I'd like to know why," Betty said indignantly.

"So would I. Doesn't it seem strange to you that he hasn't tried to see me since his return?"

"He hasn't?" Betty faced Rosaline and for the first time her eyes seemed normal. "Yes, it is strange. He can't have been too busy at court ever since his return."

"It goes back farther than that," Rosaline said, and she risked telling her sister all about the sonnets.

"Were you having an affair with Robin?" Betty asked.

"No. Certainly not. I loathe the man."

"Then how do you account for Hal's suspicions?" Betty appeared to be almost rational. At least her questions were coherent.

"I don't. Surely he has some reason."

"We'll soon find out," Betty said with complete confidence.

"How?"

"Ask him—ask both of them."

"Oh, no," Rosaline said. "I can't do that."

"I can." Betty was still confident.

Rosaline was not sure whether or not Betty was in her right mind. She still was not sure the next day as she sat in the drawing room of the Blackfriars Gatehouse. A coal fire glowed red in the grate. Her books stood on their shelves just as she had left them. Everything was in place. She could hardly believe that she had been away. She was sitting in the window seat watching the street below, waiting for his lordship, just as she had sat a thousand times before, waiting. And always he had come—always before.

But it was different now. Although she had been unable to persuade Betty to give up her mad scheme, she had no faith in it. But Betty had found out where Southampton was staying and she had gone to fetch him after dropping Rosaline at the Gatehouse to wait for him.

Mad, impulsive, absurd, as insane as Rosaline's impetuous interviews with her father and Essex. Betty was her sister; no question about that—and there they were, Betty and Hal, getting out of Betty's caroche at the front door.

Rosaline ran into her bedroom and reassured herself by a quick intensive study of her reflection in her mirror. Her face was the same, a little more mature, a little wiser perhaps. And her figure was the same. Well, almost—her waist not yet down to its former measurements, breasts fuller, with good reason. A key was rattling in the hall door lock. Rosaline bit her lips to freshen them—there was no time to use a brush—and hurried back into the drawing room.

Her fleeting glimpse of his lordship showed him to be a little thinner, his face a trifle more severe. But then she saw nothing. He smelled the same, of musk and Virginia tobacco; and his beard was as bristly as ever.

Betty watched the reunion and waited for her chance to speak. When the lovers finally broke their embrace and backed away for a better look at each other, she had her say.

"Well, I'm glad that's settled."

"How—what was it all about?" Rosaline asked, devouring his lordship with her eyes.

"All a mistake," Betty said. "Hal came here to see you unannounced and found Robin here with me. Naturally I hid. Robin didn't even know you lived here. Hal, of course, thought I was you; he never has seemed very bright to me. So I've just straightened things out, that's all."

"But, Betty." Rosaline faced her sister. "To make such an admission! You did that for my sake?"

"Why not? Everybody in London and some people in Paris already knew all about me and Robin. Why not tell Hal? Anyway it's all over."

"Yes, thank God." Southampton spoke for the first time. The piety sounded strange on his lips. "Thank God it's all over."

"I meant my affair with Robin is all over," Betty said. "And now I must go, if you'll excuse me. Someone has to look after the baby."

She went out hurriedly, eager to return to Miranda or to leave the lovers to themselves. They had a year to recapture, twelve months apart to account for, the worst misunderstanding of their lives to reconcile. First there was lovemaking to catch up on, then a thousand topics needing to be discussed at once, so that words tumbled over words and led to hysterical laughter and more lovemaking.

It was later, much later, that his lordship had time to think of Betty.

"Betty seems to get over her infatuations rather easily," he said.

"Betty hasn't been herself since her baby died," Rosaline explained. "Her affair with my Lord of Essex was the result of an unhealthy, unnatural sort of attraction, I'm sure, not even an infatuation in the usual sense."

"I was thinking of her fondness for me, as you explained it when you first moved in here." It was dark. They were lying in Rosaline's bed, tired, relaxed, comfortable. "I believe you said she loved me so much that she gave you this apartment to make me happy, even with her rival."

"Perhaps I could have been exaggerating," Rosaline said, and squeezed his hand which she held clasped against her breast. "I really think she was so much in love with Will Stanley, so eager to be freed from her betrothal, that she gave me this place to be sure that I would take you off her hands."

"Indeed?" He spanked her bare thigh with his free hand. "I didn't know that I was such a liability, so hard to get rid of." His playfulness did not cover entirely the blow to his conceit.

"Oh, but you are. Just look at me. I'm bound to you forever, and isn't it wonderful?" She squeezed his hand again and snuggled closer into the crescent of his warm virile body.

"Is it, darling?" His question caused her to stiffen.

"I think so," she said cautiously.

"Have you thought so for the past year? It must have been a bleak, unhappy time for you, all on account of my stupid mistake."

"No," Rosaline said. "I didn't get the sonnets until August. I was happy until then, in the thought of you. I had my bad times, but the Shakespeares did all they could to keep me happy. I knew we would be together again."

"I wish I had known as much. To think that I made the entire voyage with Robin, thinking all the time that he had stolen you from me."

"Or that I had stolen him from you." Rosaline could not hide the bitterness which the very mention of Essex's name aroused in her.

"Yes," his lordship said, insensitive to her sarcasm, or intending to ignore it. "Of course I wasn't in the same ship with him. I couldn't have stood that. It would have been too awkward, too painful. But I was his champion in all quarrels, anyway, against Raleigh and Monson."

[175]

"You were ready to forgive him," Rosaline said pointedly. "To stand by him."

"I suppose so."

"But not me, not while you believed I was his mistress." There was an awkward silence.

"You have made no attempt to see me since you returned," Rosaline continued.

"I have seen little of Robin either," he said, in an attempt to justify his behavior. "Her Majesty has given Robin little credit and me none at all, though I sank a man of war and took a rich merchantman. He has been sulking at Essex House or at Wanstead most of the time. I, too, have been ill-tempered and uncompanionable. Now that everything is cleared up, we can all be happy again. I must tell Robin of my mistake. I'm sure he never understood my lack of warmth during the voyage and since."

"Yes. Explain to him, by all means," Rosaline said acidly, freeing herself from his lordship's casual embrace, which had suddenly become too warm. "We certainly wouldn't want him to suffer any more from your stupid mistake, as you call it. Perhaps you would like to go to him right now."

"No, darling." He drew her back to him. "Time with you is too precious. But I must tell him before I leave England."

"Before you leave England?" Rosaline was tense again.

"Yes. I must leave for Paris tomorrow, on a diplomatic mission with Sir Robert Cecil."

"You—going with the Secretary? Isn't he Lord Essex's sworn enemy? Is it as bad as that between you and your Robin?"

"You don't know what it's been like these last three months," he began, with a note of self-pity which Rosaline had not heard in his voice since his disgrace over the Danvers affair. "First the Queen slighted both Robin and me. Then Robin refused to attend Council and left court. I had a fight with Ambrose Willoughby; he ran to the Queen, who took his part and thanked him for pulling out a handful of my hair. It's all been humiliating. Things have been going from bad to worse."

"But the Cecils?"

"The Cecils and Raleigh have the upper hand right now, but there is a sort of truce between factions at the moment. Anyway, I asked to travel on the continent to get away from it all for a while."

"For how long?" Rosaline asked.

[176]

"The business with Sir Robert will require two or three months—but Her Majesty approved my license to travel for two years."

"Two years?" Rosaline scrambled to a sitting position. "I won't allow it."

"I planned before I knew—I mean about my mistake. I planned to join Sir Henry and Sir Charles Danvers. They're still exiled in France, you know. We were going to make an extended tour. I have permission to take ten servants, six horses, and two hundred pounds in money. It's all arranged."

"Then I'll go as one of your ten servants," Rosaline said.

"The other nine will probably be Cecil spies," he said bitterly.

"You don't want to take me. Then I'll join you somewhere, Italy maybe, where I can pass as your native mistress. You shall never leave me again for two years, or even one."

"Perhaps I can find an excuse for cutting my trip short," Southampton countered. "I am not so bitter as I was when I asked her Majesty's permission. Then I hadn't recovered you." He reached for her in the dark.

"So you don't want to take me."

"How would you get permission to travel abroad, darling?" he asked realistically. "What name would you give?"

"That's right. I am nameless—I have to remain nameless."

"And if you did go, you might not be allowed to come back to England. You may be sure that I shall be under constant surveillance, and once the Cecils got on your trail they would find out everything about us. You've no idea how miserable it is at court these days—everybody spying on everybody else. I sometimes wish I were nameless myself. If I could just disappear—with you—"

Hal had never talked like that before. Rosaline wondered how much of his discouragement was due to his mistaken grievance against Essex, or how much was due to the slights he had suffered at the hands of the Queen, or lately, how much was actually due to his love for her and a genuine yearning to make a home for her. She gave him the benefit of all doubts and petted him in the dark.

"Very well," she said. "If I must spend most of my life waiting for you, darling, I suppose I must. But do cut your trip short if you can without arousing suspicion."

"Perhaps if I make good with the Secretary, he will help secure my preferment at court. If I could reconcile him and Robin, I might even become one of the Queen's favorites in my own right.

Then I am sure that I could get you accepted at court." His reference to their long cherished hope carried, at that moment, little more conviction than a reference to some outworn myth.

"Yes, darling, I'm sure you could."

"Anyway the Queen can't live forever," he said, revealing his own lack of faith in gaining Her Majesty's favor. "She's sixty-five years old, already in her dotage. What England needs is a king—a young man on the throne."

Perhaps even more clearly than her husband, Rosaline sensed the beginnings of Essex's ambitions in the thinking of at least one of his followers. The thought frightened, yet thrilled her. She had no love for the Queen. Suppose Her Majesty did die. Suppose Essex—

"To cure the weakness and evil and corruption in England," his lordship continued. "For a time I wanted to die. I began a sonnet, composed all of it except the couplet. Now I have that. Listen!" He recited twelve lines that spoke of:

> . . . *purest faith unhappily forsworn,*
> *And gilded honor shamefully misplaced,*
> *And maiden virtue rudely strumpeted . . .*

to end,

> *Tired with all these, from these would I be gone,*
> *Save that, to die, I leave my love alone.*   (66)

"Now, my love, I don't want to die. I don't even want to go to Paris. But I must."

"Yes, dear. You must."

Rosaline lay awake long after Southampton was sound asleep. Soon he would be gone again, but this time she would feel secure in his love. He would never doubt her again; he had been too happy to find the truth. He had wanted to love her. He did love her. His joy in their reunion was sincere, unmistakably sincere. Now he did not want to leave her again.

Or did he? Was his joy in learning the truth, joy at the restoration of his beloved Robin to his unreserved affection? Did he hate to leave England now because now he could return to Essex's camp with complete loyalty? What would happen if his lordship ever had to choose between her and his Robin? She had to know that answer before she felt secure.

[178]

14

YEARS LATER ROSALINE WAS WONT TO LOOK BACK UPON LITTLE Miranda's first spring as her own greenest season. True, his lordship was in France; but his first letter, sent very discreetly by way of William Strachey, made Paris seem nearer than it had ever seemed before. The sonnet it contained showed how their reunion had restored his lordship's spirits and his sense of her preciousness to him, how he feared losing her again,

> *... to whom my jewels trifles are ...*
> *... left the prey of every vulgar thief ...* (48)

How like him it sounded! As she read his lines she remembered how he had clung to her the morning after that single night they had had together. A rigor of sensual pleasure ran through her body at the memory. His last embrace, typical of the frantic impatience of so many of their stolen moments, had all but driven her recent fears from her mind; it had rekindled that urgency which she had first learned aboard the *Ictis* and known fleetingly on the many other occasions when time seemed to be running out before love had been satisfied. Perhaps it was better that way. Perhaps that was why his lordship considered her so dear a prize, a treasure to be locked up.

His letter told of his being welcomed by Sir Charles and Sir Henry Danvers, whom he hoped to have pardoned before the end of their tour so that they could all three return to England together. Then he cautioned her against listening to scandal that might be spread by his enemies at court, now that he was abroad. Rosaline had indeed already heard stories of his escapades, mostly amorous, during the time of their estrangement. To reassure him and herself, and to caution him against the continuation of such behavior abroad she wrote of

> *... the shame,*
> *Which, like a canker in the fragrant rose,*
> *Doth spot the beauty of thy budding name!* (95)

She provided excuses.

> *Some say thy fault is youth, some wantonness;*
> *Some say thy grace is youth and gentle sport;*

then warned,

> *But do not so; I love thee in such sort*
> *As, thou being mine, mine is thy good report.*   (96)

Further to show how lightly she took the mistake he had made about her and Essex she built a whole play around a similar incident. She called the play *Much Ado about Nothing,* but Richard Burbage produced it in the spring under the title of *Love's Labor's Won* to capitalize on *Love's Labor's Lost,* which had been especially popular that year.

In fact she wrote the most joyous plays of her career during that spring and summer. Despite Burbage's insistence that she supply the Lord Chamberlain's Company with some good solid tragic material, she found that she was entirely too happy to think of tragedy, much less write of it. Everything was working out too well for her and her daughter.

Betty continued to improve under the influence of Miranda's obvious affection for her, so much indeed that by July she and her husband, the Earl of Derby, were reconciled. Betty not only induced him to live with her at Stanley Palace but also wheedled him into taking in one of the Countess Alice's former governesses who claimed that her four-year-old boy was the posthumous bastard of Ferdinando Stanley, the Fifth Earl of Derby. The little Ferdinand certainly looked like a Stanley; and the Sixth Earl, after a brief period of patently insincere grumbling about turning Stanley Palace into a sanctuary for noble bastards, was as deeply in love with the two children as Betty. A stranger would have thought that the babies were the rightful heirs of Derby.

Southampton's July letter crowned Rosaline's happiness, so accurately did it paraphrase her own feeling that the spring had lacked completeness because of his absence:

> *Yet seem'd it winter still, and, you away.*   (98)

Furthermore the Danvers brothers had been pardoned on June 30, and had been ordered by the Queen to return to England.

Though Hal did not mention the possibility, Rosaline began to hope that he would come home with them.

So during the happy months, she wrote two more plays: one based on Thomas Lodge's *Rosalynde* and the other on *Gl' Ingannati*, an old Italian play which Rosaline had always loved and which Bandello had converted into a *novella*. Soon after she sent the plays to Burbage, she received a note from him urging her to meet him and Shakespeare at the Mermaid Tavern. She rather welcomed the chance to go into the City despite the August heat, and she looked forward to spending an hour in the shadowy ordinary of the old Tavern. She, of course, went alone, since she had no wish to make things awkward for the Derbys by openly consorting with common players. Such behavior on the part of a governess would not have been proper. And she went by river boat, since Betty had taken her carriage to Cecil House in the Strand, where her grandfather, Lord Burleigh, who had died on the fourth of August, lay in state.

Rosaline went ashore at Blackfriars Stairs and stopped by the Gatehouse to pick up some books she wanted, but still she reached the Mermaid ahead of time.

"You dressing like a woman now all the time?" William Johnson asked her as he showed her to a private table partitioned off from the ordinary.

"Yes. I'm a lady now."

"You sure look like one," he said admiringly. "Do you read any more?" He seated her at her table and wiped the table, the lamp, the stools, almost everything in sight, with a clean cup towel.

"No, not publicly."

"What are you doing now?" There was no leer on his face. Obviously he expected her to be doing something honorable.

"I'm an Italian tutor for the Countess of Derby," Rosaline explained.

"Oh, yes. You did live at the Oxford place in Blackfriars for a while, didn't you?"

"Yes. We're at Stanley Palace now."

William's curiosity was satisfied.

"We could use you around here these days," he said. "The Friday Club does a lot of reading in here, but none of them can read like you."

"Thank you, Will," Rosaline said.

[181]

"There's one blabbermouth thinks he can, but—" He wrinkled his nose to show his distaste.

"Who's that?"

"A fellow named Ben Jonson."

"I've heard of him. In trouble about the *Isle of Dogs,* wasn't he?"

"In jail for two or three months last fall. Should have kept him in jail. He talks and argues so much that his companions forget to drink their ale. That's bad for business." William briskly repolished a pewter tankard.

"So I would imagine," Rosaline sympathized.

"Take you, now. When you read, they just settle back and sip—usually expensive wine. You're good for business."

"Well, if it's ever so I can, I'll read for you."

"I hope it'll be that way." He looked cautiously over both shoulders and then added, "I'll own this place one of these days."

"I'm sure you will." Rosaline resolved to read for him if he ever owned the place. He could have ruined her once upon a time, but he had kept her secret.

She heard Shakespeare and Burbage enter the Friday Street door. They were complaining about their long walk in the heat. William Johnson recognized their voices too and hurried to meet them and bring them to Rosaline's table. Then he went down into the cellar for cool bottle ale.

"Rubbish!" Burbage said, dumping two manuscripts on the table in front of Rosaline.

"Good afternoon, Will," she said to Shakespeare.

"Good afternoon. You look cool in green. I don't believe I ever saw you wear green before."

"Green isn't my color," she said, still ignoring Burbage. "But it's cool. So I borrowed this dress from the Countess."

"Rubbish, I said!" Burbage had not sat down. "If you write one more silly comedy in which a stupid love-sick wench dresses in boy's clothes and ends up marrying a duke or an earl, I'll tell all London who you are and what a fake you are."

"Fake?" Rosaline would not stand for that.

"Yes, fake. Pretending to write plays, when all you are trying to do is convince yourself and your audience that all things work together for the good of girls who wear breeches. What's the matter? Aren't you sure of his lordship?"

"I certainly am! I was never more sure of anything in my life.

[182]

And I wrote some sparkling comedy in those plays. It just happened that the girls dressed as boys in both of them."

"It just happened in *Merchant of Venice* and *The Two Gentlemen of Verona,* too, but don't let it happen again if you want me to produce your work." Burbage sat down at last, hard, to his own discomfort.

William Johnson set cool bottles of ale before them. He brought a pewter mug for Rosaline.

"The mug's been hanging in the well," he said as he poured her ale into it. "It's cool."

"Thank you, Will," she said. He left the trio alone.

"The Lord Admiral's Company could probably use a good comedy or two," Rosaline said.

"If Master Shakespeare would deal with Ned Alleyn," Burbage said. "But I don't think he will."

Rosaline looked at Shakespeare, who winked at her and smiled.

"Anyway one of the Lord Admiral's playwrights has arranged for us to produce one of his plays," Burbage continued. "We are playing Ben Jonson's *Every Man in His Humor* next month sometime. Will, here, handled it for us."

Rosaline showed her surprise as well as her disapproval.

"There *are* some good comedy scenes in your plays," Burbage admitted. "But I want you to see our new comedian, Robert Armin, in action before you rework these plays. He's a former pupil of Tarleton, but he has a style all his own. I'd like to see you rewrite the Touchstone and Feste parts for him before we produce these."

"New comedian," Rosaline repeated in surprise. "What about Will Kempe?"

"He won't stick to the book, Rosaline. You haven't been to the Theater recently, have you?"

"No."

"Then I don't think you realize what you have done with Falstaff. You have created what may well be the greatest comic character in English drama, all drama maybe."

"Not rubbish?" Rosaline asked sarcastically.

"You've written the comedy into the lines; you've given the old knight an existence in his own right. But Will Kempe won't play the part straight, the way you've written it. He still thinks he's a funny man, funnier than Falstaff."

[183]

"Will Kempe is funny. He has quite a following," Rosaline insisted loyally.

"Not as funny as Falstaff. And old Jack is picking up quite a following, too. When I first tried to get Kempe to stick to the book, he went out and got drunk. John Heminge went on and played the part straight. He was better than Kempe. I'd like to play the part myself, but I'm stuck with Prince Hal."

"You haven't let Will go?" Will Kempe was Rosaline's oldest friend, though perhaps the least reliable. She did not intend to let Burbage discharge the aging comedian if she could prevent it.

"No. He's a shareholder. He's back in the part, but he'll ruin Falstaff if he insists on improvising. I tell you, you've created a masterpiece in the old villain." Burbage, mellowed by the ale and the memory of Falstaff, chuckled good-naturedly. "And that brings us to the point of this visit. We have a rush job for you. Tell her about it, Will."

Shakespeare cleared his throat before he began.

"Her Majesty called me for another audience after our last court performance."

"Indeed? What this time, another sovereign?"

"Not yet. She wants to see Sir John Falstaff in love. In fact, she commanded me to write a play featuring him in an amatory mood."

"Oh, no! Not in love! Not Old Jack Falstaff. He was never in love in his life."

Burbage laughed aloud. "You see, Rosaline," he said. "You consider the old faker a real person yourself."

"But not in love."

"Perhaps he can pretend to be in love. He's acting all the time anyway, consciously playing a dozen parts and fully aware that everyone is on to him. He's wonderful. Sure, he can be in love."

"He has to be," Shakespeare said. "Her Majesty commands, and at once."

"I don't know," Rosaline said slowly. She had got Shakespeare into this; she was the only one who could get him out of it. "I'll try, but I can't promise anything."

"But speed," Burbage said. "You must promise speed. The Queen is waiting."

"Very well. I'll work rapidly, but I don't know how confidently. When must you have it?"

[184]

"You have a month," Burbage said. "All plays have been prohibited until after Lord Burleigh's funeral, which will be held on the twenty-ninth, I believe. But Her Majesty wants it some time before the regular court season begins in November."

"A month?" Rosaline asked again.

"We must have time for rehearsal," Burbage insisted.

"Do we still have a copy of that old play we gave at the Rose?" Rosaline asked, looking to Shakespeare for help. "About five years ago. You remember, Will—a clown courting two women at once. I played a girl called Anne Page."

"The *Jealous Comedy*." Shakespeare supplied the title. "We gave it only once for Henslowe. It belonged to Lord Strange's Men."

"Yes, that's it. Is it still in the company library?"

"It's there," said Burbage, who could always be depended upon in matters of inventory.

"Then send it to me to work from, and I'll have your play ready within a month."

Burbage relaxed after Rosaline's promise, and the three carried on a less urgent conversation over their last tankard of ale.

Rosaline completed *The Merry Wives of Windsor* on the day of Lord Burleigh's funeral. In fact, she was rereading her manuscript when the funeral cortege moved out of the Strand and down King's Street toward Westminster Abbey; and since no part of the route came within sight of her rooms in Stanley Palace in Watergate Street, she ignored the magnificent procession. Later she learned of the five hundred mourners, among whom the Earl of Essex was quite conspicuous, too conspicuous according to such observers as John Chamberlain and Robert Lytton. And from Betty she got a firsthand account of the solemnity of the ceremony and the journey to Stamford Baron, where the body of the Lord Treasurer was finally interred.

But since Rosaline harbored a deep-seated resentment against all the Cecils, she very pointedly took no notice of the occasion during the actual time of the funeral. She was at Stanley Palace with only a skeleton staff of the Derby servants most of the day. She personally fed the children their supper and put them to bed. And she was about to retire herself when the second butler knocked on the door of her suite.

[185]

"Two gentlemen to see you, Madame," he announced. "I've shown them into the library."

"Two gentlemen?" Rosaline asked. It was too much to hope that one of them was the Earl of Southampton.

"Sir William Harvey," the butler explained, "and another gentleman, a Mr. Strachey, I believe."

"Very well, I'll be right down." Her heart sank as she dabbed powder on her cheeks and touched up her lips with a tiny brush. Only bad news could have sent his lordship's close friends to seek her out at such an hour on such a day. His lordship was surely in trouble, or ill, or dead. She hastily got a light cloak out of her wardrobe closet, not for warmth but for disguise. Of course she must go to his lordship. She hurried downstairs and ran to the door of the library. There she paused, composed herself, and entered the room as calmly as she could.

The two men had obviously come by boat; yet both wore hip length riding boots and showed signs of having ridden far and hard. Their doublets were dusty, and their rapiers still hung ready.

"Good evening, Madame Rose," Strachey greeted her respectfully, but his eyes lighted up with a warmth not apparent in his speech.

"Good evening, Mr. Strachey. How are Frances and little Will?"

"Well, thank you. You know Sir William Harvey." He indicated his companion, who bowed low before her.

"Do I?" Rosaline asked.

"Yes, my dear," Sir William answered her and then asked by signs if he could speak freely in the privacy of the library. Rosaline nodded, and he continued, "I know all about you. In fact, I remember you quite well, and favorably, from your readings at the Pipe and Tabor and at the Mermaid. I thought then that you were entirely too lovely to be a boy."

"Thank you, Sir William." Rosaline was relieved to learn that she did not have to pretend.

"And as I told you at the Mermaid, I felt that I should reread your poetry—or Master Shakespeare's, as you chose to call it. I have read or heard all of it several times since."

His inflection of *all* caused Rosaline's eyes to show a flash of momentary fear.

"Your secret is safe with me, my dear," Sir William assured her, sensing her uneasiness. "I consider you one of the marvels of our

[186]

age. Believe me, I shall do nothing to spoil your career."

Rosaline wondered if Sir William was deliberately keeping the conversation away from Hal, flattering her to prepare her for the bad news.

"I see that his lordship has taken you into his confidence, Sir William," Rosaline said. She was not sure at the moment that Southampton had been wise in doing so.

"Yes, though I discovered what an unusual person you are quite apart from his reports," Sir William went on in the same vein. "I have learned of your remarkable intelligence and sensitivity from your poetry, all for myself."

"But surely it's not my poetry which brings you here this evening, Sir William." She was impatient to be on her way to Hal. She had shown her impatience by standing with her cloak thrown over one arm. She had not even invited her guests to sit down.

"No, my dear," Sir William said gently. "And perhaps, yes, it is your poetry which brings us. Your deep feeling, your personal worth, and your superior intelligence make our task at once more difficult and easier."

"And your task is?" Rosaline was beginning to grow weary of Sir William's prelude.

"To discuss his lordship," Sir William said, "who as you know is the gentlest, the most amiable, the most generous and lovable young nobleman in all England."

"Yes, Sir William." Rosaline could agree with all he had said.

"As well as one of the most impulsive, and sometimes most self-willed, if I may say so."

Sir William paused. Rosaline said nothing but stood ready to leave as soon as the gentlemen had made known the real purpose of their visit.

"We three love him," Sir William continued. "And I am doubly interested since I hope to marry his mother, the Countess, who has been alone since the death of Sir Thomas Heneage, some three years ago. It is we, then, who must stand by his lordship."

William Strachey and Rosaline nodded, he uneasily, she impatiently.

"The death of Lord Burleigh leaves a sort of vacuum at court," Sir William went on. "You probably know much of the present political tension. There will be a struggle, a life and death battle for power. Sir Robert Cecil will, of course, try to succeed his father as the Queen's right hand. Sir Walter Raleigh, Sir Robert Sidney, the Lord Admiral, possible the Bacons, will support him. You no doubt know where our interests lie."

"With the Earl of Essex," Rosaline said, the very name bitter in her mouth. Every time unpleasantness came into her life, Essex was hovering nearby.

"Yes. So it is urgent that nothing happen right now that would prejudice Lord Essex in the eyes of the Queen. You understand that. That is why I am glad to be talking to an intelligent young woman."

"I understand that perfectly. I have no intention of embarrassing either of their lordships. You say that you know all about my relations with the Earl of Southampton. Surely you must know by now that I shall not disgrace him at court. For five years I have remained anonymous, with no more real existence than a ghost. I shall not change now."

"Good," Sir William said, but not with the air of relief which Rosaline had expected. "I knew that we could depend on you not to make a scene."

"And why should I make a scene?"

"That, my dear, is the difficult part." Sir William came closer to Rosaline, and his face assumed the kindest, yet the most miserable expression which she had ever seen. "His lordship is now in London. He and the Danvers brothers arrived today."

"In London, where?" Rosaline asked eagerly. She started to throw the cloak around her shoulders.

"He is in the cellars at the Steelyard."

"And you're to take me to him."

William Strachey suddenly became interested in some books in a shelf behind Rosaline. He moved away from her.

"Yes, my dear," Sir William answered. "I'm to take you to him, but not before I have explained to you that he plans to marry Elizabeth Vernon in the morning and return to France at once."

"Elizabeth Vernon!" Rosaline exclaimed. "But he can't. He's already married to me."

"That's the way he feels about it, too," Sir William said. "He considers himself bound to you. But during his estrangement from you last winter it seems that he went a little too far with Mistress Vernon. She is with child."

Rosaline merely stared at Sir William.

[188]

"As you know," he went on, "Mistress Vernon is cousin to Lord Essex. He sponsored her at court. She has been at Essex House for some time now, pleading ordinary illness to explain her absence from court. When Her Majesty learns the truth it will be very bad, even if the lady is married to his lordship. If she is not, the affair will be disastrous for all of us, for him, for Lord Essex—all of us who look to him as our champion. Especially for you, my dear."

"Especially for me. It's a disaster for me anyway." She let her arm drop. Her cloak hung limp from her hand and dragged on the floor as she turned and walked slowly half the length of the library to an outside window.

"And his lordship wants to see me?" she asked without looking back at Sir William. "Why?"

"He loves you, my dear. I'm sure of that. He wants to hurt you as little as possible."

"His lordship is only going through the form of the ceremony in the morning," William Strachey said, interrupting Sir William Harvey. "He considers his marriage to Mistress Vernon as a purely temporary expedient. He has no intention of consummating the union."

"Consummating the union!" Rosaline spun around and glared at William Strachey, who looked even more miserable than Sir William, if that were possible. But she was sorry that she had shouted at him. These men were certainly not to blame for what had happened. They were trying to be kind.

"Her Majesty would never agree to a divorce," Rosaline said more calmly, "consummation or no consummation, though I believe that is no longer a point in question."

"Her Majesty won't live forever," Strachey said. Southampton had said the same thing. "When Lord Essex is in power, he will agree to an annulment, I'm sure."

"And the lady his own cousin?"

"Lord Essex is not so strict as Her Majesty in moral matters," Strachey offered as an unconscious gem of understatement.

"Do you know of this idea of his lordship's, Sir William?" she asked.

"Yes. He feels as Mr. Strachey says he does. But I thought perhaps it would be better to let his lordship explain to you himself."

"Then he actually believes that he can go through a ceremony

[189]

with Elizabeth Vernon, satisfy Her Majesty, exonerate Lord Essex, then have it all rescinded at some future time and claim me as his only wife?" Rosaline was surprised at the coldness of her own voice. It was as though she were outlining a plot or synopsizing a play for Richard Burbage.

"He believes that sincerely," Sir William said. It was difficult to tell whether or not he believed it himself. "I hope he can do as you say. We none of us want to hurt you. We'll all look out for you."

"I'll look out for myself, thank you," Rosaline said, her chin in the air and her cloak neatly hung on her arm once more, well clear of the floor. "I am fully capable of taking care of myself and my daughter."

"We are well aware of that," Sir William said. "But we don't want to lose you. His lordship doesn't want to lose you. He really has no choice in what he is doing in the morning. You must understand that."

"No, I suppose he hasn't," Rosaline agreed glumly, "not this late. Perhaps there *was* a time when he had a choice. Shall we go?"

"Are you ready?" Sir William asked. Rosaline understood that he was not referring to her being dressed for the journey. He had done his best to prepare her.

"Yes," she said, "I think you can trust me to behave intelligently." She smiled as she used the term stressed earlier by Sir William.

Rosaline walked between the two men out into Watergate Street and around to the Stanley Stairway down to the Thames. Both men were most considerate of her, solicitous of her every comfort. They practically carried her down the steps and lifted her into the waiting wherry.

It was cool on the river, with just a hint of light fog in the night air. Traffic was heavy, and Rosaline was thankful that the trip was slow and the river too noisy for conversation.

She agreed with Sir William that there was no point in her making a scene. She could gain nothing by embarrassing his lordship. She had no claim on him that would be considered for one moment by Her Majesty, or Lord Essex, or Elizabeth Vernon, or the dowager Countess of Southampton, none of whom, presumably, knew of her existence. And there were certain advantages to anonymity; if she were to do some planning of her own she would have much more freedom of action. She was an intelligent young woman. Sir William had made much of that. She should be able to devise some plan to protect her interests. It would depend largely on Hal.

The cellars of the Steelyard were famous, or notorious, for all sorts of things. Gourmets went there for choice smoked salmon and ox tongue and salty caviar and anchovies, or for rare cheeses and dry Rhenish wine. Appetites of other kinds were satisfied by opium and laudanum, sometimes by hashish or bhang. And old rakes, long since jaded by the stews in Bankside, might be furnished with a "blue goose," or some other French delight equally bizarre. Or a man could simply hide there and be sure that anyone who saw him would be more likely to keep his secret than to admit visiting the Steelyard Cellars.

Sir William and his party followed a malodorous attendant through the most nearly respectable dining area and down a damp labyrinthine tunnel to a private cellar. Strange odors seeped out of the caves along the way and stranger sounds echoed down far reaches of the side passages. Rosaline was surprised, then, to find his lordship's cubicle brightly lighted, and furnished quite comfortably. She saw the Danvers brothers for a moment and then found herself clasped to Southampton's breast.

"Rose, darling, I thought you'd never get here," his lordship said breathlessly, and closed his mouth over hers before she could speak.

Even as she kissed him she realized that she could be quite intelligent about him then and henceforth. In fact, she began to think of some quite intelligent possibilities while she still clung to him.

15

ALTHOUGH THE QUEEN LEARNED OF THE WEDDING AT ONCE AND ordered the Earl of Southampton to return to England, he delayed for two months his departure from Paris. During that time the worst possible reports of him came to England. Instead of behaving like a happy bridegroom and a dutiful subject, he gambled too heavily and lost, and he became embroiled in half a dozen quarrels which ended just short of dueling. There were no rumors concerning him and women, but almost every other charge of debauchery was made against him.

When he did arrive in England, early in November, he was immediately clapped into Fleet Prison, where he remained until the new Countess was delivered of a baby girl (named Penelope after Lord Essex's sister) on the eighth. He was free by the end of the month, though denied admittance to court. Further reports were that he avoided his bride and generally led a miserable life through the Christmas holidays.

He made no attempt to see Rosaline. She was still somewhat undecided as to what was the right thing to do. For the benefit of those who were privy to his lordship's affairs she wrote a sonnet of generous abnegation, that began:

> Farewell; thou art too dear for my possessing,
> And like enough thou know'st thy estimate:

and ended,

> Thus have I had thee, as a dream doth flatter,
> In sleep a king, but waking, no such matter.   (87)

By giving a copy to William Strachey, who seemed to have been appointed to watch over her and who never doubted the sincerity of her poem, she managed to get it into the circles where the "Shakespearean" sonnet sequence was being passed around. His lordship's most intimate friends should find her sentiments suitably touching. Other fanciers, who still thought the poems written by a man, might find it quite conventional, a thing to be admired for its technical grace. His lordship—his lordship might make of it whatever he would.

Rosaline, upon analyzing her feelings, decided that annoyance was uppermost, followed by chagrin, anger, and bitterness, in that order. She was annoyed by his lordship, but could not find it in her heart to blame him severely. She knew his character; she should have known what to expect of him. There was certainly no viciousness in him, despite reports of his recent conduct. It was possible that he was simply stupid—at best, lacking in foresight.

Burbage's recurring cynicism was the source of her chagrin, that and her own cocksure answers to his reminders. Perhaps that was why she had always been so quick to come to Hal's defense. He was always in need of defense. And her anger invariably centered itself on the Earl of Essex, and from there shaded into bitterness. She hated Essex for what he was and for what he did to people like Hal, or Betty in her time of illness. It was Essex, the exploiter of weakness, against whom she wanted revenge; and she discovered that she *did* want revenge, a sort of compensation which she had never understood before.

But there was little that she could do at the moment, nothing in fact but wait until things changed with the Queen and with Essex and with the Earl and Countess of Southampton. She could certainly plan against that day. And plan she did, driven by annoyance and chagrin and anger and bitterness, until she began to grow morbid, almost ill.

The expiration of the Burbages' lease on Giles Allen's property where the Theater was built came as a godsend. At least, the urgent message which Rosaline received to meet the Chamberlain's Company shareholders at the Mermaid Tavern interrupted her painful introspections. It came the day after Christmas, a crowded day, since the company was performing at court in the evening.

She arrived about noon and found the rest of the company assembled. She knew all of them: Richard Burbage, William Shakespeare, Thomas Pope, Augustine Phillips, John Heminge, William Kempe, and Cuthbert Burbage, who was not a shareholder in the troupe but who had inherited the Theater upon the death of James Burbage. The men, seated but still wearing their hats and coats, looked glum indeed. They rose and greeted Rosaline, then sat down again around the massive common table which Will Johnson had moved for them into the private room.

Richard Burbage, by tacit agreement leader of the group in all things, started his explanation at once.

"You are familiar with the terms of my father's original lease on the land where the Theater now stands—that my father or his heirs had the right to tear down the building and move the timber at any time before the expiration of the lease."

The members of the group nodded. Obviously the terms were

being repeated for Rosaline's benefit. It was an old story to the others.

"Unfortunately," Burbage continued, "my brother Cuthbert, relying on a verbal agreement with Giles Allen, has allowed the Theater to stand beyond the expiration date. We have got intelligence that Allen intends to tear down the Theater and convert the timber and furnishings to his own use. He insists that, since the building has been allowed to stand beyond the fixed date, the right and interest of the Theater is, both in law and in conscience, absolutely invested in him."

Burbage sneered at the legal language of Allen's claim.

"Is there a record of Cuthbert's agreement with Allen?" Shakespeare asked.

"None. One witness, now dead, and Allen's wife, who is as greedy as her husband."

"Is there anything we can do?" asked John Heminge. "Everything we have is tied up in that building: our patronage, our art, our stage properties."

"Giles Allen has gone to the country for the Christmas holidays," Burbage said significantly. "He isn't expected back until after Twelfth Night."

"What good is a week?" Thomas Pope asked. Like most low comedians, he was a chronic pessimist.

"We could tear the building down in less time," Burbage suggested.

"With our own hands?" Pope asked. "I'm no carpenter. Anyway it's your building. Yours and Cuthbert's."

"But all our fortunes depend on it," Heminge reminded Pope. "I never want to work for a man like Henslowe again—one who keeps the actors always in his debt."

"Nor I," Phillips chimed in, "but what would we do with the building if we did tear it down?"

"I have a tentative plan," Burbage said. "I have made arrangements for a site near the Church of St. Mary Overies in Bankside, across Maiden Lane, south and east of the Rose. Sir Nicholas Brend will lease us the land for thirty-one years."

"That's a better site than the present one," Heminge said, "nearer the center of London, easier to get to by land or water."

"And Peter Street, a master carpenter, will move the building for us," Burbage continued.

"Then why this meeting?" Pope asked.

"Simple," Burbage said. "Money. It all costs money, and Cuthbert and I have been saddled with the Blackfriars Theater, which has never opened, as well as the Theater. We have no money, nothing but expenses."

"Money!" Pope snorted.

"How much?" Heminge asked.

"Three or four hundred pounds," Burbage said. "And I have still another plan. My brother and I will put up the timber and furnishings of the Theater as half a syndicate against four hundred pounds as the other half, all partners to be housekeepers as well as shareholders in Lord Chamberlain's Company."

"It sounds good," Heminge said, "except for the fact that none of us have any money."

"Can you raise any?" Richard Burbage asked. "Cuthbert and I are mortgaged to the hilt already."

"How much money do I have, Will?" Rosaline asked, speaking for the first time.

"Something over a thousand pounds," Shakespeare said with some pride. "You never seem to spend any and I've managed your principal right well, added a little to it now and then, in fact."

"I'll back the company," Rosaline said.

They all looked at her. All except Richard Burbage seemed surprised. Rosaline was reasonably sure that Burbage had staged the entire performance to get the exact results which he had achieved.

"I mean I will lend the other five of you eighty or a hundred pounds each," she said, to make it clear to Burbage that she was backing the Lord Chamberlain's Men, not the Burbage brothers. "You may pay me back out of your earnings. Can I do that, Will?"

"Yes," Shakespeare said. "At a fair rate of interest, of course."

"Of course," Rosaline agreed. "Is it an acceptable proposition?"

"Indeed it is," Heminge said enthusiastically.

The others except Will Kempe were equally happy with the arrangement. Kempe, whom Rosaline wanted to help above all the others, seemed most reluctant to accept her offer. Perhaps he was too well aware of his sorry record in paying back borrowed money. If she could only give him a share outright. But he would never allow that.

Rosaline let Shakespeare represent her as usual, and the com-

[195]

pany chose John Heminge to act as treasurer and see that suitable agreements were drawn up. It was then that Rosaline was reminded that she was still nameless. She directed Shakespeare to see that the partners were bound to each other, but left their debts to her unsecured. The actors, not fully understanding her motives, were much impressed by her faith in their integrity. So they were bound more tightly to her than any legal instrument would have tied them.

Two days later Peter Street with twelve sturdy workmen began dismantling the Theater while the Lord Chamberlain's Men stood by, armed with swords and daggers to protect the wreckers from Allen or his friends. Although Giles Allen reported that the job was carried out in "most forcible and riotous manner," he was certainly exaggerating. He was not in London during any part of the dismantling. Actually a few schoolboys playing in Finsbury Field threw some snowballs over the brick wall; but otherwise the Theater came down in a manner befitting its dignity, and the timber was hauled down to the Thames. Giles Allen ultimately hailed Street and the Burbages into court but lost his case against them. Three weeks later the timber had all been floated across the river and Peter Street was ready to begin work on the new Globe Theater, the first playhouse in England to be owned by the acting company which occupied it.

Rosaline was drawn to the construction of the Globe as a child to a new toy. Since Betty had practically appropriated her baby and Elizabeth Vernon had snared her husband and Shakespeare was given credit for her poetry, she had nothing she could call her own. The Globe, much of which she designed or collaborated on, was the only tangible thing in which she had ever held a proprietary interest. Consequently she spent all her spare time in Bankside, peering over Peter Street's shoulder, it seemed, at every stage of the project.

At first she went dressed as a woman. Then, when she felt that she was becoming conspicuous, she ransacked the company wardrobe and reassumed her disguise as a boy. She was proud of her figure, which had returned to its almost boyish slenderness, all except her bosom, which she could certainly no longer risk in apprentice jackets but had to encase in stiff non-revealing doublets. But she rather enjoyed reverting to her old self.

She was reminded of that other world of which she had become a part by such incidents as the marriage of Sir William Harvey to the Dowager Countess of Southampton, and young Southampton's departure for Ireland with Essex. She drew some satisfaction from Derby's opinion that Essex had unwittingly maneuvered himself into an impossible position by accepting command of the English forces in Ireland after opposing the appointment of all other qualified candidates. Derby felt that the war in Ireland was hopeless, the graveyard of all military men who went to challenge the rebel Earl of Tyrone.

And Rosaline was pleased, maliciously pleased, to learn that Essex had appointed Southampton General of the Horse in defiance of Her Majesty's stated orders to the contrary. She was pleased not at the advancement of her husband but at the discomfiture which Essex was storing up for himself in the future. She had given up hope for her own happiness during the Queen's lifetime, and she had little hope for a true reconciliation with his lordship beyond that time. So all she could do was count Essex's troubles as part of her revenge. In the meantime there was the Globe rising in Bankside, and Rosaline was happiest while she watched the tall cylindrical building grow foot by foot.

Betty, however, thought that Rosaline was running away from her grief. In May, the Little Countess of Derby moved her household to a cottage on the Cecil estate at Castle Heningham, in Essex; she took little Miranda and Rosaline, who preferred to stay with the Globe but could not deny her ladyship.

Rosaline managed to find time to rework the two plays she had written earlier. She found herself becoming more astringent in her comedy; how her outlook had changed! She ended by giving the plays the rather cynical titles of *As You Like It* and *What You Will*. With Robert Armin cast as Touchstone and Feste, they were sure to please the audience of the new Globe when it opened in August, but they were no longer suited to her taste.

Betty read both plays, but her manner was so mysterious that Rosaline could not tell whether or not she liked them. Betty kept the manuscripts to herself until near the end of June, refusing to allow Rosaline to send them on to Burbage. She insisted on having the Earl read them and finally had to promise Rosaline a surprise to hold the plays an extra week.

The surprise turned out to be a dark handsome young man

about Rosaline's age. Betty brought him to the summerhouse, where Rosaline was working.

"This is John Marston," she said eagerly, "a young friend of his lordship, recently of the Middle Temple. You two have so much in common. His mother was Italian, too. And he has written some satires under an assumed name—W. Kinsayder. I've told him all about you. He is as eager to know you as I am to have you meet him."

John Marston bowed and stood quietly by with a faint smile playing on his lips while her ladyship chattered on through her lengthy introduction. Rosaline wondered just how much Betty had told him about her.

"Buon giorno, signorina," Marston said with an accent that was far from authentic.

"Signora," Rosaline corrected him. "My husband is in Ireland with the army. I am very happy to know you." She would have to be careful until she learned what Betty had in mind—*all* that she had in mind. Surely her ladyship was not trying her hand at matchmaking.

"Now, for the big surprise," Betty said, motioning for the others to sit down along the trellised wall of the summerhouse. "I wanted William to break the news, but he's out hunting. Anyway I've talked him into financing a revival of Paul's Boys and arranged for you two to write for them."

Rosaline looked at Betty in astonishment and then back at John Marston, who seemed to know all about her ladyship's plans and to approve them.

"But we—I can't do that, Bet—my lady," she said in protest. "My work is already promised."

"Oh, fie!" Betty said. "You don't have to write for the common players. Paul's Boys will perform only at court and the right places, and you'll never have to go to those horrible Bankside theaters again. Children's companies are fashionable. And you can both use Mr. Marston's name. Anyway I've promised Mr. Marston that you would look over some of his plays and work with him."

"Very well," Rosaline agreed hopelessly. "I'll do that much. But I can't write for his lordship's new company. I hope he isn't depending on me."

"We'll see," Betty said confidently. "Now why don't you two get acquainted?"

She rose hurriedly and disappeared down a path toward the cottage.

Rosaline and John Marston looked at each other in an awkward silence. Neither smiled.

"Mr. Marston, I'm afraid her ladyship has made a mistake," Rosaline said.

"Perhaps." John Marston seemed suddenly at ease.

"She means well, but what she plans is impossible because—oh, for a number of reasons. How much has she told you about me?"

"A lot," he said easily. "That you were once an actress, that you know the theater exceptionally well, that you have written the poems and plays generally ascribed to William Shakespeare, that oaf from Stratford."

"Will Shakespeare is no oaf," she said heatedly. Her dislike for John Marston crystallized at that moment.

"He's no poet either, or dramatist. I've met him."

"But he is one of my dearest friends. I'll hear nothing disparaging said of him."

"And you're her ladyship's dearest friend, I believe she said." Marston's smile carried not the least hint of pleasantness. "I fear that her ladyship has not really told me all about you, *signora*."

Rosaline studied his face, fearing to believe the meaning she got from his words.

"Was Viola Nigrone your mother?" he asked suddenly.

"Yes." There was no point in denying it.

"She was my mother's cousin," Marston said, triumphantly it seemed. "So, you see, I know as much about you—or about your parentage, let us say—as does her ladyship. Or does she know?"

"She knows," Rosaline said wearily. "She can be trusted. What do you intend to do about our secret?"

"Nothing," Marston said. "Nothing, so long as I am employed as a dramatist for Paul's Boys. I am no more eager to claim kin to crazy old Monarcho than you are to have Sir Robert Cecil learn of your identity."

"I'm sure that her ladyship will see that you write for his lordship's company. And I am sure that you don't really want to work with me."

"No. I admire your work very much, but it is not the sort of thing that I want to do. I'm more interested in satire, topical subjects that appeal primarily to the courtier."

"I thought as much." Rosaline stood up and walked across the floor of the summerhouse. "The idea of collaboration was strictly hers, I suppose?"

"Not exactly. When I learned that his lordship planned to revive Paul's Boys, I looked for the best avenue of approach. It seemed to be by way of her ladyship—and, of course, I felt that you and I should meet, since we have so much in common."

"You already knew about me?" Rosaline faced Marston and toyed with a vine intertwined in the trellis.

"I surmised when I learned her ladyship had added an Italian governess to her household. And if you intend to reveal everything to her ladyship you might tell her that her new chaplain is really George Fenner,* one of Father Parson's spies."

"Does he know who I am?" Rosaline asked.

"No. He would have no background for suspecting anything of your relation to the de Veres, but if you leave manuscripts in the way of his snooping he might learn more than you want him to know. I merely pass this information along as evidence of my own good faith."

"And because once my secrets are known to others you lose your means of blackmailing me and her ladyship."

"You should write thrilling plays for the groundlings, *signora,*" Marston said with a smirk.

"I do," Rosaline said. "And now surely you will excuse me. I should like to speak to her ladyship."

He rose and bowed acknowledgement of her request.

"*A rivederla domani,*" he said.

Rosaline looked at him quizzically for a moment, wondering what he meant by *domani,* literally *tomorrow* or something more sinister.

---

* Two letters written by George Fenner on June 30, 1599, from Castle Heningham contain statements that the "Earle of Darby is busy penning commodyes for commoun players." Largely on the strength of these letters, which might refer to anyone's manuscript plays at Castle Heningham at the time, a number of scholars have ascribed Rosaline's plays to William Stanley, Sixth Earl of Derby. See *Shakespeare's Identity* (1952), by A. W. Titherley, for the most recent and exhaustive treatment of this absurdity.

"*Addio*," she said with an air of finality. Then she turned and hurried down the path Betty had taken.

She found her ladyship sitting on an ornamental bench by the duck pond, feeding bread crumbs to the swans.

"Well, how do you like him?" Betty asked brightly, trying to maneuver her farthingale so Rosaline could sit down beside her.

"Not at all." Rosaline sank down on the cool grass of the pool bank. "He is simply a blackmailer, a distant relative of mine—on the Nigrone side—who intends to force his lordship to produce his plays or expose me as your bastard sister."

"So he knows who you are?" Betty sobered immediately.

"Yes, even more than you told him, which was too much."

"Very well. I'm sure William will take care of him one way or the other—not that I care if the world knows that you're my sister."

"Are you sure, Betty?" Rosaline asked. "Aren't you ashamed of me because I write for the public theaters? Isn't that why you wanted his lordship to finance Paul's Boys, so my work would be respectable if I ever were discovered?"

"Indeed not!" Betty was indignant. "I wouldn't be ashamed of you, no matter what you did, and if everyone knew all about us. I thought that you might be happier, that maybe you might win the approval of influential people and—I don't know what I thought. But I tried to help."

"I know you did," Rosaline said, relieved that Betty really did not care whether or not she wrote for the children. "The public theater is really my home, Betty. I'm realizing it more and more every day. I like it, every bit of it—the sentiment, the sensation, the occasional lyricism, the high tragedy, the low comedy, even the bluntness and obscenity demanded by the groundlings and stinkards in the pit."

Betty was listening intently.

"Yes, I love it," Rosaline went on. "And I must write for it, on its own terms, if I write at all. Can't you understand that, Betty?"

"Yes, watching you, I think I can."

"I should like to play again, when the Globe opens. Maybe I'm yearning for a make-believe world to substitute for the real one that is growing more intolerable with every blackguard I meet, men like Marston—and Lord Essex." The bitterness of her memory erased at one stroke the near happiness of the past two months.

"Then if you want to play again, do it," Betty said. "If I wanted to and I were you—and I often wish I were you—I'd certainly play until someone stopped me."

"I don't mean regularly," Rosaline continued, "but occasionally, so I can keep the feel of the theater in my bones. I suppose I always have that idea in the back of my mind. I always write parts for me: Rosaline, Hermia, Hero, Sylvia, Nerissa—and now I know that I wrote Celia and Maria for me in these new plays."

"Do you want to go back to London, Rosaline?" Betty asked. "Now, I mean?"

"Yes, I think I do. I want to be there when the Globe opens."

"Then we'll all go," Betty said.

16

ROSALINE DREW HER CLOAK TIGHTLY ABOUT HER AS SHE CLIMBED THE Paris Garden stairs directly across the Thames from Blackfriars. A light chill fog hid the sun, as well as the worst of the sordid waterfront stews and taverns lining the riverbank eastward toward Winchester House. A few early theater-goers had crossed in the tilt-boat with her, mostly students and apprentices coming early to pre-empt choice standing room in the pit; some of them joggled her deliberately, making exploratory contacts to see whether or not it would be worth their while to pay the extra sixpence for a seat in the goose roost.

Her face masked and her figure hidden by the hooded cloak, she might well have been the courtesan they took her for; but when she engaged a sedan chair to carry her over the marshy ground to the Globe, her extravagance marked her as a lady of high quality or a quean of high price, either of which rendered her inaccessible to groundling admirers. As the bearers took their places, Rosaline drew the curtains, not because the brothels along the way particularly offended her, but because an open sedan chair was an invitation to the wealthier gallants and a distinct annoyance to the local harlots who resented competition and voiced their resentment most pungently.

Without even looking through the peepholes, Rosaline could plot the progress of her chair as the bearers headed south on Lambeth Road. To her right she could hear the dogs barking in Paris Garden, and to her left, farther away, the fainter yelps of the mastiffs in the Beargarden. The dogs were all hungry, starved to make them vicious for the bull-baiting and bear-baiting later in the afternoon. The Swan, located less than a furlong south of Paris Garden stairs, was quiet, since the Globe was the only playhouse active in the Liberty of the Clink that fall.

By the stench of the drainage ditch Rosaline knew when it was time for the porters to turn east on Maiden Lane, and she braced herself for the jolt she would feel when they stepped across the storm sewer. After the jolt she opened the right curtain and looked out into the orchard land. The trees were bare, of course, but there was still some green in the marsh grass around their roots, and the air was fresh, even perceptibly drier than the river air had been.

At the Globe, she met her erstwhile boat companions, who had gone the length of "vice row" and doubled back to approach the theater from the east end of Maiden Lane. Far from sated, they paused long enough to watch Rosaline step out of her sedan chair and to voice their disappointment when she revealed no more than a red leather boot. She paid her porters, gathered her cloak around herself again and approached her beloved Globe. She stepped under the sign of Hercules holding up the world and read the inscription *"Totus mundus agit histrionem."* Then she passed through the gentlemen's entrance and paid admission to the gatherer, a hired actor's wife who, of course not knowing her connection with the Globe, exacted full price before admitting her to the stairs to the twelve-penny rooms.

She made her way to a room on the second floor near the stage. She took her customary seat at the rail and looked across the stage and down into the pit. The three balconies were perfect circles, though the back walls were hexagonal, and the stage, jutting out from the south side of the theater, extended halfway across the pit. Directly across the stage from Rosaline, four early patrons sat around a deal table and played at primero and drank bottle ale.

Above them, in a similar room on the third balcony a grey-haired old man was deeply absorbed in a pamphlet printed on yellow paper. Two girls hawking apples and roast chestnuts were already doing a lively business in the rapidly filling pit.

Rosaline opened her cloak, though she did not remove it. No one took any notice of her until the musicians filed into the music room on the third balcony, directly over the stage and protected by the shadow, or heavens, which extended over half the open top of the amphitheater. The leader looked her way and waved to her before he began the concert. The trumpets sounded a fanfare, and the mixed consort of viols, cornets, and woodwinds started into a spirited country dance.

Rosaline tapped her foot lightly and fingered the tune on the railing in front of her as though it were the keyboard of a virginal. She remembered the sonnet his lordship had written, playfully envying the jacks of the virginal at the Blackfriars Gatehouse:

> O'er whom thy fingers walk with gentle gait,
> Making dead wood more blest than living lips. (128)

At the memory she involuntarily looked toward the back of the theater, to a lord's room on the second balcony opposite the center of the stage. Southampton would soon be there, in the same seat he had occupied nearly every day since Essex's unauthorized return from Ireland about the end of September. Essex himself had been under house arrest most of the time, but Hal and the young Earl of Rutland were free, though presumably in rank disfavor with the Queen. At any rate both of the young Earls spent all their spare time at the theater or in the company of actors and playwrights at the neighboring taverns, Southampton perhaps hoping for a chance meeting with her and Lord Rutland paying for professional readings of some plays he had written.*

Sometimes the Earl of Rutland was accompanied by his recent bride, the former Lady Elizabeth Sidney; but the Countess of Southampton was never seen in the company of her husband. Rosaline found some satisfaction in that state of affairs, though

---

* His close association with Southampton and the Lord Chamberlain's Men has caused Roger Manners, Fifth Earl of Rutland, to be proclaimed the author of Rosaline's works, especially by certain German and Belgian scholars.

[204]

she was never quite sure whether it was because the situation left some hope for her ultimate reunion with Hal, or because she enjoyed watching him suffer the unpleasant consequences of his attachment to Essex. There were still some facets of her emotional nature which she did not fully understand. Lately she had been taking stock of herself, more seriously than ever before, but still the very sight of her husband upset whatever conclusions she thought she had reached.

That Southampton haunted the Globe had disturbed her at first, but after several days of dividing her attention between the lord's room and the stage she thought she had become calm enough to regard both with equal objectivity. At times it seemed as though the whole thing were a play acted on two stages. She would find herself setting a situation involving Hal and then providing a logical dramatic solution. Then she would pull herself up with a start and the grim realization that she had no control whatever over her husband. Others held the strings to that particularly handsome puppet. And he *was* handsome, that same handsome youth who had so fascinated her as a green young girl. As she watched him from behind her disguise, she would grow more and more bitter by the minute, until his lordship dominated the entire theater, as he had dominated her life. Every day it happened that way.

William Shakespeare suddenly appeared in the balcony beside her.

"I brought your pot of coals," he said. "It gets colder and colder up here."

"Thanks, Will," Rosaline said, grateful for the live coals and for his interruption of her thoughts.

"And this," Shakespeare added, producing a sheaf of tattered, dog-eared player's parts.

"What is it?"

"An old tragedy by Thomas Kyd. *Hamlet.* You remember it."

"Oh, yes. A pretty gruesome revenge play as I recall, with ghosts and floating daggers and drownings and all sorts of things."

"That's it," Shakespeare said. "We'd like you to rework it for us."

"I might be able to do something with such a play," Rosaline said, with an involuntary glance toward the lord's room.

"That's what Dick Burbage thinks, that you are now ready to write tragedy, and that this is the one to work on."

"A pox on Dick Burbage!" Rosaline exploded. "He still thinks I changed my mind in the middle of *Julius Caesar* and wrote the last part to justify his lordship's following Lord Essex in defiance of the Queen."

"Didn't you?" Shakespeare's eyes twinkled.

"Of course not. We presented the play a week before Essex arrived in London. You know that."

"Yes, I know that," Shakespeare said. "I know, too, that with your sources of information you might have known months ago that Lord Essex planned to march on London with three thousand men, until Sir Christopher Blount talked him out of it."

"No, I didn't, Will. I guess I have been expecting something like that for a long time but I don't think I ever identified Hal with Brutus, or Essex's followers with the conspirators in the play."

"Oh, well, it doesn't matter," Shakespeare said casually.

"Yes, it does matter, too," Rosaline said with spirit. "I won't have Dick Burbage reading my mind, or claiming to."

Shakespeare laughed.

"And I don't want his lordship affecting my work without my knowing it," she said soberly, just barely audibly.

Shakespeare did not laugh at that or at Rosaline's next remark.

"And I won't have my plays interpreted as political pieces. Politics is no fit subject for the arts. I even wrote *King John* without a single reference to the *Magna Carta*. No, I don't write political tracts." Again her voice trailed off; and Shakespeare, at the sound of the trumpets heralding the start of the play, hurried off.

When Rosaline scanned the audience again, Southampton and Lord Rutland were in their customary seats. She looked back quickly at the stage. No matter how she studied the effects of her lines and dramatic devices on the listeners, she could never resist watching for the appearance of the first actor at the beginning of a play. Once the gaily painted woodwork of the Globe was hidden by the motley dress of real people, it became part of the workaday world which men hated; it was dull and unbearable until the first player, dressed in the finery for which London actors were famous, strode across the empty stage and spoke his first thrilling lines.

At that moment, Rosaline was always part of the audience, as eager to be lifted out of herself as the most unhappy drudge in the pit. She understood that yearning for escape into a gloriously romantic world of fine clothes and lords and ladies. That was why she always wrote of the nobility, of kings and queens, of dukes, earls, and countesses. No commoner was ever so common but that he identified himself with royalty. But for a trick of fate, he would have been a duke. The life of the playhouse kings and queens was the fairyland of rich and poor alike, their refuge from London as it was. If commoners should appear upon the stage at all they must of necessity be clowns or drudges, for such were all *other* commoners except each one who knew in his heart that he was noble-born.

Rosaline's moment of transport was soon past, however, because the play of the day was the first part of *The Seven Deadly Sins,* an old morality which the actors had played all their lives. The company did not have a full manuscript or even actors' parts for it but relied on a single plot board for the prompter and the memory or improvisation of the players to carry the action through. The performance was listless and uninspired, a fill-in for Thursday, the regular day for bull-baiting and bear-baiting at Paris Garden and the Beargarden. Without Will Kempe, who had left the company and forfeited his share in the Globe within a month of its opening, the old play had no sparkle to it. Only the stinkards in the pit guffawed loudly at the obscenities and coarse jests of Tom Pope, who was known to accept favors from the queans in the goose roost in return for stimulating business for them by his suggestive performances on days such as this.

Rosaline looked once at Southampton; and then wondering whether she had come to see him or the play, which she had known would not be worth the trip across the Thames, she rose angrily, tucked the bundle of manuscript inside her cloak, and practically ran to the stairs. She caused a commotion in the balcony which drew indignant complaints from the pit and gave Tom Pope an opening for a highly scabrous monologue.

Outside she saw the sedan chair propped up in front of the nearest tavern, and after picking her way across the mud in Maiden Lane she rehired her porters, at double price, to carry her back to Paris Garden Stairs. She fully expected to have to pay four fares to get a wherry back across the river at that time of the afternoon; but when she opened the curtains of her chair at the top of the wharf, a waiting waterman called, "This way, my lady. We have room for one more."

She hurried down the stairs and allowed the waterman to help her to a seat in the sternsheets. When the waterman cast off and the rowers dipped their blades into the Thames, she looked up to meet the eyes of her fellow passengers facing aft—the Earls of Southampton and Rutland.

"The play was disappointing, wasn't it, my lady?" Southampton said, either not recognizing her or pretending not to recognize her in her mask and hood. "His lordship and I were just commenting on it when you led the way out of the Globe."

"Most tiresome," Rosaline said. "Then you saw me leave?"

"We were in the theater," Rutland said with a laugh. His meaning was clear enough.

"Thursday is always bad," Rosaline said, trying to keep her voice from throbbing with her heartbeat. "I should not have come."

"Nor we," Southampton said, "unless, of course, we hoped to see something besides the play."

He knew who she was. He had known all along; perhaps he had known who she was for several weeks. She said nothing.

"What we really regret," his lordship continued, "is missing the openings of *As You Like It* and *What You Will,* or *Twelfth Night,* as I believe it was later called. I understand they were brilliant comedies."

"Quite," Rosaline said.

"We heard of an especially fine performance by some unknown boy who played Celia and Maria only once each. As an habitue of the Globe would you perchance know anything about him?"

"Nothing, my lord," she said softly. She had played the parts only once, on the opening of each play; then Burbage had refused to let her take the risk again. She was worth much more to the Globe as a writer than as an actress.

"We were in Ireland at the time," his lordship continued. "We should like to locate the boy for some private readings. None of the actors seem to know anything of his whereabouts. We thought the patrons might."

"I can tell you nothing of the boy, my lord," Rosaline said. She certainly was not going to begin another clandestine affair with his lordship on his own terms.

"Perhaps it's just as well," Southampton said sadly, and then added, half-facetiously, for the benefit of the waterman, "Lord Rutland and I would be dangerous companions for the lad at the moment. We are in disgrace with the Queen and under constant surveillance by Her Majesty's and the Secretary's spies. Anyone not already established as a respectable citizen would be suspect if he so much as read for us, I'm afraid."

"Then surely you wouldn't want to put the boy in jeopardy," Rosaline said as the boat nosed into Blackfriars Stairs.

"No, my lady," Southampton said, as he helped her onto the pier. His pressure on her arm was all the physical contact he made. She encouraged no more. "We should not want the boy investigated as thoroughly as our acquaintances are being questioned right now. He might find it embarrassing."

"I'm sure he would," she said, and started to climb the hill at the lower end of Blackfriars Street.

After bowing their farewells, the two Earls ordered the waterman to row eastward to the Steelyard.

Rosaline wondered what his lordship would have done had she agreed to a "private reading." There had been a time when she trusted him implicitly. There had been a time when she would have gone to him recklessly, without a thought for Her Majesty's spies. But now a new tension was in the air. Essex was sure to make his bid for power soon. If his lordship rode to success with Essex, then would come the time for her to hold him to his promises. Aside from the danger of exposure, she could not afford to waste her hold on him in a cheap liaison while he was married, even though he was estranged from his wife. That would not be the intelligent thing to do.

And if Essex failed in his bid for power, however he made it, Rosaline wanted no record of conspiracy. She had powerful friends in the Earl and Countess of Derby; but she could hardly expect them to protect her if she were involved even remotely with persons accused of sedition. No, she must not see his lordship, not even to find out how sincerely he wished to protect her by staying away from her. She must plan for the future.

But her immediate planning was interrupted. At the Gatehouse she found the Derby caroche waiting for her. The coachman had a message from the Earl urging her to come to Stanley Palace at once. The Countess was desperately ill and kept calling for Rosaline.

17

THE LITTLE COUNTESS OF DERBY WAS ILL FOR OVER A YEAR: THE FULL period of her pregnancy and a few months afterwards. And Rosaline stayed with her at Stanley Palace the whole time, rarely going into the City and never once crossing the river. But for his confidence in her the Earl of Derby would have canceled his long-planned journey to Rome, which indeed he did postpone for three months, until it seemed that Betty was improving. Then he went to Italy but cut his visit short in order to be at home for the birth of the baby girl, whom they named Elizabeth after her unfortunate earlier sister.

During her entire illness Betty insisted that Rosaline stay as near her as possible. It seemed that she felt that in some mysterious way Rosaline, who had borne a healthy, happy, lovable little girl, would give her strength to do the same. After all Rosaline was her sister, a near blood relative. So Rosaline slept in her ladyship's magnificent bedroom, shared her food trays, rubbed her bed-cramped back, felt the first life when little Elizabeth kicked at the walls of the womb, and spent long hours just watching over her ladyship while she slept.

At last Rosaline had the leisure to take stock of herself. That she did, in the only way she knew how: by writing of herself playing many parts before many people in many situations. And instinctively looking at herself from the point of view of the audience, from a seat in a twelve-penny room at the Globe, she quite unconsciously cast herself as a man, since truly significant things happened only to men, or so the theater audience seemed to think. A woman could live and suffer and struggle and die, while men looked on and nodded sagely, agreeing that such was her lot but never seeming to care enough to bemoan her misery or applaud her bravery.

Kyd's play gave her the framework in which to delineate her character, but the Hamlet she created during those long months of tense inaction outgrew the revenge motif within the first few weeks. His indecision rising from his extreme sensitivity, made manifest the moment he said "A little more than kin, and less than kind," immediately set him off from all other men who had ever sought revenge. And from that point he reflected or was reflected in the many mysterious facets of Rosaline's own nature. He was playful, sometimes tragically so, and brutal, lovingly so to the ill-starred Ophelia, and generous and pitiful and arrogant and witty and wise and solicitous and exacting—everything a man could be, in a delicately balanced relation to every person he met, each in turn but a reflection of himself. He could say, "Man delights me not," and yet weep at "The imminent death of twenty thousand men/That for a fantasy and trick of fame/Go to their graves like beds."

Not until she had already woven the mousetrap play into the texture of *Hamlet* did she realize how heavily she was relying upon *Hamlet* itself to clarify her own role in the tragedy, or comedy, which was being acted during her brief moment on the stage. "All the world's a stage," his lordship had said, and she had given the line to the melancholy Jaques in *As You Like It*. Now she understood what it meant; she was making her entrances and exits, playing her many parts—in Stanley Palace, in the Blackfriars Gatehouse, in the Globe, at Titchfield and maybe one day at Whitehall —or in the Tower.

By Christmas Betty was well again, and her little Elizabeth was just as healthy and ravenous in her appetite as the infant Miranda had been. And the newest Lady Elizabeth Stanley was not one to scorn the most famous bosom in England. The hearty pull she exerted on her mother's breast was a sweeter compliment than any gallant had ever paid the Little Countess. The effect was little short of miraculous; and although Betty steadfastly refused to allow either Miranda or Ferdinand to be removed from the Derby household, it was quite apparent which child had finally succeeded in making a whole woman of her again.

When the Derbys went to court for the holiday season, Rosaline of course stayed behind at Stanley Palace to look after the children, who already had every sort of nurse and attendant that Betty considered even remotely helpful. Consequently, Rosaline was able to put the finishing touches on her latest tragedy for the Lord Chamberlain's Company. Then she shut herself away from the household for an afternoon and read *Hamlet* through from beginning to end at one sitting.

When she had finished, she sat perfectly quiet for nearly an hour, reviewing her play in its totality. She still was not sure of her future decisions, but she did know more about herself than she had ever known before. She wondered if other readers would feel the same, find themselves in *Hamlet,* perhaps reject suicide as he had done, or maybe put off their personal problems until it was too late. Of one thing Rosaline was sure: after she had written *Hamlet* and read it through, she herself would never be quite the same again.

She wrapped the manuscript and sent it by courier to William Johnson at the Mermaid Tavern, with a note instructing him to forward the bundle to William Shakespeare or Richard Burbage at the Globe if neither of the actors happened to drop into the Mermaid, as was their almost daily habit.

January passed, with Rosaline still in charge of the children. After Betty's recovery and the completion of *Hamlet,* she found herself with little to do. She listened to court gossip, usually passed on by the servants. She had made no especial attempt to keep up with the Earl of Southampton, but she did know that he had returned to Ireland with Lord Mountjoy the preceding spring, that he had left Ireland and gone to fight in the Low Countries during the summer, and that he had returned to London in October. Essex House had become a hotbed of malcontents of all sorts: political refugees, religious recusants, intellectual misfits, and some downright outlaws. Southampton presumably was a cut above most of Essex's current followers; but even he had lately become involved in street brawls, the most serious of which was his altercation with Lord Grey early in January. Swords were drawn in that fray, and one of Southampton's men lost a hand. Lord Grey reported to the Queen first and seemingly won her ear. At any rate his lordship was in disgrace with Her Majesty again, or so the backstairs gossip had it.

Rosaline, however, let Southampton drop from her thoughts

when she got the urgent note asking her to meet her actor friends at the Mermaid on Friday, February 6. From the tone of Burbage's brief summons she gathered that something was radically wrong with *Hamlet* or that such little changes as she usually made at Burbage's suggestion had to be made at once. Possibly the company was eager to produce the play immediately, maybe at court before the Lenten season began.

Again she arrived at the Mermaid first, well ahead of time. William Johnson was as solicitous of her welfare as ever, though he seemed to have given up hope that she would read for his customers again. He showed her to a private table, where it was safe for her to remove her mask, and brought her a bottle of very special canary wine which he said he had been saving for her.

Even sipping very slowly, she had almost finished her first glass of canary by the time Burbage and Shakespeare arrived. To her surprise, neither of them carried a bundle of manuscript, nor did Burbage seem to have his usual bundle of complaints. Instead he lifted her up from the bench and kissed her solemnly on both cheeks. Without speaking, he stepped aside and bowed while Shakespeare followed suit.

"What's all this about?" Rosaline asked, completely nonplussed by the courtly greeting she had received.

"*Hamlet*," they said in concert.

"*Hamlet?* What about *Hamlet?*" As though she did not know! She felt a warm glow of satisfaction rising in her blood.

"*Hamlet* is wonderful," Burbage said reverently.

"Well, I must say that sounds strange coming from you, who once threw my manuscripts on this very table and shouted, 'Rubbish!' "

"I've changed," Burbage admitted humbly. "No one who ever hears *Hamlet,* or reads it, aye, or plays it, will ever be quite the same again."

Rosaline was startled by Burbage's words, an exact expression of her own earlier thoughts. Her satisfaction at his compliment was mixed with the old annoyance at his uncanny ability to read her mind. She looked to William Shakespeare for confirmation of Burbage's opinion. Too frequently Burbage's compliments concealed barbs, just as his sneers often masked a measure of grudging admiration. Shakespeare nodded soberly. Burbage meant what he said.

"What do you want changed?" Rosaline asked, sitting down again and motioning for the men to do likewise. "Surely something is wrong."

"Nothing," Burbage said. "Not a thing. I hardly see how you could add or take away, or even transpose a single line and make any improvement on *Hamlet* as it stands."

"It can't be that good."

"Well—of course we haven't staged the play yet." Burbage sounded more natural when he started hedging. "There may be something that will have to be altered slightly. But I can play Hamlet myself, just as I see him now."

"Good. I'm glad to hear that," Rosaline said. "But why your urgent message? Surely you didn't call me down here just to compliment my play—or to kiss me. Neither of you ever seemed to care before." She played a coy scene broadly, in the manner of Sam Gilburne, a boy "actress" apprenticed to Augustine Phillips.

Both men laughed at her mimicry.

"Sammy's doing better now," Shakespeare said. "He may learn to portray women very well about the time his voice begins to change." He chuckled again.

"Nothing like you, though," Burbage said. "By the way, we need a competent boy quick. Do you know where we might find one?" His meaning was clear. Now she knew why he had called on her.

"Perhaps," she said cautiously. "For what part?" She had not written Ophelia or Gertrude for herself. In fact she had written no part for herself, unless it was Hamlet, and there was not the remotest possibility that Burbage wanted a boy to play Hamlet.

"The queen in *Richard II*," Burbage said.

"That old play? You haven't played it for years," Rosaline said, frowning.

"That's why we need you. None of the boys know the play and no one of them has time to memorize the queen's part. Do you remember the role?"

"Why, yes—I think so. A few hours with the manuscript and I think I could play it. But why the hurry?"

"We have a special request for a revival of the play. Some gentlemen are paying forty shillings over and above our regular receipts."

"When?"

"Tomorrow afternoon."

[214]

"Tomorrow afternoon?" Rosaline's eyes opened wide in disbelief. "Why, that's impossible."

"We'll walk through the play in the morning. The rest of the cast are studying their heads off. You can read the part overnight." He produced a small actor's roll from the sleeve of his coat. "There's not much to it."

"Who are these gentlemen so eager to see the play on short notice?" Rosaline took the scroll and began to unroll it. It consisted of the queen's lines pasted together to form one continued strip of paper.

"Let me see," Burbage said. "They were Sir Charles Percy and Sir Joscelyn Percy and Lord Monteagle and two or three others. They're responsible men; they'll pay the extra shillings."

"Wasn't this one of Lord Essex's favorite plays?" Rosaline asked, looking up from the manuscript. "It seems to me that Lord Derby told me it was brought into the commission hearing last year when Lord Essex was placed under house arrest."

"I don't know," Burbage said.

"What about the deposition scene?" Rosaline asked. "Remember? We had to cut out nearly two hundred lines in Act IV when we gave the play at court."

"We'll play it all," Burbage said. "The gentlemen insisted upon it."

"Yes. I'm sure they did." Rosaline had recognized all the men as followers of Lord Essex. "I think perhaps they are more interested in the abdication scene than any other part of the play. Do you think it's wise to oblige the gentlemen?"

"Why not? It's true that Lord Essex's followers claim that Her Majesty is influenced by evil advisors, just as Richard was, but we've given the play before in its entirety. I don't see why we can't do it again, so long as it's in a public house and not at court."

"What do you think, Will?" Rosaline addressed her question to Shakespeare. "In my place would you play the queen?"

"I don't know," he said. Rosaline was immediately sorry that she had asked him to make her decision for her. "You'll be so heavily made up that no one would recognize you. And if there should be trouble, the entire company would swear that you had no part in the play, I'm sure of that. Sammy would admit playing the queen."

"Do they need the money?" She was still looking to Shakespeare for her answers.

"Some of them—yes." He hesitated. "Especially the hired men. We played at court only twice during the Christmas season, and Her Majesty was somewhat niggardly both times. And the weather has been bad for the Globe this winter—"

"I'll play," Rosaline said, turning resolutely to face Burbage. "What time is the walk-through reading in the morning?"

"Nine o'clock."

"I'll be there. See that I have my private dressing room." She rose to leave. She had a part to memorize.

"Certainly, Your Majesty." Burbage bowed her out.

18

ROSALINE HAD KNOWN FROM THE BEGINNING THAT THE REVIVAL OF *Richard II* was more than a nobleman's caprice. From the moment she stepped onto the stage and said, *"How fares our noble uncle Lancaster?"* she had felt the tension in the audience. And since she had had no more lines or business in her first scene, she had surreptitiously taken stock of the patrons.

The Globe was full, an exceptionally large crowd even for Saturday afternoon. But it had been augmented mostly by noblemen. She had recognized Sir Gelly Meyrick, Lord Monteagle, and Sir Christopher Blount, each in a different part of the house with what amounted to a noble claque seated around him. There had been others, too, of equal stature but strangers to her. It had been with relief that she had not found the Earl of Southampton in the audience.

As she sat nervously in the library at Stanley Palace that Sunday morning, she relived the anxiety with which she had awaited the fateful scene in Act IV, the tense expectancy which she had shared with half the audience. She heard again the deliberate applause of the noblemen when Bolingbroke commanded:

"Fetch hither Richard, that in common view
He may surrender. So we shall proceed
Without suspicion."

And she remembered the skill with which the claques seated
about the Globe had kept up their infectious applause until the
groundlings and stinkards and Winchester Geese and students and
apprentices all seemed to rise in a tremendous spontaneous ova-
tion at Richard's ultimate deposition. The effect had been sickening then; it was still sickening. The audience did not know what
it was doing. The common people had been innocently applauding
a scene in an old history play. But their actions might well have
been construed as wide popular endorsement of Lord Essex's plot
to seize the reins of government, a plot which at that moment—
on that Sunday morning in February—was in full swing.

"You do still love him, don't you, Rosaline darling?" Betty
asked. She seemed as tense as Rosaline herself as the two sisters
sat in a window seat in the library and looked out into the courtyard of Stanley Palace.

"Of course I still love him," Rosaline replied. That was the
answer Betty expected of her. She would not disappoint her audience. "I don't know how deeply, or how mistakenly, but I do
know at this moment that I don't want him to be killed. I couldn't
bear that."

Rosaline rose and walked the length of the library and back to
the window.

"I've hated him," she continued. "I've been vexed with him,
I've even pitied him, I think. I don't know. I may hate him now.
But I don't want him to die. After a woman has borne a man's
child, I don't think she could ever want him to die. It's like losing
a part of herself."

"Yes," Betty said, nodding. "When I've been most terribly angry
with William I've never wished him dead. But do you actually
want him back with you? That's different from just wanting him
not to die."

Rosaline stopped her pacing and looked appreciatively at Betty.
In her pleasure at Betty's saying something cogent, even a little
complicated, she almost forgot her own troubles for a moment. It
was good to have a rational sister.

"Honestly, I don't know, Betty," she said at last.. "I would love to be in his arms right now if he were as he used to be—or maybe as I used to think he was. I don't know how much I was in love with him or how much I loved my idea of him, which might have been as much my own creation as Hamlet is."

She turned and walked away again.

"But you aren't through with him," Betty said.

"No, I'm not through with him," Rosaline said, but she was not sure herself what she meant.

"Here's another courier," Betty said suddenly. "William's talking to him. We'll know more in a minute." She rose and joined Rosaline and both of them stood with their hands on a table, as though they might need support, and stared at the door into the hall.

Presently the Earl of Derby entered.

"What's the news?" Betty asked.

"The Lord Keeper, the Earl of Worcester, Lord Chief Justice Popham, Sir William Knollys—all of the Queen's deputation, in fact—are being held prisoner in Essex House," his lordship said. "Essex has gone into the City. He hopes to enlist the aid of the Lord Mayor and Sheriff and some of the militia trainbands."

"Will they join him?" Rosaline asked.

"I doubt it," his lordship said with a mirthless smile. "Cheering a popular hero and rising to aid him in rebellion are two quite different things. But Essex doesn't know that, or won't believe it. No, I doubt that he can raise five hundred men."

"Will he need more? This is Sunday and the Palace is lightly guarded, isn't it?"

"It was. If he had attacked at dawn he could have cut the Palace off with two hundred men. Now, I don't know. The Lord Admiral and Lord Grey have assembled three companies of foot and some sixty horse, and the Earl of Cumberland and the Bishop of London have raised some forces. I don't know how strong."

"Has there been any fighting so far?" Rosaline asked.

"No, and no further word of Southampton," his lordship said considerately. "He and Rutland and Bedford are with Essex, or were when he entered the City."

"Thank you, my lord," Rosaline said. She left the Earl and Countess in the library and went to her own suite. She tried to sleep, tried to read, tried to interest herself in the children, but all the time her mind was on the rebellion and her ears attuned for the arrival of another courier. She tried to find out which side she was on, whether or not she wanted Essex to win. His lordship had promised that once Essex was in power she would be acknowledged as the Countess of Southampton. She had believed him when he said it; that is, she had believed that he meant what he said. She still believed him, though she doubted that his plans could be carried out. She still considered Essex the chief obstacle to her happiness, and at the thought of him her old hatred began to gnaw.

Actually she wanted Essex to be defeated, to be killed if possible, though capture would mean certain execution for him and for his followers. "Aye, there's the rub," she found herself repeating. If Essex was unsuccessful, Southampton, too, would be beheaded. So she had to be on the side of Essex, her arch-enemy. She had to hope for his success and then deal with him when the time came. Once she had made her decision she went downstairs again.

Other couriers came and went throughout the afternoon. News came that Essex had given orders for the release of the Lord Chief Justice, and that Sir Ferdinando Gorges had altered the orders before transmitting them to Sir Gelly Meyrick, who had then released all the prisoners from Essex House and taken them to safety by boat. Essex and his party had returned to Essex House, found the Queen's deputation gone, and barricaded themselves for a fight to the death. Essex House was surrounded; the Earls of Cumberland and Lincoln, with Lords Burleigh and Grey and others, were leading forces from the landward. The Lord Admiral and Lords Cobham and Effingham were in command of the river forces, with Sir Robert Sidney and Sir Fulke Greville already inside the garden on the river side.

Rosaline wondered momentarily if Sir Fulke was seeking death and his dear "Philip" by going to the forefront of the siege. But she was tired and perhaps just a little hysterical, because she repeatedly found herself dramatizing the situation quite objectively and working out solutions which would be effective on the stage.

It was midnight before the final word came; and when it did come the courier was William Strachey, who, after a brief report to Lord Derby, sought out Rosaline. She admitted him to her upstairs sitting room and ordered supper and ale. His clothes were awry, his boots muddy, his face smudged, and his blond hair frightfully disheveled. From his downcast expression, she expected to hear the worst.

"Sit here, Mr. Strachey," she said, leading him to the most comfortable chair in the room. "Your story can wait until you have refreshed yourself."

"You are too considerate, Madame Rose," he said gratefully, "but I know how anxious you must be to hear how his lordship acquitted himself."

Rosaline cleared off a deal table and set it before his chair. Then she brought a sewing stool and sat down across the table from him.

"Then you must eat while we talk," she said when she was finally settled.

A serving woman brought a whole roast capon, still warm, and a loaf of bread and a pitcher of ale. William Strachey tucked a napkin in his ruff and tore a leg off the roast fowl.

"Where shall I begin?" he asked. "How much do you know already?"

"The last I heard was that Essex House was surrounded. That was about dark."

"Well," he began after getting control of his first bite of capon, "Sir Thomas Cecil, the young Lord Burleigh, was the first to enter the courtyard. His men broke open the gate and stormed the barricade. Two of his men were killed—the only casualties suffered by the Queen's forces, I believe."

"Where were you?" Rosaline asked, when he paused to drink from his tankard. "In Essex House?"

"No," he said, wiping his lips. "I would not be here now if I had been. Lord Essex had far more men outside than inside Essex House. I was in a steeple of St. Clement Danes Church across the Strand. I could see little through the smoke of the torches, but I heard much, especially after the Lord Admiral sent Sir Robert Sidney to call for surrender.

"At the trumpet call, everything became as still as death; so I could hear clearly from my perch. His lordship answered for Lord Essex. 'To whom shall we surrender?' he asked. 'Our adversaries? To do so would be to run headlong to ruin.' He was marvelously defiant."

Strachey looked up from his meal and his eyes glowed with pride. Rosaline found herself wondering if he were sincere in his devotion to Southampton, or if his admiration might be feigned for her benefit. She had no cause to doubt his loyalty, except that she was consciously planning to behave as he expected—to please her audience, she admitted somewhat guiltily to herself.

"Before Sir Robert could answer, his lordship went on, 'To the Queen? To confess guilt? If the Lord Admiral will give us hostages for our security, we will appear before the Queen. If not, we are every one of us fully resolved to lose our lives fighting.' He was magnificent!"

"Was he successful?" Rosaline had not intended to sound cynical, but she felt almost as though she had said "dramatically effective."

"The Lord Admiral refused to grant hostages, if that's what you mean, Madame Rose."

"That's what I mean." She had almost got out of character, become too objective for an anxious wife.

"The Lord Admiral did agree to a truce to let the ladies leave Essex House," William Strachey continued. "And he agreed to his lordship's request that Lord Essex's forces be allowed an hour's time to refortify the house after the ladies had departed."

"What ladies?" Rosaline asked.

"Lady Essex, Lady Penelope Rich, and some of their women. The Countess of Southampton is at Itchell, and has been for some time, Madame Rose."

"Thank you, Mr. Strachey," Rosaline said. Strachey seemed happy to report that the Earl and the Countess were still not living together.

"That was about nine o'clock," Strachey said. "For the next hour the Queen's forces kept bringing up ordnance from the Tower—cannon and a great store of powder and shot. To us outside it became apparent that the men in Essex House faced certain slaughter if the besieging forces brought their full strength to bear upon them."

William Strachey paused long enough to sever the other leg from the capon. He dipped it into a bowl of tart sauce and bit into the dripping flesh.

"We could harry the attackers for a time from our places of vantage," he continued a moment later, "but we could not have prevented their destroying Essex House and everyone in it. And certainly there were wiser heads inside; so a little before ten o'clock my Lord of Southampton and Lord Essex appeared on the leads and stated new terms of surrender.

"First, they wished to be used as honorable prisoners. Second, the Lord Admiral must report faithfully to Her Majesty what they should say for themselves in their own defense. And third, they must be allowed to have divines to instruct them in religion during the time of their imprisonment."

"That sounds ominous," Rosaline said, of the last condition.

"The leaders knew that they faced almost certain execution, Madame Rose. Surrender could only postpone their death. They made the offer to protect their followers."

"And were the terms accepted?" Rosaline asked. She still did not know the fate of his lordship.

"Yes, Madame Rose. The Earl of Essex further requested that his punishment be made severe and that of the others diminished. Then about ten o'clock he surrendered his sword to the Lord Admiral."

"And his lordship?"

"He, too." Strachey seemed to lose his appetite. Famished, he had eaten ravenously during his account of the siege, but the denouement made food distasteful.

"Where is he?" Rosaline asked.

"At Lambeth Palace. It was too dark for the Lord Admiral to risk shooting the arches of London Bridge, and evidently he was afraid to take Lord Essex to the Tower by land. So his lordship and Lord Essex and several others were sent upstream to Lambeth Palace and left in the charge of the Archbishop. About another hundred nobles have been dispersed to the various prisons about the city or placed under house arrest and quartered with men known to be loyal to the Queen—and to the Secretary."

"What will happen to them, Mr. Strachey?"

"They will be tried."

"And then?"

"We can't wait till then," he said, lifting the table to one side and rising to his feet. "We must begin now to try to save his lordship's life."

"We?" Rosaline asked. "What possibly can I do?" She too rose and followed William Strachey as he strode across her sitting room.

"His lordship will be tried by a jury of peers." He stopped pacing and turned to face Rosaline. "We must use whatever influence we can to get as many of those peers as we can to recommend clemency. Sir William Harvey is already riding into the counties to enlist whatever aid he can. The Countess, his lordship's mother, is rushing letters to all her friends and family connections. You, Madame Rose, can influence at least two Earls."

"I? Two Earls?"

"Of Derby and of Oxford."

"Why the Earl of Oxford?" Rosaline asked abruptly, stiffening at his words.

William Strachey blushed red and sputtered incoherently. She had caught him off his guard.

"Why the Earl of Oxford, Mr. Strachey?" she repeated.

"Through her ladyship, the Countess of Derby," he explained lamely. He was far from convincing.

"No, Mr. Strachey. That was not your reason for saying that I could influence Lord Oxford's stand. Why did you say it?" She pressed him as urgently as Richard Burbage had been wont to press her. Perhaps she had learned a lot from Burbage.

"He is very solicitous of your welfare, Madame, very fond of you, I think. He—he may even love you."

"Love me?" Rosaline was raising her voice. "I've seen him once in my life."

"Lord Oxford wouldn't be the first man to fall in love with you at first sight, Madame Rose; or the last, I'll wager." William Strachey was recovering his aplomb.

"Why do you say that he has been solicitous of my welfare, Mr. Strachey."

"Because, Madame Rose, I have been in his employ for several years."

"I thought you were one of his lordship's secretaries—his Maritime Secretary, I think he called you."

"Yes, Madame. But my father used to be in service with Lord Oxford and I have long had the confidence of the de Veres. When you, Madame, declared your intention of marrying the Earl of Southampton, Lord Oxford sent for me and set me the task of looking after you, in case his lordship should value you too lightly."

"Then you know who I am," Rosaline said softly. A lot of things began to arrange themselves in her memory. It did seem that William Strachey had always been standing by.

[223]

"Yes, my lady," Strachey said.

"Well, don't call me 'my lady.' It might become a habit—a dangerous habit." She was unnecessarily severe, because she had not had time to become accustomed to the idea of Lord Oxford's concern for her. "Does his lordship know my real parentage?"

"No, Madame. And he never shall, if I must tell him and if you don't want him to know."

"I wonder," Rosaline said, studying Strachey's apparently open, honest face. "Just where do your loyalties lie, with my Lord of Oxford or my Lord of Southampton? Suppose their interests clash?"

"Fortunately they have not clashed so far. If they ever do, I think my loyalty will be to you, Madame Rose, the better part of both their lordships."

His answer surprised Rosaline, not only by its boldness but by the distinct conviction of sincerity that it carried with it. His face was never more open, his eyes never more candid.

"I am not sure that I consider being spied upon as the essence of loyalty, Mr. Strachey," Rosaline said.

"I beg your forgiveness, Madame. I am no longer spying on you. I feel that you want to save his lordship from execution. I have broken faith with Lord Oxford because I believed it to be to your advantage. Believe me, Lord Oxford will welcome your calling on him for help."

"I don't like to call on him for anything," Rosaline said. She turned and walked away from Strachey.

"He is very well aware of that, Madame Rose. That is why he employed a spy to look after you rather than do it openly. He recognizes and respects your sense of independence. I am the one at fault, if your pride has been injured."

"Perhaps I'm not so capable after all," Rosaline said, keeping her back to Strachey. "You did get me away from Titchfield before I became involved in the Danvers affair. You were standing by in Plymouth when his lordship failed to return from Cadiz, you—"

"I was not inside Essex House tonight because you might have needed some help if the players from the Globe had been arrested today for the play they presented yesterday afternoon."

"That was part of the plot!" Rosaline said, turning to face Strachey again. "I knew it from the beginning. I felt it."

"Yes, and it isn't over yet. Somebody will be brought to task for that performance. Now that I've confessed to being a spy and no doubt destroyed my usefulness to your father, will you use all the influence you can in behalf of his lordship?"

"Indeed, I shall," Rosaline said. She found herself more than eager to please her audience. "Did you doubt for a moment that I would stand by him?"

"No, Madame."

"Thank you, Mr. Strachey, for your confidence. And you may be sure that I will not tell my father that you broke your trust. You may go right on spying on me." She managed a confidential smile at William Strachey.

"You've no idea how happy you are likely to make my Lord of Oxford," he said soberly. "If he thinks that you are coming to him of your own volition, I think it will lighten a burden that has lain on his heart for many years. I shall never tell him that I suggested your actions."

"Neither shall I," Rosaline said. Already she was planning her next performance. Obviously William Strachey was pleased. What kind of audience would the Earl of Oxford be?

19

AS ROSALINE ALIGHTED FROM THE DERBY CAROCHE, SHE REMEMBERED her first visit to Lord Oxford eight years before. Betty's six white horses were a far cry from the two hired nags which she and Will Johnson had ridden to Hackney.

She too had changed; how much not even she could have told. But she was dressed in her finest: a red satin farthingale with an overlay of sheer black lace, all exquisitely fitted to her still slender figure by the Countess's favorite dressmaker. She wore only pearls for ornament, and few of those, because her features required little embellishment to render them more striking than the doll-like faces of her English sisters. And her hat, a recent importation from

Italy, would have suited no other lady in the realm half so well.

All of this elegance had its effect upon her welcome, which, except for the Oxford butler's slightest show of surprise at her not being the Countess, was an impeccable compliment to a lady of quality. She was shown directly into the presence of the Earl. Her father was again in the library, but this time he rose and met her at the door.

"Come in, my dear," he said, recognizing her immediately, though he had seen her only that once, so far as she knew. "I was rather expecting you." He looked slighter, frailer, and a little greyer than she remembered him.

He bowed low over her hand and kissed her gloved fingers. The butler, properly impressed, took her cloak and withdrew discreetly.

"You expected me, my lord?" Rosaline asked as her father showed her to a farthingale chair near the fireplace. She wondered if William Strachey had made his routine report after promising her that he would not mention their conversation the night before.

"Yes." His lordship remained standing. His gentle hazel eyes roved over her person fondly. "After the battle you put up for young Southampton in the beginning I certainly didn't expect you to desert him in his time of trial, unless you have had a change of heart. Have you?"

"No, my lord," Rosaline said softly. She was acting already, and she knew it. "I have had no change of heart. I pray you, do what you can for him. I have no claim upon you, my lord. I make no threats, as I did last time. I merely beseech you."

"You *have* changed. No handsprings this time?" His lordship chuckled, and his tone was gently teasing.

"No, my lord." She had a vague feeling that he knew she was giving a performance, more studied in its way than her rash juvenile acrobatics had been. She smiled at him and repeated, "No handsprings, not when a life is at stake. This is serious."

"Yes, my dear," his lordship said, taking his eyes off her for the first time. "This is serious. How well I know! I sat on the special commission at the trial of Mary, Queen of Scots. And I sat in judgment on Phillip Howard, Earl of Arundel. Treason is serious business."

"But his lordship is not guilty of treason, my lord. Surely the worst charge against him would be misplaced affection—for Lord Essex." The name sounded bitter, tasted bitter.

"And you know about misplaced affection, Rosaline." His eyes held no censure when he settled his gaze upon her again. She hardly noticed that he had used her name.

"Yes." Her voice was low. It would have carried to the galleries, however. "If misplaced affection is a crime, then I too should be on trial."

"You are, my dear."

She looked up at her father, startled. He was not behaving as an audience should. He was participating in the scene, injecting lines not in the script. He was watching her, too.

"I'm going to take you to the trial with me, you and Betty. You will have a chance to see men, desperate men, fighting for their lives, men—or one man at least—whom you consider very dear to you."

"And I shall be on trial?"

"Yes. And you will be your own judge, to decide whether you are living or dramatizing that experience."

Rosaline felt her cheeks redden under her father's steady gaze. How did he know? Because he was her father? Because he had known her mother?

"But you will do what you can for his lordship?" she asked, sincerely she thought.

"According to the evidence. Peers of England have certain obligations in matters of this kind—"

"And of other kinds," Rosaline reminded him.

"Yes, and we find them onerous at times. I certainly do. And I am sure that young Southampton has spent more hours in anguish than you'll ever know. I understand his torment better than you do. Perhaps I even have more sympathy for him right now than you have, my dear. I was forced to give up your mother because I was an Earl with obligations. So is he."

"Perhaps." Rosaline was willing to follow her father's lead, at least a little way. "He always insisted that he was supporting Lord Essex because Essex, once in power, would make it possible for me to be recognized."

"Did you believe him?" Lord Oxford had taken a stand directly in front of her.

"Yes."

[227]

"Good. From the reports I get on him, I am inclined to believe that he meant all he said. I hope so. If the evidence points that way, we'll do all we can for him."

"Thank you, my lord." Rosaline rose to leave.

"I'm afraid I shall exact more than mere thanks for my favors."

"Anything you wish, my lord," Rosaline said, though she could not guess what he wanted.

"I have heard and read much of your work. I'm proud of you."

William Strachey was thorough, Rosaline admitted to herself. Obviously she had no secrets from her father.

"I wrote some plays long ago," his lordship said, getting her cloak for her and helping her into it. "Sponsored a company of players, in fact. I wonder if you would go over some of my old manuscripts with me." His lordship offered his arm to show her to the door. He probably read the surprise in her face.

"Yes, my lord, if you wish," she said.

"It seems that we Oxfords must employ you in some professional capacity in order to enjoy your company." He was talking easily as the two of them went out into the long hallway. "Betty considers you an invaluable Italian tutor. You've done wonders for your sister, Rosaline. Derby and I are grateful."

Rosaline could think of no comment that would be pertinent. It was hard to dramatize a situation of which her father was a part.

"I have no doubt that you will be an equally satisfactory play dresser," he went on, "equally good for me—if you'll accept a commission to collaborate with me on my plays."

Rosaline could hardly refuse. "I should like to collaborate with you, my lord," she said.

"Thank you, my dear," he said, as they reached the front door. "After the trial is over and things settle down, we shall try working together."

His voice ended on a wistful note. He said no more until he had helped her into the caroche. Then he studied her face for a long time, as though memorizing it, and said, "Goodbye, my dear. You are so like your mother."

He closed the door and stood by, watching, until the coachman drove away.

Rosaline settled back against the cushions with a feeling of annoyance. Not at her father's treatment of her; no one could have been more gracious. Indeed she was inclined to believe William Strachey's statement that the Earl was really fond of her, or at least solicitous of her welfare. But he annoyed her by raising some doubts as to the absolute perfidy of the Earl of Southampton, just when she had conditioned herself to look upon her husband as a weak, misguided youth willing to sacrifice her happiness and her daughter's legitimacy. That position afforded her a firm cynical basis, a point from which to view his lordship intelligently and to exploit his weakness as Essex had done. She recognized far back in her mind the idea that she was doing all this to get him into her debt for his very life.

And now her father had re-opened the possibility that Southampton had been suffering hours of anguish, roving the battle-fronts, living apart from his Countess, staying away from England, and finally joining in the desperate schemes of Essex and risking his life, all because of her. Such a hypothesis had as much surface validity as her own explanation of his lordship's behavior. It was disturbing, especially when she had to admit that she wanted with all her heart to believe in her father's estimate of Southampton. After all, Lord Oxford had lived through—or with—an analogous situation, with her mother. Perhaps he secretly admired Southampton for taking the risks which he himself had been unwilling to take in his own youth.

She hesitated to condemn a man without proof of his perfidy. She had already anticipated her problem in *Hamlet,* and she found herself no better equipped to deal with it than Hamlet had been. If she were only a little more reckless, or a little more gullible. But the curse of Hamlet was upon her.

The trial might well provide her with the proof which Hamlet had tried to find in his mousetrap play. The trial, the trial was the thing. Or was she already dramatizing it, as her father feared she would? It was a trial for treason against the Queen, not for infidelity to an acrobat.

20

WESTMINSTER HALL WAS DECKED OUT IN STATE FOR THE TRIAL OF the Earls of Essex and Southampton on Thursday, February 19. The trial area was arranged in a square, at the top of which was the Canopy of State over a stool to be occupied by Lord Treasurer Buckhurst, who was serving as the Lord High Steward of the trial. On two sides of the square were arranged elevated benches to accommodate the jury of peers, nine earls and sixteen barons. The seats were so placed that the lords could see all other participants in the trial as well as one another.

On the floor level, the Clerk of the Crown and his assistants sat in front of the Canopy of State; and judges from the King's Bench and Common Pleas took places below the jury benches so they might be ready to advise the lords on points of law. At the lower side of the square, the Queen's counsel, consisting of the Attorney-General, the Solicitor-General, the Recorder of London and half a dozen more solicitors and sergeants, completed the formidable array of notables which the indicted Earls had to face.

The lesser dignitaries were already in their places when Rosaline and the Countess of Derby were ushered to the seats reserved for them in the spectators' section of the hall. There were perhaps two hundred people outside the trial area, persons related to the defendants, as well as state representatives like M. de Boisisse, the French Ambassador. A third of the spectators were women, all masked for the occasion, as were Rosaline and Betty. The people were richly dressed, rivaling in color the flags of peers and the broadcloth and satin and painted canvas hangings bought especially for the occasion.

Shortly after Lord Oxford's daughters were seated, the jury filed in, led by the Earl of Oxford. When they were in their places, the Lord High Steward entered, preceded by seven sergeants-at-arms, who set down their maces and called three times for silence. Then the Lieutenant of the Tower was commanded to bring forth the prisoners.

Everyone in the room stood while the procession made its way to the trial area. Lord Thomas Howard, Constable of the Tower, came first. He was followed by Sir John Peyton, Lieutenant of the Tower, and the Gentleman Porter bearing the symbolic executioner's axe. Then came the two prisoners. Dressed in the height of fashion and but little depressed by their ten days of incarceration, they proceeded to their places behind the Queen's Counsel, where they kissed hands, embraced each other, and signaled that they were ready to trust in the Queen's justice. As soon as Lord Thomas Howard had completed his duties as Constable and joined the other jurors, the Lord High Steward sat down under the Canopy of State; and with a sibilant rustle of fine cloths and the soft scraping of shoes the audience took their seats.

The reading of the roll of peers proceeded without interruption down to the name of Lord Grey. At that point the Earl of Essex nudged Southampton and laughed derisively and then asked if the defendants had the right of challenge, a right allowed all commoners. He was not thinking of himself, he said, but of the Earl of Southampton, who had reason to distrust Lord Grey as his mortal enemy. Lord Essex was informed that peers of England were above challenge, and the reading of the roll continued. Next came the indictments, to which both Earls pleaded not guilty.

Rosaline could not help feeling that she could have done better than the principals in the trial were doing. Despite the elaborate setting, the illustrious names involved, and the high seriousness of the charges, the proceedings lacked drama. Richard Burbage would have been much more effective than was Attorney-General Coke in his longwinded preamble listing treasonable precedents: the riotous apprentices of 1595, Bradshaw and Burton in 1597, and so forth. His rhetoric was florid but stilted. Rosaline agreed with Essex's point that such a speech was slanderous sophistry, typical of orators in a corrupt state; but she was annoyed by Essex's delivery, which was so weak that the point was passed over as a mere quibble.

The presentation of evidence was equally dull. Lord Popham's account of the imprisonment of the Queen's deputation in Essex House and Raleigh's account of his meeting with Gorges on the Thames, both of which held great dramatic possibilities, were repeated with no more spirit than the reading of a recipe for bread pudding.

The Earl of Southampton began in the same vein. His description of the meetings at Drury House was dull, though Rosaline was stirred by the very sound of his voice. Perhaps his speech aroused so many memories that she paid little attention to his early statements. He did awaken her from her reverie, however, when he began his own questions.

"Mr. Attorney," he said, "what was planned at Drury House, though far from treason, was never carried out. What was carried out was never planned. It was entirely unpremeditated. I ask you,

[231]

sir, is a thing planned and not executed, or a spontaneous thing executed but not planned, treason?

"I knew nothing of my Lord of Essex's plans when I joined him this morning. I did not draw my sword all day—"

"But, my lord," Attorney-General Coke cut in, "you did have a pistol."

"Mr. Attorney," his lordship said impatiently, "it is the uncivillest thing in the world to interrupt a man who is speaking for his life!"

Rosaline felt like applauding his lordship's audacity, and indeed a ripple of assorted sounds of appreciation ran through the room.

"I took the pistol from a man in the street," his lordship continued, "to keep him from causing trouble. Then I found that the pistol had no flint; it would not have hurt a fly. Indeed, Mr. Attorney, I myself would not have hurt a fly. I was moved only by love for my Lord of Essex, not by any treasonable intentions."

Southampton at least gained favor in some quarters by his plea. Rosaline was left in her dilemma, however. She would almost have preferred that his lordship admit an attempt to seize power (that he might use it for her sake) than claim that he was moved solely by love of Essex. He could be a most exasperating person; in fact, he had been most exasperating. Yet he presented the noblest bearing in court that day.

The depositions of Sir Charles Danvers and Sir Christopher Blount and the Earl of Rutland and Lord Monteagle did nothing to raise those gentlemen in Rosaline's estimation. She was beginning to believe that the lords and ladies of her plays were far nobler creations than the real live lords and ladies of England. Her noble villains, especially as portrayed by Richard Burbage, were magnificent in their villainy. The conspirators against Caesar were cut from finer cloth than any of the squirming witnesses who had testified so far, either in person or by deposition. Not one of them could have held the Globe audience.

It was apparent, however, that none of the conspirators had ever considered harm to the person of the Queen. They felt, as did Essex, that Lord Cobham and Sir Walter Raleigh and Secretary Cecil were evil men, exerting a bad influence upon Her Majesty. The uprising had been against certain Privy Councillors, not against the Queen or the State of England. In establishing that point Essex quoted Sir Robert Cecil, the Queen's Secretary of

State, as saying that the Infanta of Spain had as good a claim to the Throne of England as any other.

There was a sudden commotion behind a painted arras on one side of the Canopy of State. A weak, delicate-looking little man, hunchbacked and splayfooted, shambled across a corner of the court area and knelt before the Lord High Steward.

"Uncle Robert!" Betty gasped under her breath.

Rosaline tensed at the name and stared at the repulsive little Secretary. For the first time she was looking at one of the hated Cecils in person. She was glad that he was so ugly, so horribly misshapen: it justified her long-festering hatred for him. She was gratified to find that he stooped to eavesdropping, like shameless old Polonius—no more honor than one of his hired spies.

"I am no swordsman," he whined at the Lord High Steward, "no earl, but I challenge his lordship's statement from my firm position in all conscience, all innocence, all truth, and all honesty. My Lord of Essex wrongs me. I have pleaded for him. I have taken him for the humble, noble, religious lord which he has heretofore pretended to be.

"Alas, I find him a wolf's head in a sheep's garment—an ambitious, aspiring traitor conniving against the State. I pray you, my Lord High Steward, as Master of this court, to give my challenge force, to require that my Lord of Essex prove the charge against me."

"What is the source of your information, my lord?" Lord Buckhurst addressed his question to the Earl of Essex.

"My Lord of Southampton heard the remark," Essex answered.

Rosaline resented Essex's forcing Southampton to take sides on the issue. She herself would have hated to side with either man. Essex or Cecil, what a loathsome choice either would have been!

"My Lord of Southampton, did you hear the remark?" Lord Buckhurst asked.

"I heard it repeated, my lord," Southampton said. If only he could convict both Cecil and Essex of treason, Rosaline mused hopefully.

"By whom, my lord?"

"I'd rather not say, my lord."

"My lord, your life, my Lord of Essex's life, and Mr. Secretary's integrity are all at stake. I feel that you must answer."

Essex and Southampton whispered together for a few seconds

[233]

and then Southampton named Sir William Knollys as his inform-
ant. Sir William was called in hastily and questioned. He denied
repeating any such remark, or even having heard anything of
similar nature. The whole thing finally came back to the seditious
book dedicated to Essex in 1595. Father Parsons, writing under
the name of Doleman, had discussed the Infanta's claim. Sir
Robert Cecil had commented, "Is it not strange impudence in
that Doleman to give equal right in the succession of the crown to
the Infanta of Spain as any other?"

Rosaline was disgusted with the proceedings. Her own title,
Much Ado About Nothing, would have been a highly apt description of the nonsense introduced so far. Her only satisfaction was
in seeing Essex confounded, but that satisfaction was marred by
the fact that the victory went to Cecil. She began to grow restless.
This trial for treason was pure farce. And there had been critics,
among the classicists, who had censured her for introducing comic
scenes into her tragedies!

Essex's elaborate scene of begging forgiveness from Cecil for
falsely accusing him went beyond farce: it approached nausea.
The Attorney did make sense in his two questions: Is it treason
to offer by force to remove a Privy Councillor, and is it treason
for a subject to try by force to make a passage to the presence of
a Prince? Getting an affirmative answer to each of those, both of
which the conspirators admitted as their aims, Attorney-General
Coke continued with points so silly and irrelevant that Rosaline
turned her attention to the variety and patterns of masks worn by
the ladies present.

Francis Bacon enlivened matters for a little while, and won
Rosaline's respect, by giving the only cogent review of the day, a
clearcut account of the charges, the evidence, and the arguments.
The fact that he used several phrases right out of Rosaline's poems
and plays perhaps aided him in both his achievements.

As soon as Bacon finished his summation, the prisoners withdrew and the peers retired to their compartment behind the
canopy. The Lord Chief Justices and the Lord Chief Baron went
in to the jury to advise on points of law. Then ale and biscuits
and tobacco were passed to all those present, both participants
and spectators. The hall hummed with subdued conversation,
though almost no one was willing to commit himself on the out-
come of the trial. Rosaline and Betty whispered a few half-believed

assurances. Rosaline's chief feeling was one of disappointment, at the general unimpressiveness of the nobility on parade, and the hollowness of all that pertained to the two on trial.

After half an hour the peers returned to their benches. The Sergeant-at-Arms began at once to question them for their decision.

"Whether is Robert, Earl of Essex, guilty of this treason whereupon he has been indicted, as you take it upon your honor, yes or no?" he asked first of Lord Thomas Howard, the junior peer.

Lord Howard bent forward, laying his left hand upon his right side, and said, "Guilty, my lord, of high treason, upon mine honor."

Little gasps escaped the womenfolk here and there about the hall at that first expression of judgment, which was followed in turn by a unanimous verdict of "guilty" as the Sergeant-at-Arms questioned each lord in ascending order, to Lord Oxford himself.

The Sergeant-at-Arms began again, "Whether Henry, Earl of Southampton...." Again the verdict was unanimous: Guilty.

Betty sobbed quietly and clasped her hand over Rosaline's gloved fingers. Rosaline made no sound at all. She was not deeply moved, not even bitter that her father and Lord Derby had concurred in the decision after both had promised to help Southampton. She had already learned to distrust the word of a peer. The whole trial was too sorry a performance to be taken seriously. Surely no man was ever really put to death by so unsatisfactory a procedure.

The prisoners were brought in again, with the same stately pomp shown in their first procession to the trial area. They remained standing, with the Lieutenant of the Tower and the Gentleman Porter beside them.

The Clerk spoke first to the Earl of Essex.

"What do you have to say for yourself, my lord, that you should not have judgment of death?"

"For myself nothing," Essex said. "But I urge the jury of peers to intercede for my Lord of Southampton, who, as he says, is guilty of no crime but loyalty to a beloved friend."

"And you, my Lord of Southampton," the Clerk continued, "what do you have to say for yourself that you should not have judgment of death?"

"My Lord Admiral, my Lord High Steward, I do plead for my life. I pray you to intercede for me to Her Majesty. Since I am found guilty of treason by law, and by judgment of my peers, I submit myself to death, yet not despairing of Her Majesty's mercy, which if she please to extend it, I will with all humility receive."

The Clerk, after noting Southampton's answer, turned the prisoners over to the Lord High Steward. Lord Buckhurst reread the indictment and the plea of not guilty. Then he addressed the two Earls directly.

"Robert, Earl of Essex, and Henry, Earl of Southampton, you have been found guilty upon God and your peers. Since there is no sufficient reason against punishment, you shall be led back whence you came, remain there during Her Majesty's pleasure; then drawn on a hurdle through the city to the place of execution; there hanged by the neck, taken down alive, your bowels taken out before your eyes, your bodies quartered, your heads and quarters to be disposed of at Her Majesty's pleasure. May God have mercy on your souls."

"How horrible!" Betty said with a shudder.

Rosaline sat perfectly still. The simple, direct, medieval phraseology of the sentence had brought the full force of the trial home to her. What had been hidden in pompous verbiage became a clearcut image, the image of a naked, bleeding body, disemboweled and quartered, to be disposed of at Her Majesty's pleasure! His lordship's body, the white and gold body which had been the temple of her pleasure. *Pleasure* was the discordant word. *Pleasure,* indeed! Rosaline felt faint for the first time in her life.

21

"AND THAT, MY DEAR, IS WHY WILL DERBY AND I HAD TO VOTE 'guilty' on both men." The Earl of Oxford leaned against the mantel and held his side as he looked down at Rosaline, seated on a farthingale chair in front of the fire. "Robert Cecil and the Earl of Nottingham, the Lord Admiral, are the most powerful men at court. They control all monopolies and land rates on which the peers are dependent for their income."

Rosaline sat staring into the fire. She had not yet removed her gloves or her hat. She was haunted by the brutal words of the sentence and the image they evoked. She had sat just as still in the coach all the way out to Hackney after her father had insisted that she come home with him so that he might explain his and Lord Derby's seeming defection.

"Had we voted contrary to the other peers," he went on, "we would have become immediately suspect ourselves and been placed under close surveillance by Cecil's spies. Then we could have done nothing further to aid young Southampton. Essex *was* guilty. Had his coup succeeded, heads would be rolling now in the palace gardens."

"I hold no brief for Lord Essex," Rosaline said in a monotone. She held no image of his quartered body either, though such an image would not have disturbed her. It was not that she was squeamish in such matters; she had seen executions at Tyburn, traitors' heads stuck on pikestaffs above the Surrey gate of London Bridge, pirates drowned as the tide came in over their staked-down bodies at Execution Dock below Wapping Old Stairs in Limehouse. But Hal—

"I'm inclined to believe Southampton's plea," her father continued. "I doubt that he was consciously guilty of treason. Let's see, how old is he? You're twenty-six, aren't you?"

"Yes. His lordship was twenty-seven last October."

"He's old enough to know better," Lord Oxford said. "But I doubt that he does. He's never seemed very mature to me. Anyway, we'll do all we can for him. Nothing short of Her Majesty's intervention can save Essex. But Essex is the one they're after. Once he's out of the way, the Cecil faction may be more inclined toward clemency. Every man they kill makes a few more enemies for them."

"But what *can* we do, my lord?" Rosaline looked up at her father for the first time. "The sentence has been pronounced." She shuddered.

"It won't be carried out, not literally." His lordship smiled reassuringly at Rosaline. "Essex will simply be beheaded—the rest of the charge will never be applied to him. We shall try to gain sympathy for Southampton, young Rutland, and some of the others who are little more than misguided youths. We'll have to find out from them the most likely quarters where such sympathy

[237]

may be roused. Lady Southampton has many friends. And we ourselves are not without friends," he said, with another smile. "I'm not very active any more, but I can counsel. That's why I brought you here and asked Betty to move her household to Hackney tomorrow. My Countess Elizabeth and my children are in Bath for a while. We can all live here and work and plan together."

"That is most generous of you, my lord."

"Don't forget my fee. You must dress some plays for me in return." He sounded almost jocular.

"I won't forget, my lord. May I go to his lordship tomorrow?" Rosaline found it strange to ask anyone's permission to do anything.

"How will you manage it? I won't ask if you can manage. I'm sure you can, but how?" Oxford stood up straight, drew a deep, unsteady breath, and moved away from the mantel. It seemed that some sort of pain had passed.

"I don't know just now. But I'm sure a man I know can find a way."

"Who is the man?"

"William Strachey, a friend of mine and of his lordship, but not implicated so far, as I understand."

"William Strachey?" If Lord Oxford felt any surprise at hearing the name of his spy, he concealed it perfectly. "My dear, I certainly can't prevent you from trying to see Southampton. If I could, I wouldn't. Long ago I forfeited my right to direct your life, but do you love him enough to take the risks?"

"I don't know, my lord," Rosaline said, rising. "I must take the risks to find out. Good night, my lord."

"Good night, my dear. There's a maid outside waiting to show you to your room."

Rosaline turned back at the door and curtsied. He bowed formally, and followed her with his eyes until she went up the stairs.

The next morning Rosaline found William Strachey waiting for her when she came down to breakfast. His presence would have surprised her had she not already known his connection with her father.

"I learned that you were here, Madame Rose," he said, for the benefit of the Earl. "I came early to take you to his lordship, if you are free to go, and if my Lord of Oxford will permit it."

"I'm free to go, oh, yes, I'm free," she said, eagerly enough for Strachey, she hoped.

"And I have no authority over Lady Derby's governesses," Oxford said to keep up the rather involved deception which was no longer deceiving anyone.

"Let's go at once," Rosaline urged.

She called for a cloak and hurried out to the hired coach which Strachey had brought to Hackney. On the way into the City, she outlined her plan. They stopped at the Gatehouse for her to change into boy's clothes and to gather up a bundle of his lordship's linen which was still stored there. Then they went down to the Thames and took a boat downstream, under the bridge, to the Tower. Strachey readily gained admission to the Tower offices and finally to his lordship's apartment near the Queen's Gallery. Captain Harte, his lordship's keeper, proved to be a longtime friend of Strachey's. He admitted the "lad" to the inner chambers, and Strachey kept Captain Harte outside with him, most fortunately for Rosaline.

"The inside doors are not locked, lad," Captain Harte said genially. "Take his lordship's linen right in to him."

Southampton had not been expecting visitors so early in the morning. He had on a rumpled dressing gown, for the Tower was cold and damp despite its apparently comfortable furnishings, and his beard and hair were still uncombed. Remnants of his breakfast —cold beef and stale beer—lay scattered on his tray. Rosaline had never seen his Lordship in such unpleasant surroundings before.

But he had eyes only for her. Taking the bundle of linen from her and dumping it on the bed, he clasped her to him almost brutally.

"You've come," he whispered. "Of all the people in the world, I knew you would be the one."

He held her close for a full minute more before he freed her sufficiently for her to kiss him. Then he clung to her again, hungrily, desperately.

"You would not let me die without seeing you again," he said.

"I'm not letting you die," Rosaline said. "I've come to see what we can do to keep you alive. We haven't much time. What can we do? Do you have any plans?"

"Yes, it's you—you are the only one," he said. Rosaline feared that he was merely rambling, until he continued. "We have one slim chance—only one, and we need an absolutely trustworthy messenger.''

He released her and peered cautiously out the door. William Strachey still held Captain Harte in deep animated conversation. Southampton closed the door into the anteroom and removed a ring from his finger. He held the ring up before Rosaline's eyes.

''Her Majesty gave this ring to Robin many years ago,'' he said significantly. ''She told him to send it to her if he were ever in dire straits and she would grant him any favor he asked.''

''Who knows of the ring?''

''Many people. That's why I have it. Robin wore it in a little black bag on a chain around his neck until a few nights ago, before—well, until Saturday night. Then he burned all the secret papers and the bag and gave the ring to me. He was sure that he would be searched if we failed. He was.''

''But weren't you searched also?'' Rosaline could not help being skeptical. Besides, she had not come to the Tower to help the Earl of Essex.

''Yes. But no one, except the Queen and Lady Nottingham, knows what the ring looks like. So no one was suspicious of a ring that I was wearing right out in plain view.''

''I see,'' Rosaline said. It was the sort of situation she might have thought up for one of her plays.

''Robin is being watched every minute by Cecil's spies, and everyone who talks to him is being searched. But you—you, my darling, are our hope. Can you get this ring to Lady Nottingham?''

''Yes, I think so,'' Rosaline said. If she could not, Betty certainly could. ''But isn't she the Lord Admiral's wife, and isn't he—''

''Oh, that won't make any difference.'' His lordship was practically scoffing. ''She's very, very fond of Robin. I might even say she's in love with him. Anyway, this is our only chance. No one outside Her Majesty's immediate circle can get to her now, and Lady Nottingham is our only hope. Will you try?'' The pleading expression in his eyes was not pretty.

''Of course, I'll try, my lord. You know I'll try. I'll get the ring to Lady Nottingham.''

''Yes, I know you will. Dear competent, dependable Rose. Then Lady Nottingham—''

At the sudden quiet outside, marking the end of Captain Harte's conversation, Rosaline hastily kissed his lordship, gathered up an armful of soiled linen, and opened the door herself before the keeper became suspicious.

"I'll bring this back as soon as the laundress finishes it, my lord," she said, backing out of the door.

"If I still need it by then," his lordship said, more in self-pity than in grim facetiousness.

"You'll need it, my lord," she reassured him, and hurried past the keeper without a backward glance.

"Got everything, lad?" William Strachey asked.

"Yes, Mr. Strachey."

"Then we'll be going. Thank you, Captain Harte. Give my greetings to his lordship."

"That I will, Strachey. And I hope you may see him again, alive. The restrictions may be lifted after a few days."

"I hope so." Strachey, sensing Rosaline's impatience, fell into step beside her as she hurried down the corridor.

"We must get to Stanley Palace before her ladyship leaves for Hackney," she whispered. "Is the river quicker?"

"If we get a wherry with some extra rowers."

"Then do that," Rosaline urged.

They rushed through the formalities of being signed out of the Tower on the river side and hurried down to Tower Wharf, where they chartered a fast wherry. Rosaline had never seen the river so busy. It seemed that all the winter traffic had been held up for the thaw and then released at once, all going downstream. Strachey offered to pay the rowers for extra speed, however, and in time the wherry pulled up to Stanley Stairs.

Rosaline had forgotten that she was dressed as a boy, and was chagrined that she had to depend on Strachey to gain her admission into her own home. He took her in, past a startled butler, and then he and Betty did enough shuffling to make her be forgotten by the servants. Back in her own room, and in the process of changing into women's clothes, she ran through the story of the ring for Betty's benefit.

"Now, Betty," she asked, "can you go to Whitehall today, right now, and give the ring to Lady Nottingham? I'll see to moving the household to Hackney."

"Of course, Rosaline. It's only a little way. I'll call for my coach and have it ready by the time I'm dressed. I can be at court in an hour."

Rosaline helped Betty dress. Then she hurried her down to the coach and saw her off. She sighed as the coach drove away, but she knew only too well the delays still in store for Betty. His lordship had gone into detail about the maddening procedure of getting an audience with someone near the Queen at a time like this. Every woman related to any of the conspirators was probably trying to see Lady Nottingham that day. Still, Betty was Betty, and that was a comfort to Rosaline as she turned back into Stanley Palace to get the children ready for the move to Hackney.

Ferdinand was seven and a half years old then, Miranda a few months over three, and the little Lady Elizabeth just a year old. They all three considered Betty their mother, but since Betty obviously adored Rosaline, the children tolerated her and obeyed her in the absence of Lady Derby. There were two servants to each child, of course, but still it was Rosaline who got the children dressed and into the dogcart.

Lord Oxford met them out in the grounds and after a grand-fatherly welcome to the children he sent them with servants to the kennels and the foal barns while he reminded Rosaline that he had work for her.

"There is nothing we can do until we hear from Betty," he said, showing her into the now familiar library. "And it will do you no good to brood and fret. You might find it diverting to look over these old manuscripts of mine."

He pointed to two bundles lying on the large table. Dutifully, Rosaline picked up the nearest and glanced through the first few pages.

"They are not new plays by any means," Lord Oxford explained. "Or even original. Both, in fact, are based on Italian sources. The one you have there is an adaptation of *Giglietta di Nerbona* from Boccaccio's *Decameron Tales,* and the other owes a lot to Cinthio's *Epitia.*"

Rosaline knew both sources. The first was a story of the substitute mate. And she vaguely remembered an old play which had added the same sub-plot to the *Epitia.* Perhaps this was it. She wondered if it were true after all that Betty's mother had come to his lordship's bed pretending to be someone else. Certainly the plays had little to recommend them if there were not some personal association to heighten their appeal.

"I wrote them a long time ago," his lordship continued, "when my own troupe of actors was quite prominent, especially in the provinces. John Lyly was writing for me at the time. He never thought much of these plays but I believe he dressed one or two passages, maybe shook up a scene here and there. They're mostly mine, though. See what you think of them and what you think we can do with them."

"Indeed I will, my lord," she said. Already she saw much that could be done to the plays, though his lordship was by no means a rank amateur.* She sat down near the fire, with her back to the afternoon sunlight, and began to read critically. His lordship stole out of the room when she became absorbed in her work. He presumably had business with Ferdinand and Miranda.

It was dark before the Countess of Derby arrived at Hackney. The children had already been put to bed, and Rosaline and her father had supped and returned to the library to await her ladyship's arrival. His lordship had asked that the Countess be shown directly to the library when she came. He and Rosaline rose to greet her when they heard her carriage crunching along the graveled driveway.

Betty, looking more like a countess than usual, removed her hat and cloak and gloves and waited for the servants to leave before she spoke.

"I'm afraid I could do nothing for poor Robin," she said soberly, backing up to the fireplace and facing her father and sister.

"But Hal, what about Hal?" Rosaline asked.

"I'm coming to that."

*Lord Oxford's connection with Rosaline's plays has long fascinated and baffled "Shakespeare" scholars. The fact that Oxford was called "one of the best for comedy amongst us" by Francis Meres in 1598, the echoes of some of his known poetry in certain of Rosaline's plays, and the probability that Rosaline's manuscripts used for the 1623 Folio Edition were in the hands of Oxford's daughters, Betty and Susan (married to the Earl of Montgomery, to whom the Folio is dedicated) have led some serious researchers to advance the theory that Francis de Vere, 17th Earl of Oxford, actually wrote the plays. See Looney's *"Shakespeare" Identified* and the Ogburns' *This Star of England* for ingenious and voluminous developments of this hypothesis.

"Yes, let her tell it in an orderly fashion," the Earl said, only too well aware of Betty's tendency to ramble.

"I was admitted to Lady Nottingham's chamber after about a three hours' wait," Betty began, with every indication that she would stick to her story. "I asked for complete privacy. She dismissed her maids and I showed her the ring.

"She recognized it at once, but looked at me in surprise. 'But I understood that you had broken off with Lord Essex, Lady Elizabeth,' she said.

"I told her that I had indeed no interest in Robin except such as I would have in any man who was fighting for his life. I asked her if she knew of the Queen's pledge. She nodded her head, but squinted up her eyes and studied my face the way some little animal peers out of its hole at you."

Betty shrugged her shoulders as though a rigor of revulsion had shaken her body.

"Then I asked her to take the ring to the Queen and ask for Robin's and Hal's pardon. 'Young Southampton, too?' she asked. 'Yes,' I said, 'both of them.'

"She said, 'I shall have to confer with my husband, the Lord Admiral.' I nodded agreement to that, and we sat without speaking until she had sent for Lord Nottingham and he had come. Then he sent for Uncle Robert, and there we sat, all staring at the ring and at one another.

"I repeated my request, and Lady Nottingham assured the men that the ring was genuine and that Her Majesty had indeed promised Robin anything he wished should he send the ring to her.

"We stared at the ring for a minute or two more. Then Uncle Robert made the decision. 'Lady Nottingham,' he said, 'I must advise you to refrain from interfering with the course of events. Essex is guilty of treason against Her Majesty and against the state. We cannot allow justice to be thwarted by a mere sentimental whim.'

"Then the Lord Admiral spoke. 'My lady, I must forbid you to speak to the Queen in this matter, for our own sakes, yours and mine. Essex is our sworn enemy. Our lives are henceforth in danger so long as he lives. Essex must pay the penalty for his crime.'

"Uncle Robert spoke to me next; he was quite friendly. 'Who knows about this ring, Betty?' he asked.

[244]

"I'm afraid I left a rather bad impression with Uncle Robert. 'I and no one else,' I said, leaving him to wonder how the ring came into my possession. 'We are not going to let the Queen see the ring,' he said, freezing the kindness out of his face. 'Does it mean so very much to you, my dear?'

"I knew that nothing I could do would save Robin; so I said, 'I don't want to see men die. I've asked you to spare the lives of two. Obviously you will not spare Essex. You are all afraid of him.'

"They were, all three of them. I could tell. 'You are not going to show the ring to the Queen,' I said. 'And we are not going to give it back to you, either,' Uncle Robert said.

"Lady Nottingham laughed, a nasty little laugh, and said, 'Nor to you, either, Robert Cecil. I'm going to keep the ring myself.' She dropped it into her bosom and tossed her head triumphantly. 'I shall remember where it is, and so will you.'

"While they were glaring at each other, I said, 'I shall remember, too.' Then they all looked back at me. 'If you insist on killing Essex to save your own skins, you must promise me that you will all three intercede with Her Majesty on behalf of my Lord of Southampton. At least I can accomplish half of what I came for. I hope to be around court for a long time, and I have an excellent memory.' "

"You said that, Betty?" Rosaline asked.

"Indeed I did. I'm the Countess of Derby, daughter of the Seventeenth Earl of Oxford. I'm not to be intimidated by some upstart new-nobility or a base-born Secretary, even if he is my uncle."

"Bravo!" Lord Oxford said with a chuckle.

"Anyway it was Hal we were trying to save, wasn't it?" Betty asked. Rosaline never did know how seriously Betty felt about Essex. No one ever knew, probably not even Betty herself, or Essex.

"What did they say to that?" Lord Oxford asked.

"Nothing," Betty said. "But they nodded agreement. I'm positive that Hal has three petitioners close to the Queen. Uncle Robert knows that I'm half Cecil too. He wouldn't dare cross me except in the case of Essex, of whom he is in mortal fear."

"I hope you are right," Lord Oxford said.

"I do, too," Rosaline said. "And I'm so proud of you. I think you're wonderful."

[245]

Betty glowed under Rosaline's praise; and the two sisters, suddenly realizing that they were both exhausted, embraced each other and climbed the stairs arm in arm.

22

THE NEXT FEW WEEKS WERE UNEASY TIMES FOR THE HUNDREDS OF people trying by devious ways to secure pardon for the condemned men. Essex was beheaded on Ash Wednesday, February 24. Sir Gelly Meyrick was executed at Tyburn on March 13; and two days later Sir Christopher Blount and Sir Charles Danvers were beheaded in the Tower. There were no more deaths for a time, though the Earl of Southampton, Sir John Davies, Sir Edward Baynham, and John Littleton were officially listed as "condemned, awaiting execution."

Contrary to Captain Harte's predictions, discipline in the Tower became more stringent, probably because the Privy Council knew that Essex's ring had been smuggled out of one of the prisoners' quarters and they wanted to prevent any further complications. When Rosaline tried to see Southampton again, the keeper took the clean linen through the bars of the outer door and returned the soiled clothes the same way, without allowing Rosaline so much as a glimpse of the prisoner. She learned further that his lordship was allowed to see no one but his physician and his chaplain. He could not even receive letters.

So she had to postpone her carefully studied plan for renewing and re-examining her relations with his lordship in the light of reason. She continued to collaborate with her father on his two plays, though she was uninterested and did only indifferent work on the manuscripts. Instead she found her imagination playing most actively on his lordship; and in spite of her resolution to maintain a detached, intelligent attitude until she was sure of their love again, she could not help feeling fear for his life at first, then sympathy for him as a poor trapped youth, then pity and compassion for a man so completely cut off from all things dear to him, then—by that time she had all but forgotten the slights she had suffered and she looked forward only to the day when she could go to him and comfort him without a thought beyond joy in reunion.

In May the Earls of Rutland and Bedford, as well as a dozen lesser nobles, were let off with fines ranging from £30,000 downward. A month later the fines were reduced by a third, and it became apparent that the Privy Council was gradually adopting a policy of clemency. It was generally admitted that there would be no more executions; and after the death of John Littleton from natural causes, there was some hope that the rest of the condemned men might even be released to the house custody of various trusted noblemen.

The most fortunate development for Rosaline, however, was Captain Harte's request for a change of duty. Sir John Peyton, Lieutenant of the Tower, accepted the request and was empowered to find a suitable replacement. Being a longtime friend of the Dowager Countess of Southampton, Sir John appointed George Harvey, a distant relative of Sir William Harvey, his lordship's stepfather. With the news of the change in keepers came a resurgence of hope for Rosaline. Her fancy played even more freely during the latter part of June, while she was waiting word from William Strachey that plans for her visiting his lordship were complete.

The young Countess of Southampton was no longer a threat, Rosaline reasoned. As a cousin of Essex, she could have no standing at court; and now that Essex was dead his lordship owed no loyalty to the scheming woman who had trapped him into marriage. With the Essex clan in disgrace, and indeed in poverty since the confiscation of Lord Essex's estates, it would be politic for his lordship to sever all relations with the family of his former idol. Under such conditions, surely the Church and Her Majesty would be favorable to an annulment of the hasty marriage. Her Majesty might even advise it and insist upon the annulment as a condition of his lordship's return to court. So Rosaline reasoned, if such hopeful ruminations might be called reasoning.

When William Strachey finally came to Hackney to tell Rosaline that arrangements were complete, she was as eager to be on her way to the Tower as she had been to greet his lordship in the dear days before he had ever given her any cause to doubt his loyalty. Perhaps it was an unconscious realization, far back in her mind, that Essex was dead, that for the first time in many years she was to see Hal without fear of competition from his idol. Certainly Essex had always been the obstacle in her path. Now that he was gone, perhaps she could recapture his lordship's complete affection, as well as strengthen her own, which had probably suffered as much from jealousy of Essex as had Southampton's from divided loyalties.

When Rosaline was admitted to the Tower, his lordship had already been granted permission to walk in the yard, upon the recommendation of Dr. Paddy, but she found him in bed. She could not tell how ill he was, his principal trouble being a swelling in the knees which the doctor called "quartern ague." He seemed listless, and his color was bad.

"I've come to read for you, my lord," Rosaline said when George Harvey showed her into his lordship's quarters. Mere laundry delivery did not permit all the time she wanted; so William Strachey had secured permission for a page to read to his lordship, whose eyes suffered from his confinement.

"That's very good of you, lad," Southampton said. His voice was strange. Rosaline could not tell whether he was speaking for the benefit of the keeper or he had actually changed. He showed little enthusiasm at her visit.

"What would you like me to read first?" she asked.

"Anywhere you like," he said. "Master Ashton, my chaplain, has been reading Psalms."

"You mean you want me to read from the Bible?"

"Yes. It's there on the table."

"Very well," Rosaline said. She laid her own books on the table and picked up the Bible.

The keeper, probably having had enough of Master Ashton's reading, left the room immediately and went on beyond the anteroom, locking the door behind him and clumping down the long hall until the sound of his boots died away. Obviously he was well out of earshot.

"Do you still want me to read Psalms?" Rosaline asked eagerly.

"Yes."

"But, my lord—Hal, it is I, Rose."

"I know it." He made no attempt to rise.

"And you want me to read Psalms?"

"Yes. I have received much comfort from Master Ashton's reading. He was with Robin near the end. Robin forgave all his persecutors and made peace with God and man before his death. With Master Ashton's help I shall do the same."

"Have you talked to no one except Master Ashton?" Rosaline asked. She was beginning to see what a zealous divine could do to a person locked in solitary confinement for four months.

"Dr. Paddy and Mr. Harvey, my keeper."

"But, Hal, don't you want to know what's happening outside? Don't you even care about what happened to Lord Essex's ring?"

"Obviously you didn't deliver it," he said, turning his head to stare reproachfully at Rosaline. "But I forgive you, as Robin most certainly did before he died."

"Forgive me?" Rosaline could not hide her annoyance. "Your precious Robin's precious ring was delivered to Lady Nottingham within six hours after you gave it to me!"

"But Robin was executed. Surely Her Majesty—"

"Her Majesty never saw the ring. Lady Nottingham was not so fond of Lord Essex as you thought. She called in the Lord Admiral and Sir Robert Cecil, and the three of them decided to say nothing to Her Majesty."

His Lordship continued to stare at Rosaline. There was no bitterness in his expression. He seemed willing to forgive everybody concerned. His complete apathy was more disturbing to Rosaline than violent anger would have been. She wondered if Master Ashton were a hypnotist. Certainly Essex's mawkish published confession had sounded nothing like the Essex she had known.

"How does it happen that I was spared?" his lordship asked at last, almost as though he blamed someone for keeping him alive.

"Many of us who love you, my lord, have been using every means we know to influence Her Majesty and the Privy Council in your favor."

"And Master Ashton has prayed for me constantly, of course."

"So have we all, my lord. And we have resorted to other means as well. You have been spared. Now we must work for your complete pardon." She tried to sound brisk and optimistic, as though securing his pardon would pose no problem at all.

"Master Ashton, too, is urging his friends to intercede for me at court. The Bishop of London is a family friend, also. He was formerly the rector of St. Andrews in Holborn, which, as you know, is a living within the gift of my family. I feel sure these worthy men can secure the Queen's pardon when they make clear the full measure of my repentance."

"Just what do you mean by the Queen's pardon, my lord?" Rosaline asked, further disturbed by his obvious lack of enthusiasm even as he spoke.

"Her forgiveness. I must have her forgiveness before I die."

"Oh, fie," she said, drawing on Betty's vocabulary. "You aren't going to die. We aren't going to let you die."

"But I must be prepared," he said, smiling indulgently but weakly at Rosaline. "I must secure Her Majesty's forgiveness, certainly."

"Very well, if you must, you must. Now which of the Psalms shall I read?"

"The fifty-first."

Rosaline turned to the Psalm and read:

"Have mercy upon me, O God, according to thy loving kindness: according to the multitude of thy compassions put away mine iniquities.

Wash me thoroughly from mine iniquity and cleanse me from mine sins.

For I knew mine iniquities, and mine sin is ever before me.

Against thee, against thee only have I sinned, and done evil in thy sight, that thou mayest be just when thou speakest, and pure when thou judgest.

Behold, I was born in iniquity, and in sin hath my mother conceived me."

She stopped and studied his lordship's face through shrewd, narrow eyes.

"Do you hear this Psalm often, my lord?"

"Every day. It is one of our—of my favorites."

"*Ours*—meaning Master Ashton's," Rosaline said thoughtfully. "Surely then you would rather I left it to him to read to you. It is hardly the sort of thing a mistress reads to her lover."

His lordship was shocked; and slight though his reaction was, it gave Rosaline hope. At his frown, however, she returned hastily to her reading and finished the Psalm. She was sensitive to her audience's wishes, and satisfying them had long been her business. And she was not entirely without resources in the Psalms herself. She read next from the seventieth Psalm, hoping that it might instill the hope of immediate deliverance in his lordship's mind, anything to combat the feeling of resignation which possessed him.

"O God, haste thee to deliver me: make haste to help, O Lord.
Let them be confounded and put to shame that seek my soul: let them be turned backward and put to rebuke that desire mine hurt.
Let them be turned back for a reward of their shame which say, aha, aha.
But let all those that seek thee be joyful and glad in thee, and let all that love thy salvation say always, God be praised.
Now I am poor and needy: O God, make haste to me: thou art my helper and my deliverance: O Lord, make no tarrying."

Rosaline had lost none of her dramatic art during her recent inactivity. She was still in full command of her voice, mistress of the boldest inflections and subtlest nuances. Master Ashton would be hard driven henceforth to match her rendition of the Psalms; and given her choice of selections, she was perfectly willing to meet him on his own ground.

Before she left, Southampton was sitting up on the edge of his bed, listening intently, or at least watching the movement of her lips as though the words had taken on new meaning. He hardly noticed, or at least did not seem to resent, her slipping directly from the Psalms into some sonnets of her own which she had written to comfort him. Then, hearing the keeper's boots echoing in the hallway, she rose and crossed over to the bed. She clasped Hal to her—he seemed so thin, so much smaller—and kissed him lightly on his sallow cheeks. Before he could decide whether to clutch her to him or push her away, she was gone. She met George Harvey at the barred outer door and ran down the corridor like a schoolboy finished with his lessons.

William Strachey was waiting for her at Tower Wharf.

"How was his lordship?" he asked her as he helped her into a loading tiltboat.

[251]

"He looks ill, but I'm afraid his worst sickness doesn't show in his face."

William Strachey led her to a seat well aft, while the watermen waited to make up their load.

"And the condition is being aggravated, I believe," she went on. Recently she had been finding it easier and easier to talk to William Strachey. He came nearer than anyone else to knowing all her secrets and to sharing her attempts to help her husband.

"By what?"

"By Master Ashton," she said bitterly. "If he keeps his hold on his lordship he will surely force him to deny me as a partner in an unholy union. Another four months under that man's influence and his lordship will not be recognizable as the man we knew in Titchfield and Blackfriars. He'll be a psalm-singing Puritan as bigoted as—as Josiah Norton."

"Not his lordship!" Strachey objected.

"Yes, unless we—unless I can counteract Master Ashton's pious influence."

The tiltboat, all seats filled, creaked and groaned as the five rowers eased it away from the wharf and headed it toward midstream. The sun was low enough to shine under the canopy into Rosaline's eyes when the boat headed west again. She decided not to try to get back to Hackney that evening, but to spend the night at the Gatehouse.

"I have every confidence that you can do that," Strachey reassured her.

"You mean be an antidote to piety?" she asked with attempted gaiety. There was no reason for her to burden William Strachey with further troubles of her own.

"Yes, Madame Rose." Despite the crinkling at the corners of his eyes, he spoke soberly. "I assure you that I have never found anything unholy or impious in you. You are the best answer I know to the sanctimonious puritanism which Master Ashton mistakes for piety. I know him well."

"Thank you, Mr. Strachey," she said. She felt obligated to return his compliment. "How are Frances and little Will?" she asked. She had not thought of them for several months.

"Little Will has a little brother, Edmund," he said.

"Congratulations!" she said. "I didn't know. Frances must be delighted."

"Frances is dead, Madame Rose."

"No. Oh, William, how could I have been so negligent not to have asked sooner? When?"

"Two months ago. You've had your own worries."

"But I was fond of Frances. I shall never forget our voyage on the pinnace, from Plymouth to London."

"She was fond of you, too, Madame Rose. She considered you an excellent lady."

"Thank you. And the boys, where are they?"

"With their aunt at Crowhurst. In time they will enter the household of Sir Edmund Bowyer, Frances's half brother."

"Then they will have a good home."

"Yes, until I can provide them with another."

"What do you plan to do?"

"Stay in London until his lordship is released, then go to Virginia, if some of his former plans are ever worked out."

Virginia. His lordship's plans. If she could only get him to Virginia, away from his chaplain and his Countess and his memories of Essex. But she was only dreaming. And she was still dreaming when the tiltboat made its stop at Blackfriars Stairs.

Rosaline was perfectly capable of directing her thoughts, however, when the occasion demanded. She began her campaign against Master Ashton on her very next trip to the Tower. She introduced more secular reading and more gentle shocks to stir his lordship out of his lethargy; and she studied his moods carefully, fitting herself into them, no matter how morbid. When at last his lordship was prompted to write a sonnet, albeit a very dismal one about death:

Bare ruin'd choirs, where late the sweet birds sang,   (73)

she humored him by replying in kind, promising,

Your monument shall be my gentle verse,
Which eyes not yet created shall o'er-read;
And tongues to be your being shall rehearse,
When all the breathers of this world are dead;
   You still shall live (such virtue hath my pen)
   Where breath most breathes, even in the mouths of men.   (81)

[253]

As long as he took pleasure in self-pity and resignation, she fed him cues which allowed him to revel in his misery. Then as he brightened, helped by his walks through the narrow strip of sunlight in the Tower court, she brightened with him. She had him in very good spirits by the time his mother was permitted to see him about the middle of August. He was much improved by his mother's visit, in turn, and Rosaline kept him gaining steadily until Michaelmas.

Rosaline had won George Harvey's complete confidence by that time, and the keeper, thinking her a boy of course, let her spend as much time with his lordship as she liked. She had begun introducing erotic poetry into her reading and encouraging intimate contacts, so that by the time the anniversary of the *Ictis* came around she was ready to make her supreme bid against Master Ashton's pious endeavors. And she was successful.

On Michaelmas day she came late in the afternoon; and as soon as George Harvey left, she reminded his lordship of passages from *Love's Labor's Lost*. He readily remembered his lines, and they re-enacted their performance together. It was but a step farther to memories of the *Ictis*. Then Rosaline was in his arms, and for a time the apartment in the Tower held all the enchantment of the master's cabin of the *Ictis*. So long denied, their passion surged again. Hal seemed to be his carefree eager self, far from the physical wreck which Rosaline had started rebuilding some three months before.

She felt that she had scored on Master Ashton, until her return on his lordship's birthday. Then she was greeted by a sonnet on lust:

The expense of spirit in a waste of shame . . . (129)

"Oh, no, my lord!" she said, when she read it. "Surely you can't consider our love as lust." She thought she had brought him farther along than that.

He merely stared at her reproachfully, with the expression he had worn that first day, back in June.

"Has Master Ashton seen this?" she asked.

"Yes. He thinks it is quite good. He wants a copy of it."

"I'm sure that he does. Did you tell him why you wrote it?"

"No." His lordship looked away guiltily. "I was ashamed."

"You were ashamed!" she practically shouted. "Ashamed of our love, the finest, purest thing in either of our lives. Hal Wriothesley, you can be the most exasperating man in the world."

"I can, can't I?" he said sheepishly. For a moment there was a flash of his former self. "Oh, Rose, half the time I don't know what I am doing or what I think. Master Ashton is trying to help me. So are you. I'm sure of that. So are lots of people. I appreciate it all—but sometimes I don't understand it all. Can you be patient with me? As patient as Master Ashton?"

"Yes, yes—of course I can, darling," she said, and buried her face in his waistcoat. He no longer smelled of sickness. He had begun to smoke his pipe again. He smelled like her husband. "I can be patient. But don't ever refer to our love as lust again."

"Very well, darling," he said into her hair. "I've had news that Her Majesty is relenting. For a birthday message my mother wrote me that we can expect a surprise from the Queen within a few days. I'm sure it means more freedom of some kind or another. We can be together more."

Neither of them could have guessed that at that very moment a letter was being drafted by the Privy Council to "Mr. George Harvey, Esq., having charge of the prisoners in the Tower in the absence of Lieutenant," for delivery on October 11. It read:

> *Whereas Her Majesty is informed that the Earl of Southampton is of late grown very sickly, in the which respect Her Highness is pleased that for his comfort the Countess his wife shall be permitted to have access unto him; these are therefore accordingly to will and require you to suffer her at convenient times to repair unto him, for which these shall be your warrant.*

23

"IT WAS ALMOST AS THOUGH ROBIN WERE BACK, RIGHT HERE IN THE room with me," his lordship said. "I had forgotten how much Elizabeth favored him—the same hair, the same brow, the same eyes—mouth a little softer, but recognizable."

He spoke freely of his wife's visit to the Tower. His expression was one of joy, marred now and then by a momentary cloud of grief at some memory of his beloved Essex. Rosaline sat perfectly still with her book lying unopened in her lap. She watched the emotions play in his face. She winced at the most exuberant passages in his description of the Countess. She shrank before the task which had doubled or trebled now that the Countess had become a tangible adversary, perhaps even an ally of the pious Ashton.

"She was dressed in the height of fashion, she assured me. I had forgotten what a beautiful woman really looked like." He chuckled softly and let his eyes stare over Rosaline's shoulder as he remembered the vision.

"You mean with her clothes on," Rosaline reminded him somewhat tartly.

"What?" he asked, bringing his eyes to bear on her, but not quite focusing his attention.

"I said you mean that you've forgotten what a woman looks like with her clothes on. The Countess has me at a decided disadvantage as long as I have to masquerade as a page boy in order to visit you, my lord." She kept her voice steady. "I suppose she did keep her clothes on?"

"Yes," his lordship said soberly. "Yes, she was quite proper and formal. We have not been intimate for some time. I was not with her much before—before Robin's death."

"I know that, my lord," she said, relenting a little. It was true that he had seemed to avoid his Countess, to be trying to keep his vow with Rosaline, before the rebellion.

"She came in state, with a footman and a maidservant in attendance. Her visit was more like a duty call. I don't know whether she wanted to come or not. But she came—and it was like a breath of home." Southampton was chastened, his spirits damped. He rose and walked around the stool on which Rosaline sat.

Rosaline was sorry that she had punctured his bubble. Of course he missed life at court. Of course he missed the noble ladies with whom he had associated all his life. That was what he had meant by a breath of home. Rosaline represented something else.

"She'll come again," Rosaline said softly. Perhaps it would be better to finish the battle right in this prison cell than to risk a campaign in the open after his release, when all the splendor of the court would be arrayed on the side of the Countess. Here, in the Tower, it was only the Countess and Master Ashton—as though they were not enough!

"Yes," his lordship said. "Whether it's her idea or my mother's, she'll come again."

"And again. It's her idea, my lord. And she'll have her idea of what the Queen meant by granting her access to you for your comfort, too."

The Countess did come again, of course, and again. At first she came about once a month. Then, upon Master Ashton's advice, she began coming more often. Rosaline knew instinctively that the chaplain had urged her to make more frequent visits.

"You told Master Ashton about me, didn't you, Hal?" she asked on her next visit.

"Yes," he said. "Not that you are the little page who comes to read to me. But I told him about you and your baby and how it was outside."

Rosaline was aware that his lordship considered Miranda *her* baby. Indeed he had never seen the child.

"And he advised you to forget me and to renew your bonds with your church wife. Is that it?"

"Yes."

"Why did you do it?"

"The yearning for confession, I suppose. I—Rose, you've never been cooped up like this, all alone with just the shadows of the world coming through like—like Plato's cave."

"No."

"Things don't look the same in here. One loses perspective. My memory is not always clear or accurate."

"But you do remember that I love you, don't you? That I've given my life to you—that I run a terrible risk every time I come to see you? Is all that clear to you, Hal?"

"Yes. I remember that, especially when I'm with you. Yes, Rose, you are the realest thing of all."

Rosaline was convinced that she could hold her own so long as she was present in person. It was during her absence from the Tower that doubts arose. And she had to grant his honesty in writing down his thoughts during those periods, though she read his sonnets with sinking heart. She caught the first hint of her possible infidelity which Master Ashton had planted in his lordship's mind. She could readily appreciate the chaplain's inability to understand how a woman like her could be faithful. A woman who would exchange her virtue for a pagan love knot would sell it again for some other trifle.

Certainly the suspicion was there, tacked onto his lordship's testament of love for her which ended,

> *Thou mayst be false, and yet I know it not.* (92)

So she was the one to be suspected of being of "inconstant mind." He was the faithful lover. How clever of the pious Master Ashton to reverse the lovers' positions. How adroit he was at introducing doubt into his penitent's mind. Such were the insidious methods of Puritans. One day they would undermine every stable institution in England if they were not stopped—the Church, the State, everything. She, for one, would not give up without a struggle.

But she watched the suspicion grow in spite of all that she could do. On her visits she convinced Hal that she loved him. By her manner, her words, her wholehearted physical surrender to him when they had sufficient privacy in his bedchamber—by every means at her disposal she tried to convince him. Time and again she succeeded, only to be met in her next visit by some sonnet compounded of love and suspicion. One went too far in hinting at possible hypocrisy on her part:

> *So shall I live, supposing thou art true,*
> *Like a deceived husband . . .* (93)

She had to answer that one:

> *Canst thou, O cruel! say I love thee not,*
> *When I against myself with thee partake?* (149)

There were other poems, bitter ones, vituperative ones, penitent ones, sonnets of all kinds recording his lordship's struggle. She could tell every time that Master Ashton had counseled his lordship on the evils of the flesh. She could read the chaplain's admonitions concerning conjugal obligations. She knew when Master Ashton discovered that his lordship was trying to reach a decision on his wives before he was released from prison, and she could guess when the chaplain and the Countess began collaborating.

She knew, too, when his lordship first took his Countess to bed in the Tower. Even before he confessed to her, she drew the correct inference from his sonnet of remorse that began:

Love is my sin... (142)

"Whatever gave you the idea that I have profaned my lips or sealed false bonds of love, my lord?" she asked angrily, when she read it. "Whose bed have I robbed of its revenue?"

"I'm no fool, Rosaline," his lordship said defensively. "You are a beautiful woman, a maddening woman. Surely men are attracted to you. And you outside, free, alone."

"I see. Men are attracted to me. So I am false to you. What kind of reasoning is that?" She flared at him over the sheet of paper which she still held in her hand.

"I know how hard it is to resist temptation. I—"

"Elizabeth Vernon has at last decided to strip off her clothes and meet me on my own ground, has she?"

"She knows nothing about you," he said evasively.

"She must. She's no fool. She may not know that I have 'access to you for your comfort,' but she knows very well that I exist, waiting for you on the outside perhaps. I asked, has she?"

"Yes, Rosaline. I couldn't very well refuse—she's my wife."

"And you find it hard to resist temptation," Rosaline repeated his admission.

His lordship turned away from her, refused to meet her gaze or even defend himself.

"Perhaps I find it impossible to resist her. Still I love you, Rose. In spite of everything."

"In spite of what?" she asked, but she did not wait for an answer. She rushed out into the anteroom and called for the keeper to unlock the door.

"His lordship does not wish me to read to him today," she explained.

Back at Stanley Palace, she took time to re-read and reconsider the most recent sonnet and the half-dozen others in similar vein. Then she picked verses at random in her commonplace book. She tried to piece together a coherent picture of Hal's feeling for her. She tried to read continuous meaning into his poetry, to find the sequence of his thought, to establish some sort of permanent pattern in his nature. And as she began to evaluate his work, she found her annoyance receding. Once she had assumed a critical, objective attitude, she found that she was no longer seething inside. The process of analyzing his character calmed her.

In the intensity of her struggle to hold his lordship she had all but forgotten that she had fully intended to deal with him intelligently. But it all came back to her as she read, her promise to Sir William Harvey and William Strachey that night they had taken her to the cellar of the Steelyard—and her promises to herself. And here she was, following her feelings in all their vagaries, never once taking the intelligent view.

The Countess of Derby came up behind Rosaline sitting in the garden, her commonplace book open in her lap.

"Do you want to talk to me about it, Rosaline?" she asked.

"Oh, Betty. I thought you were still at court." Rosaline closed her book and made room for her sister to sit down beside her. Betty was dressed quite simply, without hoops.

"I came home last night," Betty said. "Do you want to talk?"

"About what?"

"About whatever is worrying you."

"Nothing is worrying me," Rosaline said, brightening consciously.

"Very well. I'm becoming a very sympathetic comforter. You might as well take advantage of it, if you ever are worried."

"Whom have you been comforting?"

"Her Majesty," Betty said. There was no boasting in her voice. "She has been unhappy ever since Robin was executed, a year and a half ago now. You know that she hasn't sat on the throne since his death."

"No, I didn't know that." Rosaline studied her little sister, the Queen's confidante. How far she had come!

"Well, she hasn't. She stumbled last October when she went to open Parliament. Her robes were too heavy for her. I think she considered it an omen. She hasn't been well since."

"She's an old woman," Rosaline said.

"But it's grieving over Robin that's killing her. That's why she likes to talk to me," Betty said with a mirthless little laugh. "It really isn't very flattering. She seeks out Robin's mistresses or suspected mistresses as her confidantes. I suppose she wants those who were most intimate with him to talk about their intimacies. There's a lot I don't understand about Her Majesty. But I don't mind. I feel so sorry for her. She's really pathetic."

"Do you think I'm pathetic, Betty?"

"Heavens no, Rosaline. I can't imagine your being pathetic. I can't imagine your not being equal to whatever you have to face. I just thought you might want to talk. We haven't talked in a long time. First you were busy with Father at Hackney. By the way, what about his plays?"

"Burbage has already produced both of them. *All's Well That Ends Well* and *Measure for Measure,* we called them. They were billed as Shakespeare's."

"How were they?"

"Not good—not bad. I'm not proud of them."

"Then you've been spending so much time with Hal, or worrying about him," Betty went on, her father's plays quickly forgotten. "I miss you, Rosaline. So does Father, I think. Why don't you go to see him occasionally?"

"I—I'm sure he doesn't miss me. It—it's so awkward. Maybe after Hal is free—I don't know." Rosaline's reluctance was apparent.

"Very well. You don't want to talk. Anyway the children need me. I've been at court for over a week." Betty hugged Rosaline around the shoulders and went off in the direction of the children's playground.

So Betty could not imagine her not being equal to whatever she had to face. Neither could she, Rosaline discovered, if she set her mind to it—not her heart, her mind. And now her mind was clear, at least on some things. She would not lose by default. Her own integrity, her daughter's legitimacy, and sheer stubborn pride demanded that she be acknowledged as the rightful Countess of Southampton. Aside from feelings, aside from love, pure rational intelligence required her to hold Southampton by whatever means she could employ.

She never crossed his lordship again, never chided him, never even mentioned his Countess. Instead she used every trick that she had ever learned in the theater, every line, every gesture which was supposed to betoken undying, unquestioning love. At first Southampton showed mild surprise, then masterful appreciation.

Then he composed a sonnet almost incoherent in its vituperative accusations:

In loving thee thou know'st I am forsworn . . . (152)

Still, he admitted that he loved her in spite of himself. He welcomed her eagerly each time she came to the Tower, and he vented his physical passion upon her hungrily, desperately, sometimes brutally, whenever he had the opportunity. Despite what he felt in her absence, what he wrote during his periods of remorse, Rosaline had a powerful hold on him.

But her victory was far from sweet. For the first time, she began to feel ashamed of her relations with his lordship. Everyone knew perfectly well that the Countess was granting him all wifely favors on her visits to the Tower, making the most of her "access to his lordship for his comfort." And since the practice was quite common among lords imprisoned in the Tower, the Countess's actions were above reproach. She was his wife. She was being dutiful. And she was providing the Tower staff with a very tantalizing vicarious romance, for Elizabeth Vernon, Countess of Southampton, was a beautiful woman; even Rosaline had to admit that.

So Rosaline found herself in the position of a servant girl carrying on a backstairs affair with the master of the house. And even though she was sure that his lordship preferred her to the Countess, she felt cheap and common because she had to allow him to make love to both of them. Still she could not give up her struggle, no matter how degrading it became. She had prior claim. She would hold onto it at any cost.

His lordship was struggling too. He was fighting an inner battle equal to her own. And he was suffering. The pain was apparent in his face. The strain was telling on his body and in his conversation and in what little poetry he wrote. But he deserved to suffer. Carrying on with two women! Too weak to deny either of them!

The strain began to tell on Rosaline too, and in her work. She moved to the Gatehouse to get away from Betty, whose worry over her manifested itself in annoying oversolicitousness and a constantly open invitation to talk over her troubles. Rosaline was not one to talk over her troubles; she preferred to write about them.

She deliberately began work on a play about Troilus and Cressida. She knew Boccaccio's *Filostrato* well, and Chaucer's *Troilus and Criseyde,* and various translations of the *Iliad.* The story had seemed to be always in the back of her mind, for she had made numerous references to it in her early plays. Now it seemed a perfect vehicle to carry her shame, to dramatize her degradation and his lordship's weakness and depravity, to expose and debase heroes like Achilles and Hector and Agamemnon and Essex—Essex always, whatever the hero's name—who brought corruption into the world and strumpeted good women like Cressida and Rosaline.

So between her visits to the Tower, Rosaline stayed at the Gatehouse and berated mankind in a reckless, strident diatribe. Forced to be loving and gentle during her hours with his lordship, she threw off all control when she returned to the Gatehouse. There she wrote with complete abandon the loudest, bitterest poetry of her career. She was the promiscuous Cressida, the obscene Pandarus, the harping Thersites, the ineffectual Cassandra all at once, screaming at the top of her voice, venting her rage on herself and on the world that forced her to be what she was.

Week after week she kept up the dual debasement of herself, meek and mild and forgiving in the Tower, loud and vulgar and vindictive in the Gatehouse. All through the fall and the holiday season she kept to herself, except for her visits to the Tower. And in her solitude she grew prouder and prouder of her success in both fields. She was sure that she had convinced the prisoner of the sincerity of her love in the face of his abuse. And she was equally sure that in cheapening and debasing Chaucer's Criseyde she had at last given to the world the true picture of strumpeted virtue.

Throughout it all she was scrupulously careful to show no feeling, no emotion, except complete adoration for his lordship. Even when he tried to test her, she divined the purpose of his excessive abuse and reacted as though he were caressing her. To his subtle accusations, his sly questioning, his attempts to catch her off guard, to lure her into flaring up at him and giving him a chance to put her on the defensive again, she bore up as gently and smiled as sweetly as Master Ashton in his most pious moments.

She was proud of her performance. It was the best performance of her career, and she had given it when her best had been demanded. She had no idea that his lordship could see through her pretenses, until he confronted her with his sonnet on the peculiar abilities of actors:

. . . who, moving others, are themselves as stone . . . (94)

They were standing when he showed her the sonnet. Both of them had on heavy coats, for it was a cold damp day in early March, and the long winter chill still pervaded the Tower apartment. In his arms his lordship held a cat, a gift from his Countess to keep him company, and stroked the purring animal while Rosaline read the sonnet.

She looked up at him with perhaps the first completely honest expression she had worn in his presence in half a year.

"At last you've thrown my profession up to me, my lord," she said. "I thought that was the one thing you would never use against me."

"Nor would I, if you had never acted with me. I thought it was understood that you would never pretend with me."

"And you think I have, my lord?" Rosaline was colder than the weather warranted. She shivered.

"Yes, Rose. I think you have. Just recently—two or three months, maybe—I've sensed that you were not sincere in all your actions."

"But you accused me of every kind of infidelity long before that." Rosaline laid the sonnet aside and clapped her gloved hands to restore circulation.

"Yes. Perhaps you were acting long before that. You may have been pretending with me all along."

"How can you say that, my lord?" she asked. Her question was not asked in a tone of shock. She began to pace the room to keep warm, and she talked calmly, as much interested perhaps in her shortcomings as an actress as in his lordship's skepticism. "Surely you can't believe that my manifestations of love are false."

"That is the part hardest to disbelieve. But Master Ashton assures me that a practised courtesan can counterfeit the subtlest reaction of a devout wife."

Rosaline held her temper—once she would have made him swallow his words tartly seasoned with comments of her own.

[264]

"Does your Master Ashton consort with practised courtesans, my lord?" she asked, as sweetly as she could.

"Of course not."

"But he *is* an authority on such women."

"I said that your lovemaking was hardest to doubt. But when I tested you in other things, Rose, you reacted in ways which I know are quite foreign to your nature. You've stood for abuse here in the Tower that would have sent you into a rage at the Gatehouse."

"It could be, my lord, that I love you so dearly that I would submerge everything in my nature to please you," Rosaline said. She stopped her pacing and faced him.

"If you can consciously submerge the very fire in your temperament, which I know well, I would say that you were proving yourself to be a consummate actress. That, I believe, is what disturbs me most. If you can be gentle in the face of my reference to practised courtesans, which I know would start a virtuous woman to seething inside, then how can I trust any of your outward expressions of emotion?"

Rosaline studied his face as he spoke. He hardly looked like himself; and his very manner of speech, not to say his words, was strange indeed compared to his former conversation. He sounded very much like a seminary student practicing theological disputation. He kept right on.

"The fact that you can deceive the world, even the guards of this prison, by your perfect impersonation of a boy is proof of your ability to appear to be what you are not."

"How much more have you told Master Ashton about me?" Rosaline asked, when his lordship paused in his monologue.

"Nothing more. But he knows about actresses."

"As well as courtesans," Rosaline said. "But, my lord, he doesn't know me, not unless you have told him who I am."

"I have not done that." She believed him.

"My lord, why have you suddenly—no, not suddenly—taken this course with me?" Rosaline asked. "I've seen it coming for some time. Are you trying to rid yourself of me? Where have I failed you? What could I have done that I haven't done? What have I done that I shouldn't have done?"

Her questions coming all at once, and after months of unquestioning passivity on her part, caused his lordship to frown in some perplexity. Not even Master Ashton could have had ready answers for all of them.

"Have I so cheapened myself by coming here that you are ashamed of me at last?" she went on. "Do I make so tawdry an appearance beside the Countess's regal person that I have become physically repulsive to you? Do I need fine clothes and attendants to make my entrances effective? My lord, it is not I who have employed the accoutrements of the stage to dazzle you in your sordid prison house. I have come to you simply, lovingly, naked—literally naked—without resorting to a single artful device to make me more attractive than I naturally am."

His perplexity deepened.

"If you don't love me, if you don't want me, in my natural state, my lord, there is nothing I can do. But please, my lord, don't accuse me of hypocrisy. Don't say that I am not what I seem to be."

He dropped the cat onto his bed and pressed his right hand to his forehead, covering his eyes.

"I don't know, Rose; I don't know," he said miserably. "When you're here, you seem so dear. But then, when I'm alone—"

Or with Master Ashton or the Countess, Rosaline thought.

"When I'm alone, I begin to doubt that you ever had one sincere feeling for me."

For a moment Rosaline felt sorry for him. He was having to face a problem, a very real one, without the childish optimism of his idol Essex to reassure him. Rosaline wondered what would have happened if he had had to face the problem ten years before, when he had first met her. It might have made a man of him.

Now she did not give up hope. She was pleased, in a way, that his lordship had seen through her more obvious pretensions. It showed a clarity of perception that had not always been present in his thinking. She could explain her acting on the grounds that she was trying not to upset him during his unhappy time. If he had actually sensed her insincerity, he might now examine more closely the behavior of his Countess and his chaplain.

As soon as she reached the Gatehouse she sat down to draft a reply to his sonnet. She wrote rapidly, beginning:

> *Alas, 'tis true I have gone here and there*
> *And made myself a motley to the view . . .* (110)

While she was still considering revisions, she heard a coach rattle to a stop on the cobblestone below. Presently the Countess of Derby admitted herself, obviously in a highly nervous state.

"Oh, Rosaline, I'm glad I found you in," she said, throwing off her cloak. She was in full court attire. "I've driven all the way from Richmond."

"What is it, Betty?" Rosaline asked, rising. "What's happened—Miranda?"

"No—the Queen, and it's all my fault." Betty was close to tears. There were signs that she had been closer earlier.

"Sit down. Tell me what is your fault."

Rosaline led her sister to a seat before the fire and helped her get her elaborate court dress into a chair.

"It's about the ring—Robin's ring."

"Very well—Robin's ring. Now tell me about it." Rosaline sat down on a stool beside Betty and held her sister's hand.

"Her Majesty called me in again, and began talking about Robin. Oh, Rosaline, she was so pathetic! 'If he had only asked for mercy,' she said. 'If he had only appealed to me.'

"Rosaline, her heart was breaking. I know it was. 'If he had loved me at all,' she said, 'he would have asked me to forgive him. But, Lady Elizabeth, he never relied for a moment on the love I bore him. If he had only swallowed his pride and asked for mercy.'

"What would you have done, Rosaline? She was so pathetic. She was grieving herself to death. Rosaline, I couldn't let her die thinking that Robin never called on her for forgiveness and mercy.

"So I said, 'Oh, Your Majesty, he did call on you. He did. He sent his ring.'

"She stiffened in her chair and clawed at my hand. She frightened me then, but I told her all about the ring.

"Then she made me go with her to see Lady Nottingham, who was on her deathbed, for the very same reason, I think. Remorse over hiding the ring, I mean.

"Lady Nottingham verified my story and produced the ring. Oh, Rosaline, it was awful.

"Her Majesty just barely made it back to her chamber. There she sank down into some pillows on the floor. She wouldn't even let them take her to her bed. She just lay there on the pillows, listless, resigned, hopeless. I just know she's going to die, and it's all my fault."

"But you did it for her, Betty," Rosaline said soothingly. "You said yourself that you didn't want her to die thinking that Lord Essex had not asked her mercy."

"I didn't want her to die at all, Rosaline. Lady Nottingham died within an hour after Her Majesty's visit. I did that, too. Don't you see, Rosaline?" Betty burst into tears at last.

Rosaline eased her stool up against Betty's chair and held her sister to her. After a time Betty's quick tears gave way to long shuddering sobs. Then the Little Countess sat up, wiped her eyes, and blew her nose on one of Rosaline's linen kerchiefs. She looked at Rosaline, who had risen and stood by the mantel gazing down at her dry-eyed.

"Rosaline, you aren't even crying?" Betty said reproachfully.

"No."

"But, Rosaline, Her Majesty is dying. I just know she is."

"Perhaps. She's a very old woman."

"And you don't care? Oh, Rosaline, don't you have any feelings at all?"

Betty sniffed again and dabbed at her eyes. Rosaline stared at her sister for a moment and then turned to examine her own frowning reflection in a wall mirror.

24

THE QUEEN LINGERED FOR TWO WEEKS. SHE NEVER MOVED FROM HER pillows and she never ate or slept again after her visit to Lady Nottingham. The plague, too, grew worse all over the city, spread like sympathetic inflammation. The theaters were closed on March 19 by order of the Privy Council. All London seemed to lie inert, in a state of catalepsy, until, between two and three o'clock on the morning of the twenty-fourth, the Queen died at Richmond.

Then everything sprang back into motion at once. Sir Robert

Carey rode north before dawn to inform King James of Scotland that he was the new King of England. Sir Henry Danvers took the news to Ireland, and all of the British Isles began to hum with rumor and prophecy and conjecture. The Tower, especially, underwent a transformation. Since it was filled with political prisoners who most likely would be freed by the new monarch, discipline was relaxed, and friends of the men inside flocked through the gates and crowded the corridors.

Rosaline hurried to the Tower herself, but she could get nowhere near his lordship's cell. Even had she been able to get there, she would have faced almost certain discovery by some of his lordship's visitors. So she made her way back to the crowded wharf and boarded a tiltboat loading for westward passage. Inconspicuous in her page's costume, she took a seat well aft and read the sonnet she had written in anticipation of his lordship's release:

> *Not mine own fears, nor the prophetic soul*
> *Of the wide world dreaming on things to come,*
> *Can yet the lease of my true love control . . .* (107)

Hal no doubt would regain his health after his release; but when she last saw him he had looked haggard and worn.

At Blackfriars Stairs she disembarked and began the long climb up Ludgate Hill toward the Gatehouse. She was tired, more so than the exertion should have made her, by the time she reached her apartment.

She began to wonder whether or not she really wanted his lordship to be released.

She did not go near the Tower again, but she began spending her afternoons in the Mermaid Tavern just to hear the news that the patrons brought in from various quarters. William Johnson more than once sent special runners to find out what was going on in the Tower, though he had more than he could do, what with the host lying ill with the plague and the barmaids afraid to come to work. Such was her mood, however, that she felt called upon to repay his favors at once. She worked for a time as a barmaid, and then when the host died she arranged for William Shakespeare to lend William Johnson enough of her money to buy the tavern for himself.

It seemed like forever, though actually she waited little more than two weeks for news of his lordship's release, which was effected on April 9. William Strachey brought the news to the Gatehouse. Rosaline was not dressed, though it was near midday, and she received him in her morning gown.

He seemed ill at ease, he who was usually so stable and dependable, as he told her the news.

"He went with his mother directly to the Savoy," Strachey said. "He could hardly have done otherwise, Madame Rose. The Countess had chartered an elaborate barge, and the entire family were waiting by the wharf."

"The entire family?" Rosaline asked, indicating a chair for Strachey.

"Yes, Madame Rose. His mother, Sir William Harvey, Lord and Lady Arundel, Lady Penelope Rich and—"

"And—" Rosaline prompted. She sat down on a low stool.

"And the Countess and little Lady Penelope," Strachey finished, staring into the few coals glowing in the grate. "He really had no choice, Madame."

"He never seems to have a choice," Rosaline said, with a show of impatience. "Or he never exercises one."

Strachey made no comment.

"Mr. Strachey, you are always going out of your way to make apologies for his lordship. Are you really that fond of him?"

"I have my loyalties," he said. "I try to hold to them. I know that he has no wish to hurt you, Madame. If I can soften any of the buffets by assuring you that he is not his own master yet—"

"Yet?"

"Not until he has made his place secure with the King."

"Mr. Strachey, I waited ten years for his lordship to make his place secure with Her Majesty. Must I go through all that again?"

At last he faced her.

"I don't know, Madame. I hope not. Knowing how much you care—"

"Don't be too sure, Mr. Strachey. I'm not so sure myself that I care that much. You may tell his lordship that, if he doesn't wish to come and hear it in person." She rose, putting an end to the conversation.

Strachey stood up and walked directly to the door. There he bowed formally.

"I may not see his lordship for a few days," he said. "He's riding north to meet His Majesty."

Rosaline nodded as Strachey went out the door. It was not until after he had gone that she wondered whether or not Hal had sent Strachey. Strachey had not said so, and she had not thought to ask him directly. Just who had sent him? Southampton? Oxford? Or had he taken it upon himself?

Rosaline tried to avoid the swirling backwash of the change of monarchs. Floods of poetry lamented the passing of Elizabeth and complimented James. Rosaline contributed not a line to either, though all literary London wondered at "Shakespeare's" silence. She remained aloof, just as she had refused to participate in the feud which had been raging between Ben Jonson and John Marston and Thomas Dekker for the past two or three years, though "Shakespeare" had been attacked in the lively "war of the theaters."

After Henry Chettle publicly urged "Shakespeare" to,

> Drop from his honeyed muse one sable tear
> To mourn her death who graced his desert,

Will Shakespeare himself came to Rosaline and asked her to write something in memory of Her Majesty.

Still she refused, and she offered no eulogies or orations or interludes to be included in the welcome planned for King James. Instead she tried to shut herself away at the Gatehouse, where she worked on *Troilus and Cressida*. Disgust for herself prompted her to give Pandar the bitterest of all her words to end the play:

> As many as be here of Panders' Hall,
> Your eyes, half out, weep out at Pandar's fall;
> Or, if you cannot weep, yet give some groans,
> Though not for me, yet for your aching bones.
> Brothers and sisters, of the hold-door trade,
> Some two months hence my will shall here be made;
> It should be now, but that my fear is this,—
> Some galled goose of Winchester would hiss.
> Till then I'll sweat, and seek about for eases;
> And at that time bequeath you my diseases.

[271]

She sent her manuscript to Richard Burbage and then sat at home brooding while Southampton received honor after honor from his new monarch, honors which he shared with his Countess, Elizabeth Vernon, cousin and living image of Robert Devereux, late Earl of Essex. First his lordship carried the Sword of State before His Majesty at Huntingdon. Then he had all his titles restored, with added offices, such as Governor of the Isle of Wight and Steward of the Royal Demesne, worth £6000 a year. He was at last made Knight of the Garter. Then, and most painful of all, Rosaline learned that his Countess was with child again. Obviously his lordship's household was finally in order. And Rosaline was no part of it, not even a mistress kept on the side.

While she was still brooding in solitude, Richard Burbage came to call. He brought the manuscript of *Troilus and Cressida* with him and laid it casually on the center table when Rosaline asked him to sit down. She found that she was very glad to see him, so lonely had she been of late.

"What do you think of the play?" she asked, feigning an eagerness which she really did not feel.

"It's no good, Rosaline," Burbage answered, almost sorrowfully.

"No good?"

"It has no heart in it, no feeling."

Rosaline was stunned by his words, not that she resented his criticism of her play—she trusted his judgment—but his words echoed the very ones used by Hal in the Tower, the words of Betty when she had informed Rosaline of Her Majesty's illness, even the sentiment Shakespeare had hinted at when she refused to write an elegy for the Queen. She merely stared at Burbage.

"It is just a crowd of angry, ugly, cowardly people running around screaming at one another," he continued. "Nobody cares what happens to any of them. There may come a time when a play about dull, unworthy, uninteresting people doing nothing significant can find an audience; but there is no such audience in England at present."

"No feeling, did you say?" Rosaline brought him back to his original comment.

"No feeling. It hardly seems possible that the author of *Romeo and Juliet* could have written it."

"Or of *Hamlet?*"

"Or of *Hamlet*. Not that *Hamlet* has deep feeling. I've played the title role too often. It isn't feeling; it's intellectual magnificence that carries Hamlet to the heights. This play has none of that either."

Rosaline could not resent Burbage's frankness. At times she distrusted him, when he was driving her. But at the moment he seemed to be offering nothing more than honest opinion.

"Then I was losing feeling as far back as *Hamlet*," she said, rising. She walked the length of the room, then turned to Burbage almost savagely.

"Richard Burbage," she said, "you are the third or fourth person who has told me that I lack feeling. I'm getting tired of it. I feel as deeply, more deeply than any of you. I've known jealousy and love and hate. I've been hurt by ambition and ingratitude and sheer blind stupidity. And I've borne it all with the patience of Griselda."

"Don't take it out on me," Burbage protested with a shrug of his shoulders. "All I said was that your play has no heart in it. I didn't say that his lordship—"

"There you go! I didn't mention his lordship. You're just sitting there gloating because you always said that he would desert me. Well, he has. Gloat!"

"I'm not gloating. All I ever suggested was that you cultivate your literary talent to fall back on—"

"When his lordship no longer wanted to push me back on a featherbed! I remember! Very well, Richard Burbage, his lordship has pushed me back on a featherbed for the last time. And I don't need my talent either. I have money. I have friends and position." She turned her back on Burbage and looked out the window into Blackfriars.

"A lot of good money will do you," Burbage said. "I know you better than you know yourself. I've played the best parts you ever wrote. When I said that you needed your talent to fall back on I wasn't thinking of money or friends or position. Perhaps it has something to do with integrity—our kind of integrity." He rose and joined Rosaline at the window.

"Integrity," Rosaline repeated. Then she softened. "Dick, I've always identified my love with my integrity. It was all I had. I've clung to it, fought for it with every ounce of my being. Now that it's gone I have nothing, nothing. I'm a cheap little vagabond with a bastard daughter."

Her shoulders slumped.

"I guess that's why I got so angry when you said I lacked feeling," she went on. "Perhaps it's true. I don't know whether I never had feeling or the feeling has all been squeezed out of me. Even my little Miranda. I hardly know her; I don't even know whether I love her or not, or whether she loves me."

"You had feeling to spare when you created Juliet. Yes, and old Jack Falstaff, bless his old roguish heart."

"Did I, Dick?" she asked, looking up into his face.

"Indeed you did," he said, more kindly than he had ever spoken before. "And there are passages of exquisite tenderness in *Twelfth Night* and *As You Like It*, inserted probably before you turned cynical and reworked them."

"But I thought you never cared for those plays."

"I wanted you to write tragedy," he said. "I felt that you were wasting your time on comedy. I still want you to write tragedy."

"Do you think I can?"

"It's the best way I know to find out whether or not you've got feeling."

Rosaline narrowed her eyes at Burbage. Her body began to tense again.

"Is this what you've been leading up to all the time, Richard Burbage?" she asked. "Did you come here to trick me into writing tragedy for the Lord Chamberlain's Men?"

"The King's Men," Burbage corrected her. "Since May 19 we have been the King's Men, Grooms of the Chamber."

"Oh yes, I'd forgotten. Very well, tragedy for the King's Men. Did you?"

"You're the one who was boasting a few minutes ago about feeling more deeply than any of us, and bearing your hurt with the patience of Griselda. How should I know whether you can still write tragedy or not? *Troilus and Cressida* is certainly not very promising. I won't know till I play one of your parts."

Burbage walked away from her as though he were uninterested, if not actually skeptical of her ability.

"Do you feel what I write?" she asked, following him as he walked.

"Certainly, if there's any feeling in it."

"There you go again!" she said. "Very well, if you feel what I write I'll show you. I'll tear your insides out. I'll show you and

[274]

his lordship and his Countess and anybody else who will listen. I'll write such concentrated human passion into your parts that you'll come crawling to me, begging me to stop! I'll show the world whether or not I have any feelings! And if you have any feelings, I'll rip them to shreds."

"Good," Burbage said, so calmly that he enraged her still further. "Which one shall we begin with? Jealousy?"

"Jealousy? Yes, jealousy, jealousy in a darkling like myself. But it will have to be a man—so you and your superior male audience can share in his misery. What's the name of that jealous Moor in Cinthio's *novella?*"

"I never heard of him," Burbage said.

"Well, you will. I shall call him Othello, and if you are any sort of actor with any feeling at all, the whole world will hear of the Moor of Venice and his jealous love for Desdemona."

25

AFTER ROSALINE BEGAN WORK ON THE TASK SHE HAD SET FOR HERSELF she reckoned time in acts and scenes and lines, not in years and months and days. It was not that she shut out the real time she lived in or shunned the people she knew. It was rather that she lived with Othello and Iago; indeed she *was* sometimes one, sometimes the other, sometimes both; or both were but extensions of herself, as were the loyal Emilia and Desdemona, "chaste and heavenly true." She felt every passion, shared in every cynical thought turned on honesty and goodness in the play. But she was not unaware of the Coronation Procession in March, postponed a year because of the plague. She knew when the Countess of Southampton bore her second daughter, Anne, in April. And she was not insensitive to the final illness and death of the Earl of Oxford in June.

That scene was real to her. She sat in Lord Oxford's curtained bedroom and heard his last words to his daughters. He had insisted that Betty bring her to Hackney; so she had taken her place with Lady Susan and Lady Bridget. Betty stood beside her husband across the bed from the three sisters.

"Betty and William already know what I have to say," his lordship began. He was propped up on pillows, and his eyes were bright, feverishly bright, but his voice was weak, and he kept a hand pressed against his side.

"Briefly—Rosaline, whom we have all learned to love, is your sister, your eldest sister, my daughter, born out of wedlock." His words carried no apology.

No one spoke or seemed shocked by his statement. Rosaline suspected that Betty had already told the younger girls about their dark mysterious half-sister.

"She has not wished to be recognized," his lordship continued. "I have let her have her way, as indeed I have had to let her have her way in everything." He smiled at Rosaline. "Like her mother before her.

"But I do want you to know about her. I—I've tried to watch over her, after a fashion, from a distance. We can't claim her, if she doesn't wish to be claimed; and she feels that she would make things awkward for the rest of you if I acknowledged her.

"Be that as it may, I do have to explain her legacy. Over ten years ago she came here to plead for a young man's freedom. We granted it but exacted an earnest of five thousand pounds as a token of good faith. Unfortunately the young man has broken faith. That earnest, which by careful husbandry has grown to something over seven thousand pounds, rightfully belongs to Rosaline."

His lordship again turned his attention to his darkest daughter.

"If I had given it to you sooner, my dear, you would have wasted it trying to buy the young man's way out of trouble. And you would have accomplished nothing. You may have it now—or William, Lord Derby, will continue to hold it in trust for you."

Rosaline nodded. She meant that she agreed to the latter plan, which Betty had already outlined to her.

"So I had to tell you. You girls will all be taken care of. Your half-brother, Henry, will of course succeed to the title and the bulk of the Oxford properties. I will explain to his mother, since we can keep no records of Rosaline's affairs unless we want to reveal her secrets to the Crown.

[276]

"I wish, my dear, I could have done more for you. I wish you had called upon me more often, called upon my love—all our love, which I assure you is genuine family affection."

The scene was clear. It was real. It happened. Her sisters hugged her and showed her sincere affection. She took her place in line and kissed her father before she left. She listened to his almost pathetic expressions of gratitude for the time she had spent with him working on his plays. And in a sentimental mood she had felt guilty of neglecting him, giving him cause to hate her for not being a true daughter to him. Such was her ability to play turnabout and make herself the offender. In that mood she addressed a sonnet to him:

Accuse me thus: that I have scanted all
Wherein I should your great deserts repay;
Forgot upon your dearest love to call,
Whereto all bonds do tie me day by day;
That I have frequent been with unknown minds,
And given to time your own dear-purchas'd right ... (117)

Betty, who delivered the poem, said that he cherished it. Within a week he was dead.

His death was real, but not so real as the death of Desdemona. It was not so dramatic as Othello's suicide, his dying words, whatever they might have been, not so effective as Othello's:

I kissed thee ere I killed thee. No way but this—
Killing myself, to die upon a kiss.

And though many mourned the passing of the Earl of Oxford, few were deeply touched, as all London was touched by the death of Richard Burbage's Othello. While the family grieved for a week at the loss of a father, thousands wept repeatedly, month after month, at the smothering of chastity and the triumph of jealousy over the darkly magnificent Moor of Venice, "for he was great of heart."

Rosaline turned next to liars in love, to love without illusion, to death itself as a lover—not the lyric young love of Romeo and Juliet, but the mature, experienced passion of Antony and Cleopatra. Again, for her preponderantly male audience, she made

Antony the stronger of the two. But it was from Southampton that she drew her character of Cleopatra, fickle, spoiled, willful, too weak and cowardly to make a decision, yet passionate withal.

Rosaline convinced the Globe audience that such love, under such conditions, was possible, possible though tragic. She knew that she convinced the patrons, because she went to the Globe again and again, every time *Antony and Cleopatra* was played, and she sat in the audience, in the twelve-penny rooms and in the six-penny rooms, in the lords' rooms and in the pit. She watched the listeners, studied their reactions, sensed their tensions, heard their sighs, sometimes felt their heartbeats. She knew that she touched them. They felt with her, felt what she had found in her heart and put into her poetry. They believed in her passions. So did she, more than in the ecstasy she had once known aboard the *Ictis*. The play was more real.

And when the audience, and Richard Burbage, clamored for more, she caught their fever, developed a thirst herself for feelings never before captured in poetic drama. She roamed the streets of London, listening to the shouts of joy in the very young and the cries of misery in the very old. She rode for hours in hired boats up and down and back and forth across the Thames, with her ears always attuned to the troubled singsong of her fellow passengers.

She went regularly to the Beargarden and the bullpen and watched the vicious mastiffs nip and tear at the tethered beasts until the ring was blood-spattered. She watched men urge the dogs on, pay for the privilege of whipping the enraged bears with their own hands. She looked into men's eyes and watched their jaws slacken and their mouths water when they were possessed by the bloodlust. Sometimes she followed them to the brothels and heard them wear out their passions in the cribs while she sat in reception rooms and fed coins to the blind and crippled musicians, or lost them at dice tables.

Richard Burbage tried to stop her from taking such risks—she was becoming too valuable a property to be let loose in London, prey to any footpad or cutthroat. He himself came to the Blind Cupid and took her home one Thursday in February.

"What were you looking for in there?" he asked gruffly as he led her out into Maiden Lane and headed toward the Thames.

"Passions, feelings—that's where they are rawest. Soon I will catch up with them, all of them. I'll catch them and tie them in a bundle and sell them to you for your playhouse."

"Have you been drinking?" he asked in alarm. He wrapped her coat about her.

"Yes," she said. "Blood. I've been drinking blood all afternoon at the Beargarden. Then I followed my drinking companions to the Blind Cupid. Dick, have you ever seen what blood, deliberately drawn blood, does to a person? Have you ever watched a man try to cleanse himself of it?"

"No," he said. "Neither have you." He deftly shifted her to the wall and walked between her and the Bankside ruffians. Fortunately most of them knew him by sight and greeted him as a friend.

"Oh yes, I have," she said. "And soon you will, too. You'll show the world what it means to have blood on your hands and on your conscience. You'll find out what it means to try to hack your way through a world where witches speak in riddles and blood is everywhere and a man can no longer sleep. That is, if you have any feeling."

"What are you talking about, Rosaline?" Burbage said. They had reached Winchester Stairs.

"Macbeth, the man who murdered sleep." She allowed Burbage to help her into a waiting wherry. He wrapped a blanket around her coat, against the spray that blew off the rowers' dripping paddles.

"Macbeth—a play, I presume. How are you sleeping these nights?" he asked.

"Alone, if that's what you mean," Rosaline answered. "Not very well, if *that's* what you mean, but I shall when I finish *Macbeth*. At last I'm catching up."

"Catching up," Burbage repeated. "You've said that before. Just what do you mean?"

The wherry cut into the cold north wind, which blew foully over the city and then across the river.

"Dick, all my life I've felt that I was walking beside a high board wall," Rosaline began more calmly, once she was settled in the sternsheets and huddled against Burbage. "Life was going on on the other side of the wall, but I was always shut out—a little girl without a home, roaming England in a wagon, being schooled under trees and in dressing tents, never living like other children.

"Then a girl, dressed as a boy, hiding always, never living in the open. When my chance came, I threw it away—on an earl, no less. I lived alone, seeing his lordship now and then, getting little glimpses of court life, or home life, through cracks in the high board fence.

"My baby was never my baby. I had to borrow a home for her, or lend her to Lady Derby. I glimpse her only now and then through cracks in the fence.

"Dick, do you know what I mean by being walled off from life and love and every normal feeling by a high board fence?"

"Yes, Rosaline, perhaps I do," he said sympathetically. "The way you explain it, I think I understand."

"But do you know how to see it all? Do you know how to catch up with life on the other side of the fence?"

"No."

"Did you ever run along a fence peering through the cracks? The faster you run, the faster the boards go by. Did you ever notice that the faster you go the more you can see?"

"Yes. Every child learns that trick."

"That's the secret, Dick. If you run fast enough you get a steady view of what's going on on the other side of the fence. That's what I'm doing. I'm catching up with the view."

"Isn't it quite a pace?" Burbage asked. The wherry was well past midstream. Already the buildings on the north bank were knocking off some of the wind.

"Yes, Dick. You just wait and see. You'll be Macbeth. You'll not be getting a steady image—not yet. Things are still blurred and sketchy, all except the blood, but you'll understand. You'll see that I'm catching up with the view."

"Can you keep up the pace, Rosaline?"

"Oh, Dick, I have to. Of course I can keep it up. I must show you and Bet—the Countess, and Will Shakespeare—and his lordship—that I taste life and feel every passion men have ever known. I'm no freak. I'm a real, living person, a woman. You yourself once said that I was a freak, a woman, or a genius."

"My mind is still open on the matter," Burbage said with a chuckle. He squeezed her shoulders playfully and helped her up Blackfriars Stairs. "Don't take yourself too seriously, Rosaline. You're doing fine, especially on your last two plays."

"*Macbeth* is better," Rosaline said as the two climbed Ludgate

[280]

Hill. "And the next one will be better, and the next one still better. I'll see more and more."

"Just don't run too fast."

Burbage stopped at the foot of the stairs to her apartment. She faced him for a moment.

"The heartbreaking part of it is that the wall is still there, Dick," she said. "Even when I see it all I may not be a part of it. I may still be looking through a wall. My feelings aren't counterfeit, are they, Dick? They're real, aren't they?"

"They are real the way I read them," he said. "As real as life itself."

"But you read them on the stage. How I envy you and Winifred and your little Julia."

"And little Richard, coming along, we hope." Burbage drew his muffler around his throat. He still had far to go out into Shoreditch.

"I hope so, too," Rosaline said, and hurried upstairs to work on *Macbeth.*

She finished the play on March 26, the day on which James Wriothesley was born to the Earl and Countess of Southampton, a month and three weeks after Rosaline's thirtieth birthday, had she reckoned time by such a calendar.

Macbeth was an immediate success, both with the men who played it and with the heterogeneous audience that flocked to the Globe. It was so successful that Rosaline began to distrust the acclaim of the mob. She feared that she might be defeating her own purpose. As she sat in the theater day after day, studying Burbage's projection of bloodstained Macbeth and watching the rapt expressions on the faces around her, she began to wonder whether she was actually portraying deep feeling or merely pandering to the bloodlust and accompanying guilt which she had followed from the Beargarden to the brothel. Was she, after all, only depicting a better bearfight?

And she began to loathe the crowd she had appealed to as judges of her work. What did they know about human feelings? Lusts and appetites, yes—but pure human passions, what did they know? They, the mutable, rank-scented many, were no fit judges of her. They wouldn't even know when they were being held in contempt. Or would they?

While *Macbeth* was running before the wind, applauded on

every hand, Rosaline set out coldly and deliberately to bait the mob as they had baited the bears and the bulls in Paris Garden. For them she wrote *Coriolanus*. She finished the play in four months, carried on by the momentum generated during the composition of *Macbeth*. Then she sat back and watched Burbage as Coriolanus, proud, cold, aloof, impersonal, pour out abuse on the unwashed multitude who were presumptuous enough to sit in judgment on poetic drama and human passion. She, like Coriolanus, spurned their verdict, even when it was all praise. She reveled in the epithets which Burbage hurled at the stinkards, and she smiled smugly when the crowd cheered him for reviling it.

But she could not ignore Burbage after the first performance.

"You slipped up that time, my lady," he said. "There's a lot of talk in *Coriolanus* but about as much feeling as there is in a frozen fish. I know—I've just been Coriolanus for two cold-blooded hours."

Rosaline glared at him in silence. After all the searing lines she had given him to blister the stinkards with, lines which surely he wanted to read.

"What happened to the view on the other side of the fence?" he asked.

What about the view? Very well, she had attended to the crowd. Now she would attend to Mister Burbage. She would find out if he had any heart in him, if he were fit to judge her passions. After all she had done for him! Providing him with the material which had made him the most widely acclaimed tragic actor in the world, the superior of the great Edward Alleyn!

She began with the old story of King Lear, piling sensation on sensation, torture on torture. Resting from almost total exhaustion, just after sending Lear and his fool out into the wild night, she came across the published quarto of Ben Jonson's *Sejanus* containing William Strachey's sonnet. It ended:

> *If men would shun swoll'n Fortune's ruinous blasts*
> *Let them use temperance; nothing violent lasts.*

The warning against violence, against extremes, seemed almost a personal message to Rosaline. She remembered how steady and dependable Strachey himself had been, and she suddenly wanted to see him. He had not been near her since her breach with

Southampton and the death of her father. Presumably he had no further business with her, but she missed him. So on a quick impulse, she wrote him a note commending him on his poetry and asking him to call.

She was in the midst of Lear's mad trial in the old farmhouse when Strachey came. He was formal, as usual, and the humorous crinkles around his eyes had set into permanent lines, but his voice was as warm and comforting as ever.

"You are a most surprising man, Mr. Strachey," Rosaline said after she had served him a glass of wine.

"What is the surprise this time?" he asked.

"The sonnet. I had no idea that you wrote poetry. Published too!"

"That's not the first," Strachey said, modestly however. "I had a poem in Francis Mychell's *View of France,* published last year."

"Indeed? I don't know that book." Rosaline spoke politely, while she let her eyes rove over Strachey's familiar countenance and long, somewhat ungainly, legs.

"You wouldn't, Madame Rose," he said. "It is of little interest. Then, like everyone else, I have a sheaf of unpublished sonnets."

"I'd like to read those."

"Some of them perhaps," he said with an unaccustomed shyness. "I brought seven or eight of them along." He drew a roll of manuscript out of his sleeve and handed it to Rosaline.

She unrolled the paper and glanced over a poem that ended:

> *In others' works thou dost but mend the style,*
> *And arts with thy sweet graces graced be;*
> *But thou art all my art, and dost advance*
> *As high as learning my rude ignorance.* (78)

"I wrote those some years ago, Madame," Strachey explained self-consciously when Rosaline looked up.

"To me?" Rosaline asked in rather tardy recognition of his subject.

"Yes, Madame. I know it was presumptuous."

She read a second:

> *I grant, sweet love, thy lovely argument*
> *Deserves the travail of a worthier pen,*

[283]

Yet what of thee thy poet doth invent
He robs thee of and pays it thee again.
He lends thee virtue and he stole that word
From thy behavior; beauty doth he give
And found it in thy cheek; he can afford
No praise to thee but what in thee doth live. (79)

"The others are all the same, Madame Rose," Strachey said when she looked up again. "I wrote sonnets to you, but really I couldn't compete with so worthy a rival as his lordship. He was the better poet and the better man. You needn't read the other six, since you know what they are about."

"Oh, but I shall. I want to. And don't belittle yourself. Your poems are quite as good as his lordship's, and you, Mr. Strachey—"

"I have one more," he said, producing a fresh piece of paper. "Madame Rose, I have never been very far away from you. I've stayed in the background while I've watched you drive yourself too hard. Now I must go away for a time."

"Where?"

"To Constantinople, as secretary to Sir Thomas Glover, the Ambassador."

"How wonderful!" Rosaline forced her enthusiasm. She found that she really did not relish the idea of his leaving London. He had always been around in times of trouble.

"It is simply that my Lord of Oxford is dead, and my Lord of Southampton has no need for me at the moment," Strachey explained. "I have no business watching over you either, Madame, but do take care of yourself while I'm away. And take this last poem of mine as a warning."

He rose and walked toward the door, still holding his latest sonnet in his hand. He was perspiring in his embarrassment, not at all like his usual calm self. Rosaline joined him at the door, and then he gave her the paper.

"Thank you, Mr. Strachey," she said. "I shall be duly warned. I'm glad someone worries about me. I shall miss your watching over me. You will write from Constantinople, won't you?"

"Yes, Madame, if I may."

"I shall look forward to your letters. I've never been to the East." She herself felt stiff and formal in his presence for the first time.

William Strachey agreed, and then he was gone. Rosaline read his warning, except for one word, where his moist thumb had smudged the ink during his stubborn insistence on holding onto the poem until the end of his visit. Like so many of Hal's it was about death, but death as she saw it, not as Hal had feared it. So William Strachey read all the tragedy that she had put into her work. He saw death hovering over it all, the essence of tragedy, the end, perhaps the aim of the passions. She had to write of death while she was catching up with life. That was what death was: catching up with life. But now William Strachey was on his way to Constantinople, and Lear was on his way to madness.

She returned to Lear. She understood him. She understood how a man could make one mistake, just one error in judgment, one misplacement of trust or affection, and pay for it for the rest of his life in pain upon pain, misery upon misery, until the tension was intolerable or made tolerable only by the sheer force of poetry. She continued to strain emotions to the breaking point and hold them together with the magic of words. She prevented a broken heart by a metaphor, held onto sanity with an iamb. Repeatedly she fended off the unbearable with a deft conceit. Then it was over. Lear caught up; he learned, he regained his sanity, but too late. His heart burst " 'twixt two extremes of passion, joy and grief."

Rosaline finished the play for Christmas and it was performed at Whitehall on Saint Stephen's Night, December 26. Rosaline did not see it, and it was nearly a year before it was played again; but Richard Burbage reported indirectly on the performance. He simply called on Rosaline and suggested that she give up tragedy for a while, try a comedy perhaps and return to tragedy after she had taken a rest. That was all he said, except a word or two suggesting that she might find material for a serious comedy in the story of Apollonius of Tyre.

Rosaline ostensibly followed Burbage's suggestion. She began working on Apollonius, whom she called Pericles, but she also continued to write the story of *Timon of Athens,* in which she intended to finish what she had begun in *King Lear.* If she read Burbage's reactions right, she had just missed the ultimate in tragedy in her last play. She felt that Lear was all that Burbage could stand; and almost in a gloating mood she set out to create a Timon that would tax Burbage to his limits. If she could do that, and he could project to his audience, then she would have shown the world, and herself, that she knew all about human feeling. No one could ever again accuse her of counterfeiting.

So she worked for a year. There were interruptions such as the birth of Betty's son, James, and Strachey's return from the Levant. And there were periods when she accomplished nothing. But she stuck with both projects. She poured bitterness into every scene of *Timon,* bitterness which overflowed into the scenes in *Pericles.* Yet there was hope in *Pericles,* the joy in reunion, a glimpse of a world less grim than the one she was holding to a steady image in *Timon.* But she shut it out. It had no place in her work until *Timon* was finished. Indeed she tore up the first two acts of *Pericles,* only to go right ahead with the rest of the play. It was as though one half of her insisted on cursing in the person of Timon and the other half yearned for the hope of Pericles.

Christmas came again, and the Thames was frozen solid for weeks. An elaborate frost fair grew on the river, stall by stall, until it seemed that every entertainer, every confectioner, every mountebank in all England had set up shop on the ice. Punch and Judy shows vied with dancing bears, religious relics competed with oriental herb remedies and hot roasted chestnuts tempted customers from the glacé stalls.

River traffic was carried by sleds. Wherries were set on runners and pulled by horses, and all manner of ingenious ice boats were devised to haul merrymakers. And since the Thames became the center of London, the bankside enterprises—brothels, cockpits, bullpens, theaters—all profited. It was then that *King Lear* was presented at the Globe, just when the people were tiring of ordinary pleasures, for *King Lear* was never ordinary.

Rosaline herself did not know how extraordinary it was until she saw it, the third day of its run. She had been wrestling with *Timon* and *Pericles* the first two days and nights, too intent on her work even to eat, much less to cross the ice to the Globe. But on the third day she went, with William Strachey, and they sat in a lords' chamber with Winifred Burbage, who was also seeing *Lear* for the first time.

"I had to come," Winifred said, when the other two joined her. "Dick has been so enthusiastic and yet so strange about this play that I had to see it."

"I haven't seen it either," Rosaline said. "I've been too busy."

"I have," Strachey said. He ventured no further comment.

The women had only a minute to look around the audience. It was all familiar to both of them: the unruly groundlings in the pit, the finery of the gentlemen in the balconies, the masked ladies, and the brazen unmasked courtesans in the goose roost. The platform stage, the "heavens" black-shrouded for tragedy, the musicians' loft. It was all the same, until Burbage came onstage and said:

"Meantime we shall express our darker purpose."

From that moment, the Globe was different. Burbage was different, or seemed so to the two women who knew him best. Or perhaps he was the same, intensified beyond all measure, himself so concentrated that he seemed like another. For two hours they watched him suffer all the anguish that could be written into the part of a mad old king.

Winifred suffered with him. Rosaline gloated at the strain the part put upon him. The audience below and around them, transported, forgot to applaud. At Albany's words:

> *"The weight of this sad time we must obey,*
> *Speak what we feel, not what we ought to say.*
> *The oldest have borne most; we that are young*
> *Shall never see so much, nor live so long,"*

the people filed out as if they too were a part of the dead march. There were no *bravo's*, no plaudits for Burbage's finest performance.

Winifred turned to Rosaline as the house emptied.

"He mustn't play it again tomorrow," she said.

"Why?" Rosaline asked. "He was wonderful."

"It takes too much out of him. That's why I had to come. Now I know. Let's go to him."

The three went downstairs and into the large tiring room. Burbage was already half-dressed in his street clothes.

"You mustn't play it again tomorrow," Winifred repeated.

"I don't intend to," he said, just barely nodding to his other two guests. "Never again will I walk on that stage three days in succession bearing the dead Cordelia in my arms, and say, '*Howl,*

[287]

howl, howl, howl! O, you are men of stone.' I won't do it three times in one week, do you hear me, Rosaline?"

"Yes, I hear you. Very well, don't. But just wait until I finish *Timon of Athens.* Then you'll see real tragedy, the real task I've set for you."

"Timon?" Burbage snapped. "Have you written another tragedy? I told you not to!" He crossed over to Rosaline and shook her by her shoulders. "You can't go beyond *Lear.* You know that. Only your superb blank verse holds *Lear* together. Otherwise it is unbearable. If *Timon* goes further—if you try to carry tragedy further—the play will fall apart. Do you hear me? It will fall apart. So will I. So will the audience.

"So will you," he added softly, and gave her shoulders one last gentle shake.

26

FOR SEVERAL HOURS ROSALINE HAD LAIN VERY STILL AND WATCHED the strange man in her room. She did not know how long she had been in bed; indeed it had taken at least an hour of surreptitious spying to convince her that she was really in her own bedroom in the Blackfriars Gatehouse. The furniture had been rearranged, with her bed placed in the sunlight, which hurt her eyes, and new thin curtains over the windows and some tables and stools, even a second bed, moved in—pieces which did not belong in her boudoir.

But the man was strangest of all. When her eyes became better accustomed to the sunlight, she was able to make out his features. He was a short man, about thirty years old. His complexion was olive, as dark as her own, and he had little round black eyes set in an equally round face. His hair, too, was as black as hers, but somewhat coarser, as best she could tell. And though she was dark herself, she shared the Englishman's distrust of Latin coloring.

That was why she had feared at first that she was in the Tower and that he was her jailer, that and the fact that he spent much

[288]

time copying from her commonplace book and the loose leaves of sonnets stuck here and there between its pages. Even after she had assured herself that she was in the Gatehouse, she could not account for his presence there. Obviously he was her keeper and she was a prisoner in her own house. No one else came into the room. It was he who brought food for her, hot broth and cool milk, and then went away and left her alone. She ate while he was out of the room. She did not want him to know that she was awake.

Later she shut her eyes, not too tight, not tight enough to show strain, when he came near her, and then she watched him through half-open eyes until he was looking the other way, or absorbed in his copy work, and then she raised her eyelids and studied him carefully. She had to find out all she could before she spoke, lest she reveal some secret which he had not already learned.

The first time he held her arm she thought that he was going to put manacles on her, but she tensed herself and held her tongue and kept her eyes shut. After a while he let go of her. The same thing happened a second and a third time. Then her curiosity got the better of her and she deliberately tried to surprise him.

"Who are you and what are you doing?" she asked pointedly, and opened her eyes wide and challenged him when he grasped her wrist.

"I'm William Harvey, and I'm counting your pulse," he said, favoring her with what he no doubt considered a good-natured smile.

"Oh no, you're not!" she snatched her arm away. "I know Sir William Harvey, and you're not at all like him."

"I didn't say *Sir* William Harvey." He chuckled easily and continued to smile down at her. "Harvey is a fairly common name and every second man in England seems to be called William these days."

"Sir William is a gentleman," she said. "He wouldn't copy out of my book without my permission."

"So you've been watching me." He nodded approvingly. "That's good. I will ask your permission before I take my copy out of here. And if it will reassure you, I can tell you that I am here at Sir William's insistence. He is a distant relative of mine, my godfather, in fact."

"And why would he send you here to spy on me?" she asked with a show of petulance.

[289]

"Perhaps because I am a physician—Physician Extraordinary to King James—a very good physician, I might say, and Sir William seems to be quite fond of you. He wanted you to have the best care available, he and your sister."

"My sister?" Rosaline asked in alarm.

"Her ladyship, Countess of Derby."

"Her ladyship told you that I was her sister?"

"Yes. Now don't worry. I'm your physician. As such I must learn all I can about you and I'm bound to keep everything I know in strictest confidence. You have nothing to fear from me. Now, may I spy on you to the extent of determining the rate of your pulse?"

Rosaline reluctantly extended her arm and allowed him to count her pulse. Actually she felt too weak or too tired to resist. Simply talking seemed to tire her. When he released her wrist again she had had time to collect her wits and regain some strength.

"Have I been very ill?" she asked.

"Yes, Madame, very ill."

"For long?"

"For over a month."

"A month—but that's impossible. I don't remember—"

"No, Madame. You don't remember. It's just as well. That's one of the great mercies. Now all the unpleasantness is past and you can start remembering again."

"Did I—did I talk much?" she asked fearfully.

"Yes, but to no one who should not have heard," he assured her. "Now, would you like to rest awhile? We can talk some more later."

"Yes," she said. She wanted to do some thinking before she did any more talking. Despite the physician's seeming good nature and apparent high spirits, Rosaline was still distrustful. But she found it difficult to think, and with the sun out of her eyes at last she dropped off to sleep.

When she awoke she ate the supper which William Harvey brought to her, and she rather looked forward to talking to him after she had eaten. But he refused conversation until she had finished all the food on her tray; so she decided to be a little caustic.

"I consider myself fortunate to have so extraordinary a physician attending me," she said. "Physician Extraordinary was the term, wasn't it?"

"Yes. Also Fellow of the Royal College of Physicians, candidate for Physician to St. Bartholomew's Hospital. You are fortunate indeed, fortunate to be alive after the way you've abused yourself, driven your body and your heart for the last five or six years."

"I too am fortunate to have such a patient," he said gently after he had parried her thrust. "In fact we have a lot in common. We seem to be interested in the same thing." He removed her supper tray.

"What is that?" Rosaline asked, mollified by his manner in spite of herself.

He sat down in a chair beside her bed and crossed his short legs uncomfortably.

"The human heart," he answered. "For years—at Caius College, Cambridge, then at Padua, and now in my work here—I have been most interested in the heart. I've studied the hearts of dogs and pigs and serpents and frogs and lobsters and shrimps and oysters, even embryo chicks. I think that I am on the verge of a discovery concerning the heart and its function which may revolutionize anatomical theory. I already know a lot about the organ and its function in the lower animals.

"But I have not been privileged to lay bare the human heart and reveal its workings as you have done." He faced Rosaline solemnly. "There are laws against vivisection which prevent me from doing physically and literally what you have done emotionally and figuratively. How I envy you your understanding of the human heart!"

"You are speaking of the poems in my book?" she asked. "Many of them are by friends of mine—Mr. Strachey, Master Shakespeare—"

"Master Shakespeare," Harvey repeated, his eyes twinkling, impishly now. "I know all about Master Shakespeare from his own lips, and from Mr. Burbage. Madame, you have many devoted friends who have been most helpful to me during your illness. They made my diagnosis."

"Then you know all about me?"

"All? No. I doubt that anyone will ever know all about you, Madame, though many may spend their lives trying to learn. I know what your friends and relatives know. I know what some brilliant men, men like Sir Francis Bacon, think of your work."

"Sir Francis Bacon," Rosaline repeated in dismay. He was brilliant; he was the patron of learning in many fields; he claimed to have taken all knowledge for his province; but he was an opportunist who would betray his own mother to secure advancement for himself. If he knew her identity and wanted to trade on it—he and Sir Robert Cecil—

"He has heard or read all of 'Master Shakespeare's' work," Harvey said. "He is deeply impressed by much of it. We spent hours discussing the plays, especially the later tragedies, while I attended him during his recent illness. But, Madame, he has never heard of you, and I'm sure that he never will hear of you. Still Sir Francis Bacon* is perhaps the most astute and assiduous student of your work, unless it is Mr. Burbage or myself."

"And what does the brilliant man think of my work?" Rosaline asked weakly. After the Essex trial she had respected Bacon's intelligence if not the man himself.

"That you have portrayed the passions of man more convincingly and more deeply than any other dramatist of our time, perhaps of all time." His eyes were steady now, keen, focused on hers to emphasize the gravity of his statement.

"You wouldn't say that I was without feeling then?" she asked. She was almost willing to accept his verdict.

"You without feeling, Madame?" He laughed aloud. "Absurd! You are *all* feeling. If anyone ever felt, it was you, Madame, until you became numb with overwork and trying too hard and getting too cold at the frost fair." He stood up, to mark the end of the time he would allow her to talk.

"Was it my heart?" she asked. "I mean my illness."

"Possibly—part of it. We don't know much about the heart. It was your lungs. You have had pneumonia. And you were worn out. But now that's all over. You'll get well again, better than ever."

"How long?" she asked with what little strength she had left.

*Echoes of Rosaline's phraseology in Bacon's Essays and commonplace book prompted Mr. William Henry Smith, in 1857, to advance the theory that Bacon wrote the plays and sonnets. Since that time there has been a steady stream of "Baconians" to keep the hypothesis alive. Nathaniel Holmes, Ignatius Donnelly, Mrs. E. W. Gallup and Sir Edwin Durning-Lawrence have been some of the most articulate champions of Bacon.

[292]

He looked at her for a moment as though undecided. Then with a nod, to himself perhaps, he spoke.

"It will be a long time, Madame," he said. "You are intelligent and you sound rational today, for the first time. I think you will understand."

Young William Harvey sounded like his godfather when he appealed to her as an intelligent woman. She braced herself for the worst.

"You must rebuild what you have been tearing down for five or six years," he said seriously. "It will take time, several months, maybe a year or two, but you will recover."

"Thank you," she said, and closed her eyes. She rather welcomed the idea of lying where she was for several months, maybe a year or two. The worst was not so bad after all. "I think I shall sleep now."

"And when you wake," Harvey said, half to himself, "I want to know what you meant by the 'natural gates and alleys of the body,' Madame. Hamlet is not the only man who has been trying to solve the riddles propounded by the ghost of his father."

Rosaline lost consciousness while William Harvey was repeating lines from *Hamlet*:

"And in the porches of mine ears did pour
The leperous distilment; whose effect
Holds such an enmity with blood of man
That swift as quicksilver it courses through
The natural gates and alleys of the body,
And with a sudden vigor it doth posset
And curd, like eager droppings into milk,
The thin and wholesome blood."

27

William Strachey took Rosaline to the cottage at Castle Hening-ham as soon as she was able to travel. None of her family went along, because, unknown to her, the little Lady Elizabeth Derby had died just before her eighth birthday and the Countess Elizabeth, pregnant again, was prostrated by the death of her second namesake. The Earl of Derby, however, sent along a competent staff of servants who were devoted to her ladyship's "Italian governess."

A number of other things were kept from Rosaline. It was long afterwards that she learned that John Marston had been imprisoned in Newgate during her illness, had blackmailed the Earl of Derby into securing his release, and had used some of his information to force the Earl of Southampton to promise him the living of Christchurch in Hampshire as soon as he had taken Orders. Marston then used the promise of the living to win the hand of one Mary Wilkes, daughter of King James's chaplain. And quite understandably his connection with the Royal Chaplain made it easy for him to take Holy Orders. So was Rosaline's most dangerous "cousin" silenced by her friends while she lay unconscious or convalescent.

Some things she was told. Young William Harvey, her physician, asked her permission to allow Thomas Thorpe to publish his copy of her commonplace book under the title of *Shakespeare's Sonnets*. Out of gratitude, she agreed to the publication and to the dedication to William Harvey which read:

To the only begetter of these insuing sonnets, Mr. W. H., all happiness and that eternity promised by our ever-living poet wisheth the well-wishing adventurer in setting forth.   T. T.

The quarto volume was issued in May of 1609, about a year after Rosaline's removal to Castle Heningham. Rosaline remembered the date well; she received her copy of the book about a week after William Strachey sailed for Virginia on the *Sea Venture*, one of the nine ships in the expedition headed by Sir George Somers and Sir Thomas Gates. And since she had begun to miss him, the only one at Castle Heningham to whom she could talk freely, she had immersed herself in the sonnets with none-too-happy results. She found herself reliving her life with Southampton, subjecting herself again to the stresses which had wrecked her.

She remembered in time that she was an "intelligent" woman. But in her loneliness, she had no one to turn to except herself; and her resources were the very emotions which she was trying to avoid, or language, sheer language for its own sake. Half-fearfully she considered writing a new play. Burbage had turned her *Timon of Athens* and *Pericles, Prince of Tyre* over to George Wilkins, who had got them into shape for production; and anyway William Harvey had forbidden her to work on either of them again. He had, indeed, forbidden her to work on tragedy at all.

So she began slowly, cautiously, to write a romance about the ancient British King Cymbeline and his daughter Imogen. And although she could not help identifying herself with Imogen, the most faithful of all the wives she had ever created, she concentrated on poetry rather than on feeling and managed to hold onto her emotional stability, even if her language did at times become so obscure that she had trouble recapturing her meaning on second reading. She spent almost a year on *Cymbeline,* a lonely year as she realized when she read her finished manuscript and felt the full impact of the yearning she had unconsciously written into the recognition and reunion scenes. In places the play echoed the same longing that had pervaded her earlier story of Pericles. Yet there was throughout a serenity which comforted her, a placidity which assured her that her storm had passed. She no longer feared to write.

In the fall she began a dramatic version of Greene's *Pandosto,* another story of separation and reunion. Her original plans, however, were interrupted by two happy events. First she received a long detailed letter from William Strachey. Addressed to "an excellent lady," it gave a vivid account of the shipwreck of the *Sea Venture* in the Bermuda Islands, and the ten months which the crew spent in that delightful place building ships to take them on to Virginia. She was fascinated by Strachey's descriptions of the islands and more than ordinarily pleased by his thoughtfulness in writing so voluminously to her.

The second pleasure was an extended visit from Miranda. When the court season opened at Whitehall, the Countess of Derby, now recovered from her grief at the death of her daughter and happy over the birth of her second son, Robert, entered into social activities with more enthusiasm than she had ever shown before. Consequently, Miranda, then a grave young lady of thirteen, began to feel that she was a burden on her gay and beautiful aunt. She asked to visit her mother at Castle Heningham, and with Dr. Harvey's approval she moved into the cottage with Rosaline early in November.

It was then that Rosaline learned for the first time that young Ferdinand Stanley had also gone to Virginia with Sir Thomas Gates.

"He is going to make a home for us," Miranda said seriously, her big black eyes solemn at the pronouncement.

"What do you mean by *us?*" Rosaline asked as the two of them sat before an open wood fire in the cottage kitchen. She was just getting acquainted with this lovely honey-haired daughter of hers.

"I mean him and me. We'll be married, of course," Miranda said.

"Oh, I didn't know that," Rosaline said.

"Ferdinand will tell you when he returns. When he comes after me, I mean."

"Let's see, how old is Ferdinand?"

"He's seventeen. But he convinced Uncle William that it was time he was striking out for himself."

"And old enough to be married, I suppose. But what about you, Miranda? Aren't you a little young?"

"In a year I'll be as old as your Juliet," the child said pointedly.

"So you will," Rosaline said, smothering a surprised chuckle. "And in three years, say, when Ferdinand's twenty—"

"If you insist, Mother," Miranda said dutifully. "But if Ferdinand makes a home for us before then—"

"Don't you feel that you have a home, dear?" Rosaline asked.

"Not really, Mother," Miranda said gravely. "We know the truth about us and about you, and we appreciate all that Aunt Betty and Uncle William have done for us, but Ferdinand says that there is not really any place for us now that we are grown."

"That's the way Ferdinand feels, is it?"

"Yes, Mother. I, too. While we were babies, Aunt Betty wanted us around, just as she did poor little Elizabeth and her two little boys. She treated us like dolls, I think. She loved us—she still does, but—"

"Do you feel all this, or is it some more Ferdinand?"

"Oh, I feel it, Mother. I really do. And I'm not a doll any more. I'm a woman, or will be by the time Ferdinand makes a home for us."

"Must that home be in Virginia?" Rosaline asked. "Couldn't you have a home here in England?"

"No, Mother. In England we would always be tied to the

house of Derby in one way or another. Ferdinand's sure of that. He wants to go to Virginia or somewhere else in America where one Stanley is as good as another Stanley, and not a Derby."

"Your Ferdinand seems to have done a lot of thinking for a seventeen-year-old," Rosaline said, forgetting that at seventeen she had been an accomplished actress and a better than average playwright. "And he thinks America is the place to make a home for you?"

"Yes, he says that America is going to be a wonderful place for ambitious bastards." Both Ferdinand and Miranda accepted their status without shame.

"Ferdinand said that, did he?"

"He wrote me that in his last letter."

"I think I'm going to like your Ferdinand," Rosaline said. "I've hardly seen him since he was a little boy."

"You'll love him, Mother," Miranda said confidently. "He'll make a home for us all—you too. And he'll be rich."

"Don't worry about me," Rosaline said quickly. She still felt like an outsider, loath to accept favors even from her own daughter. "And Ferdinand *will* be rich. Don't tell him beforehand, but when you marry him you will bring him a very large dowry, five thousand pounds provided by your father."

"My father? But I thought—" Miranda bristled and looked very much like a thirteen-year-old.

"Don't think ill of your father," Rosaline said gently. "I'm sure he did the best he could. Anyway the money is already being held in trust for you by your Uncle William."

"I won't," Miranda said. "Think ill of my father, I mean. And I won't tell Ferdinand about my dowry. I'll surprise him."

"Yes, do that."

"And, Mother, will you do just one thing for me?" Miranda was still a little girl. She was prepared to wheedle if necessary.

"Yes, dear, anything. What?" What could she do for Miranda that Betty had not already done?

"Will you write a masque for my wedding? Aunt Betty has told us many times of the beautiful play you wrote for hers, *A Midsummer Night's Dream*." Miranda talked fast. She gave her mother no opportunity to refuse. "And she's always wanted to have a big wedding for me, especially now that little Lady Elizabeth is dead. Of course Ferdinand and I don't care about a big wedding. But we wouldn't want to disappoint Aunt Betty. You wouldn't want to either, would you, Mother? You will write a masque for me, won't you?"

"Yes, Miranda," Rosaline said. "I think I do want to write a masque for your wedding. I think maybe that's exactly what I want to do."

"Now?" Miranda asked excitedly, jumping up from her stool and running to her mother.

"Not right now," Rosaline said with a laugh. "Let me finish *The Winter's Tale* first. Then let me take time to write you the most romantic wedding masque that a bride ever had."

Miranda hugged Rosaline to her.

"I knew you would, Mother," she said. "I just knew you would."

Miranda's influence was felt immediately. The last two acts of *The Winter's Tale* were full, so full of Miranda in the person of Perdita that but for its grave, unhappy memories of the first three acts, the last half of the play hardly seemed to belong to the first half at all. Indeed Acts IV and V of *The Winter's Tale* became almost a prelude to Miranda's wedding masque.

William Strachey's return from Virginia the next spring contributed further to Miranda's play. Rosaline, much improved, took up residence in the Gatehouse again; and Strachey, who came loaded down with manuscripts of his own, moved into the apartment across the hall. In addition to his *True Reportory of the Wreck and Redemption of Sir Thomas Gates upon the Islands of the Bermudas,* he had already written a rough draft of his *True History of Travaile into Virginia, Brittania,* complete with a dictionary of the Chesapeake Indian language. And as secretary to Lord De la Warre, Governor of Virginia, he had taken on the job of editing a code of "Laws Divine, Moral and Martial" for the colony and a map of Virginia with descriptions by Captain John Smith and others.

In addition to all this he was full of vivid, glowing descriptions of the Bermudas, which Rosaline had chosen as the setting for Miranda's wedding masque. She had already begun the play, using his letter as the source of her first scene, a storm at sea; but for the atmosphere of the island she relied on the stories he told her and Miranda after he moved into the Gatehouse. And he was the one with whom she discussed her ultimate purpose in writing the play. Perhaps she even decided on that purpose during her first long conversation with him after his return from Virginia.

It happened in the Gatehouse. William Strachey paid a formal call, and Rosaline received him quite stiffly at first.

"It is good to see you, Mr. Strachey," she said, when they were seated in the window seat overlooking the courtyard. "I enjoyed your letter. Thank you for remembering me."

"I could have done no less," he said. "I could not be content with only an official report of so thrilling an adventure, and I knew of no one else to whom I could write a personal account and be sure of having it appreciated."

"You may be sure that it was," she said. She had forgotten how calm his grey eyes were, how soothing it was just to meet his gaze now and then. "Your letter was a—a godsend, and an inspiration."

"Hardly that, Madame Rose," he said with a self-conscious chuckle. His occasional shyness and his blond hair which refused to turn grey created an illusion of boyishness which was not at all in keeping with his position as first Secretary of Virginia. "I meant it to fill an idle hour."

"It has filled many," Rosaline assured him, "and is assuming even larger proportions as your island grows into the play I'm working on."

"Oh, a new play. What is it about?"

Rosaline stood up and walked a few steps away from the window seat. She turned and motioned for him to sit down again.

"It's a wedding masque for my daughter," she said. "And it's about me and my work, and—and his lordship."

She half turned and picked up a scarf that had been dropped on the center table.

"Have you seen him, Mr. Strachey?" she asked, without facing her guest.

"Yes, Madame Rose. Since the illness of the Earl of Salisbury, my Lord of Southampton is the senior member of the Council of Virginia, and he has always been a strong figure in the Virginia Company. I made my reports to him upon my arrival in London."

"How is he, Mr. Strachey?" she asked softly, toying with the scarf.

"His lordship has secured steady preferment, constant advancement under King James," Strachey said evasively. He rose and stared out the window.

"And his family?"

"There are now five children," Strachey said. "Three girls and two boys."

"Is he happy?"

"I don't know, Madame Rose," Strachey faced Rosaline but came no closer to her. "His lordship works hard. He is a good man, Madame Rose, but not his own master; no earl is, under an English monarch. He lives under a cloud, I believe, a grief or a sorrow; but he's not thoughtless or evil, Madame Rose. I can assure you of that."

"You've always been loyal to him, haven't you, Mr. Strachey?"

Strachey made no answer.

"Then I think you should be the first to know that I've decided to give him up," she said.

At the startled look which crossed Strachey's face, Rosaline laughed.

"No, I've not had a relapse," she said. "Of course it sounds absurd for me to say that I am giving his lordship up, I who have not seen him for seven or eight years, I who never had a hold on him. What I mean is that I am renouncing the image I have kept of him, an image which is probably more of my own making than of his person. Do you know what I mean, Mr. Strachey?"

"Yes, I think I do. Knowing him and knowing you, Madame, I can understand."

"He has dominated my life, as you well know, Mr. Strachey, and my work." Rosaline began to pace the floor. Strachey stood by the window and watched her.

"He was my Romeo," Rosaline went on, "the inspiration for all the joy that I wrote into my sunny comedies—and the source of all the bitterness that went into my tragedies. It was always to or about him or what he did to me that I wrote. He was the spirit of it all."

"I think he knows that, Madame."

"Don't stand up for him any more," Rosaline said sharply. "I don't blame him entirely. Her Majesty, by her tyranny, made him what he was, and then locked him up in the Tower. And perhaps I've held him in bondage ever since his release. Maybe that's his cloud.

"Well, Mr. Strachey, I'm releasing him and I shall tell him so.

That's what my new play is about, the masque for my daughter, *our* daughter.

"I shall write of a spirit—Ariel, I shall call him—who was imprisoned by a foul old witch. I shall free him and use him for my inspiration, or I shall have Prospero do it, and then let him go after he has presented my daughter's wedding masque. Will his lordship understand such a story, Mr. Strachey?"

"His lordship is not stupid," Strachey said gently. He had joined Rosaline in her pacing, quite unobtrusively and perhaps unconsciously.

"And in the play I shall tell all who know me that I am forsaking the life I have lived. I shall throw off the cloak of Shakespeare's name, break my staff, and drown my books in the sea. I shall cease to create magic worlds and fairy people. I shall cease to be a freak or a genius, a woman who can read and write.

"I shall tell the world that I am through with my masquerade. And, Mr. Strachey, I shall do it so beautifully and so lyrically that men will applaud for a thousand years. Do you doubt me, Mr. Strachey?"

"No, Madame Rose. But don't overwork yourself again." Strachey's voice was strained by a growing anxiety.

"I shan't, Mr. Strachey. You'll be right across the hall and you'll watch over me just as you've always done and I'll relax by watching you edit your manuscripts. And when I'm all through with the play, and my Miranda is married to her Ferdinand, I shall go away and rest forever. I shall never write another line.

"I shall become an aging, fretting mother, perhaps a doting grandmother. No—I shall never dote and I shall never live with Miranda. But I shall be an ordinary old woman, ailing and complaining."

"You could never be ordinary," Strachey said in reproof and in relief. Rosaline's tenseness was leaving her.

"No. I won't be ordinary. But I *shall* rest forever, maybe on some magic island like your Bermuda, peopled with creatures of my own imagination, a gentle place where the air will never sear my lungs and the smoke will never sting my eyes again on cold winter nights along crowded streets."

"That, Madame, is Bermuda."

"Or Prospero's island, or the Caribbees."

"Bermuda. I shall insist upon it." Strachey was no longer shy.

Rosaline was almost sure that she caught the same twinkle that his eyes had flashed that evening many years before when he had approached her in the tiring room of the Rose and invited her to read for a company of lords and gentlemen at the Pipe and Tabor.

28

SYMBOLICALLY, ROSALINE ACCOMPLISHED EVERYTHING THAT SHE SET out to do in *The Tempest,* as she titled Miranda's masque. But in planning to keep it as a treat for Miranda's wedding, she reckoned without taking Richard Burbage into consideration. Since the Burbages had taken the Blackfriars Theater back from the boys' company in 1608, the King's Men had used it as their winter quarters, playing there four or five months out of the year. So Richard Burbage was a frequent visitor at the Gatehouse while Rosaline and William Strachey were working on their respective manuscripts.

And it was no great task for Burbage to get Miranda's permission to produce *The Tempest,* which was finished a good two years before Ferdinand Stanley came back from Virginia. By promising Miranda that the King's Men would play at her wedding if she would relinquish her claim on the premiere production of her masque, he persuaded her to let him use it to open the season at the Banqueting House at Whitehall on November 1, 1611; and he used it several times at the Blackfriars Theater and the Globe before Ferdinand returned in the spring of 1613.

Rosaline humored Miranda; and very much against her will she humored Burbage, too, at least to the extent of dressing three plays for him, in violation of her resolve to quit writing altogether. She would not attempt another whole play, however, and Burbage had to be content with the few touches she added to John Fletcher's *Cardenio, Two Noble Kinsmen,* and *Henry VIII.* She kept insisting that each one was the last; but while she was marking time waiting for Miranda's wedding, which in some way seemed to mark the end of a period in her life, she continued to help Strachey in his rather ambitious work and so found it hard to refuse Burbage when he asked her aid.

It was *The Tempest,* however, not any later work, which finally brought the long hazy problem of Shakespeare's identity to the attention of the Crown. The presentation of *The Tempest* during the nuptial festivities for Princess Elizabeth and Frederick the Elector Palatine, in February of 1613, so delighted King James that he wrote a highly commendatory letter to William Shakespeare.* Shakespeare of course showed the letter to Rosaline and immediately dismissed it, because he had what he considered a much more important announcement to make—that he was now Rosaline's landlord, or one of them.

Together with John Heminge, William Johnson, and John Jackson—all friends of Rosaline—he had just bought the Gatehouse from Henry Walker, to whom Lady Oxford had willed the property upon her death the year before. Rosaline was pretty sure that the men, all of whom felt indebted to her in one way or another, had bought the Gatehouse just to be sure that her apartment would be left undisturbed during her lifetime.

King James's admiration for Shakespeare's works would not be dismissed, however, no matter who bought property in Blackfriars. In June Shakespeare got a summons to appear before His Majesty, and when he learned from Ben Jonson and Michael Drayton what was wanted of him he came straight to Rosaline again. He found her strolling in the courtyard, basking in the warm June sun.

"His Majesty wants me to work on some court masques directly under the supervision of Sir George Buck, Master of the Revels," Shakespeare explained. The dignity which his receding hairline had imparted to his handsome face and deep-set eyes was eclipsed for the moment by the agitation apparent in every feature. "His Majesty considers it odd that I have contributed nothing so far

* Although there is no copy of the letter extant, it was still mentioned by the Duke of Buckingham as late as 1709: "That most learned prince and great patron of learning, King James the First, was pleased with his own hand to write an amicable letter to Mr. Shakespeare; which letter, though now lost, remained long in the hands of Sir William D'Avenanat, as a credible person now living can testify."

to the court masques which have become so popular since he came to the throne."

"It does seem to be a lucrative field," Rosaline said. "And quite honorable work." Betty had appeared in at least three masques by Ben Jonson, and all the ladies at court sought him out to try to win parts in the casts. The masque was one route to the King's favor.

"I don't question that, Rosaline, but you know that I can't work at the Revels Office—or anywhere else."

"Then why not just say that you can't, that you've retired to Stratford?"

They walked in a regular pattern, following the cross walks in the courtyard.

"It isn't that simple," Shakespeare said. "His Majesty considers the offer as a sort of reward, as an expression of royal favor in recognition not only of *The Tempest* but of all the plays, which he seems to have heard or read and to value quite highly."

"How do you know all this?" Rosaline asked.

"From Ben Jonson and Michael Drayton. I spend a lot of time with them, since I'm here in London alone. I enjoy them. They're good drinking companions, but they may be the death of me yet." Shakespeare laughed nervously. He seemed not to be himself at all, not as Rosaline had known him, genial and carefree.

"How is that?"

"I think they may be at the bottom of all this. They might have started it as a joke, Ben Jonson, anyway. But now it's got out of hand."

"But why?"

"Well, Ben Jonson has doubted for sometime that I wrote the plays. And the better we got to know each other, the more skeptical he became, I think. At first he began praising my work, saying that I deserved a place in Westminster Abbey and would probably be buried there."

"This is high praise."

"But not too high, Rosaline. I'm convinced of that, but I can't take credit like that for your work. Acting as your agent, shielding you with my identity is one thing. Receiving royal favor and national acclaim for work I didn't do is quite another. I can't do it. I won't do it."

"And Ben Jonson started this as a joke?" Rosaline moved into a splash of sunlight in the middle of the courtyard and looked up at Shakespeare.

"At first I laughed at him," Shakespeare went on. "I told him that I could keep myself out of the Abbey. I would insist on being buried in Stratford and put a curse on anyone who dared move my bones. I even quoted him my epitaph:

> "Good friend, for Jesus' sake forbear
> To dig the dust enclosed here
> Blest be the man that spares these stones
> And cursed be he that moves my bones.

No Stratford sexton would ever disturb a grave so marked. I know how superstitious they are."

Rosaline laughed softly.

"That should keep you out of the Abbey," she said. "But you say the joke has got out of hand?"

"I've given orders to use the epitaph," he said soberly. "But that isn't all. Ben kept praising me to His Majesty, or rather my work, until the King has decided to bestow this honor upon me."

"Just take it then. It's probably a sinecure. You won't really have to write anything."

"No, it's gone farther than that. I think Ben was really trying to force my hand, to make me tell him who actually wrote the plays, or to produce the real author to work for the Office of Revels."

"But you didn't?" Rosaline asked in sudden horror. "You didn't tell him about me?"

"Yes."

"No, Will, you didn't!"

"Yes, I did. When I got the summons I talked it over with Ben and Michael. I had to. They're at court all the time. They know what to do; so I finally admitted that you wrote my work."

Rosaline sat down on a stone bench. Her strength was all gone.

"Both of them agree that we should tell His Majesty the truth. He is a patron of letters, as his sponsorship of the Bible translation proves, and he is something of a poet himself. Ben is of the opinion that His Majesty will bestow the honor on you, recognize you as the truly great poet that you are and at last give you the acclaim you deserve."

[305]

"Oh no, Will. No. I don't want it, not now. I just want to rest, to be left alone. My whole story would come out—and Hal, and Miranda. You must stop Mr. Jonson."

"It's too late, I'm afraid. We have been granted an audience tomorrow morning, St. Peter's Day, at eleven."

"We?" Rosaline sounded dazed.

"You and I and Ben Jonson."

"With His Majesty?"

"With His Majesty." Shakespeare was firm.

"Very well," Rosaline said in resignation. "If it must fall on you or me, let it fall on me. I've imposed on you for twenty years now. You've shielded me long enough. I do understand your reluctance. I'll go."

"Rosaline, I—Ben and I feel that you are about to receive an honor that is due you. It's not a catastrophe."

"I wonder," Rosaline said.

Rosaline told no one except William Strachey of Shakespeare's visit. It was Strachey who took her to Whitehall the next morning to see the King. They met Shakespeare and Ben Jonson at White-hall Stairs and walked up to the palace.

Rosaline had seen Ben Jonson many times, but never at close range; perhaps she had instinctively avoided him. He was very little taller than she, and already getting too fat. His clothes were ill fitting, and the way he squinted up his face in the sun made it difficult for Rosaline to distinguish between his natural features and some of the huge pockmarks which marred his complexion. After Shakespeare had introduced Rosaline, Ben Jonson fell into step beside her.

"So you are the genius behind Master Shakespeare's plays," he said. "I guessed long ago that Will had not written them. He's not quite up to them."

"William Shakespeare has been a great help to me," Rosaline said. She could not tell how to take Jonson's remarks. "I could not have got along without him."

"Nor he without you," Jonson said with a chuckle. "I used *genius* intentionally. Madame, you are a genius, even if Bohemia doesn't have a seacoast." He referred to her error in *The Winter's Tale,* of course.

"Mr. Jonson," she said with some heat, "some of my characters—Marcus Antonius, for instance—have qualities which the real figures never had either. That is the dramatist's license, his duty, in fact."

"True, true," Jonson admitted. "I stand reproved. I'll gladly concede Bohemia a seacoast rather than lose Marcus Antonius's eloquence." His laugh then was quite friendly.

Rosaline said no more. The walk was taking all her breath. But Ben Jonson kept up a steady monologue. She learned that he really did admire her work, that he took satisfaction in finding who had actually written it, and that he sincerely believed the King would honor her most highly.

"His Majesty is a man of literary integrity, Madame," he said. "He has good judgment and he rewards competence. I think you will profit greatly by this audience."

By that time they were inside the palace, all except William Strachey, being shown to the presence chamber by one of His Majesty's royal guards. There was no delay in their being admitted. His Majesty, most sensitive about his weak legs and shambling gait, did not share his predecessor's love for grand entrances. He preferred to be seated first in an empty room and let his subjects come to him. That morning, near the end of June, he was seated in a small airy chamber on the second floor, where he could feel the breeze blowing across the Thames.

His subjects entered the small room and sank to their knees almost within arm's reach of His Majesty. The King bade them raise their eyes; and upon the plea of Ben Jonson, who seemed on almost familiar terms with the King, he dismissed all others in attendance. Then he spoke first to William Shakespeare.

"Master Shakespeare," he said graciously, "we are most highly pleased with your work. We, as you probably know, are something of a poet." He paused.

"Everyone is familiar with *Essays of a Prentice in the Divine Art of Poesie*, Your Majesty," Shakespeare said, as he had been coached to do by Ben Jonson.

"Ah, yes," His Majesty said proudly. "That of course was written when we were quite young. We pride ourselves most as a patron of letters now. We are especially proud of our new Bible.

"And that brings us to you, Master Shakespeare. Some of our literary advisors, Mr. Jonson, for one, assure us that the body of work written by you may one day be comparable in stature to our own, or, shall we say, second only to the Bible as a monument to our age?"

Shakespeare became pale under the King's unusual praise, and Rosaline felt herself trembling—in weakness or in fear, she could not tell which. To her, His Majesty's flattery was an awful pronouncement. She feared where it might lead.

"We are therefore preparing a reward for you, a retainer from the Office of Revels, for which we shall expect more masques like your delightful *Tempest*. There will be other rewards in money, as Mr. Jonson will attest, and perhaps in time knighthood."

His Majesty paused and beamed genially down upon his kneeling subjects.

"And this is Mistress Shakespeare, I suppose," he said, smiling at Rosaline.

"No, Your Majesty," Rosaline said.

"No?"

"No, Your Majesty," Shakespeare said, with the voice control acquired during a lifetime on the stage. "This lady is the real author of all the work ascribed to me. We brought her to explain why I cannot accept the honors tendered me."

His Majesty stared first at one of the speakers and then at the other.

"Is this true, Mr. Jonson?" he asked at last. "Is it true that the poetry you have been praising was written by this woman?" His Majesty's pronunciation of *woman* made an epithet of the word.

"Yes, Your Majesty," Ben Jonson said, and then took advantage of his privileged position to give the King a brief explanation.

"Who knows of this?" His Majesty asked Rosaline when Ben Jonson had finished.

"Very few, Your Majesty," Rosaline said evenly, sensing that His Majesty might let her keep her secret. "My secret has been well kept. All who know can be trusted implicitly." She remembered John Marston for a moment, and then she remembered William Stanley, Earl of Derby, and she felt sure that Marston would never speak of her again.

"That is providential," the King said sternly. Then he rose unsteadily and walked toward an open window, holding onto chairs and the wall all the way. Ben Jonson started to rise once, perhaps to help the King, but sank back into the kneeling position, his own enthusiasm damped.

[308]

His Majesty looked out across the Thames for a full minute, then to his left, toward the City of London, then back at his kneeling subjects. He slowly turned around, shifting his weight so that he leaned against the windowsill. When he spoke, he no longer sounded like a gracious monarch. He even dropped the royal *we*.

"When I came to this throne, I followed a woman. I have been compared to that woman, to Elizabeth, every day since, in every act I have performed. She left me a state already waning in its glory, and I shall forever suffer by comparison to her." His voice trembled with emotion.

"She was not a good woman. I *am* a good man. I have given God's Word to all people in an inspired language they can understand. That Bible—King James's Bible—was to be my legacy to all Englishmen, my answer to Elizabeth, for a woman should not speak out in a church. I have done what it was not right that she should do, what she could not do. That was the glory that I did not have to share with Elizabeth—God's glory.

"Now I find that the only rival to my literary work, the great drama of our time, is also the work of a woman. I shall not permit the glory of my Bible to be shared by the secular work of a woman! That is why I said that the keeping of your secret was providential, Madame.

"I use the word literally. God has seen to it that your work has been ascribed to a man. It was His will. I am fully aware of the high merit of your work. I was prepared to reward the man who created it.

"But a woman, never!" His Majesty practically screamed. "It is against nature, it is against man, it is against God that a woman should write as you have written. I hereby decree that you never existed. Mr. Jonson, Mr. Shakespeare, I charge you to warn every person privy to this secret that to reveal it is to lose his life.

"You, Madame—I forbid you to write another line. I forbid you to claim authorship of Master Shakespeare's work. On pain of death, I forbid it!

"And I'm convinced that I am doing God's will." His Majesty pounded the windowsill with his fists. "Do all of you understand that?"

"Yes, Your Majesty."

"Mr. Jonson, you will keep ever alert for any hint of this

affair—you are in a position to do so—and you will inform me at once of any possible whisper. And you will see that every record, every reference to this woman is destroyed."

"Yes, Your Majesty."

"I will not share my glory with a woman! You are dismissed."

His Majesty turned again and looked out over the river at London, which Elizabeth had ruled at the height of its glory. His subjects backed out of the presence chamber and hurried along the corridors toward the sunshine outside. Ben Jonson had urgent business somewhere in the palace grounds. The other three boarded a wherry at Whitehall Stairs.

"What happened?" Strachey asked when he considered it safe to talk.

"I am forbidden to write another line," Rosaline said. Actually her expression was one of relief, though her eyes were still troubled.

"I shall not be honored," Shakespeare said with a wry smile. "In fact, I think it is high time that I retired to Stratford."

"It all sounds good to me," Strachey said. "Everyone should be happy."

"You weren't there," Rosaline said. "It was awful while it lasted. Incidentally, by royal decree I never existed."

"That poses a neat problem," Strachey said. "Where shall I tell the waterman to take us, other than just downstream, or is our destination non-existent by royal decree?" His gayety was a little strained.

"The Globe," Rosaline said. "Will has a performance in two hours. Let's go with him. By the way, what is playing?"

"*Henry VIII*. You know—you did some work on it."

"Oh yes, but I've never seen it."

"Winchester Stairs," Strachey directed the waterman, and the wherry began to head toward the right bank. The passengers were silent for the rest of the way and during most of the lunch they ate before the performance. Then Rosaline and William Strachey left Shakespeare at the stage door and found seats in the second balcony, just beneath the goose roost.

The Globe was a comfort to Rosaline after her experience at Whitehall. She wanted no royal recognition. This was her world; these were her people, even if she could never write for them again.

She swept the crowded balconies with long fond glances. Even the stench of the sweating groundlings jostling each other for choice standing room in the pit below was far from offensive to her nostrils. The hard bench was welcome, more welcome than a padded farthingale chair would have been, though Rosaline was dead tired from her trip upstream. And gaudy posts and railings, freshly painted in gilt and red and green for the summer season, were positively elegant by comparison to the oak-paneled wainscot along the Whitehall corridors.

The King, too, Henry VIII as played by Richard Burbage, was a far more regal personage than King James would ever be. Burbage would never drop the royal *we* to spill his personal venom over all talented women.

Rosaline had written the first two scenes of the play. She followed them from memory and then became still more deeply absorbed in the performance as it moved into Fletcher's passages. Scene Three went off smoothly and the "sweet society of fair ones" were duly assembled at the banquet hall at York Palace to welcome the king. Rosaline started nervously when the cannon was fired to herald the king's approach.

Neither she nor anyone else saw the fiery gun-wadding settle on the dry thatch roof. And with Strachey's pipe fuming beside her, and a thousand more contributing their fog to the atmosphere, the roof was half burned off before anyone noticed the smoke. The end of Act I offered the first break, the first release of the audience's attention.

Then someone yelled "Fire!" and a hundred voices echoed his warning. By that time the burning rushes had begun dropping onto the "heavens" and onto the wooden floors of the balconies. Frightened patrons, hastily brushing the burning brands off their clothes, scattered the embers still more widely.

Rosaline felt herself lifted bodily out of her seat while she stared, fascinated, at the flames, hardly distinguishable from the lurid coloring of the woodwork or the flashing silks of the nobles who crawled over the balcony railings and slid down the pillars like monkeys on poles. The terrified faces of the stinkards in the pit looked ashen, or glowed red in the cramp and press of people trying to get out the two small exits.

Strachey ran around the balcony, away from the front stairs. He carried Rosaline through one area heavy with smoke. She sucked in lungfuls of the fumes and began to cough violently. The smoke stung her eyes, too, and she closed them tight. Suddenly she felt a spray in her face and sucked in a taste of ale during a coughing spell. She opened her eyes just in time to see a drunken gallant shake his bottle of ale until it foamed and again squirt a steady spray on the burning seat of his companion's breeches. Both clowned and laughed raucously, seemingly unmindful of the burning theater.

Rosaline closed her eyes again as Strachey ducked into the lord's chamber and through the upper tiring room to the back-stage stairs. A minute later she felt cool air on her cheeks, and Strachey deposited her gently in an abandoned sedan chair across Maiden Lane from the Globe. As soon as she recovered from her coughing spell, she dried her smarting eyes and she and William Strachey sat quietly side by side and watched the Globe burn to the ground.

It was all over in less than two hours. Though no one was hurt, not a thing was left of the theater except the foundation. When there was nothing more to see, Rosaline turned to Strachey and stared at him mutely.

"Shall we go?" he asked. His hair and eyebrows were singed, his clothes scorched, and his face smudged and grimy.

"Yes. I can walk," she said.

She could walk, but she was very tired by the time they reached Winchester Stairs. Once aboard the wherry she practically collapsed in Strachey's arms and suffered another coughing spell brought on when the exertion of walking drew the smoke still deeper into her lungs.

"Now the Globe is non-existent," she said, "but not by royal decree."

Strachey made no comment.

"Part of me burned up in the Globe, Will," she said, "the only part that ever existed—despite royal decree. This is the end of something."

"The Globe will be rebuilt," Strachey said.

"But not I. I shall never be rebuilt, not what I was. I—I think I am ready to go to Bermuda, to rest forever. Will three thousand pounds take me there and keep me? That's what I'll have after Miranda's dowry is paid next month."

"I'll take you there and keep you," Strachey said.

"But three thousand pounds will help."

"Yes. But you won't need it. You can have a coral palace there for a hundred pounds."

"Then I shall be forgotten—I who never existed, or existed only in coral palaces and fairylands."

"You'll never be forgotten, not so long as men can see or hear a play, not so long as there is one theater left in the world."

"But no one will ever know who I was." She relaxed against Strachey's sturdy body—it had always been there for her to lean on when she needed it. "I don't care, but isn't it ironical that after all the names I've borne I shall not be known by any one of them? There was de Vere. And Lee and Allen and Wriothesley and Southampton—all were mine.

"And my first names. Rosa Lena and Ross and Rosaline. And, of course, you and his lordship always called me Rose. But I shall be known by none of them. I shall be known only as Shakespeare."

"That which we call a Rose by any other name would smell as sweet," Strachey said, in perfect mimicry of her own Juliet.

"William Strachey, you stole that line from me. I know I've used it somewhere." Rosaline sat up straight and faced him accusingly.

"I am not the first man to lift a line from you, Madame Rose," he said; "and I shall not be the last, I warrant."